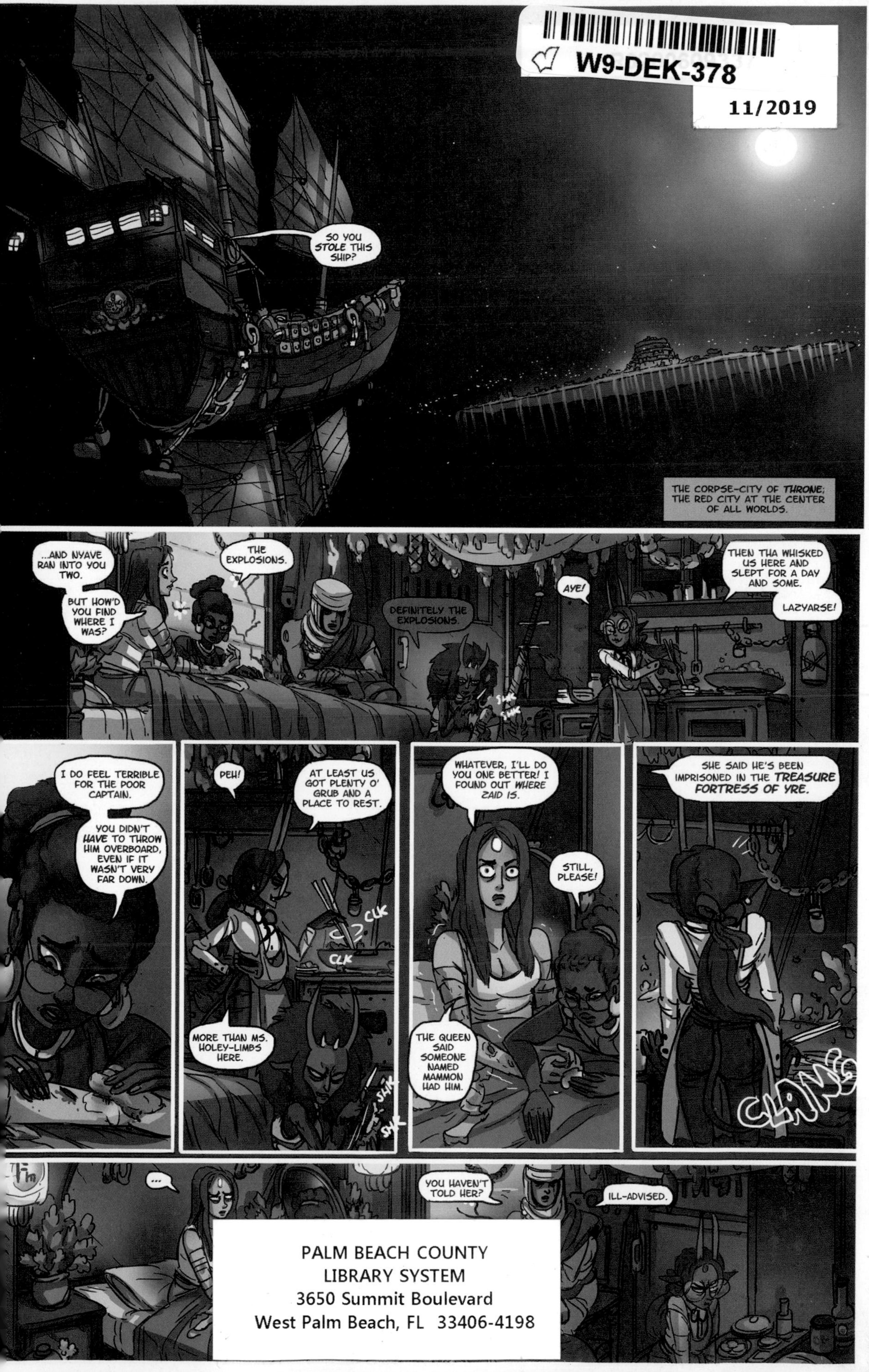
SO YOU STOLE THIS SHIP?
THE CORPSE-CITY OF THRONE; THE RED CITY AT THE CENTER OF ALL WORLDS.
...AND NYAVE RAN INTO YOU TWO.
BUT HOW'D YOU FIND WHERE I WAS?
THE EXPLOSIONS.
DEFINITELY THE EXPLOSIONS.
AYE!
THEN THA WHISKED US HERE AND SLEPT FOR A DAY AND SOME.
LAZYARSE!
SHK
SHK
I DO FEEL TERRIBLE FOR THE POOR CAPTAIN.
YOU DIDN'T HAVE TO THROW HIM OVERBOARD, EVEN IF IT WASN'T VERY FAR DOWN.
PEH!
AT LEAST US GOT PLENTY O' GRUB AND A PLACE TO REST.
CLK
CLK
MORE THAN MS. HOLEY-LIMBS HERE.
SHK
SHK
WHATEVER, I'LL DO YOU ONE BETTER! I FOUND OUT WHERE ZAID IS.
STILL, PLEASE!
THE QUEEN SAID SOMEONE NAMED MAMMON HAD HIM.
SHE SAID HE'S BEEN IMPRISONED IN THE TREASURE FORTRESS OF YRE.
CLANG
...
YOU HAVEN'T TOLD HER?
ILL-ADVISED.

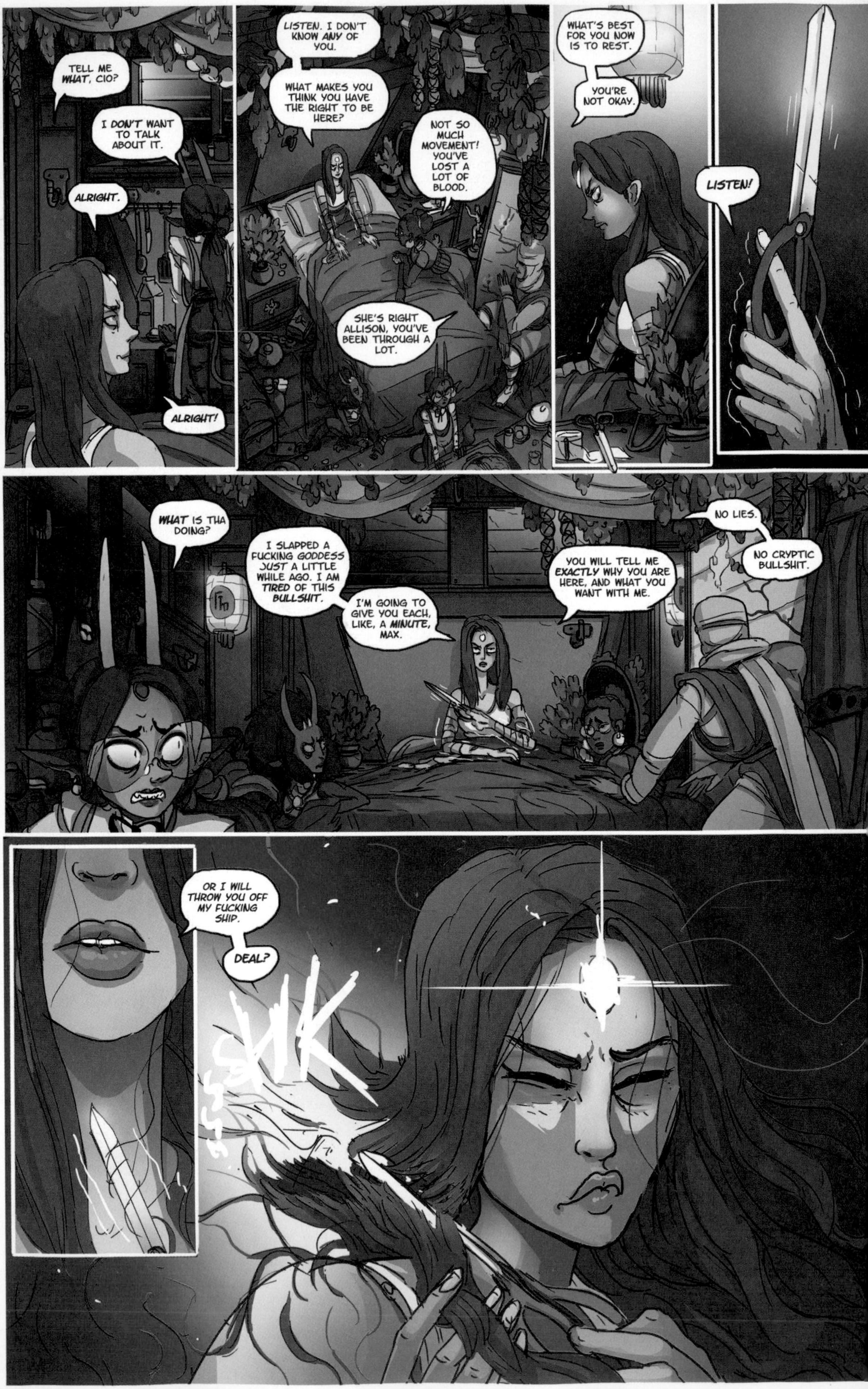
TELL ME *WHAT*, CIO?
I *DON'T* WANT TO TALK ABOUT IT.
ALRIGHT.
ALRIGHT!
LISTEN. I DON'T KNOW *ANY* OF YOU.
WHAT MAKES YOU THINK YOU HAVE THE RIGHT TO BE HERE?
NOT SO MUCH MOVEMENT! YOU'VE LOST A LOT OF BLOOD.
SHE'S RIGHT ALLISON, YOU'VE BEEN THROUGH A LOT.
WHAT'S BEST FOR YOU NOW IS TO REST.
YOU'RE NOT OKAY.
LISTEN!
WHAT IS THA DOING?
I SLAPPED A FUCKING GODDESS JUST A LITTLE WHILE AGO. I AM *TIRED* OF THIS *BULLSHIT*.
I'M GOING TO GIVE YOU EACH, LIKE, A *MINUTE*, MAX.
YOU WILL TELL ME *EXACTLY* WHY YOU ARE HERE, AND WHAT YOU WANT WITH ME.
NO LIES.
NO CRYPTIC BULLSHIT.
OR I WILL THROW YOU OFF MY FUCKING SHIP.
DEAL?
SHK

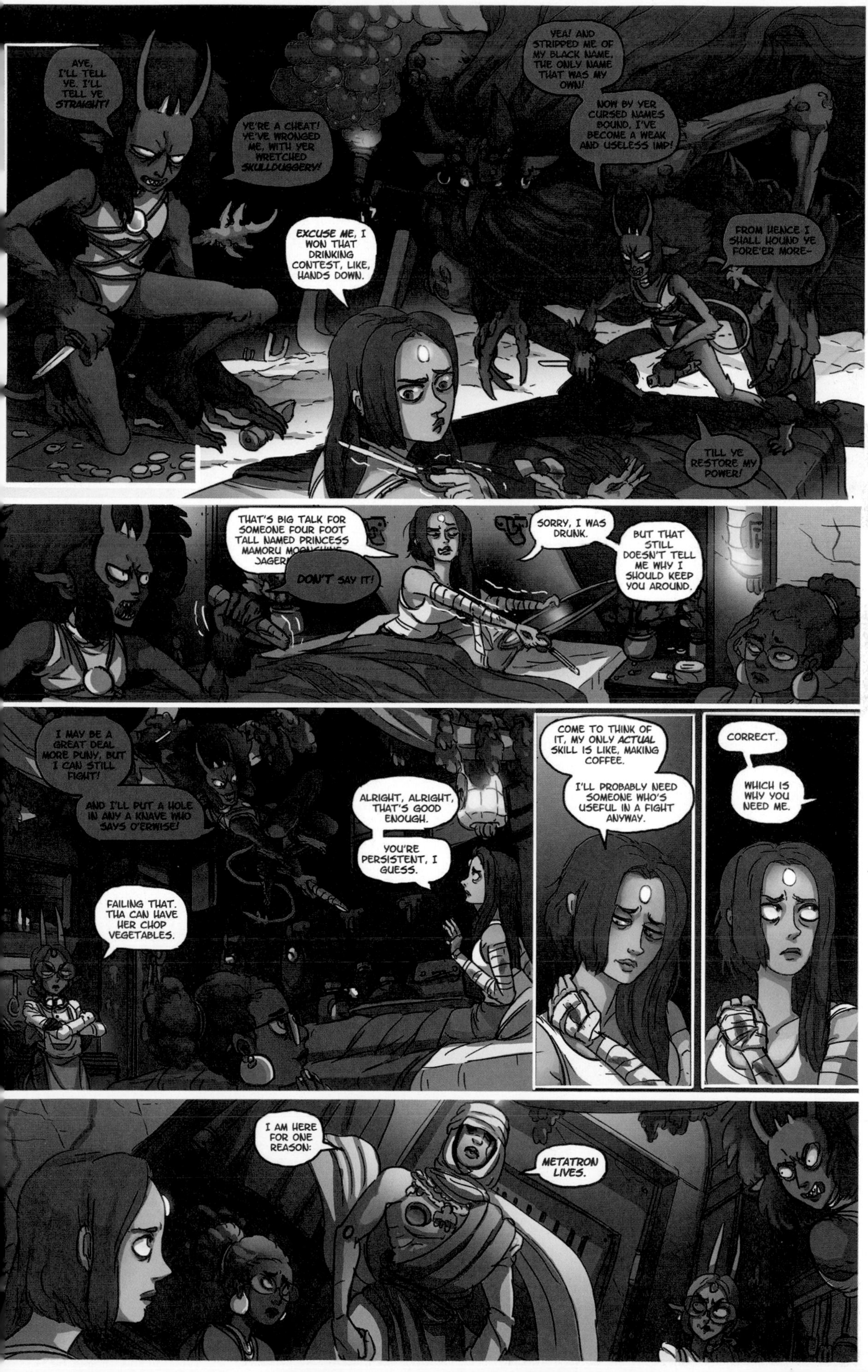
AYE, I'LL TELL YE. I'LL TELL YE STRAIGHT!
YE'RE A CHEAT! YE'VE WRONGED ME, WITH YER WRETCHED SKULLDUGGERY!
YEA! AND STRIPPED ME OF MY BLACK NAME, THE ONLY NAME THAT WAS MY OWN!
NOW BY YER CURSED NAMES BOUND, I'VE BECOME A WEAK AND USELESS IMP!
EXCUSE ME, I WON THAT DRINKING CONTEST, LIKE, HANDS DOWN.
FROM HENCE I SHALL HOUND YE FORE'ER MORE-
TILL YE RESTORE MY POWER!
THAT'S BIG TALK FOR SOMEONE FOUR FOOT TALL NAMED PRINCESS MAMORU MOONSHINE JAGER
DON'T SAY IT!
SORRY, I WAS DRUNK.
BUT THAT STILL DOESN'T TELL ME WHY I SHOULD KEEP YOU AROUND.
I MAY BE A GREAT DEAL MORE PUNY, BUT I CAN STILL FIGHT!
AND I'LL PUT A HOLE IN ANY A KNAVE WHO SAYS O'ERWISE!
ALRIGHT, ALRIGHT, THAT'S GOOD ENOUGH.
YOU'RE PERSISTENT, I GUESS.
FAILING THAT. THA CAN HAVE HER CHOP VEGETABLES.
COME TO THINK OF IT, MY ONLY ACTUAL SKILL IS LIKE, MAKING COFFEE.
I'LL PROBABLY NEED SOMEONE WHO'S USEFUL IN A FIGHT ANYWAY.
CORRECT.
WHICH IS WHY YOU NEED ME.
I AM HERE FOR ONE REASON:
METATRON LIVES.

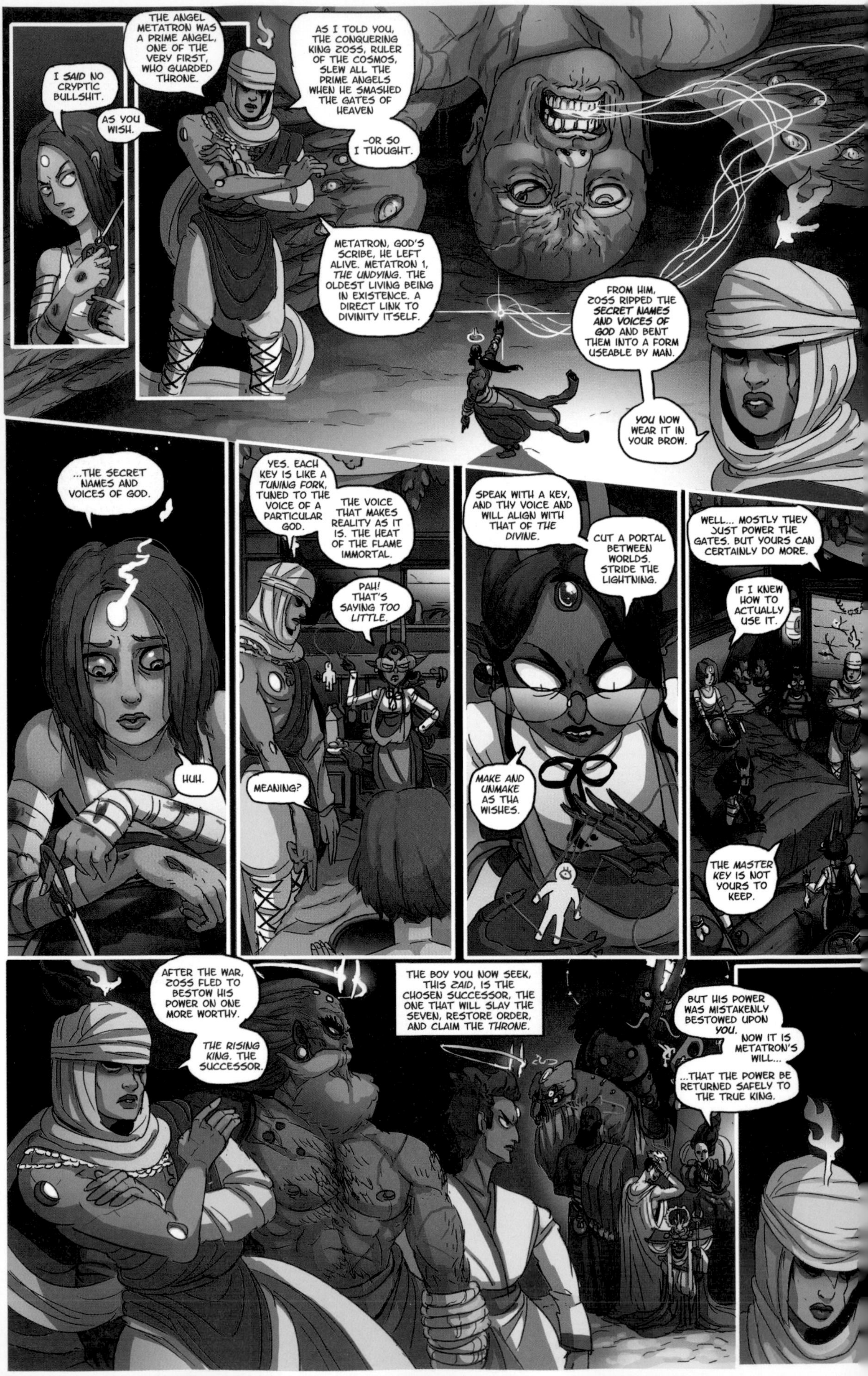

I SAID NO CRYPTIC BULLSHIT.
AS YOU WISH.
THE ANGEL METATRON WAS A PRIME ANGEL, ONE OF THE VERY FIRST, WHO GUARDED THRONE.
AS I TOLD YOU, THE CONQUERING KING ZOSS, RULER OF THE COSMOS, SLEW ALL THE PRIME ANGELS WHEN HE SMASHED THE GATES OF HEAVEN
-OR SO I THOUGHT.
METATRON, GOD'S SCRIBE, HE LEFT ALIVE. METATRON 1, THE UNDYING. THE OLDEST LIVING BEING IN EXISTENCE. A DIRECT LINK TO DIVINITY ITSELF.
FROM HIM, ZOSS RIPPED THE SECRET NAMES AND VOICES OF GOD AND BENT THEM INTO A FORM USEABLE BY MAN.
YOU NOW WEAR IT IN YOUR BROW.
...THE SECRET NAMES AND VOICES OF GOD.
HUH.
YES. EACH KEY IS LIKE A TUNING FORK, TUNED TO THE VOICE OF A PARTICULAR GOD.
THE VOICE THAT MAKES REALITY AS IT IS. THE HEAT OF THE FLAME IMMORTAL.
PAH! THAT'S SAYING TOO LITTLE.
MEANING?
SPEAK WITH A KEY, AND THY VOICE AND WILL ALIGN WITH THAT OF THE DIVINE.
CUT A PORTAL BETWEEN WORLDS. STRIDE THE LIGHTNING.
MAKE AND UNMAKE AS THA WISHES.
WELL... MOSTLY THEY JUST POWER THE GATES. BUT YOURS CAN CERTAINLY DO MORE.
IF I KNEW HOW TO ACTUALLY USE IT.
THE MASTER KEY IS NOT YOURS TO KEEP.
AFTER THE WAR, ZOSS FLED TO BESTOW HIS POWER ON ONE MORE WORTHY.
THE RISING KING. THE SUCCESSOR.
THE BOY YOU NOW SEEK, THIS ZAID, IS THE CHOSEN SUCCESSOR, THE ONE THAT WILL SLAY THE SEVEN, RESTORE ORDER, AND CLAIM THE THRONE.
BUT HIS POWER WAS MISTAKENLY BESTOWED UPON YOU.
NOW IT IS METATRON'S WILL...
...THAT THE POWER BE RETURNED SAFELY TO THE TRUE KING.

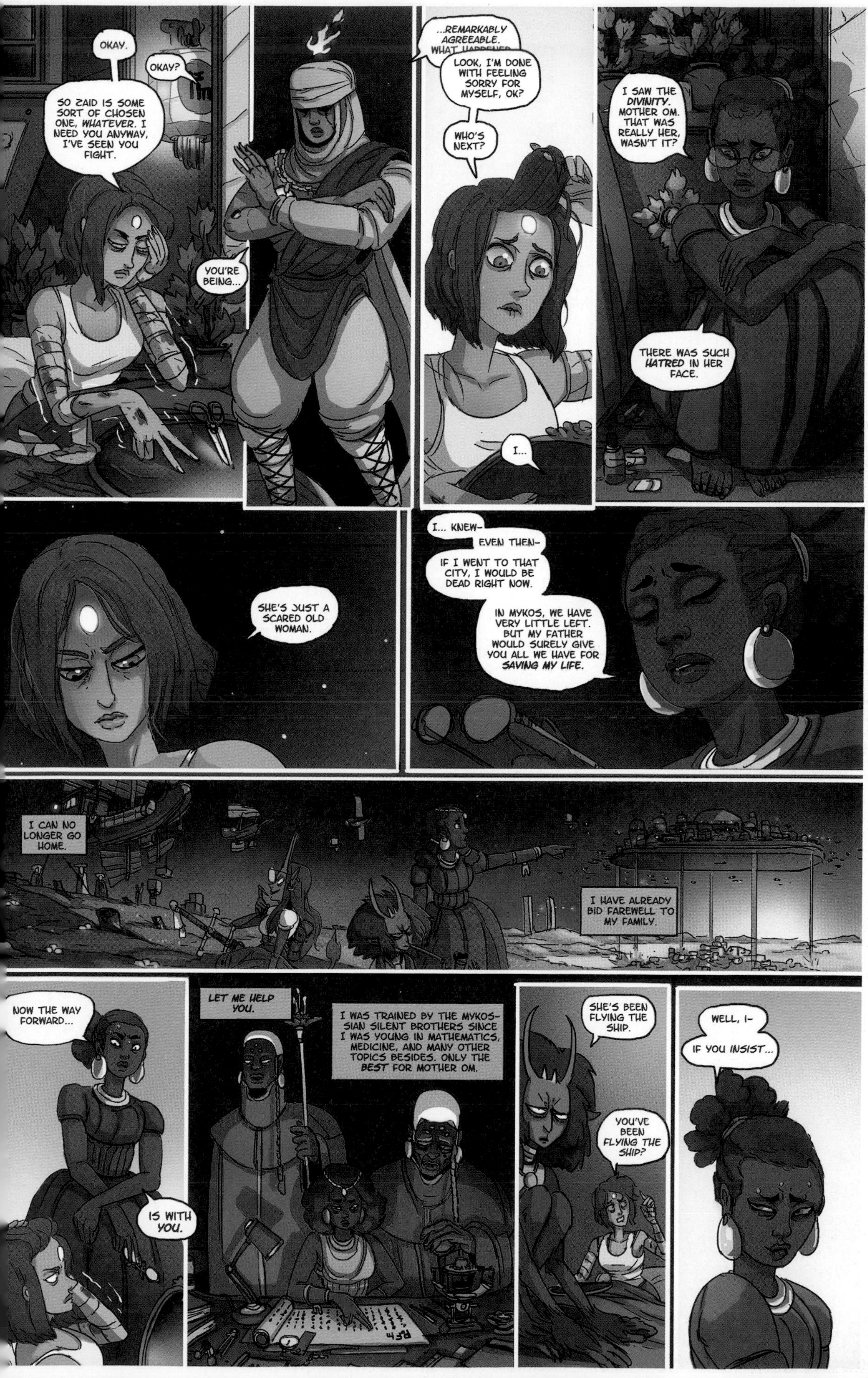
OKAY.
OKAY?
SO ZAID IS SOME SORT OF CHOSEN ONE, WHATEVER. I NEED YOU ANYWAY, I'VE SEEN YOU FIGHT.
YOU'RE BEING...
...REMARKABLY AGREEABLE. WHAT HAPPENED
LOOK, I'M DONE WITH FEELING SORRY FOR MYSELF, OK?
WHO'S NEXT?
I...
I SAW THE DIVINITY. MOTHER OM. THAT WAS REALLY HER, WASN'T IT?
THERE WAS SUCH HATRED IN HER FACE.
SHE'S JUST A SCARED OLD WOMAN.
I... KNEW-
EVEN THEN-
IF I WENT TO THAT CITY, I WOULD BE DEAD RIGHT NOW.
IN MYKOS, WE HAVE VERY LITTLE LEFT. BUT MY FATHER WOULD SURELY GIVE YOU ALL WE HAVE FOR SAVING MY LIFE.
I CAN NO LONGER GO HOME.
I HAVE ALREADY BID FAREWELL TO MY FAMILY.
NOW THE WAY FORWARD...
IS WITH YOU.
LET ME HELP YOU.
I WAS TRAINED BY THE MYKOSSIAN SILENT BROTHERS SINCE I WAS YOUNG IN MATHEMATICS, MEDICINE, AND MANY OTHER TOPICS BESIDES. ONLY THE BEST FOR MOTHER OM.
SHE'S BEEN FLYING THE SHIP.
YOU'VE BEEN FLYING THE SHIP?
WELL, I-
IF YOU INSIST...

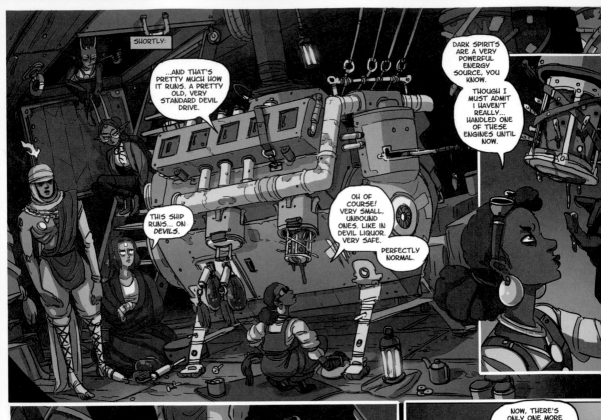

SHORTLY:

...AND THAT'S PRETTY MUCH HOW IT RUNS. A PRETTY OLD, VERY STANDARD DEVIL DRIVE.

DARK SPIRITS ARE A VERY POWERFUL ENERGY SOURCE, YOU KNOW.

THOUGH I MUST ADMIT I HAVEN'T REALLY... HANDLED ONE OF THESE ENGINES UNTIL NOW.

THIS SHIP RUNS... ON DEVILS.

OH OF COURSE! VERY SMALL, UNBOUND ONES. LIKE IN DEVIL LIQUOR. VERY SAFE.

PERFECTLY NORMAL.

OK... YOU'RE HIRED.

JUST DON'T BE SO SMUG ABOUT IT.

NOW, THERE'S ONLY ONE MORE PERSON HERE WHO'S BEEN CONSPICUOUSLY QUIET.

I'VE SAVED THY PRETTY ARSE AT LEAST TWICE NOW, OR DID THA FORGET, WOBBLE-BRAINS?

AH, HM, I SEE.

HOWEVER...

WH-WHERE-

WH-WHERE DID THA GET THAT?

OH, A NEW FRIEND BORROWED IT FROM YOU.

HMMM!

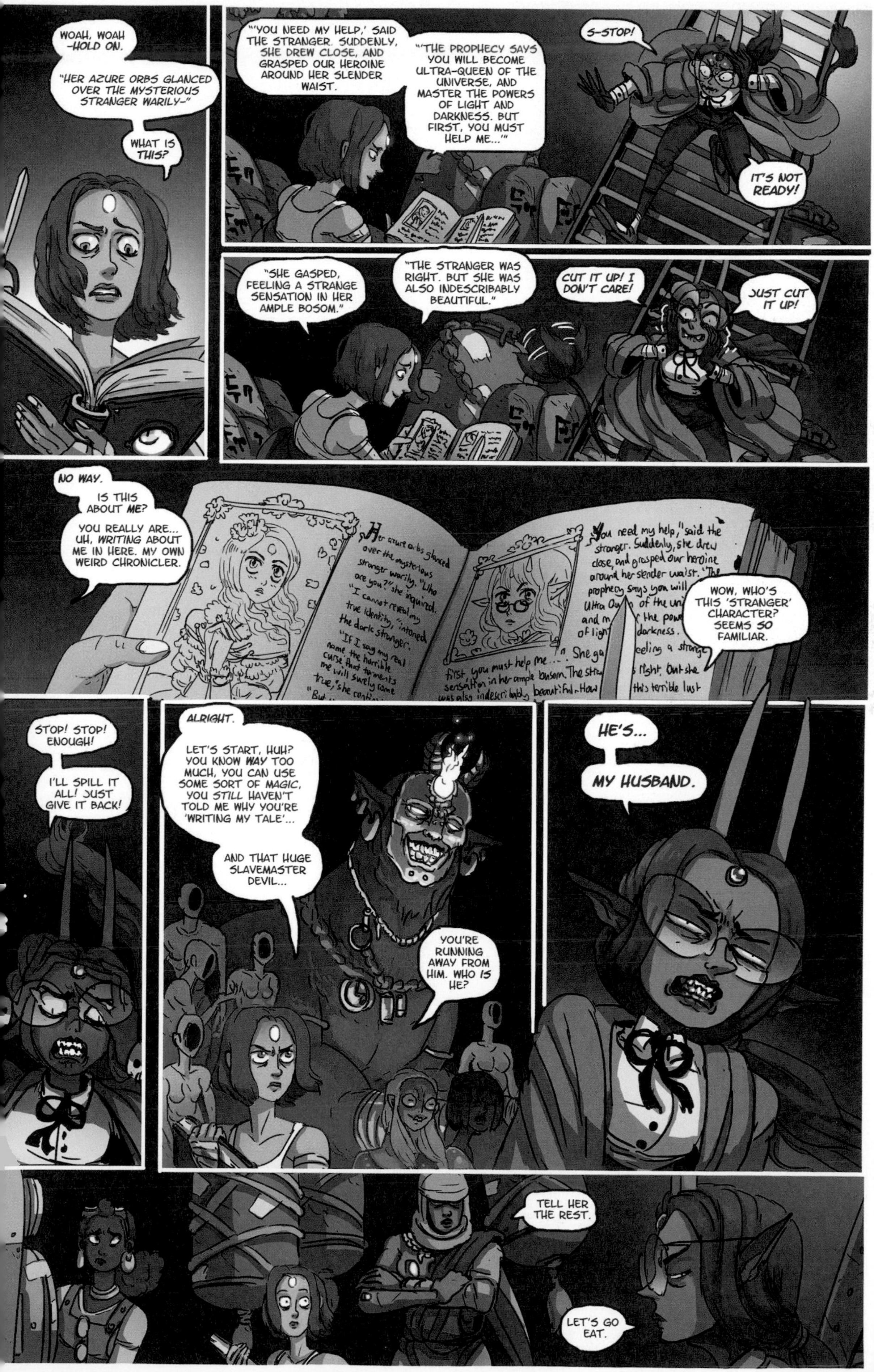
WOAH, WOAH -HOLD ON.
"HER AZURE ORBS GLANCED OVER THE MYSTERIOUS STRANGER WARILY-"
WHAT IS THIS?
"'YOU NEED MY HELP,' SAID THE STRANGER. SUDDENLY, SHE DREW CLOSE, AND GRASPED OUR HEROINE AROUND HER SLENDER WAIST.
"'THE PROPHECY SAYS YOU WILL BECOME ULTRA-QUEEN OF THE UNIVERSE, AND MASTER THE POWERS OF LIGHT AND DARKNESS. BUT FIRST, YOU MUST HELP ME...'"
S-STOP!
IT'S NOT READY!
"SHE GASPED, FEELING A STRANGE SENSATION IN HER AMPLE BOSOM."
"THE STRANGER WAS RIGHT. BUT SHE WAS ALSO INDESCRIBABLY BEAUTIFUL."
CUT IT UP! I DON'T CARE!
JUST CUT IT UP!
NO WAY.
IS THIS ABOUT ME?
YOU REALLY ARE... UH, WRITING ABOUT ME IN HERE. MY OWN WEIRD CHRONICLER.
WOW, WHO'S THIS 'STRANGER' CHARACTER? SEEMS SO FAMILIAR.
STOP! STOP! ENOUGH!
I'LL SPILL IT ALL! JUST GIVE IT BACK!
ALRIGHT.
LET'S START, HUH? YOU KNOW WAY TOO MUCH, YOU CAN USE SOME SORT OF MAGIC, YOU STILL HAVEN'T TOLD ME WHY YOU'RE 'WRITING MY TALE'...
AND THAT HUGE SLAVEMASTER DEVIL...
YOU'RE RUNNING AWAY FROM HIM. WHO IS HE?
HE'S...
MY HUSBAND.
TELL HER THE REST.
LET'S GO EAT.

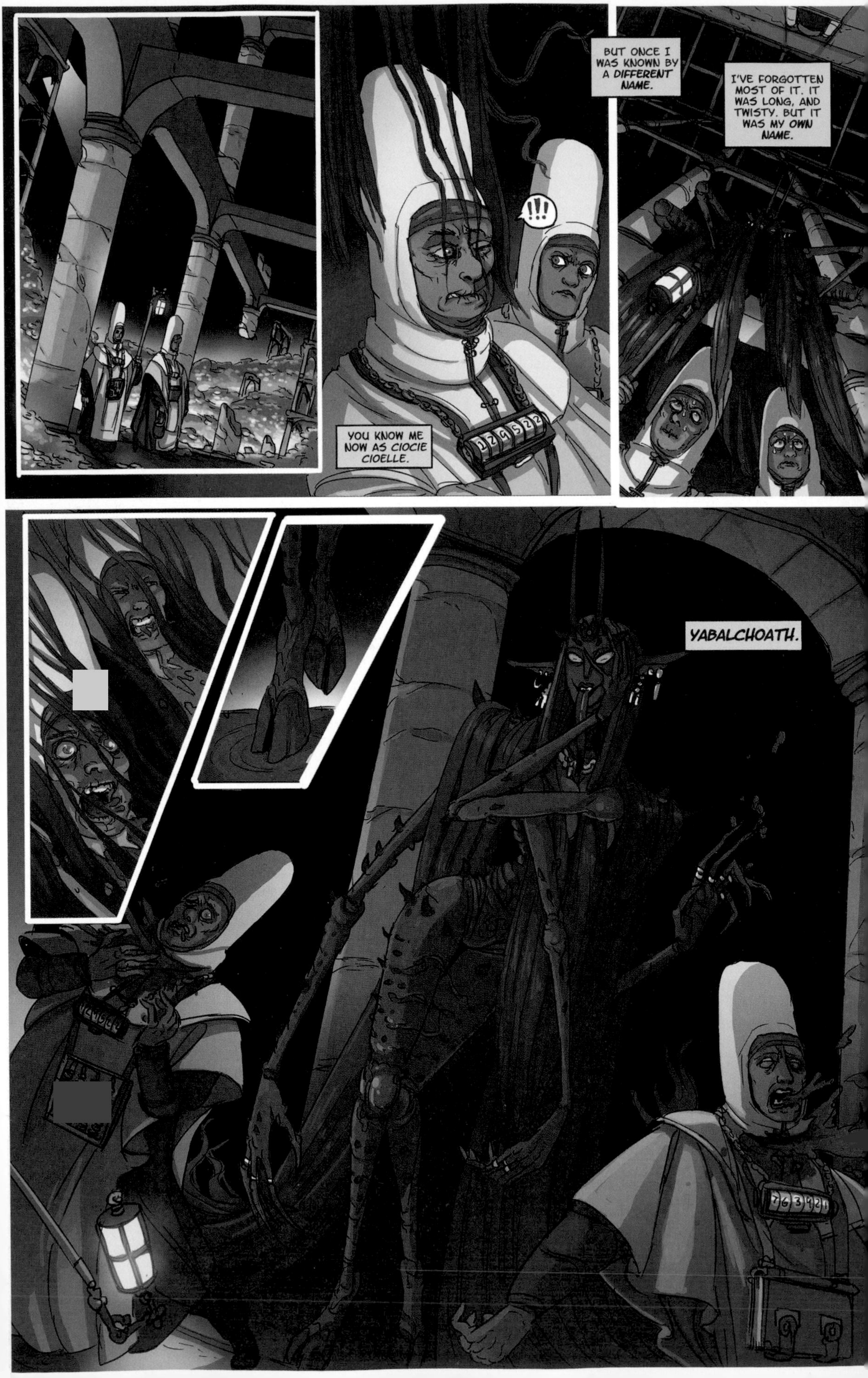
!!!
YOU KNOW ME NOW AS CIOCIE CIOELLE.
BUT ONCE I WAS KNOWN BY A DIFFERENT NAME.
I'VE FORGOTTEN MOST OF IT. IT WAS LONG, AND TWISTY. BUT IT WAS MY OWN NAME.
YABALCHOATH.

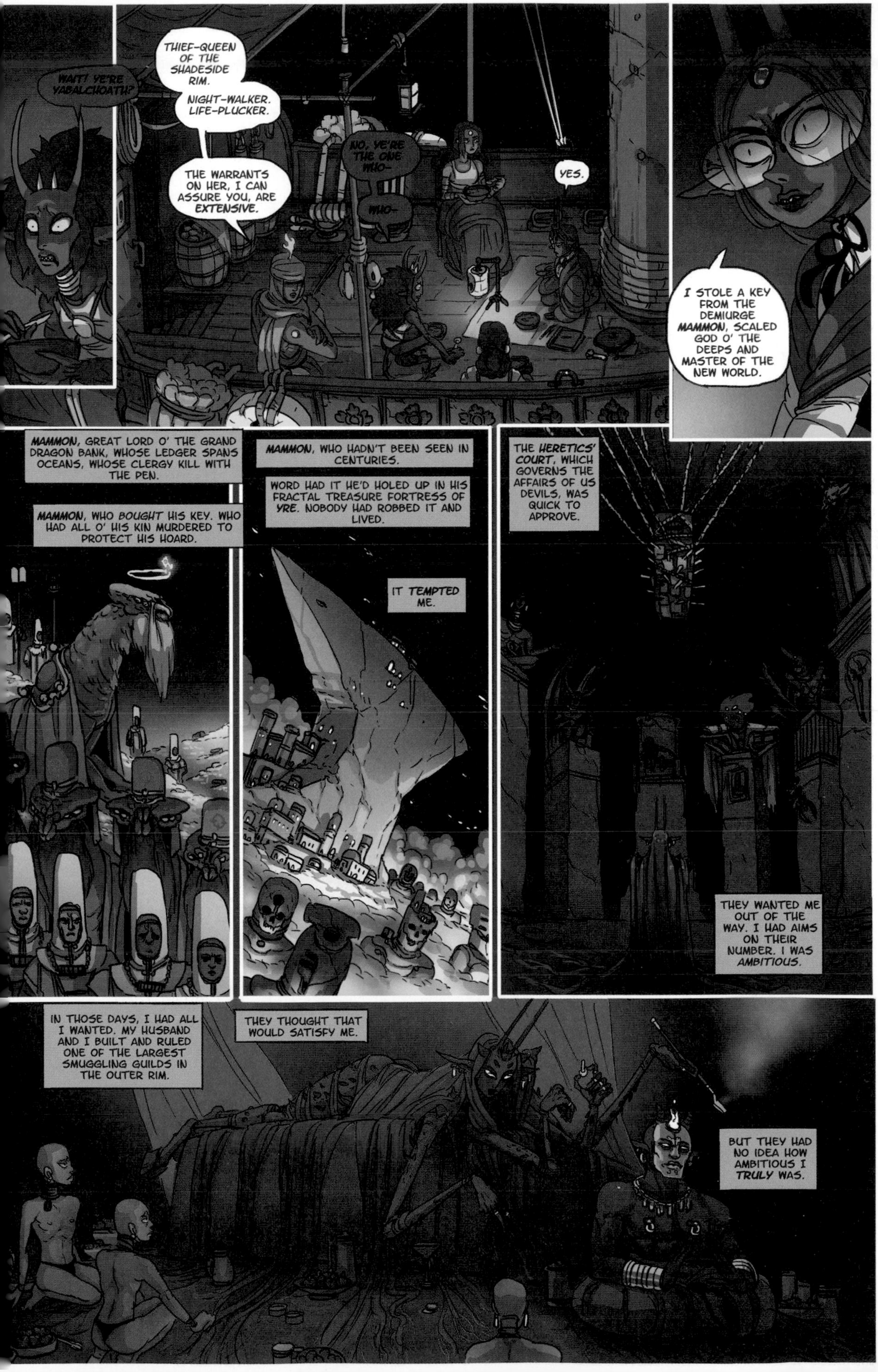
WAIT! YE'RE YABALCHOATH?
THIEF-QUEEN OF THE SHADESIDE RIM.
NIGHT-WALKER. LIFE-PLUCKER.
THE WARRANTS ON HER, I CAN ASSURE YOU, ARE EXTENSIVE.
NO, YE'RE THE ONE WHO-
WHO-
YES.
I STOLE A KEY FROM THE DEMIURGE MAMMON, SCALED GOD O' THE DEEPS AND MASTER OF THE NEW WORLD.
MAMMON, GREAT LORD O' THE GRAND DRAGON BANK, WHOSE LEDGER SPANS OCEANS, WHOSE CLERGY KILL WITH THE PEN.
MAMMON, WHO BOUGHT HIS KEY. WHO HAD ALL O' HIS KIN MURDERED TO PROTECT HIS HOARD.
MAMMON, WHO HADN'T BEEN SEEN IN CENTURIES.
WORD HAD IT HE'D HOLED UP IN HIS FRACTAL TREASURE FORTRESS OF YRE. NOBODY HAD ROBBED IT AND LIVED.
IT TEMPTED ME.
THE HERETICS' COURT, WHICH GOVERNS THE AFFAIRS OF US DEVILS, WAS QUICK TO APPROVE.
THEY WANTED ME OUT OF THE WAY. I HAD AIMS ON THEIR NUMBER. I WAS AMBITIOUS.
IN THOSE DAYS, I HAD ALL I WANTED. MY HUSBAND AND I BUILT AND RULED ONE OF THE LARGEST SMUGGLING GUILDS IN THE OUTER RIM.
THEY THOUGHT THAT WOULD SATISFY ME.
BUT THEY HAD NO IDEA HOW AMBITIOUS I TRULY WAS.

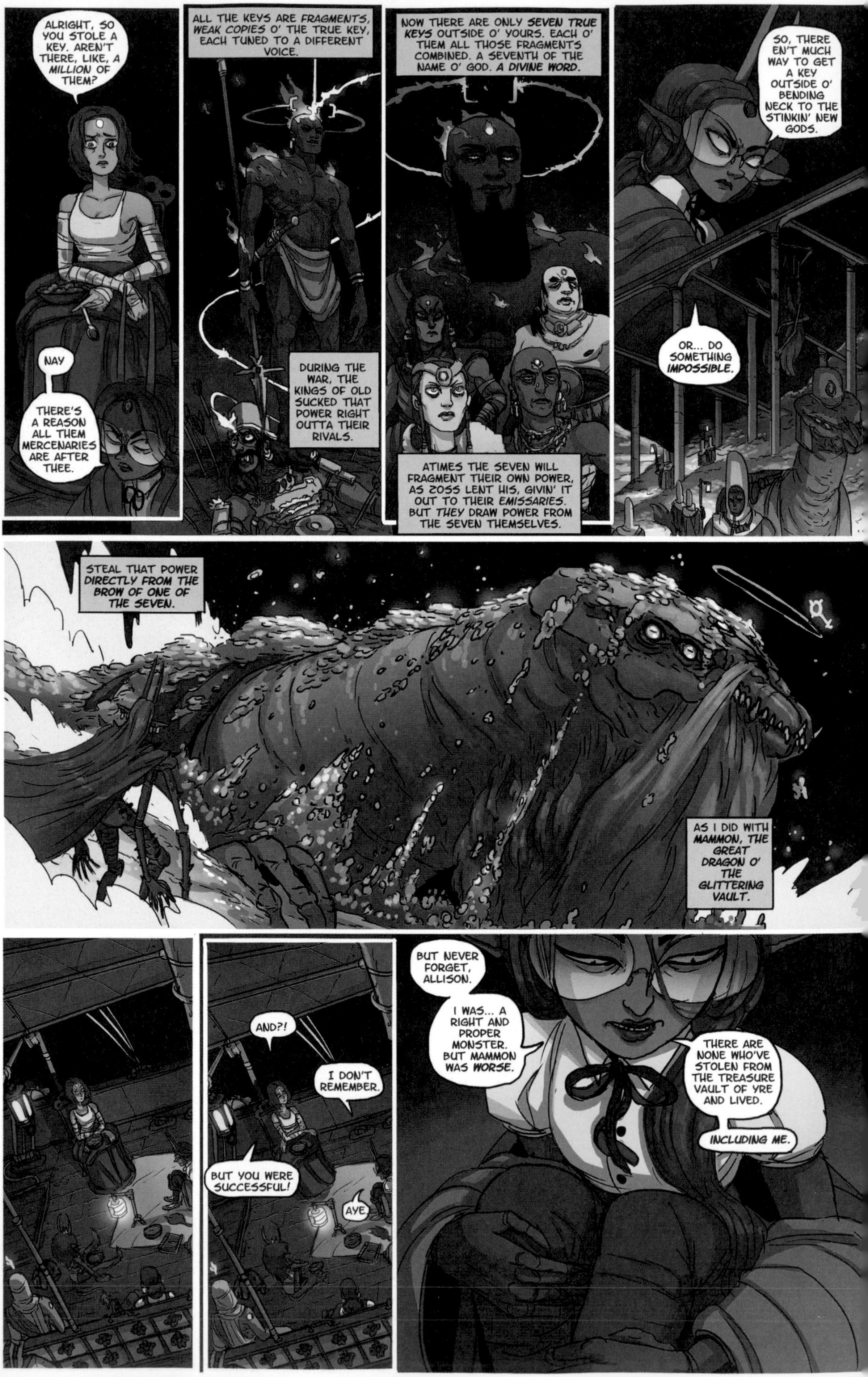
ALRIGHT, SO YOU STOLE A KEY. AREN'T THERE, LIKE, A MILLION OF THEM?
NAY
THERE'S A REASON ALL THEM MERCENARIES ARE AFTER THEE.
ALL THE KEYS ARE FRAGMENTS, WEAK COPIES O' THE TRUE KEY, EACH TUNED TO A DIFFERENT VOICE.
DURING THE WAR, THE KINGS OF OLD SUCKED THAT POWER RIGHT OUTTA THEIR RIVALS.
NOW THERE ARE ONLY SEVEN TRUE KEYS OUTSIDE O' YOURS. EACH O' THEM ALL THOSE FRAGMENTS COMBINED. A SEVENTH OF THE NAME O' GOD. A DIVINE WORD.
ATIMES THE SEVEN WILL FRAGMENT THEIR OWN POWER, AS ZOSS LENT HIS, GIVIN' IT OUT TO THEIR EMISSARIES. BUT THEY DRAW POWER FROM THE SEVEN THEMSELVES.
SO, THERE EN'T MUCH WAY TO GET A KEY OUTSIDE O' BENDING NECK TO THE STINKIN' NEW GODS.
OR... DO SOMETHING IMPOSSIBLE.
STEAL THAT POWER DIRECTLY FROM THE BROW OF ONE OF THE SEVEN.
AS I DID WITH MAMMON, THE GREAT DRAGON O' THE GLITTERING VAULT.
AND?!
I DON'T REMEMBER.
BUT YOU WERE SUCCESSFUL!
AYE.
BUT NEVER FORGET, ALLISON.
I WAS... A RIGHT AND PROPER MONSTER. BUT MAMMON WAS WORSE.
THERE ARE NONE WHO'VE STOLEN FROM THE TREASURE VAULT OF YRE AND LIVED.
INCLUDING ME.

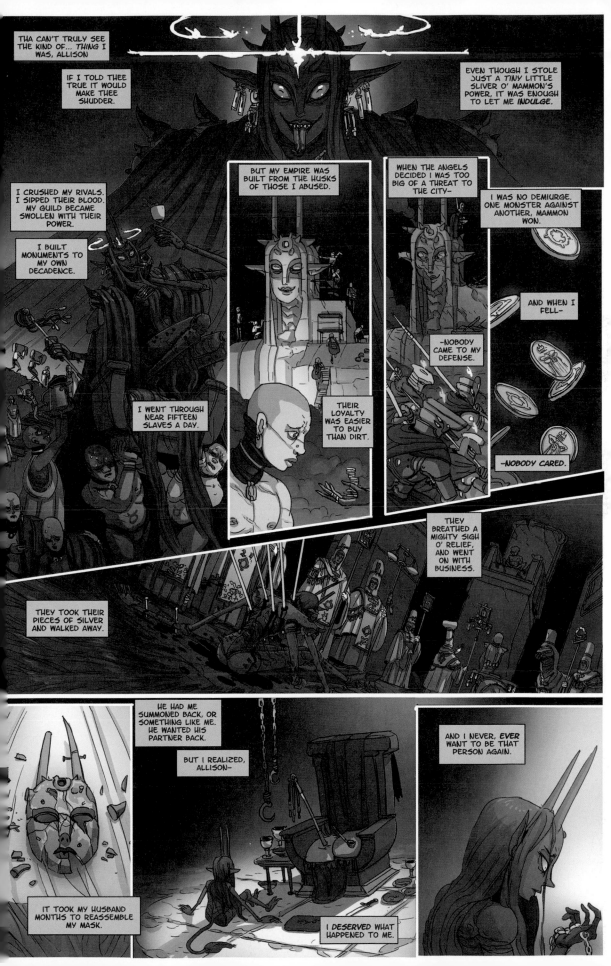

THA CAN'T TRULY SEE THE KIND OF... *THING* I WAS, ALLISON

IF I TOLD THEE TRUE IT WOULD MAKE THEE SHUDDER.

EVEN THOUGH I STOLE JUST A *TINY* LITTLE SLIVER O' MAMMON'S POWER, IT WAS ENOUGH TO LET ME *INDULGE*.

I CRUSHED MY RIVALS. I SIPPED THEIR BLOOD. MY GUILD BECAME SWOLLEN WITH THEIR POWER.

I BUILT MONUMENTS TO MY OWN DECADENCE.

BUT MY EMPIRE WAS BUILT FROM THE HUSKS OF THOSE I ABUSED.

WHEN THE ANGELS DECIDED I WAS TOO BIG OF A THREAT TO THE CITY—

I WAS NO DEMIURGE. ONE MONSTER AGAINST ANOTHER, MAMMON WON.

—NOBODY CAME TO MY DEFENSE.

AND WHEN I FELL—

I WENT THROUGH NEAR FIFTEEN SLAVES A DAY.

THEIR LOYALTY WAS EASIER TO BUY THAN DIRT.

—NOBODY CARED.

THEY BREATHED A MIGHTY SIGH O' RELIEF, AND WENT ON WITH BUSINESS.

THEY TOOK THEIR PIECES OF SILVER AND WALKED AWAY.

HE HAD ME SUMMONED BACK, OR SOMETHING LIKE ME. HE WANTED HIS PARTNER BACK.

BUT I REALIZED, ALLISON—

AND I NEVER, *EVER* WANT TO BE THAT PERSON AGAIN.

IT TOOK MY HUSBAND MONTHS TO REASSEMBLE MY MASK.

I DESERVED WHAT HAPPENED TO ME.

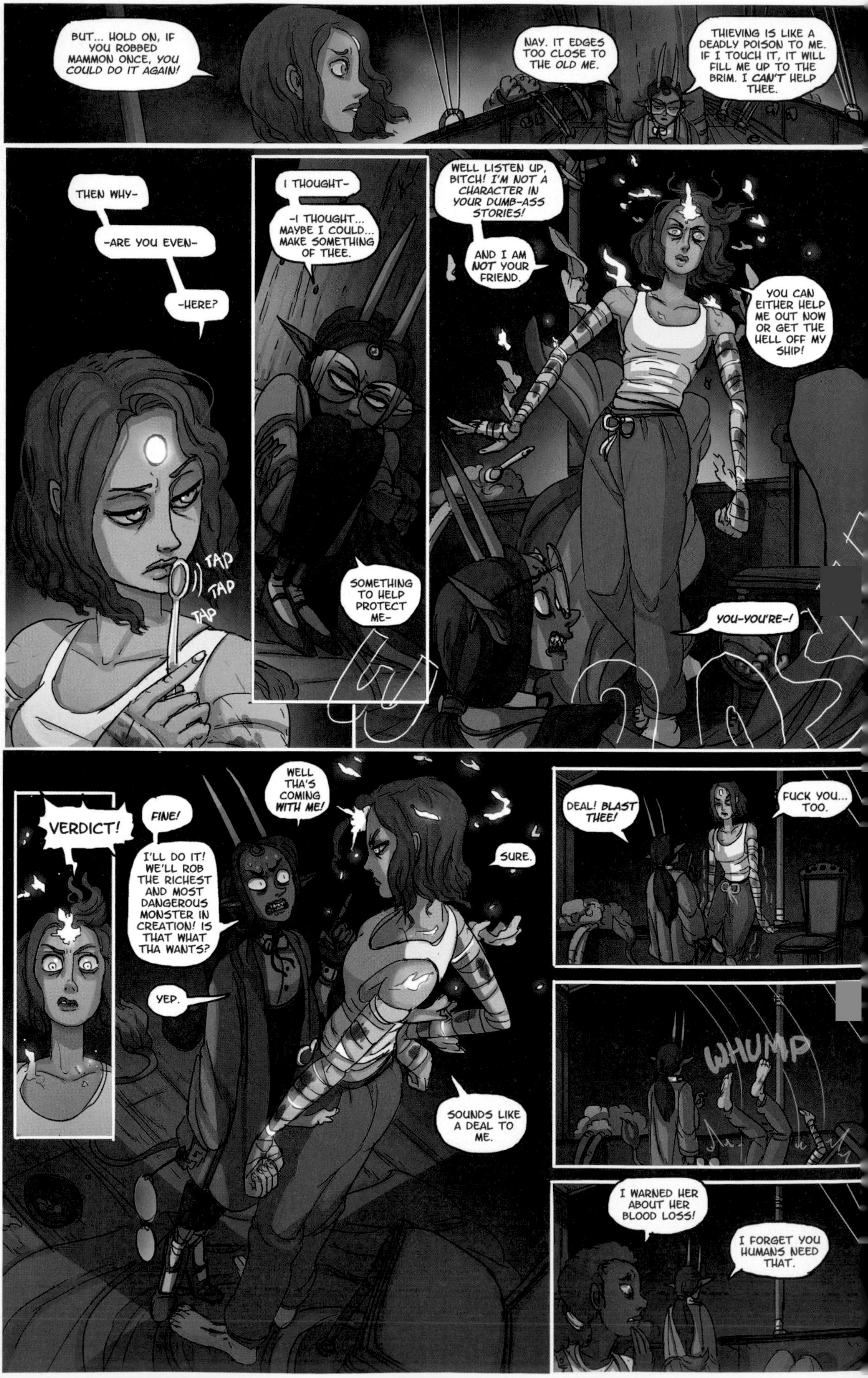
BUT... HOLD ON, IF YOU ROBBED MAMMON ONCE, YOU COULD DO IT AGAIN!
NAY. IT EDGES TOO CLOSE TO THE OLD ME.
THIEVING IS LIKE A DEADLY POISON TO ME. IF I TOUCH IT, IT WILL FILL ME UP TO THE BRIM. I CAN'T HELP THEE.
THEN WHY-
-ARE YOU EVEN-
-HERE?
TAP
TAP
TAP
I THOUGHT-
-I THOUGHT... MAYBE I COULD... MAKE SOMETHING OF THEE.
SOMETHING TO HELP PROTECT ME-
WELL LISTEN UP, BITCH! I'M NOT A CHARACTER IN YOUR DUMB-ASS STORIES!
AND I AM NOT YOUR FRIEND.
YOU CAN EITHER HELP ME OUT NOW OR GET THE HELL OFF MY SHIP!
YOU-YOU'RE-!
VERDICT!
FINE!
I'LL DO IT! WE'LL ROB THE RICHEST AND MOST DANGEROUS MONSTER IN CREATION! IS THAT WHAT THA WANTS?
YEP.
WELL THA'S COMING WITH ME!
SURE.
SOUNDS LIKE A DEAL TO ME.
DEAL! BLAST THEE!
FUCK YOU... TOO.
WHUMP
I WARNED HER ABOUT HER BLOOD LOSS!
I FORGET YOU HUMANS NEED THAT.

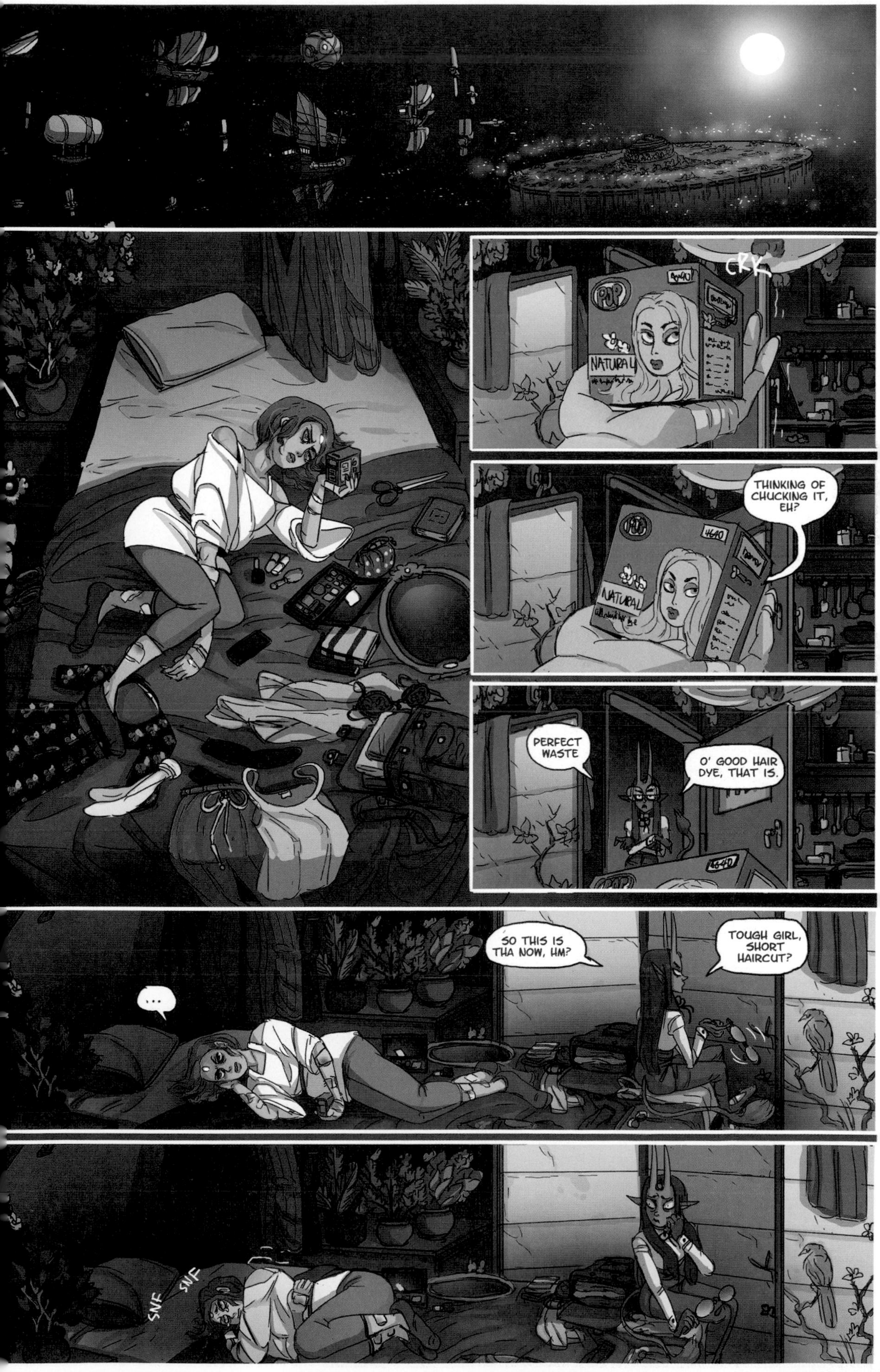
CRK
NATURAL
THINKING OF CHUCKING IT, EH?
NATURAL
PERFECT WASTE
O' GOOD HAIR DYE, THAT IS.
...
SO THIS IS THA NOW, HM?
TOUGH GIRL, SHORT HAIRCUT?
SNF SNF

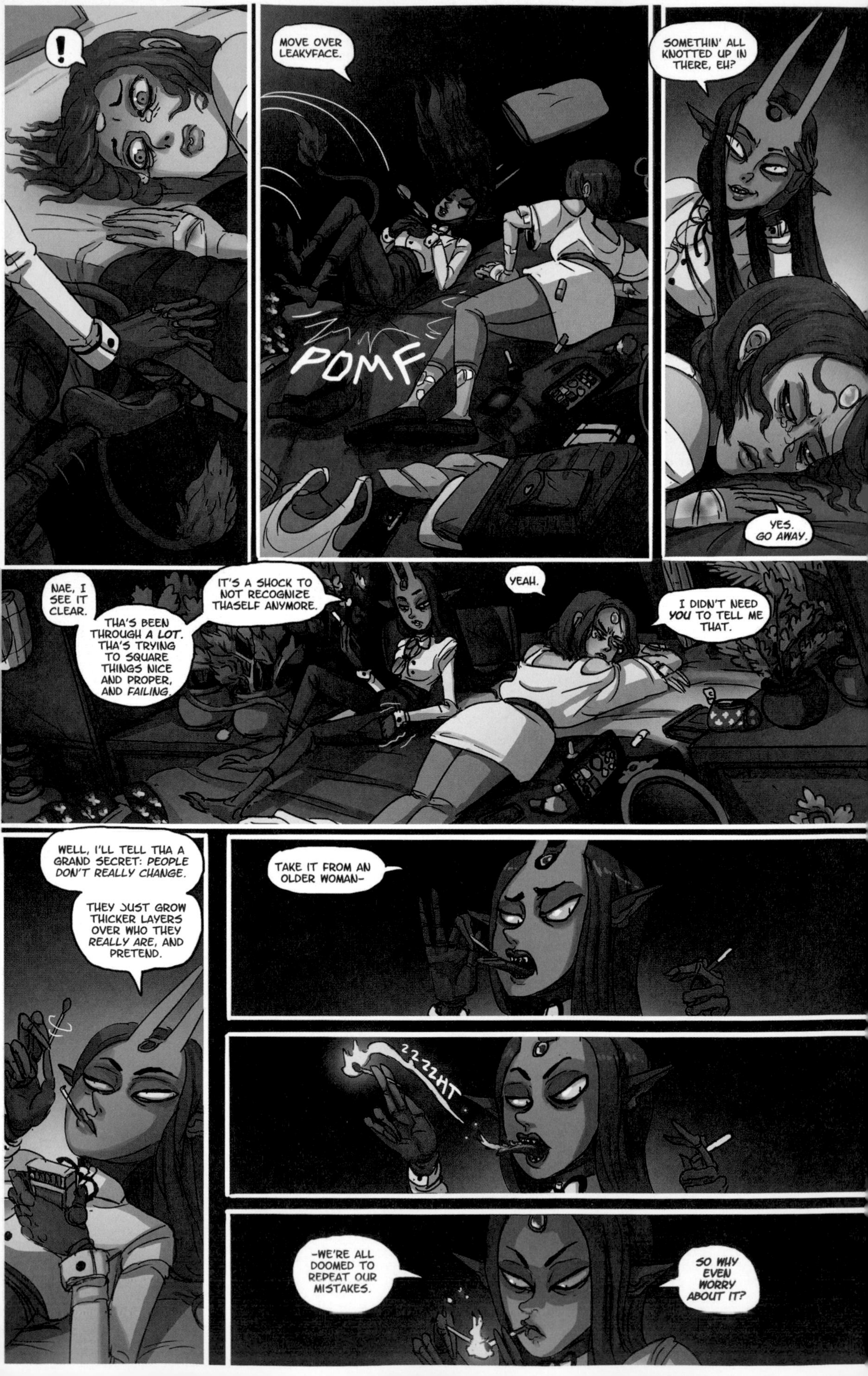
!
MOVE OVER LEAKYFACE.
POMF
SOMETHIN' ALL KNOTTED UP IN THERE, EH?
YES. GO AWAY.
NAE, I SEE IT CLEAR.
THA'S BEEN THROUGH A *LOT*. THA'S TRYING TO SQUARE THINGS NICE AND PROPER, AND *FAILING*.
IT'S A SHOCK TO NOT RECOGNIZE THASELF ANYMORE.
YEAH.
I DIDN'T NEED *YOU* TO TELL ME THAT.
WELL, I'LL TELL THA A GRAND SECRET: *PEOPLE DON'T REALLY CHANGE.*
THEY JUST GROW THICKER LAYERS OVER WHO THEY *REALLY ARE*, AND PRETEND.
TAKE IT FROM AN OLDER WOMAN–
ZZZZHT
–WE'RE ALL DOOMED TO REPEAT OUR MISTAKES.
SO WHY EVEN WORRY ABOUT IT?

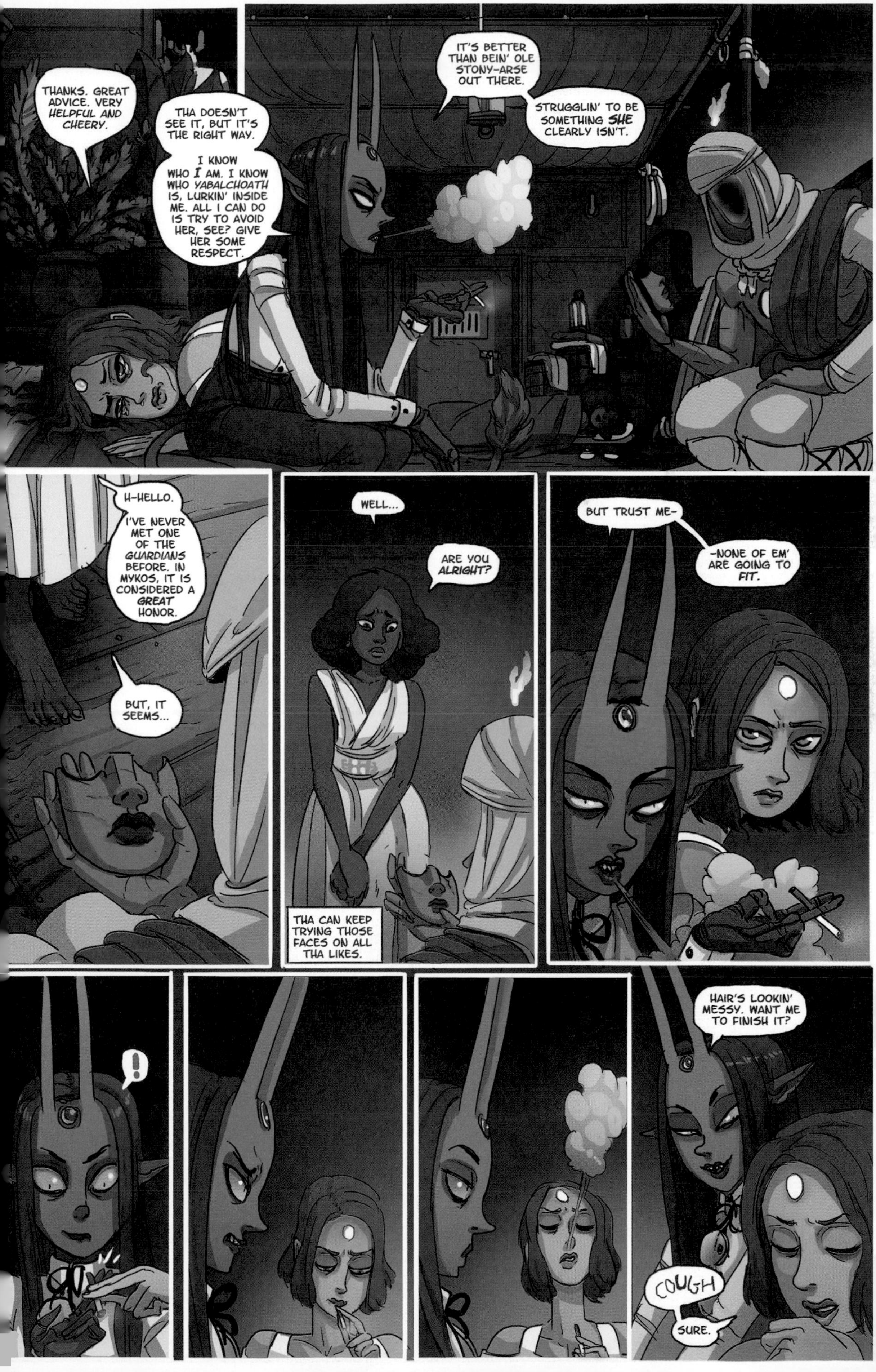
THANKS. GREAT ADVICE. VERY HELPFUL AND CHEERY.
THA DOESN'T SEE IT, BUT IT'S THE RIGHT WAY.
I KNOW WHO I AM. I KNOW WHO YABALCHOATH IS, LURKIN' INSIDE ME. ALL I CAN DO IS TRY TO AVOID HER, SEE? GIVE HER SOME RESPECT.
IT'S BETTER THAN BEIN' OLE STONY-ARSE OUT THERE.
STRUGGLIN' TO BE SOMETHING SHE CLEARLY ISN'T.
H-HELLO.
I'VE NEVER MET ONE OF THE GUARDIANS BEFORE. IN MYKOS, IT IS CONSIDERED A GREAT HONOR.
BUT, IT SEEMS...
WELL...
ARE YOU ALRIGHT?
THA CAN KEEP TRYING THOSE FACES ON ALL THA LIKES.
BUT TRUST ME-
-NONE OF EM' ARE GOING TO FIT.
!
HAIR'S LOOKIN' MESSY. WANT ME TO FINISH IT?
COUGH
SURE.

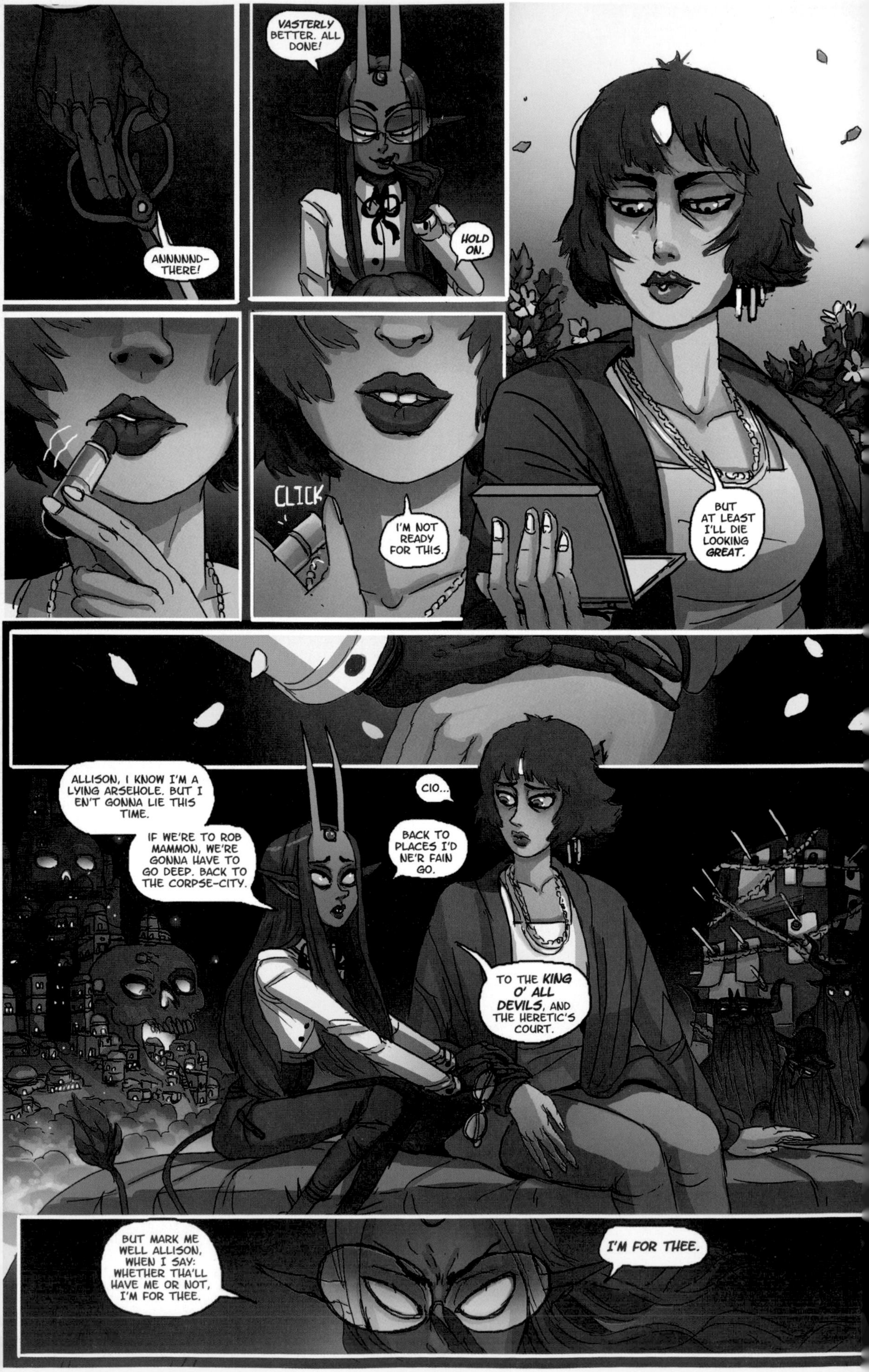
ANNNNND-THERE!
VASTERLY BETTER. ALL DONE!
HOLD ON.
CLICK
I'M NOT READY FOR THIS.
BUT AT LEAST I'LL DIE LOOKING GREAT.
ALLISON, I KNOW I'M A LYING ARSEHOLE. BUT I EN'T GONNA LIE THIS TIME.
IF WE'RE TO ROB MAMMON, WE'RE GONNA HAVE TO GO DEEP. BACK TO THE CORPSE-CITY.
CIO...
BACK TO PLACES I'D NE'R FAIN GO.
TO THE KING O' ALL DEVILS, AND THE HERETIC'S COURT.
BUT MARK ME WELL ALLISON, WHEN I SAY: WHETHER THA'LL HAVE ME OR NOT, I'M FOR THEE.
I'M FOR THEE.

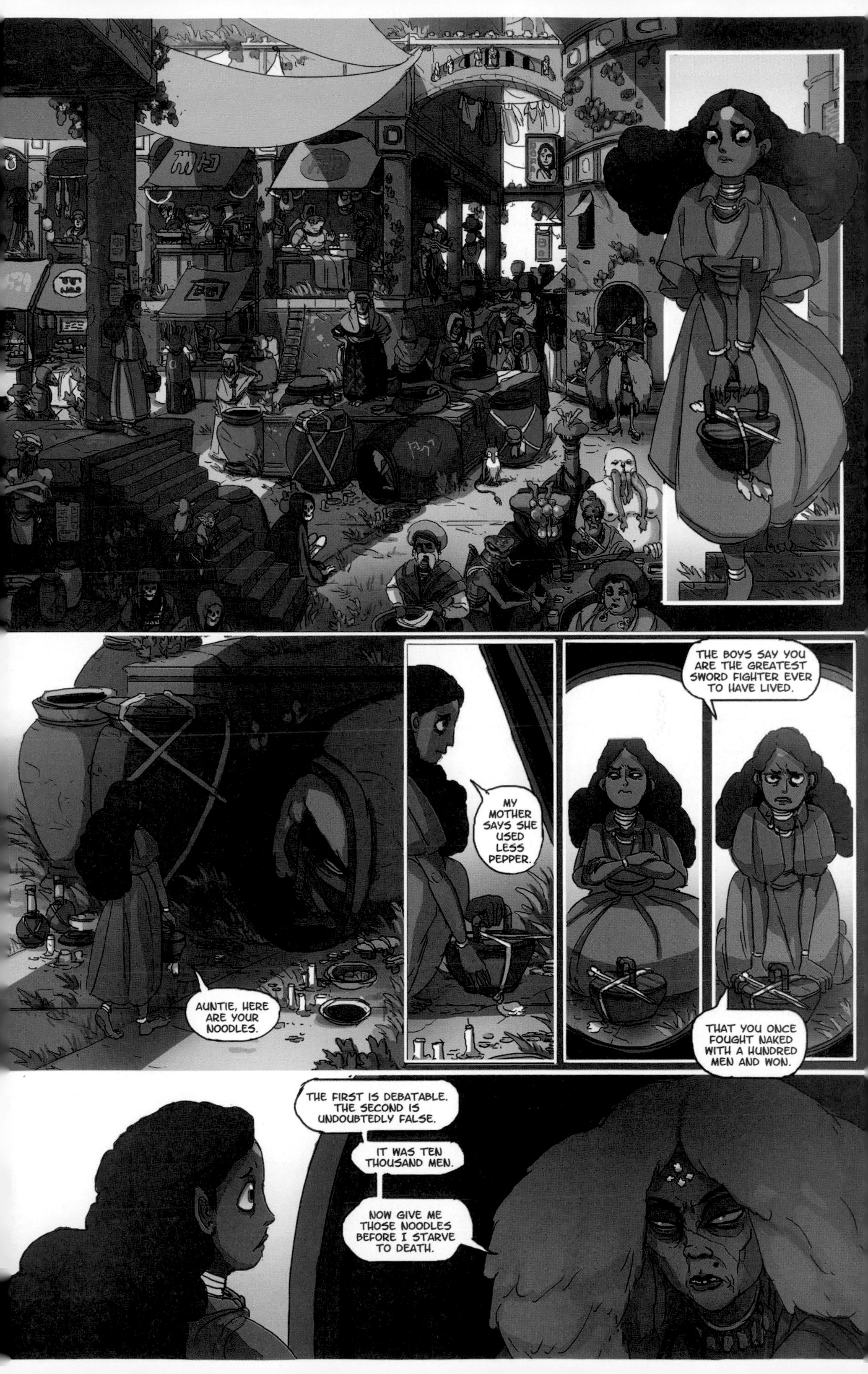
AUNTIE, HERE ARE YOUR NOODLES.
MY MOTHER SAYS SHE USED LESS PEPPER.
THE BOYS SAY YOU ARE THE GREATEST SWORD FIGHTER EVER TO HAVE LIVED.
THAT YOU ONCE FOUGHT NAKED WITH A HUNDRED MEN AND WON.
THE FIRST IS DEBATABLE. THE SECOND IS UNDOUBTEDLY FALSE.
IT WAS TEN THOUSAND MEN.
NOW GIVE ME THOSE NOODLES BEFORE I STARVE TO DEATH.

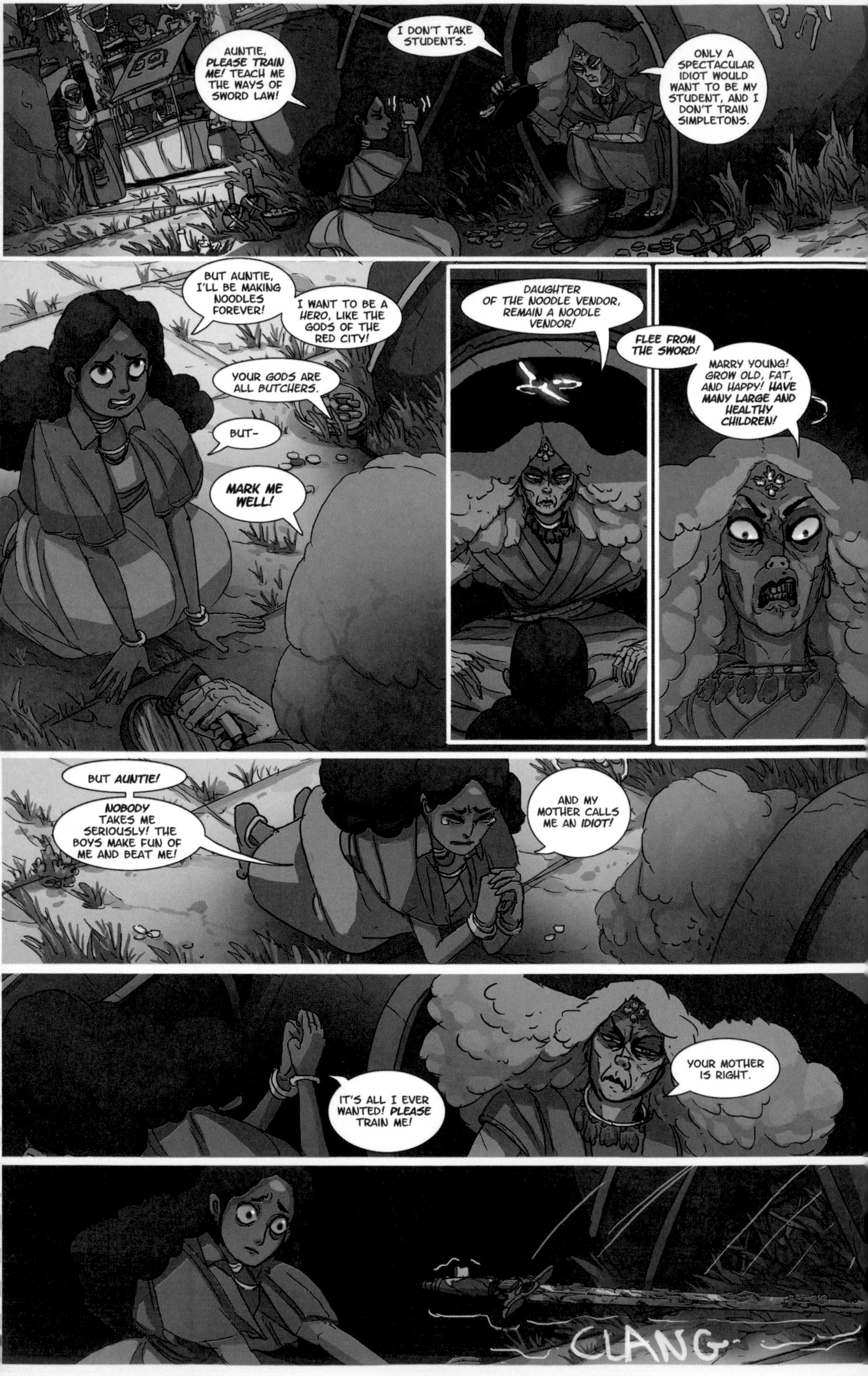
AUNTIE, PLEASE TRAIN ME! TEACH ME THE WAYS OF SWORD LAW!
I DON'T TAKE STUDENTS.
ONLY A SPECTACULAR IDIOT WOULD WANT TO BE MY STUDENT, AND I DON'T TRAIN SIMPLETONS.
BUT AUNTIE, I'LL BE MAKING NOODLES FOREVER!
I WANT TO BE A HERO, LIKE THE GODS OF THE RED CITY!
YOUR GODS ARE ALL BUTCHERS.
BUT-
MARK ME WELL!
DAUGHTER OF THE NOODLE VENDOR, REMAIN A NOODLE VENDOR!
FLEE FROM THE SWORD!
MARRY YOUNG! GROW OLD, FAT, AND HAPPY! HAVE MANY LARGE AND HEALTHY CHILDREN!
BUT AUNTIE!
NOBODY TAKES ME SERIOUSLY! THE BOYS MAKE FUN OF ME AND BEAT ME!
AND MY MOTHER CALLS ME AN IDIOT!
IT'S ALL I EVER WANTED! PLEASE TRAIN ME!
YOUR MOTHER IS RIGHT.
CLANG

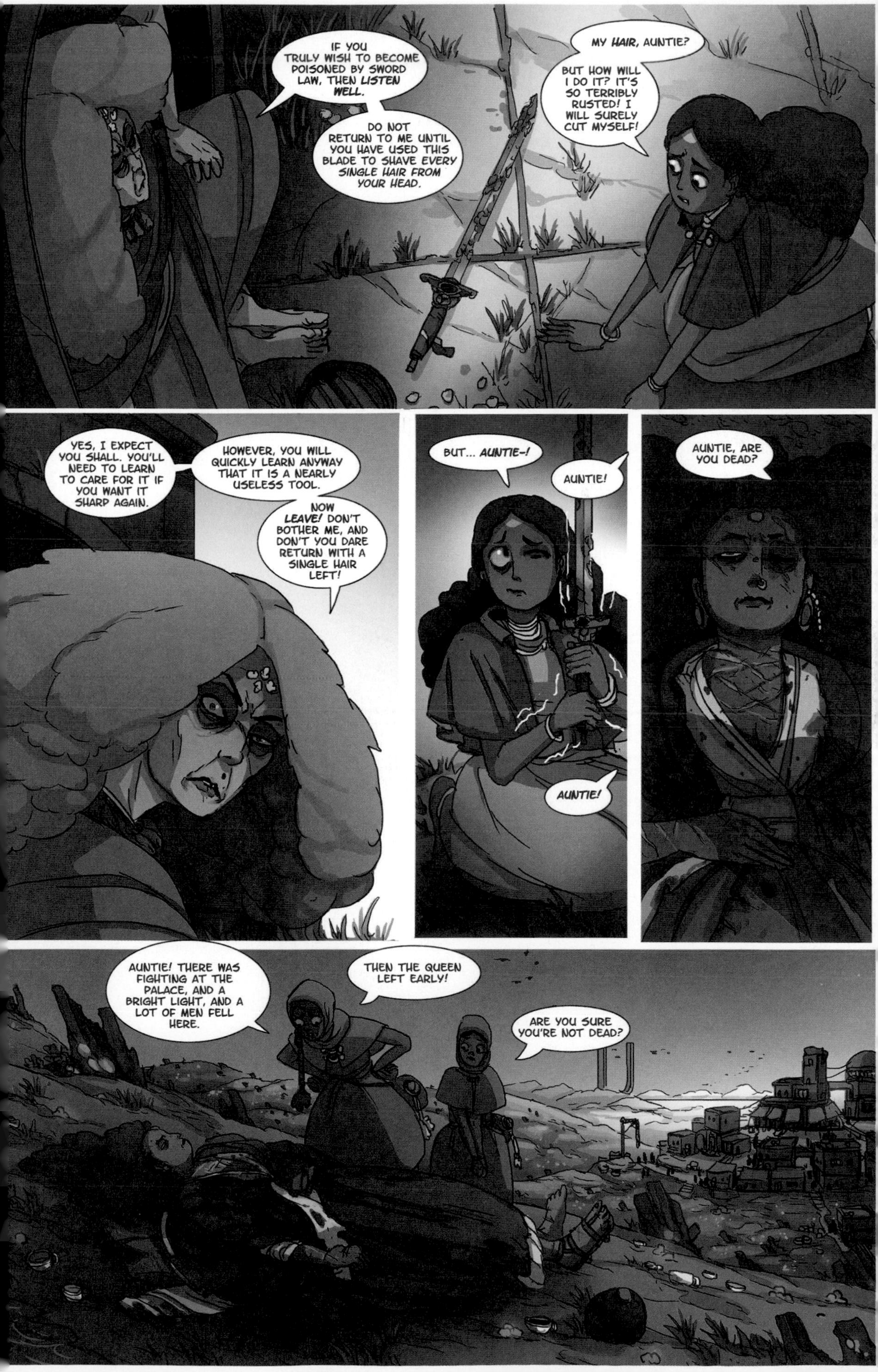
IF YOU TRULY WISH TO BECOME POISONED BY SWORD LAW, THEN *LISTEN WELL*.
DO NOT RETURN TO ME UNTIL YOU HAVE USED THIS BLADE TO SHAVE EVERY SINGLE HAIR FROM YOUR HEAD.
MY *HAIR*, AUNTIE?
BUT HOW WILL I DO IT? IT'S SO TERRIBLY RUSTED! I WILL SURELY CUT MYSELF!
YES, I EXPECT YOU SHALL. YOU'LL NEED TO LEARN TO CARE FOR IT IF YOU WANT IT SHARP AGAIN.
HOWEVER, YOU WILL QUICKLY LEARN ANYWAY THAT IT IS A NEARLY USELESS TOOL.
NOW *LEAVE!* DON'T BOTHER ME, AND DON'T YOU DARE RETURN WITH A SINGLE HAIR LEFT!
BUT... *AUNTIE-!*
AUNTIE!
AUNTIE!
AUNTIE, ARE YOU DEAD?
AUNTIE! THERE WAS FIGHTING AT THE PALACE, AND A BRIGHT LIGHT, AND A LOT OF MEN FELL HERE.
THEN THE QUEEN LEFT EARLY!
ARE YOU SURE YOU'RE NOT DEAD?

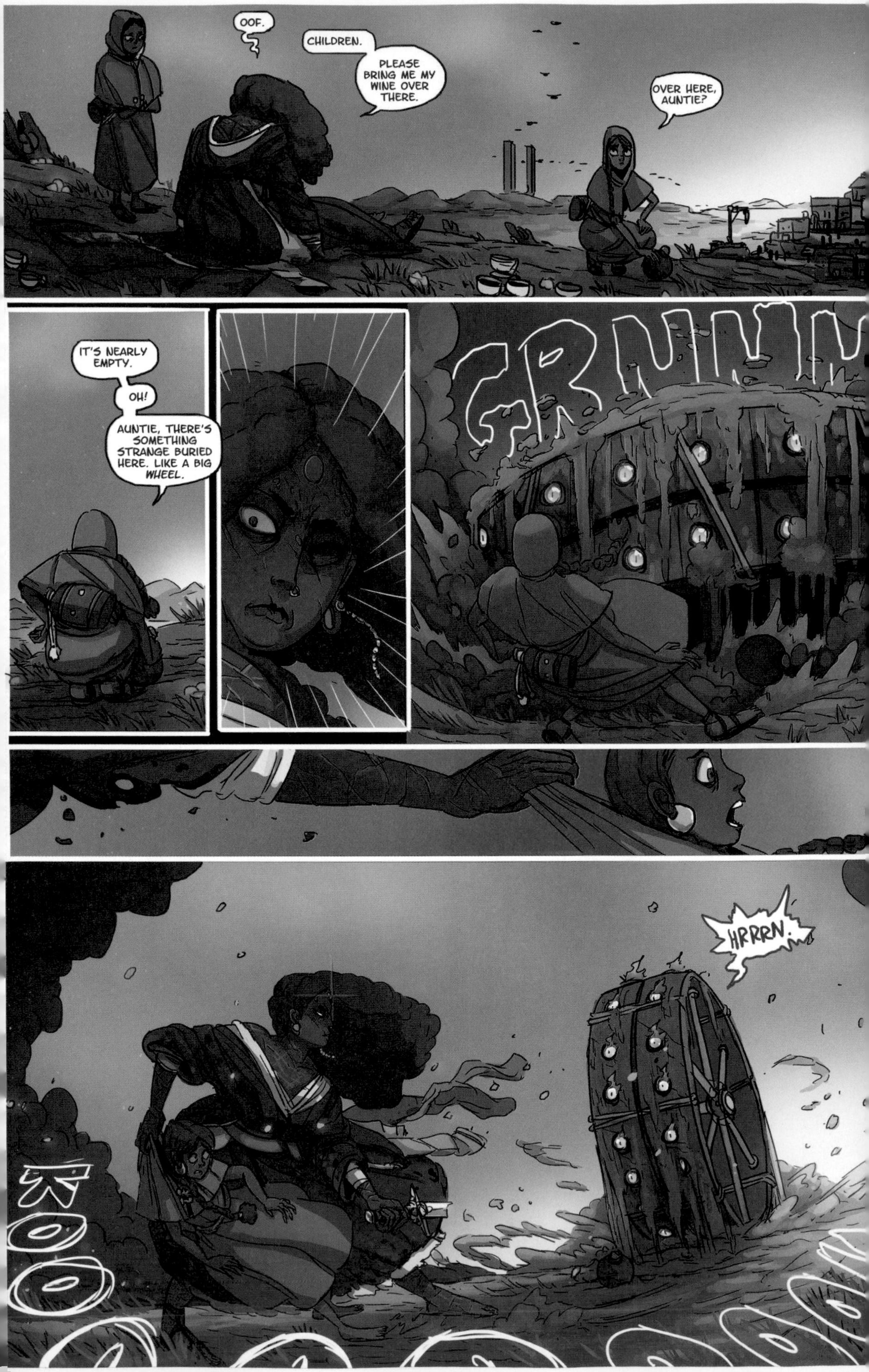
OOF.
CHILDREN.
PLEASE BRING ME MY WINE OVER THERE.
OVER HERE, AUNTIE?
IT'S NEARLY EMPTY.
OH!
AUNTIE, THERE'S SOMETHING STRANGE BURIED HERE. LIKE A BIG WHEEL.
GRMMM
HRRRN.
BOOOM

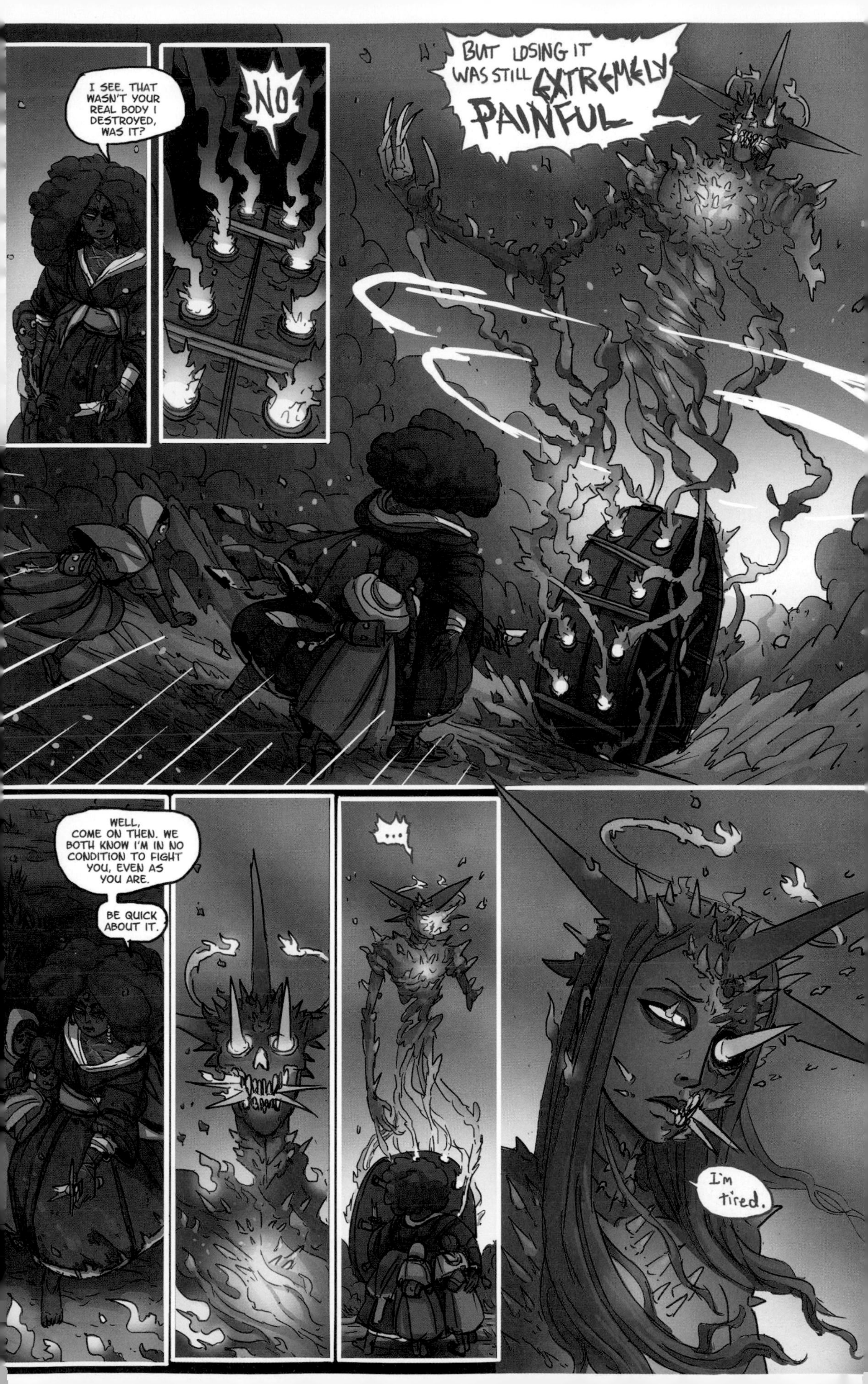
I SEE. THAT WASN'T YOUR REAL BODY I DESTROYED, WAS IT?
NO
BUT LOSING IT WAS STILL EXTREMELY PAINFUL
WELL, COME ON THEN. WE BOTH KNOW I'M IN NO CONDITION TO FIGHT YOU, EVEN AS YOU ARE.
BE QUICK ABOUT IT.
...
I'm tired.

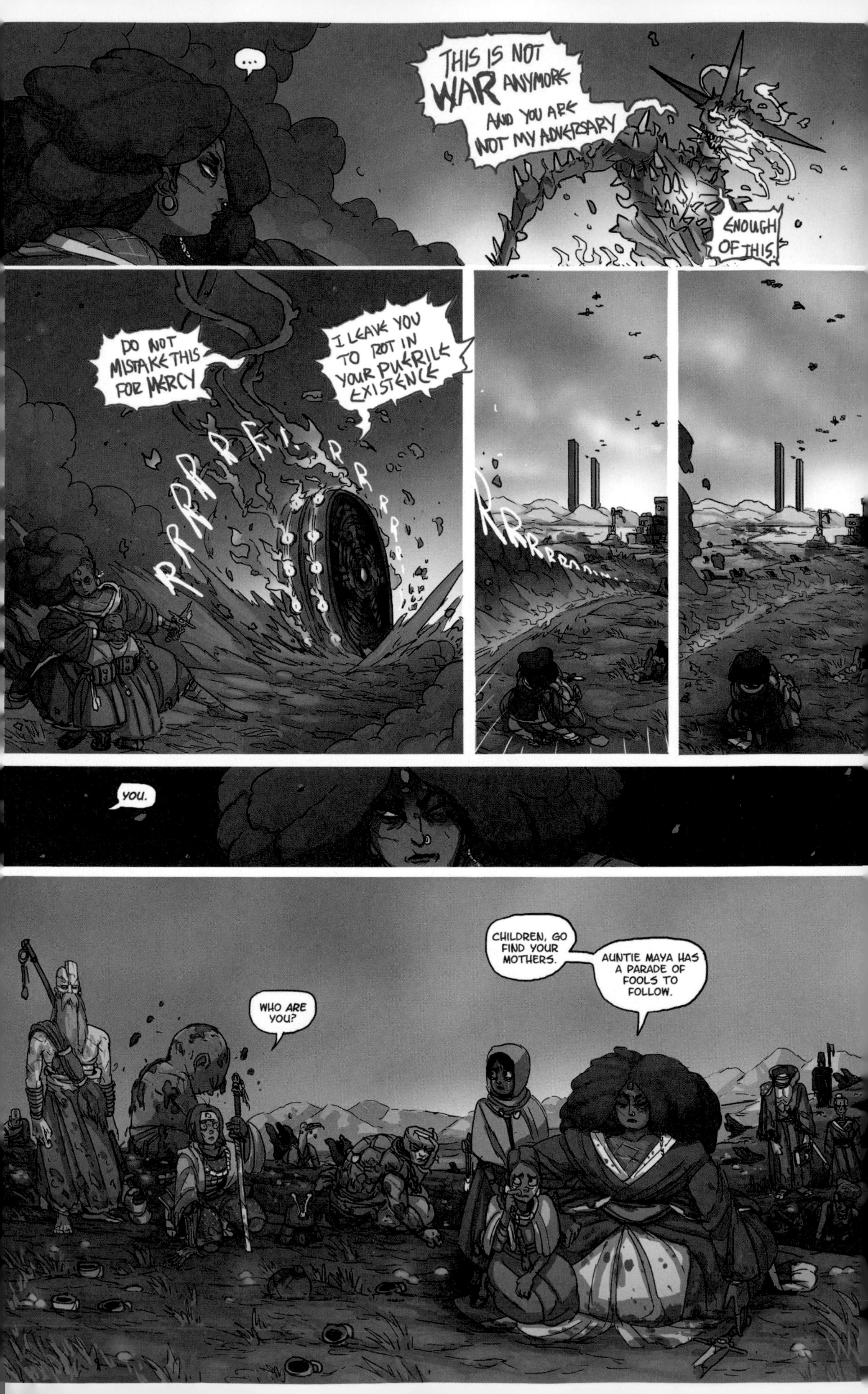
...
THIS IS NOT WAR ANYMORE
AND YOU ARE NOT MY ADVERSARY
ENOUGH OF THIS.
DO NOT MISTAKE THIS FOR MERCY
I LEAVE YOU TO ROT IN YOUR PUERILE EXISTENCE
RRRRRRR!
RRRRRRR
RRRRrrr.....
YOU.
WHO ARE YOU?
CHILDREN, GO FIND YOUR MOTHERS.
AUNTIE MAYA HAS A PARADE OF FOOLS TO FOLLOW.

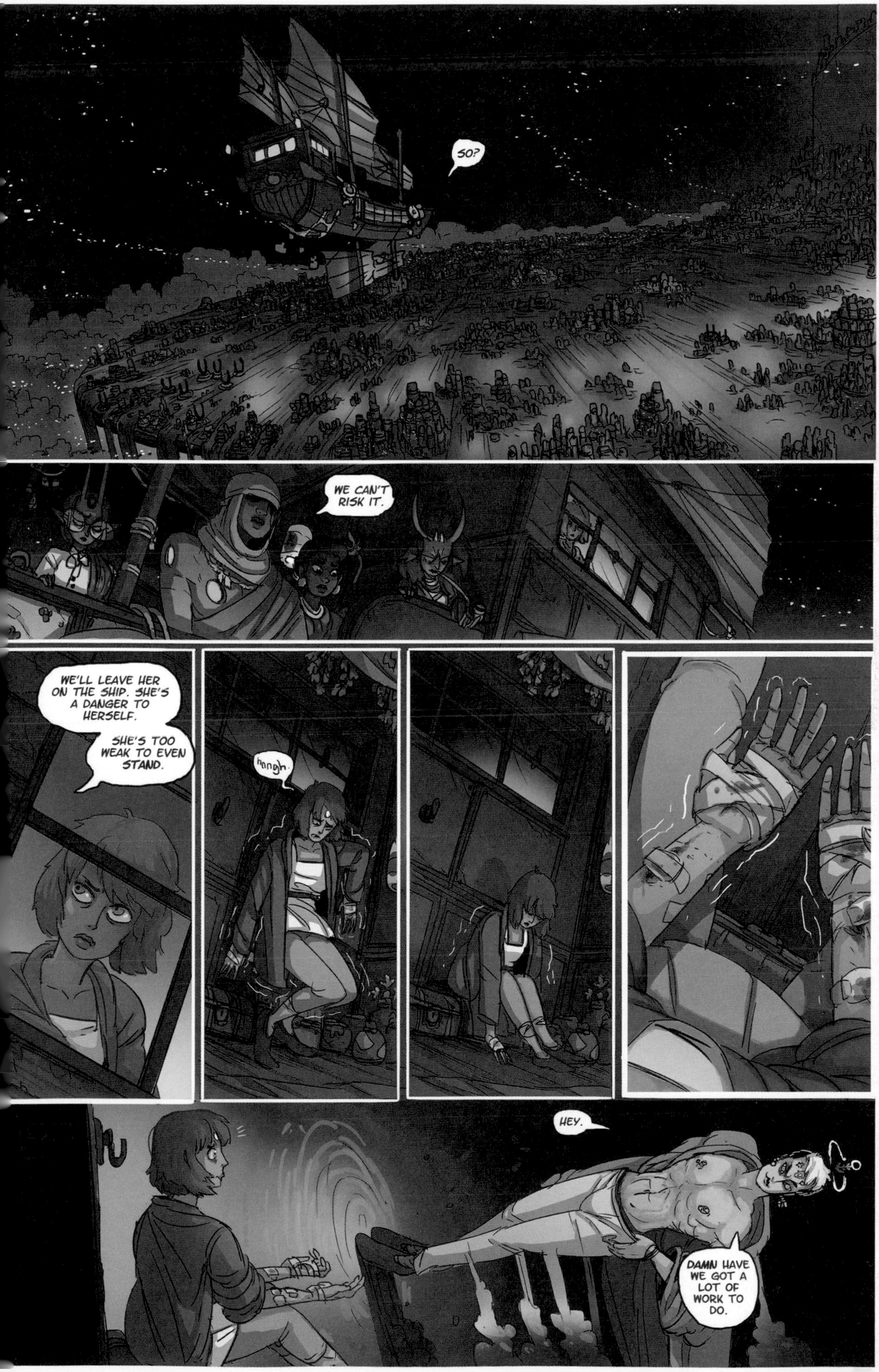
SO?
WE CAN'T RISK IT.
WE'LL LEAVE HER ON THE SHIP. SHE'S A DANGER TO HERSELF.
SHE'S TOO WEAK TO EVEN STAND.
hnngh.
HEY.
DAMN HAVE WE GOT A LOT OF WORK TO DO.

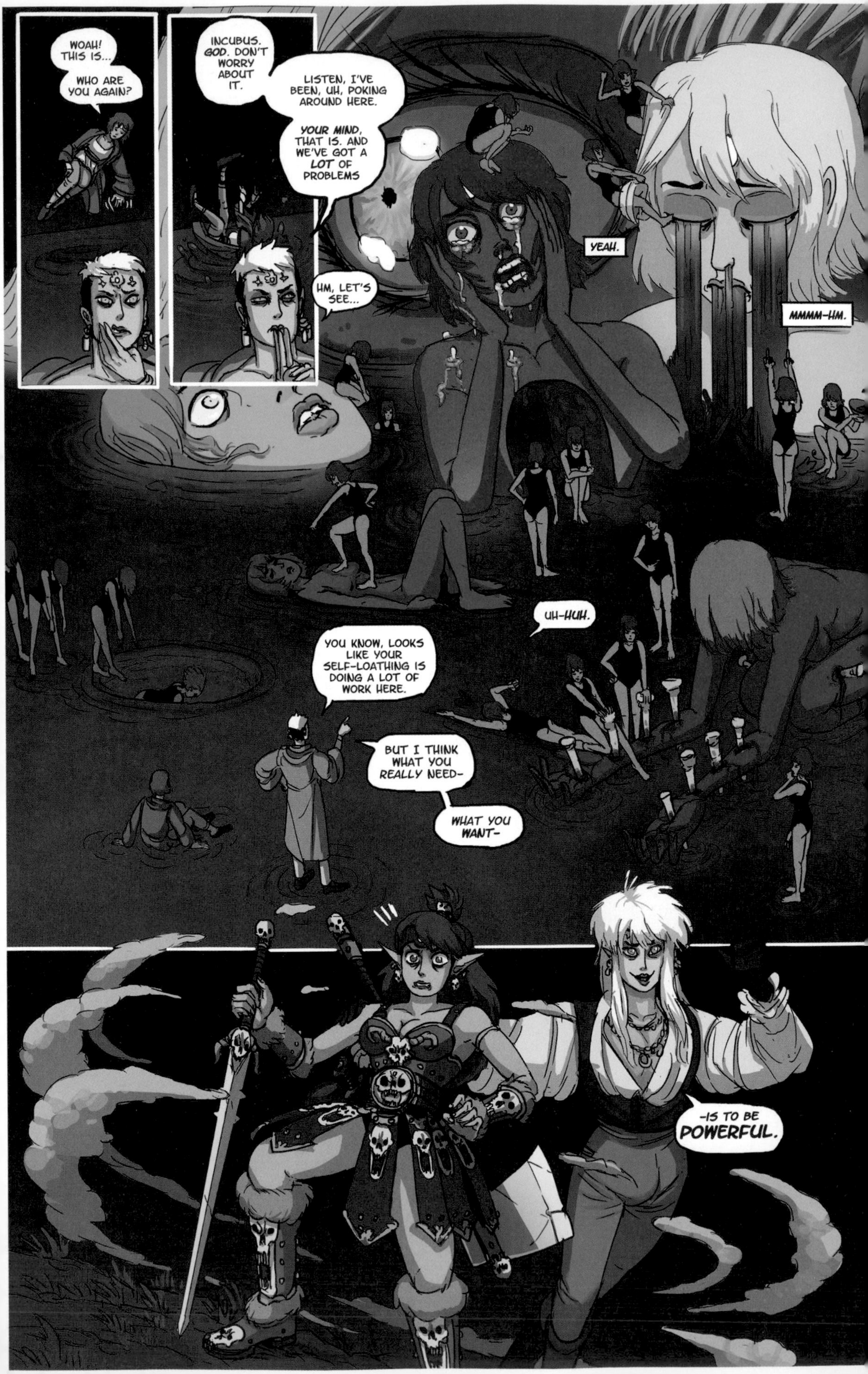
WOAH! THIS IS...
WHO ARE YOU AGAIN?
INCUBUS. GOD. DON'T WORRY ABOUT IT.
LISTEN, I'VE BEEN, UH, POKING AROUND HERE.
YOUR MIND, THAT IS. AND WE'VE GOT A LOT OF PROBLEMS
HM, LET'S SEE...
YEAH.
MMMM-HM.
UH-HUH.
YOU KNOW, LOOKS LIKE YOUR SELF-LOATHING IS DOING A LOT OF WORK HERE.
BUT I THINK WHAT YOU REALLY NEED-
WHAT YOU WANT-
-IS TO BE POWERFUL.

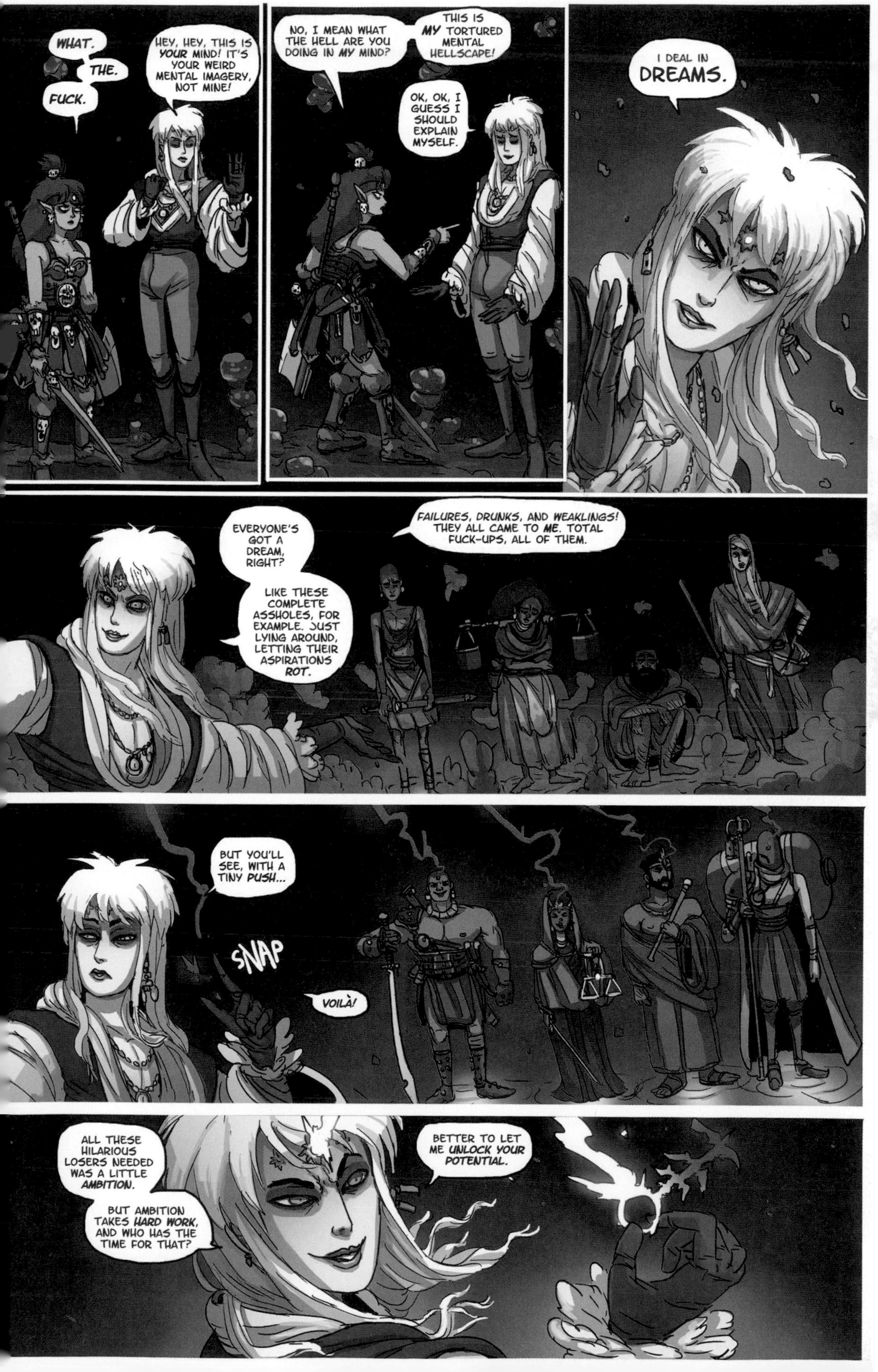

WHAT.
THE.
FUCK.
HEY, HEY, THIS IS YOUR MIND! IT'S YOUR WEIRD MENTAL IMAGERY, NOT MINE!
NO, I MEAN WHAT THE HELL ARE YOU DOING IN MY MIND?
THIS IS MY TORTURED MENTAL HELLSCAPE!
OK, OK, I GUESS I SHOULD EXPLAIN MYSELF.
I DEAL IN DREAMS.
EVERYONE'S GOT A DREAM, RIGHT?
LIKE THESE COMPLETE ASSHOLES, FOR EXAMPLE. JUST LYING AROUND, LETTING THEIR ASPIRATIONS ROT.
FAILURES, DRUNKS, AND WEAKLINGS! THEY ALL CAME TO ME. TOTAL FUCK-UPS, ALL OF THEM.
BUT YOU'LL SEE, WITH A TINY PUSH...
SNAP
VOILÀ!
ALL THESE HILARIOUS LOSERS NEEDED WAS A LITTLE AMBITION.
BUT AMBITION TAKES HARD WORK, AND WHO HAS THE TIME FOR THAT?
BETTER TO LET ME UNLOCK YOUR POTENTIAL.

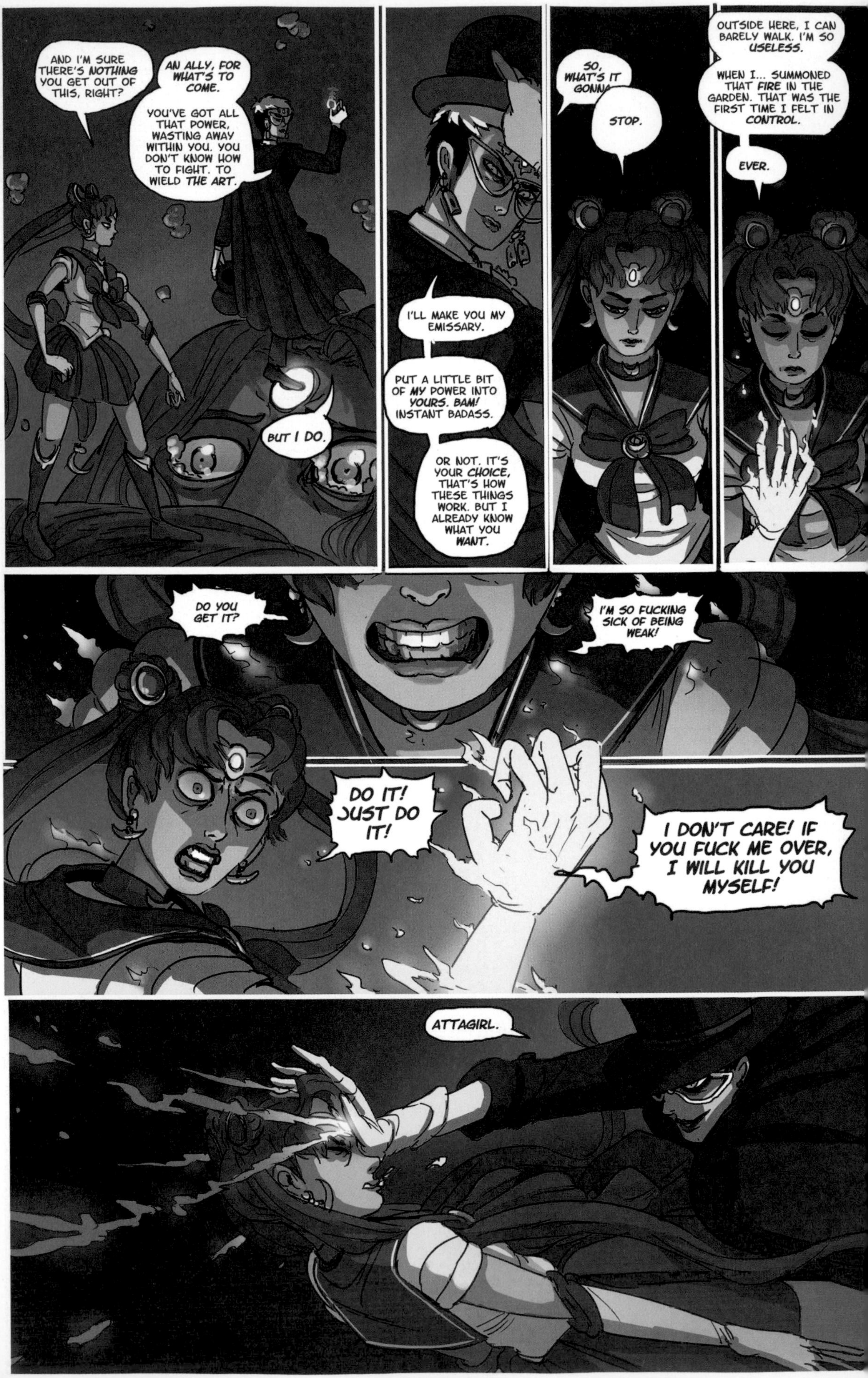
AND I'M SURE THERE'S NOTHING YOU GET OUT OF THIS, RIGHT?
AN ALLY, FOR WHAT'S TO COME.
YOU'VE GOT ALL THAT POWER, WASTING AWAY WITHIN YOU. YOU DON'T KNOW HOW TO FIGHT. TO WIELD THE ART.
BUT I DO.
I'LL MAKE YOU MY EMISSARY.
PUT A LITTLE BIT OF MY POWER INTO YOURS. BAM! INSTANT BADASS.
OR NOT. IT'S YOUR CHOICE, THAT'S HOW THESE THINGS WORK. BUT I ALREADY KNOW WHAT YOU WANT.
SO, WHAT'S IT GONNA
STOP.
OUTSIDE HERE, I CAN BARELY WALK. I'M SO USELESS.
WHEN I... SUMMONED THAT FIRE IN THE GARDEN. THAT WAS THE FIRST TIME I FELT IN CONTROL.
EVER.
DO YOU GET IT?
I'M SO FUCKING SICK OF BEING WEAK!
DO IT! JUST DO IT!
I DON'T CARE! IF YOU FUCK ME OVER, I WILL KILL YOU MYSELF!
ATTAGIRL.

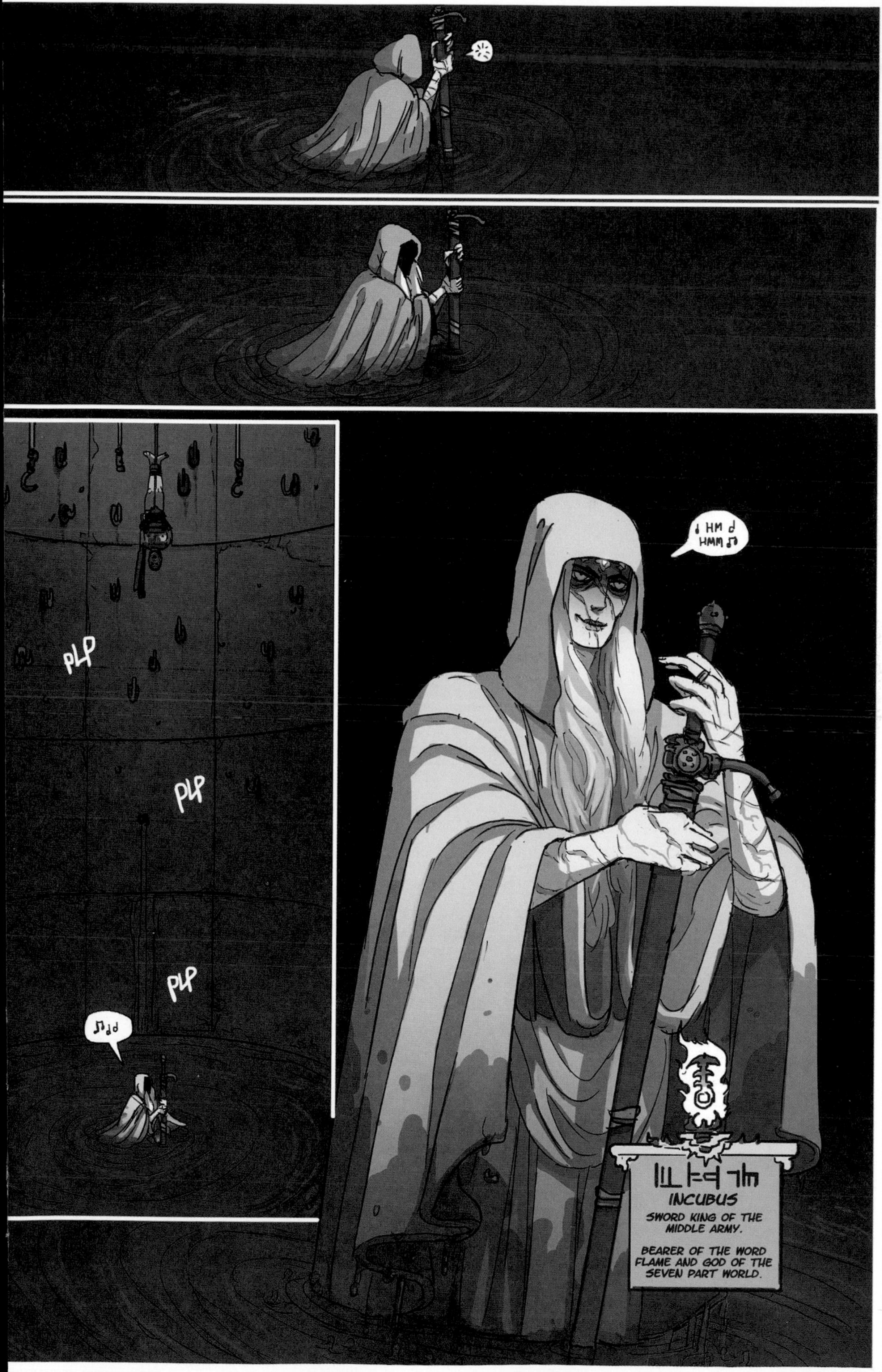
PLP
PLP
PLP
♪ HM ♪
HMM ♫
INCUBUS
SWORD KING OF THE MIDDLE ARMY.
BEARER OF THE WORD FLAME AND GOD OF THE SEVEN PART WORLD.

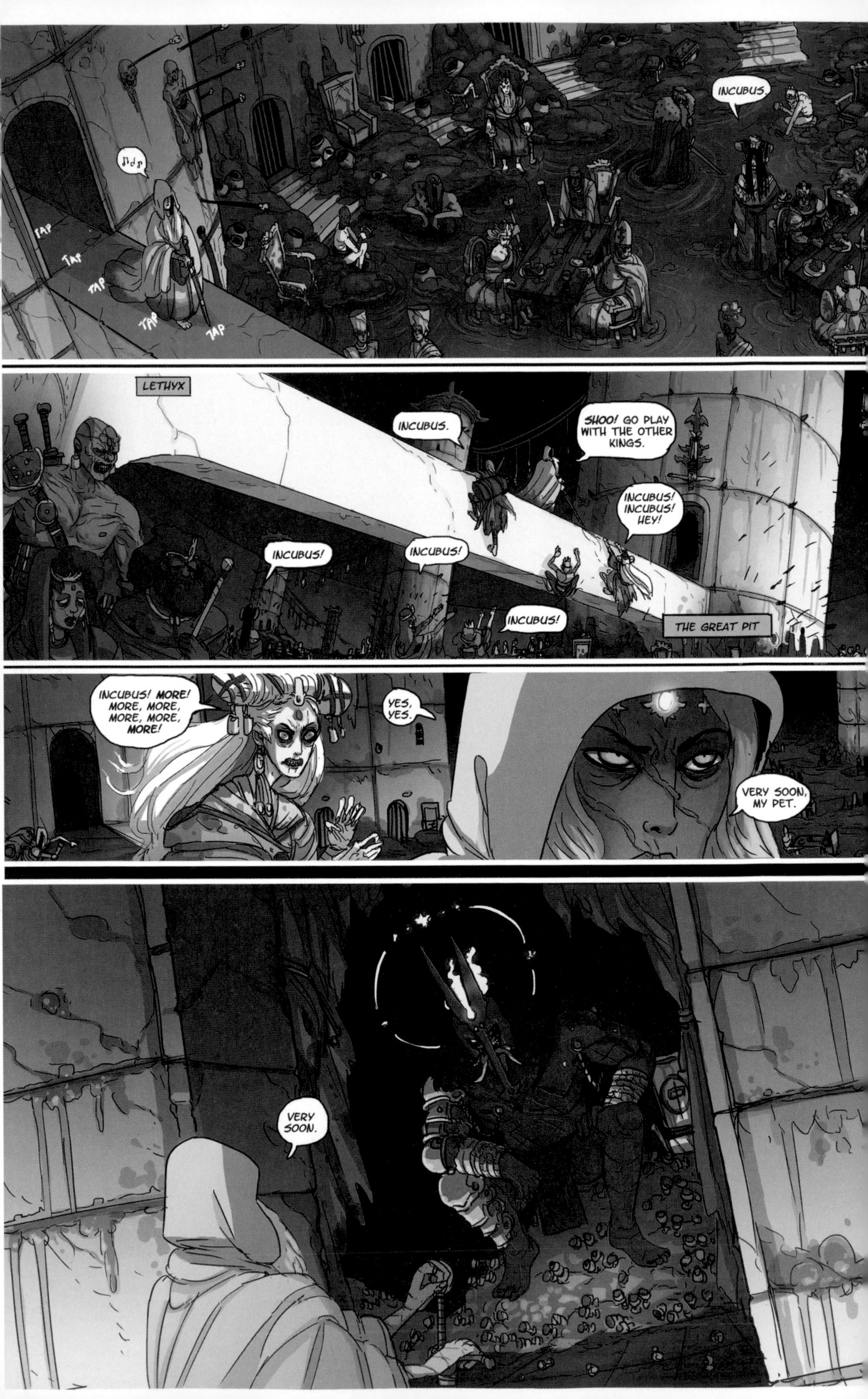
TAP
TAP
TAP
TAP
TAP
INCUBUS.
LETHYX
INCUBUS.
SHOO! GO PLAY WITH THE OTHER KINGS.
INCUBUS! INCUBUS! HEY!
INCUBUS!
INCUBUS!
INCUBUS!
THE GREAT PIT
INCUBUS! MORE! MORE, MORE, MORE, MORE, MORE!
YES, YES.
VERY SOON, MY PET.
VERY SOON.

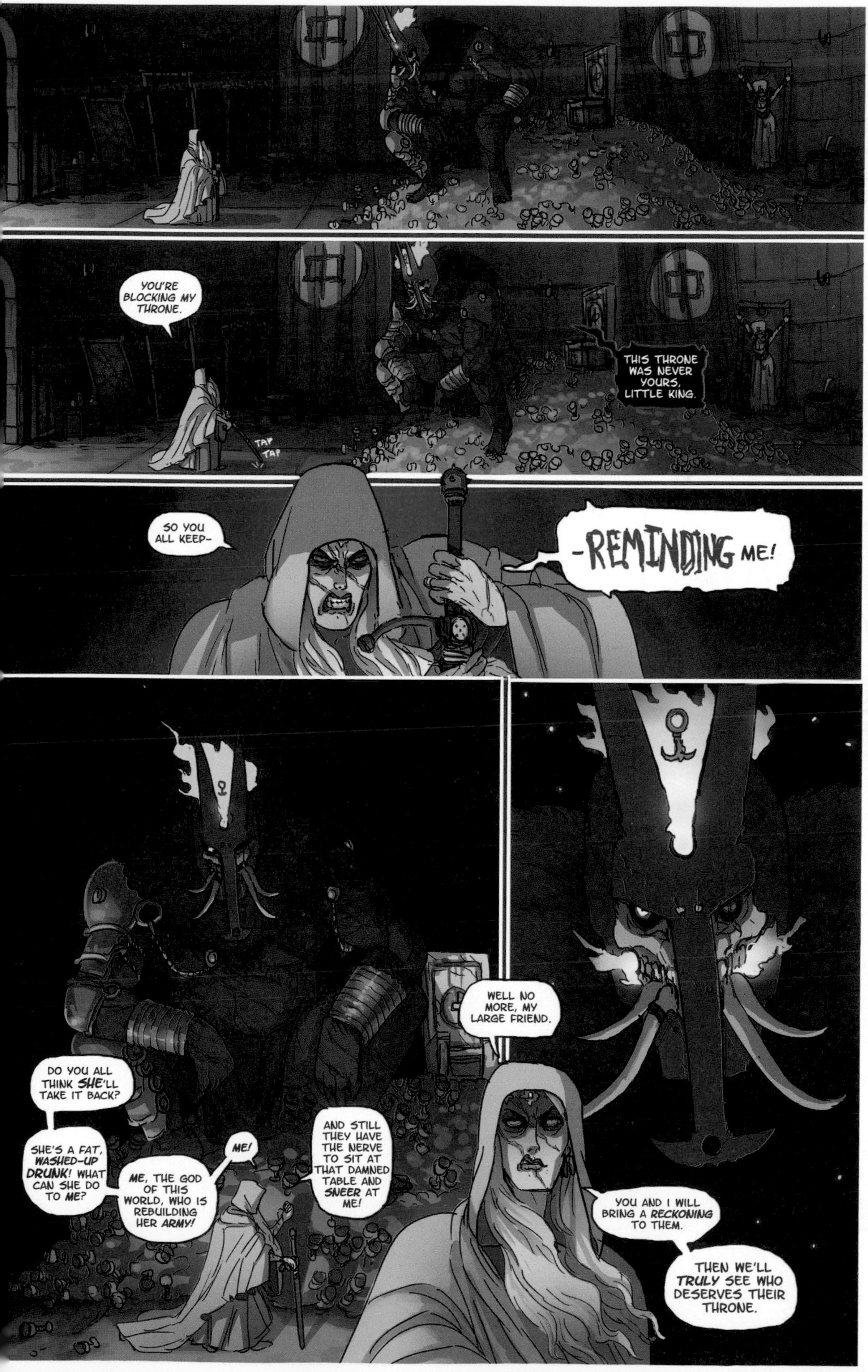
YOU'RE BLOCKING MY THRONE.
TAP TAP
THIS THRONE WAS NEVER YOURS, LITTLE KING.
SO YOU ALL KEEP-
-REMINDING ME!
WELL NO MORE, MY LARGE FRIEND.
DO YOU ALL THINK SHE'LL TAKE IT BACK?
SHE'S A FAT, WASHED-UP DRUNK! WHAT CAN SHE DO TO ME?
ME, THE GOD OF THIS WORLD, WHO IS REBUILDING HER ARMY!
ME!
AND STILL THEY HAVE THE NERVE TO SIT AT THAT DAMNED TABLE AND SNEER AT ME!
YOU AND I WILL BRING A RECKONING TO THEM.
THEN WE'LL TRULY SEE WHO DESERVES THEIR THRONE.

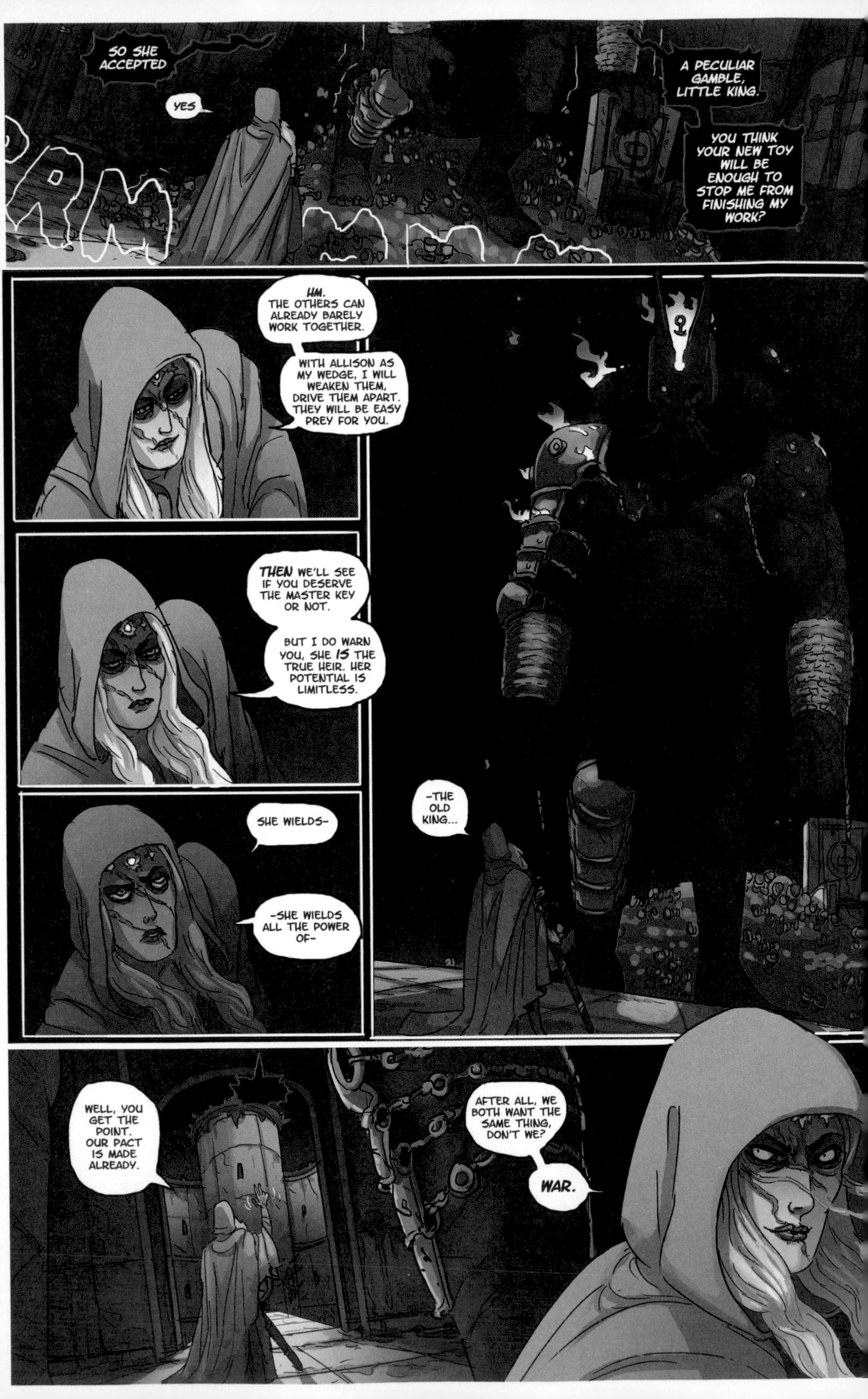

SO SHE ACCEPTED
YES
A PECULIAR GAMBLE, LITTLE KING.
YOU THINK YOUR NEW TOY WILL BE ENOUGH TO STOP ME FROM FINISHING MY WORK?
HM. THE OTHERS CAN ALREADY BARELY WORK TOGETHER.
WITH ALLISON AS MY WEDGE, I WILL WEAKEN THEM, DRIVE THEM APART. THEY WILL BE EASY PREY FOR YOU.
THEN WE'LL SEE IF YOU DESERVE THE MASTER KEY OR NOT.
BUT I DO WARN YOU, SHE IS THE TRUE HEIR. HER POTENTIAL IS LIMITLESS.
SHE WIELDS-
-SHE WIELDS ALL THE POWER OF-
-THE OLD KING...
WELL, YOU GET THE POINT. OUR PACT IS MADE ALREADY.
AFTER ALL, WE BOTH WANT THE SAME THING, DON'T WE?
WAR.

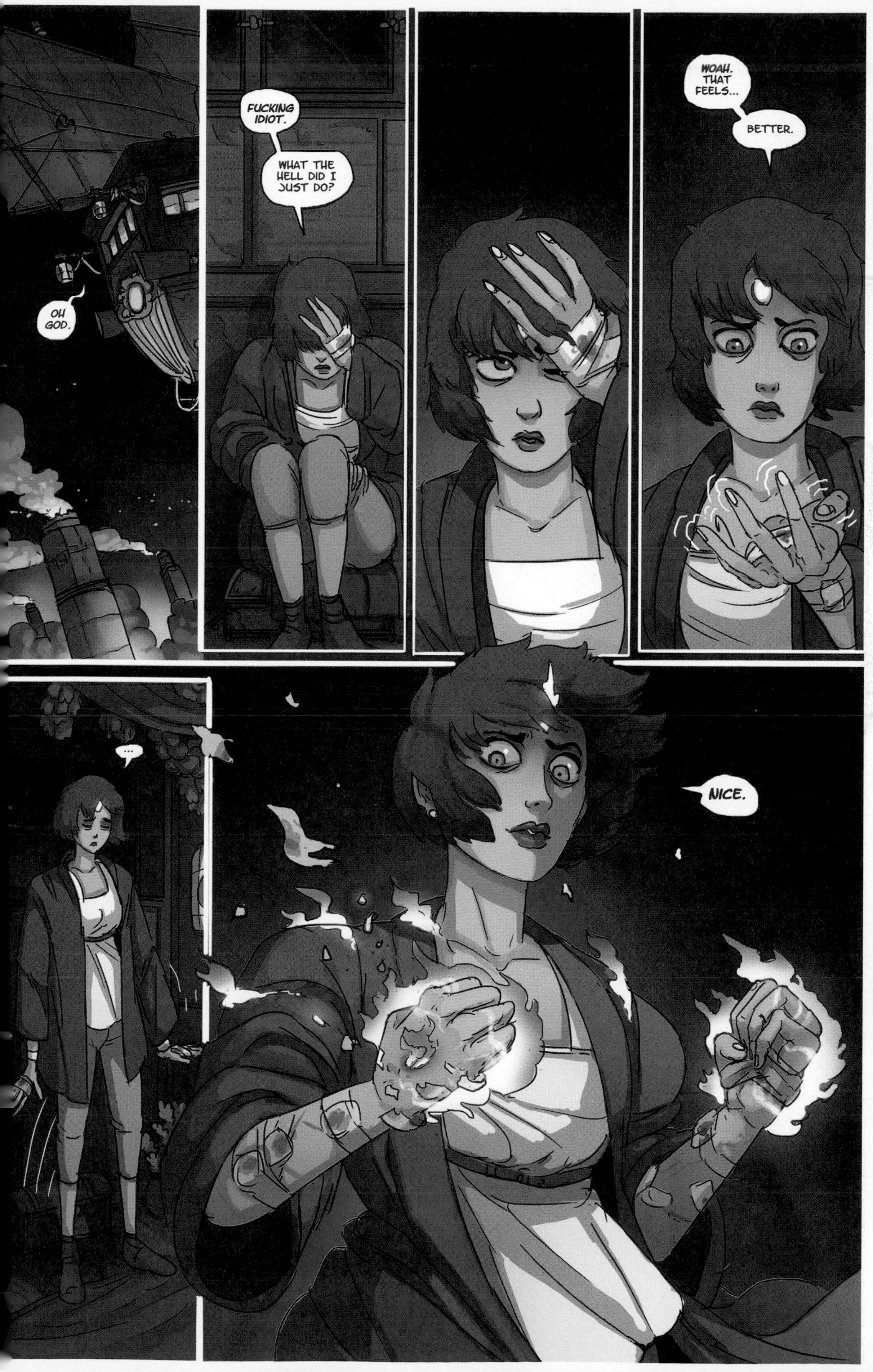
OH GOD.
FUCKING IDIOT.
WHAT THE HELL DID I JUST DO?
WOAH. THAT FEELS...
BETTER.
...
NICE.

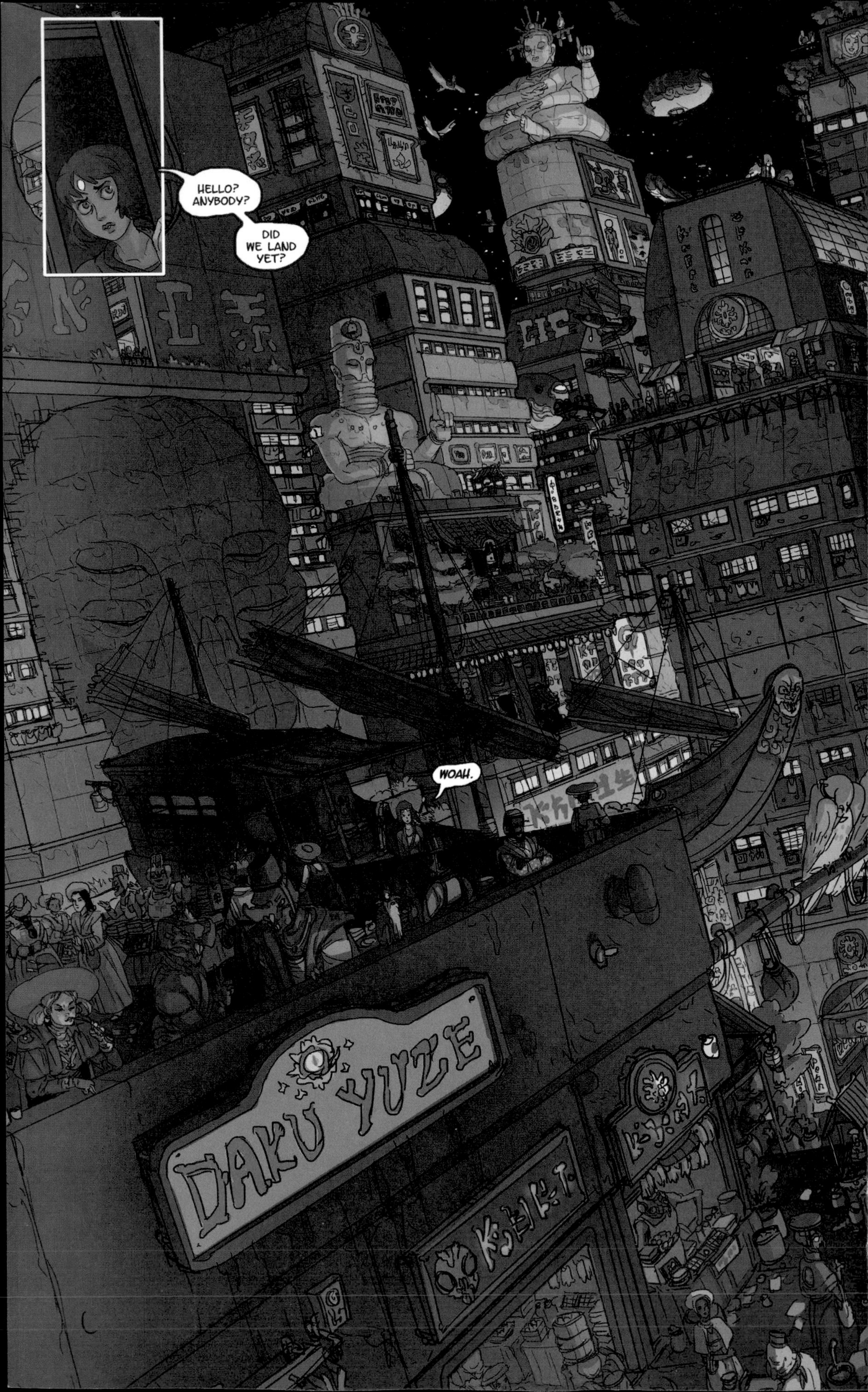
HELLO? ANYBODY?
DID WE LAND YET?
WOAH.
DAKU YUZE

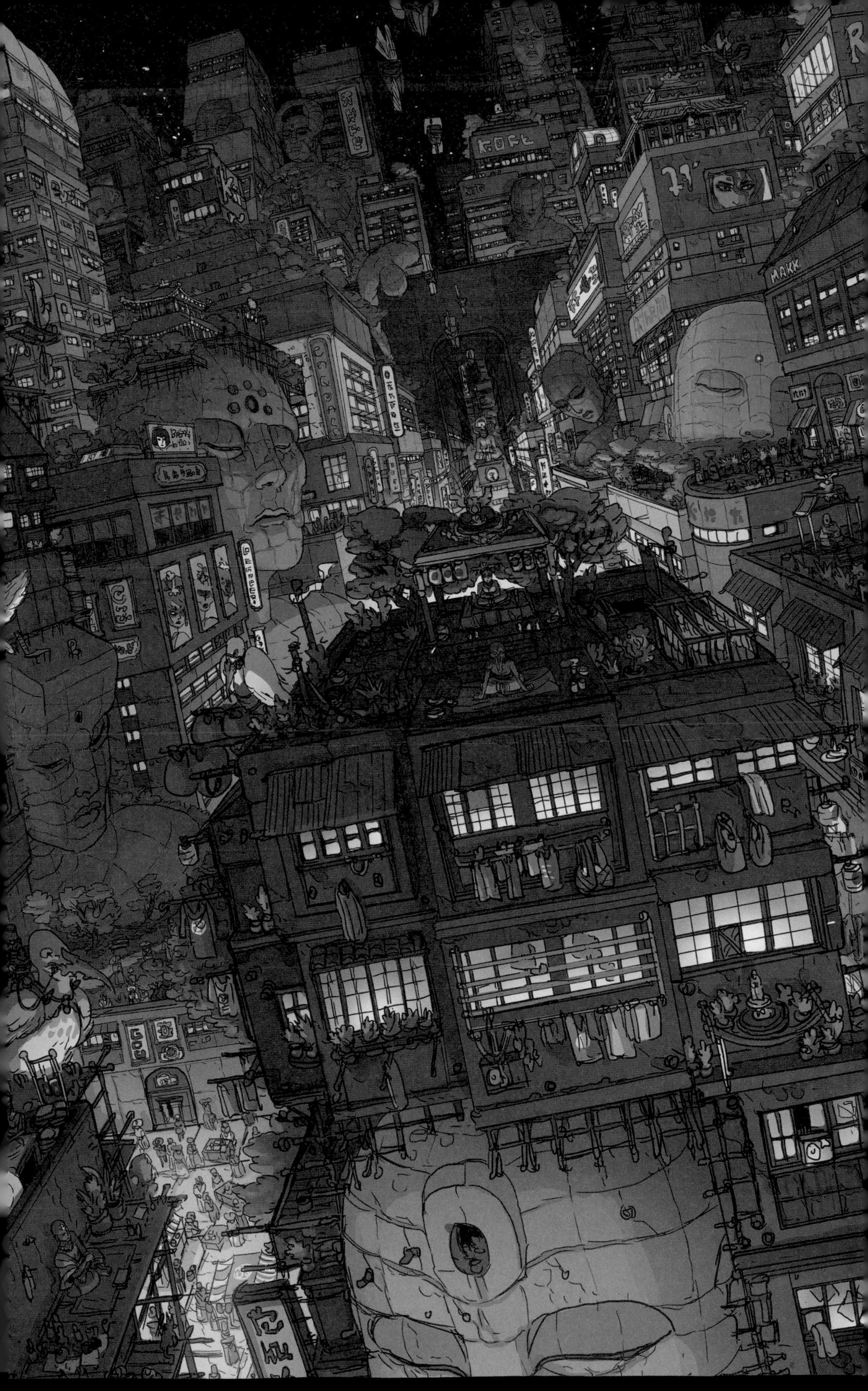

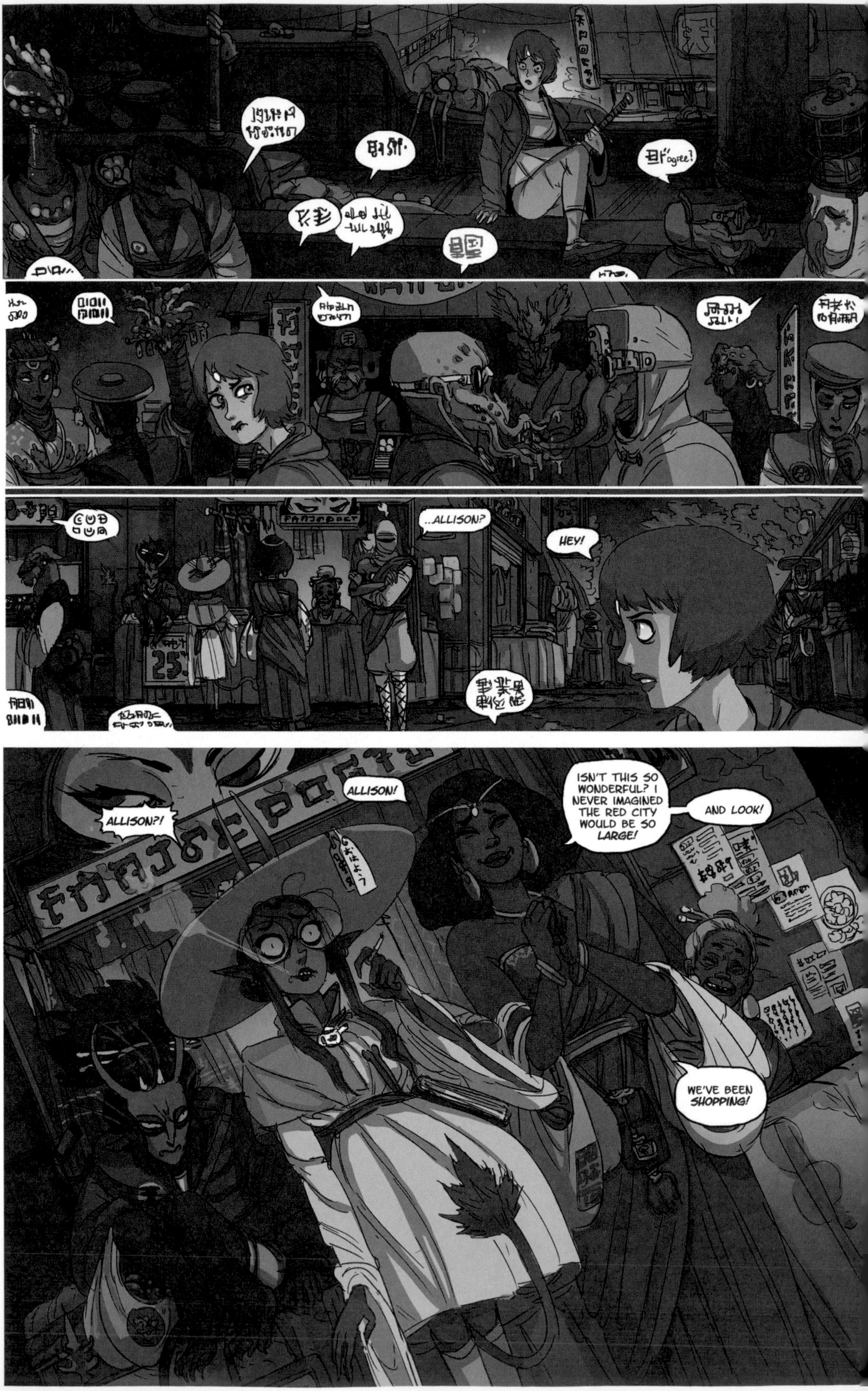

agree?
...ALLISON?
HEY!
ALLISON?!
ALLISON!
ISN'T THIS SO WONDERFUL? I NEVER IMAGINED THE RED CITY WOULD BE SO LARGE!
AND LOOK!
WE'VE BEEN SHOPPING!

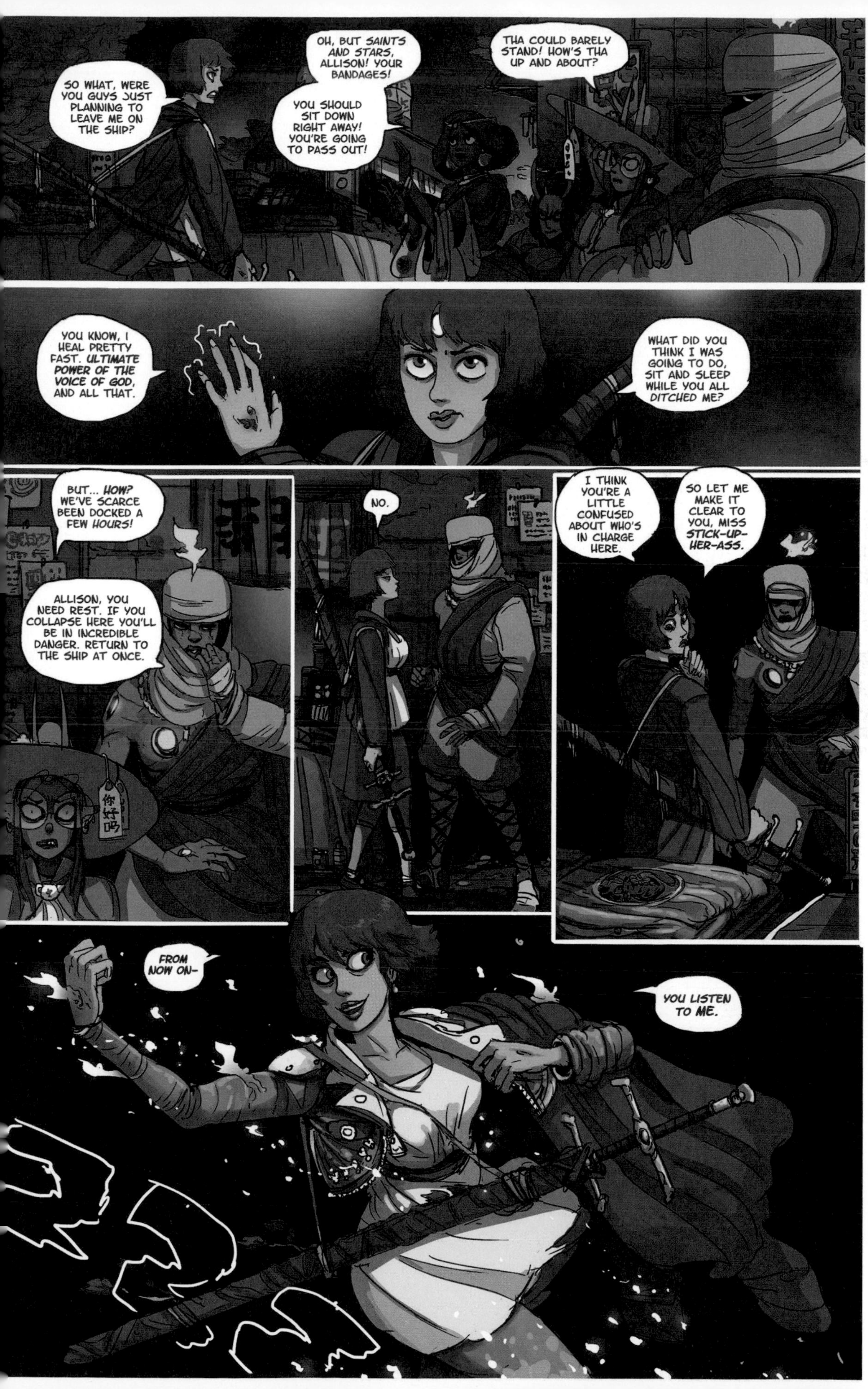
SO WHAT, WERE YOU GUYS JUST PLANNING TO LEAVE ME ON THE SHIP?
OH, BUT SAINTS AND STARS, ALLISON! YOUR BANDAGES!
YOU SHOULD SIT DOWN RIGHT AWAY! YOU'RE GOING TO PASS OUT!
THA COULD BARELY STAND! HOW'S THA UP AND ABOUT?
YOU KNOW, I HEAL PRETTY FAST. ULTIMATE POWER OF THE VOICE OF GOD, AND ALL THAT.
WHAT DID YOU THINK I WAS GOING TO DO, SIT AND SLEEP WHILE YOU ALL DITCHED ME?
BUT... HOW? WE'VE SCARCE BEEN DOCKED A FEW HOURS!
ALLISON, YOU NEED REST. IF YOU COLLAPSE HERE YOU'LL BE IN INCREDIBLE DANGER. RETURN TO THE SHIP AT ONCE.
你好吗
NO.
I THINK YOU'RE A LITTLE CONFUSED ABOUT WHO'S IN CHARGE HERE.
SO LET ME MAKE IT CLEAR TO YOU, MISS STICK-UP-HER-ASS.
FROM NOW ON-
YOU LISTEN TO ME.

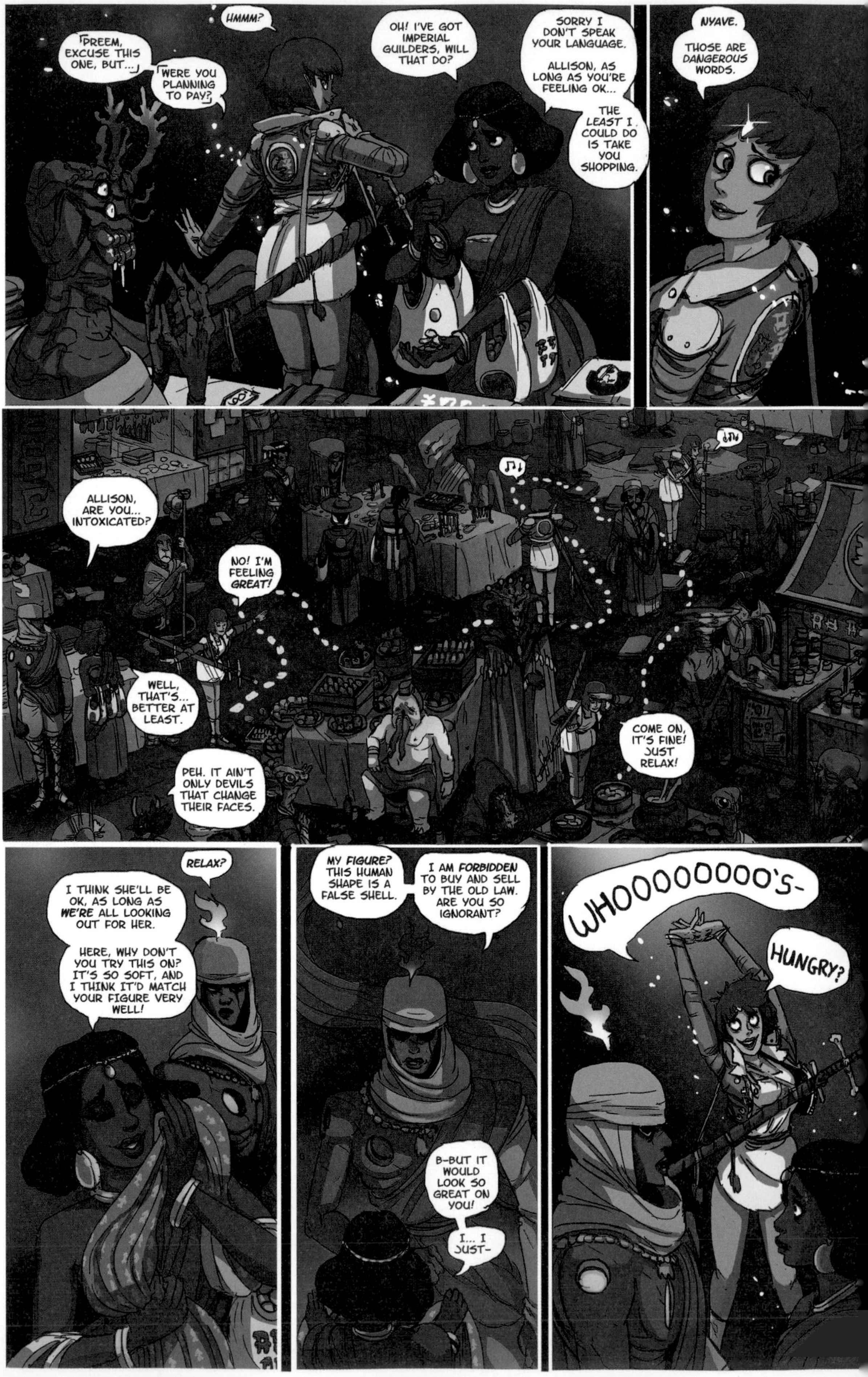
PREEM, EXCUSE THIS ONE, BUT...
HMMM?
WERE YOU PLANNING TO PAY?
OH! I'VE GOT IMPERIAL GUILDERS, WILL THAT DO?
SORRY I DON'T SPEAK YOUR LANGUAGE.
ALLISON, AS LONG AS YOU'RE FEELING OK...
THE LEAST I COULD DO IS TAKE YOU SHOPPING.
NYAVE.
THOSE ARE DANGEROUS WORDS.
ALLISON, ARE YOU... INTOXICATED?
NO! I'M FEELING GREAT!
WELL, THAT'S... BETTER AT LEAST.
PEH. IT AIN'T ONLY DEVILS THAT CHANGE THEIR FACES.
COME ON, IT'S FINE! JUST RELAX!
RELAX?
I THINK SHE'LL BE OK, AS LONG AS WE'RE ALL LOOKING OUT FOR HER.
HERE, WHY DON'T YOU TRY THIS ON? IT'S SO SOFT, AND I THINK IT'D MATCH YOUR FIGURE VERY WELL!
MY FIGURE? THIS HUMAN SHAPE IS A FALSE SHELL.
I AM FORBIDDEN TO BUY AND SELL BY THE OLD LAW. ARE YOU SO IGNORANT?
B-BUT IT WOULD LOOK SO GREAT ON YOU!
I... I JUST-
WHOOOOOOOOO'S-
HUNGRY?

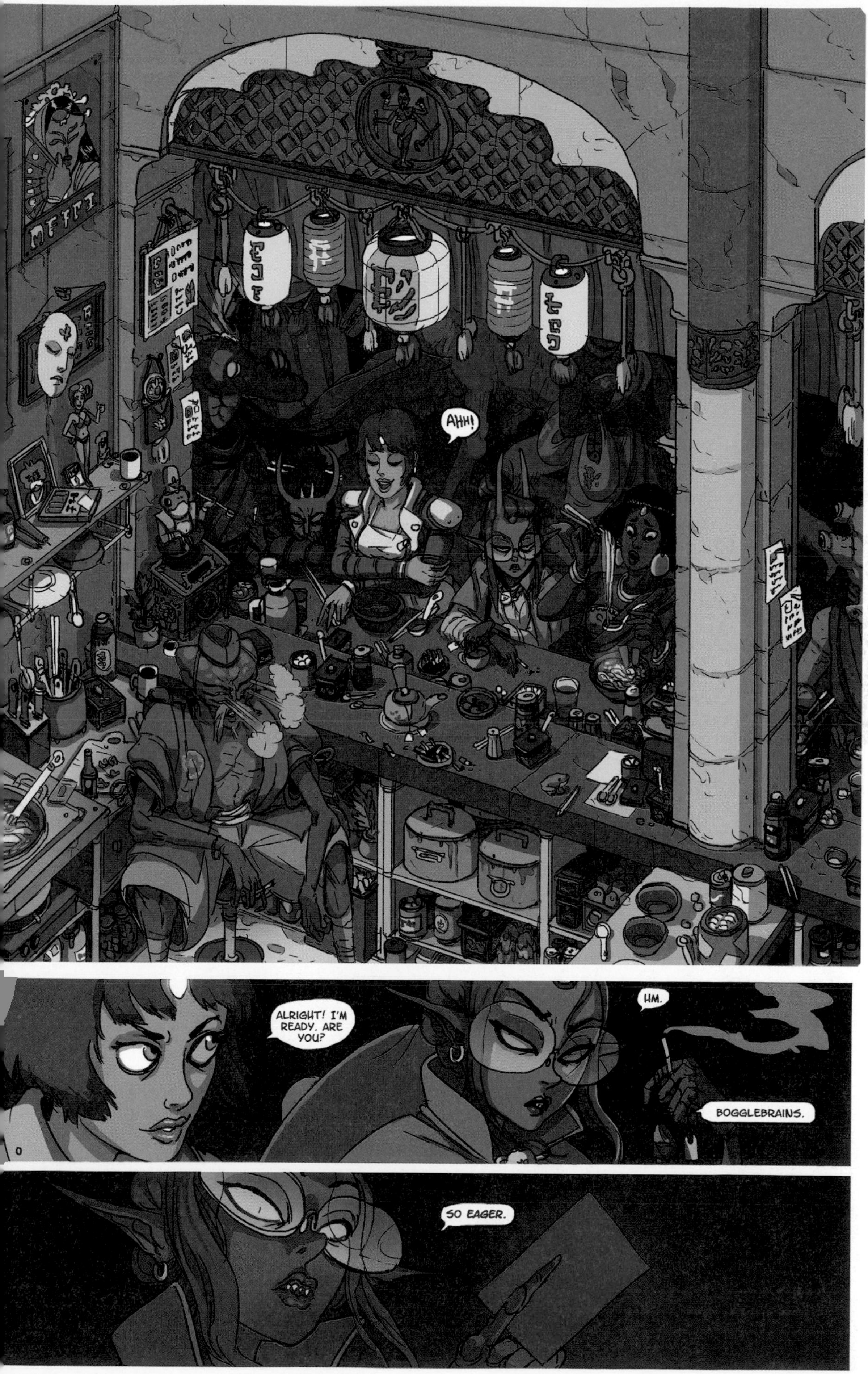
AHH!
ALRIGHT! I'M READY. ARE YOU?
HM.
BOGGLEBRAINS.
SO EAGER.

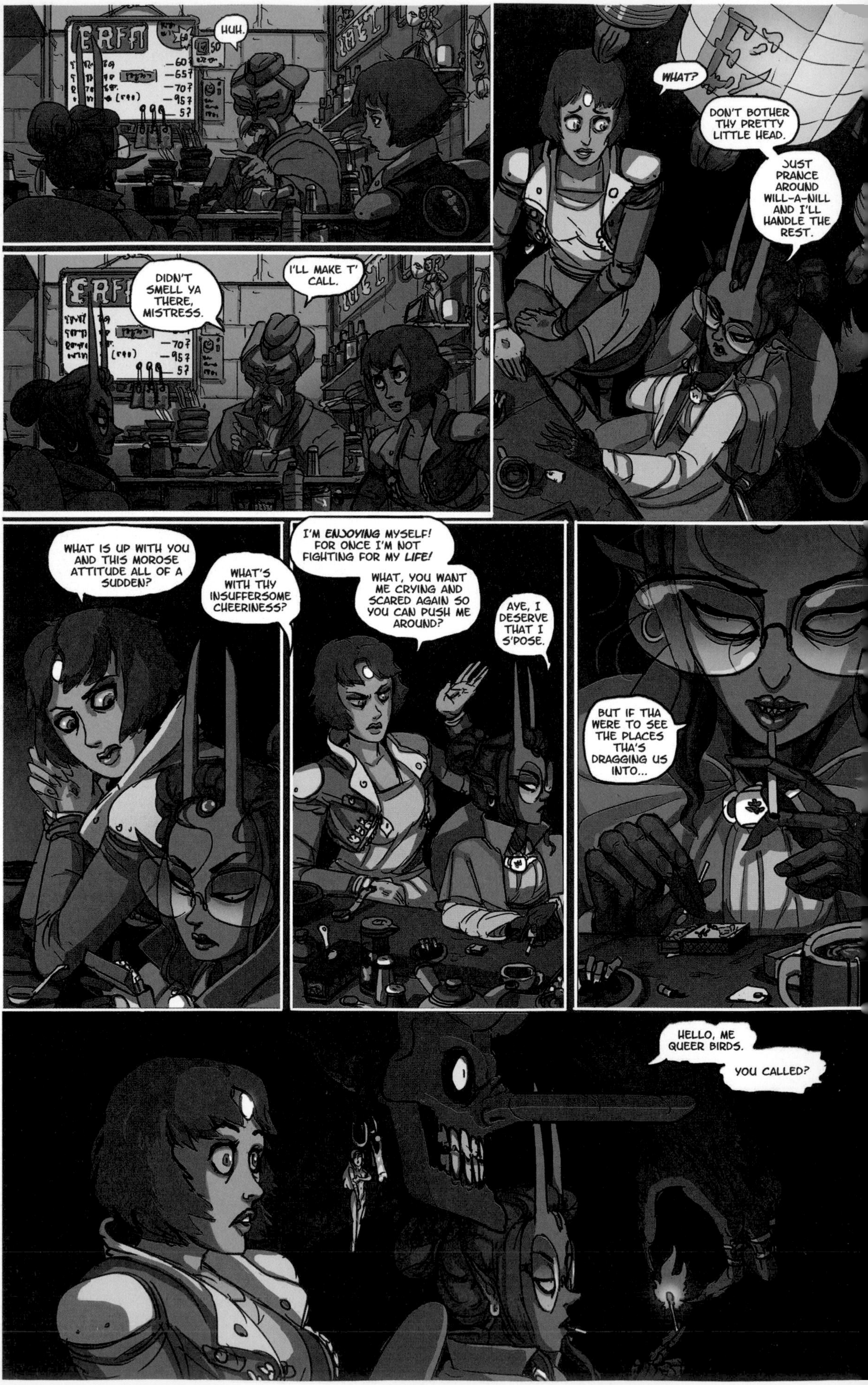

HUH.
DIDN'T SMELL YA THERE, MISTRESS.
I'LL MAKE T' CALL.
WHAT?
DON'T BOTHER THY PRETTY LITTLE HEAD.
JUST PRANCE AROUND WILL-A-NILL AND I'LL HANDLE THE REST.
WHAT IS UP WITH YOU AND THIS MOROSE ATTITUDE ALL OF A SUDDEN?
WHAT'S WITH THY INSUFFERSOME CHEERINESS?
I'M *ENJOYING* MYSELF! FOR ONCE I'M NOT FIGHTING FOR MY *LIFE!*
WHAT, YOU WANT ME CRYING AND SCARED AGAIN SO YOU CAN PUSH ME AROUND?
AYE, I DESERVE THAT I S'POSE.
BUT IF THA WERE TO SEE THE PLACES THA'S DRAGGING US INTO...
HELLO, ME QUEER BIRDS.
YOU CALLED?

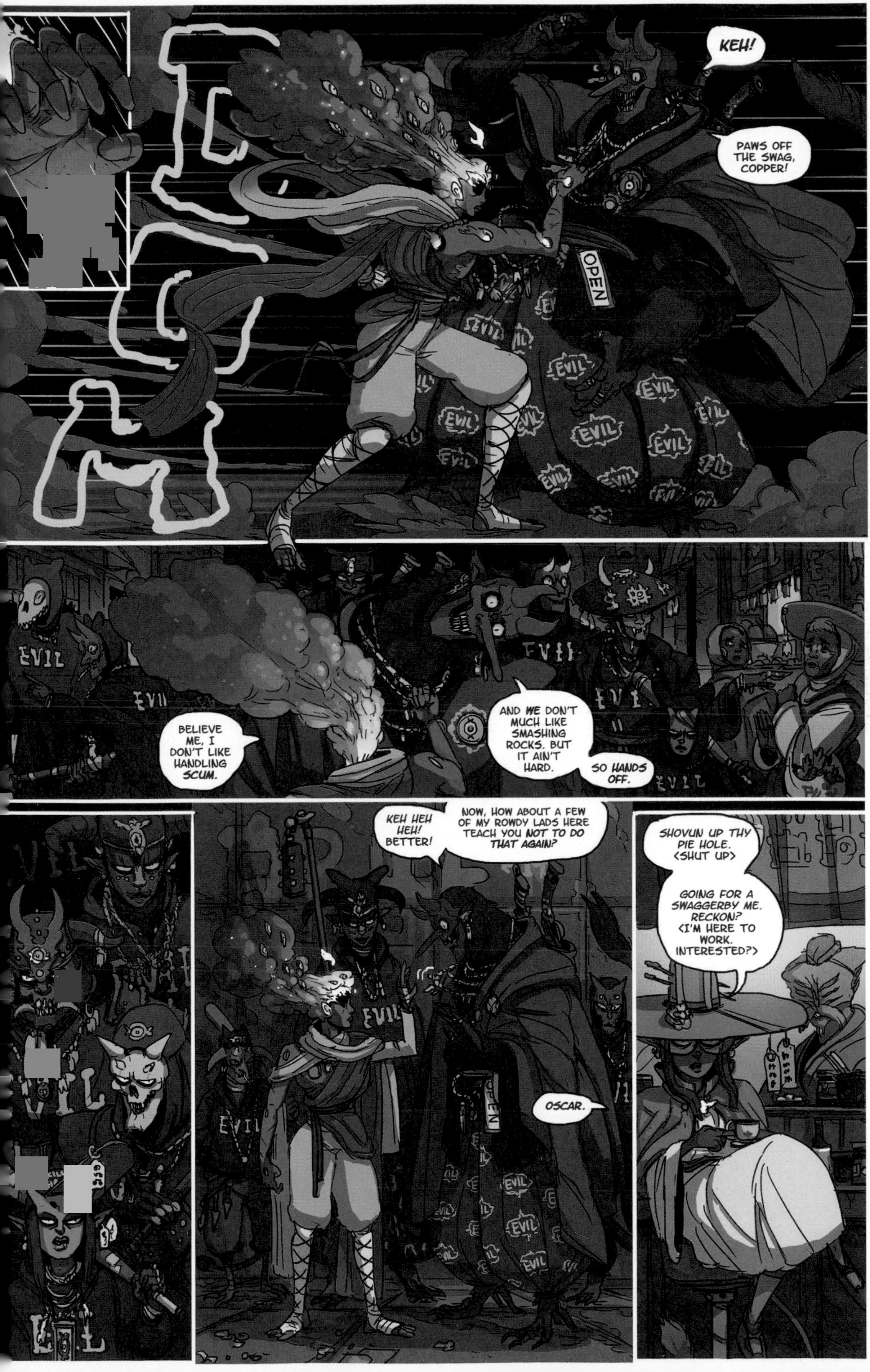
KEH!
PAWS OFF THE SWAG, COPPER!
OPEN
BELIEVE ME, I DON'T LIKE HANDLING SCUM.
AND WE DON'T MUCH LIKE SMASHING ROCKS. BUT IT AIN'T HARD.
SO HANDS OFF.
KEH HEH HEH! BETTER!
NOW, HOW ABOUT A FEW OF MY ROWDY LADS HERE TEACH YOU NOT TO DO THAT AGAIN?
OSCAR.
SHOVUN UP THY PIE HOLE. <SHUT UP>
GOING FOR A SWAGGERBY ME. RECKON? <I'M HERE TO WORK. INTERESTED?>

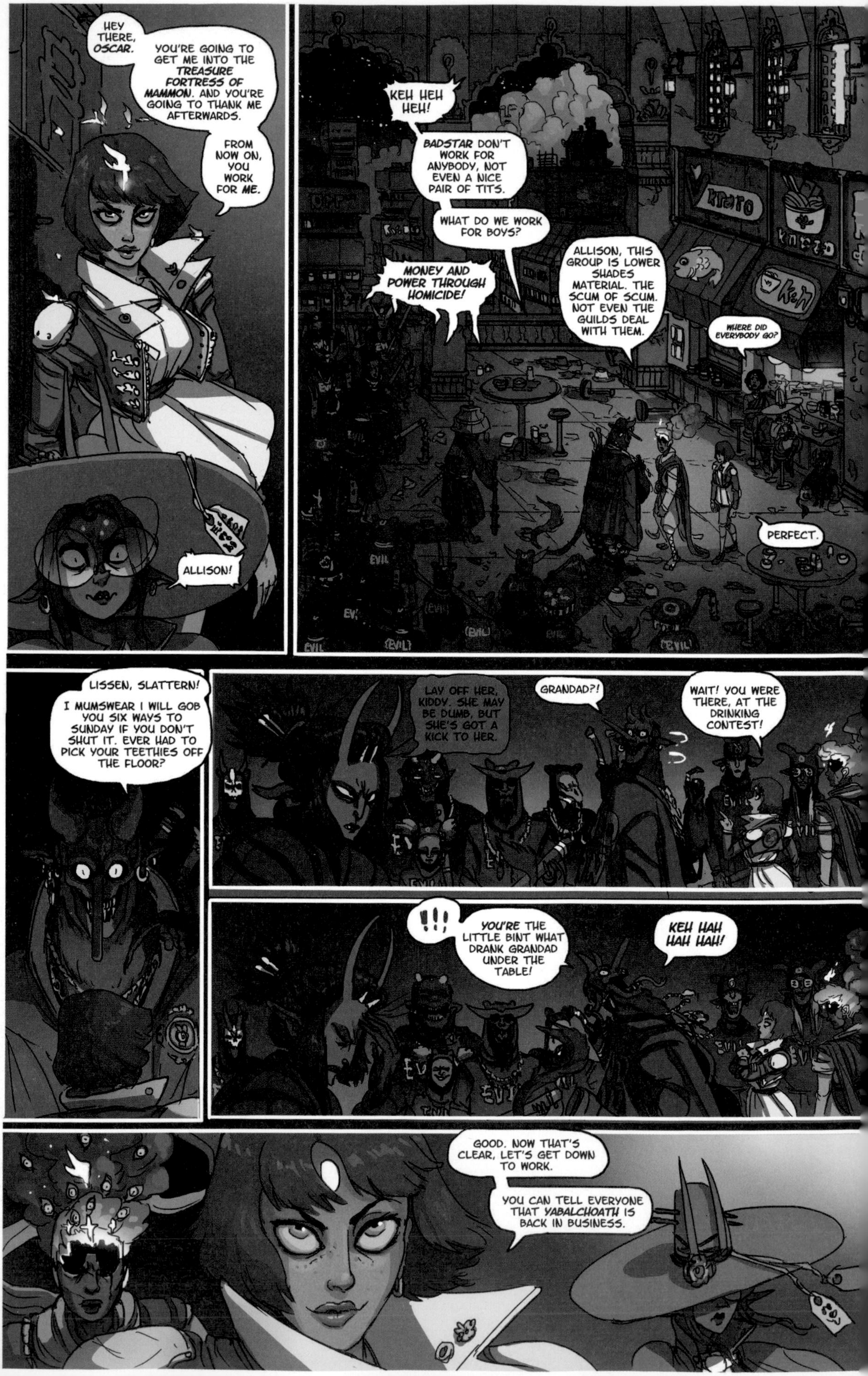
HEY THERE, OSCAR.
YOU'RE GOING TO GET ME INTO THE TREASURE FORTRESS OF MAMMON. AND YOU'RE GOING TO THANK ME AFTERWARDS.
FROM NOW ON, YOU WORK FOR ME.
ALLISON!
KEH HEH HEH!
BADSTAR DON'T WORK FOR ANYBODY, NOT EVEN A NICE PAIR OF TITS.
WHAT DO WE WORK FOR BOYS?
MONEY AND POWER THROUGH HOMICIDE!
ALLISON, THIS GROUP IS LOWER SHADES MATERIAL. THE SCUM OF SCUM. NOT EVEN THE GUILDS DEAL WITH THEM.
WHERE DID EVERYBODY GO?
PERFECT.
LISSEN, SLATTERN!
I MUMSWEAR I WILL GOB YOU SIX WAYS TO SUNDAY IF YOU DON'T SHUT IT. EVER HAD TO PICK YOUR TEETHIES OFF THE FLOOR?
LAY OFF HER, KIDDY. SHE MAY BE DUMB, BUT SHE'S GOT A KICK TO HER.
GRANDAD?!
WAIT! YOU WERE THERE, AT THE DRINKING CONTEST!
!!!
YOU'RE THE LITTLE BINT WHAT DRANK GRANDAD UNDER THE TABLE!
KEH HAH HAH HAH!
GOOD. NOW THAT'S CLEAR, LET'S GET DOWN TO WORK.
YOU CAN TELL EVERYONE THAT YABALCHOATH IS BACK IN BUSINESS.

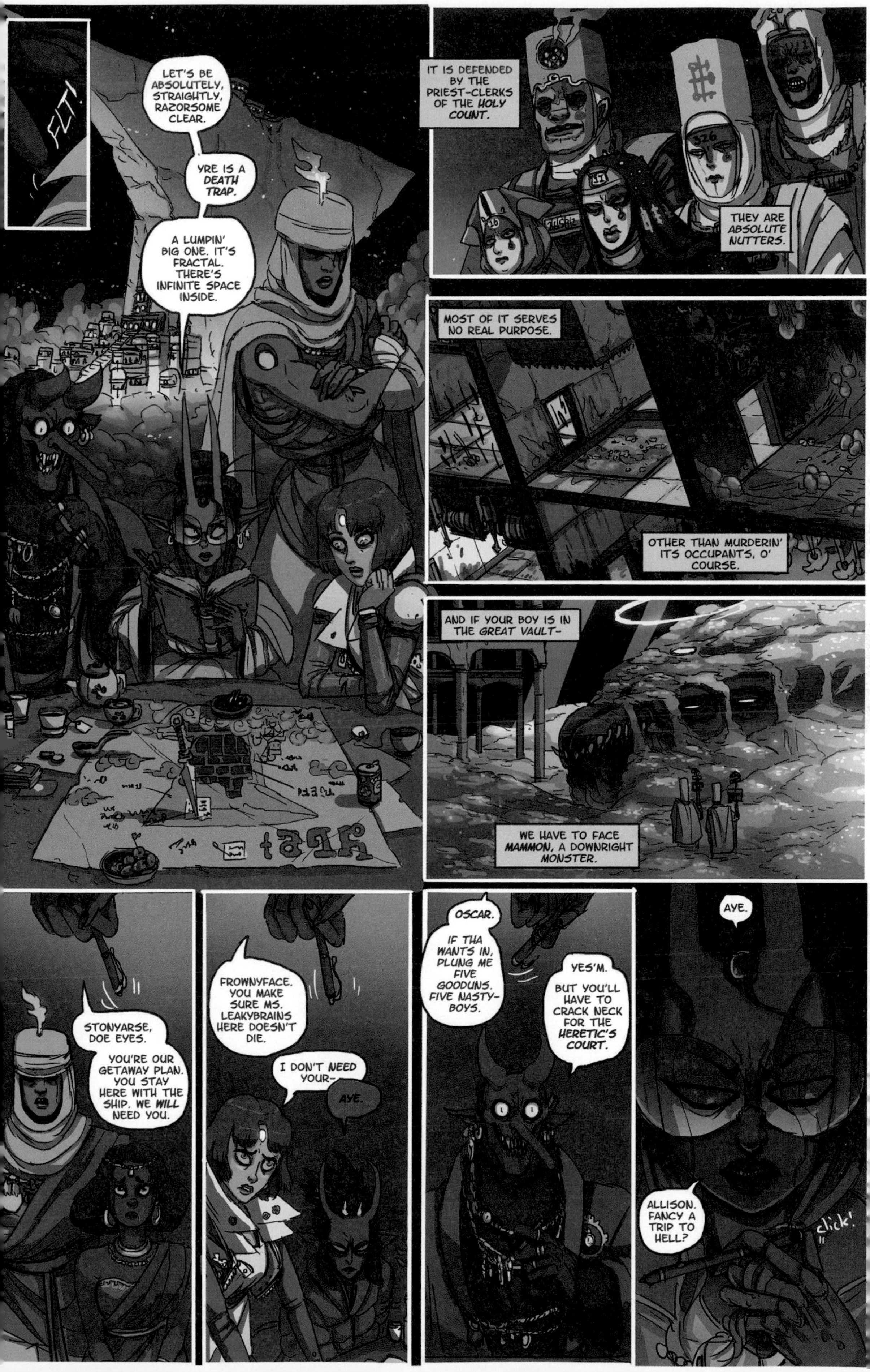
FLT!
LET'S BE ABSOLUTELY, STRAIGHTLY, RAZORSOME CLEAR.
YRE IS A DEATH TRAP.
A LUMPIN' BIG ONE. IT'S FRACTAL. THERE'S INFINITE SPACE INSIDE.
IT IS DEFENDED BY THE PRIEST-CLERKS OF THE HOLY COUNT.
THEY ARE ABSOLUTE NUTTERS.
MOST OF IT SERVES NO REAL PURPOSE.
OTHER THAN MURDERIN' ITS OCCUPANTS, O' COURSE.
AND IF YOUR BOY IS IN THE GREAT VAULT-
WE HAVE TO FACE MAMMON, A DOWNRIGHT MONSTER.
STONYARSE, DOE EYES.
YOU'RE OUR GETAWAY PLAN. YOU STAY HERE WITH THE SHIP. WE WILL NEED YOU.
FROWNYFACE. YOU MAKE SURE MS. LEAKYBRAINS HERE DOESN'T DIE.
I DON'T NEED YOUR-
AYE.
OSCAR.
IF THA WANTS IN, PLUNG ME FIVE GOODUNS. FIVE NASTY-BOYS.
YES'M.
BUT YOU'LL HAVE TO CRACK NECK FOR THE HERETIC'S COURT.
AYE.
ALLISON. FANCY A TRIP TO HELL?
click!

"Prince Kassardis was given three vessels of wine, and three wives, and three rings to gird his ring-fingers. But Kassardis' heart was heavy at his wedding ceremony, and no amount of wine could float it up from the depths it had sank to. For this ceremony held with it deadly promise, for it was custom in that part that the prince, within a week of his wedding, should choose a favorite wife. This was a marker, a battle drum of sorts, between the three wives of the great house of Ium-Am. The battle only ended when one wife stood, scarred and bloody, and the remainder were dead or exiled.

Kassardis was sick of this slaughter, and the hollow wreck of a man he called his father. His three wives were very pretty, but they were cruel as hawks. Even as he stood there besides the marriage pool, he could see the bloodlust glow behind their veiled eyes. It was for that reason he took his naming dagger and traveling cloak and fled his tower one summer night."

– TALES OF THE SILVER PRINCE

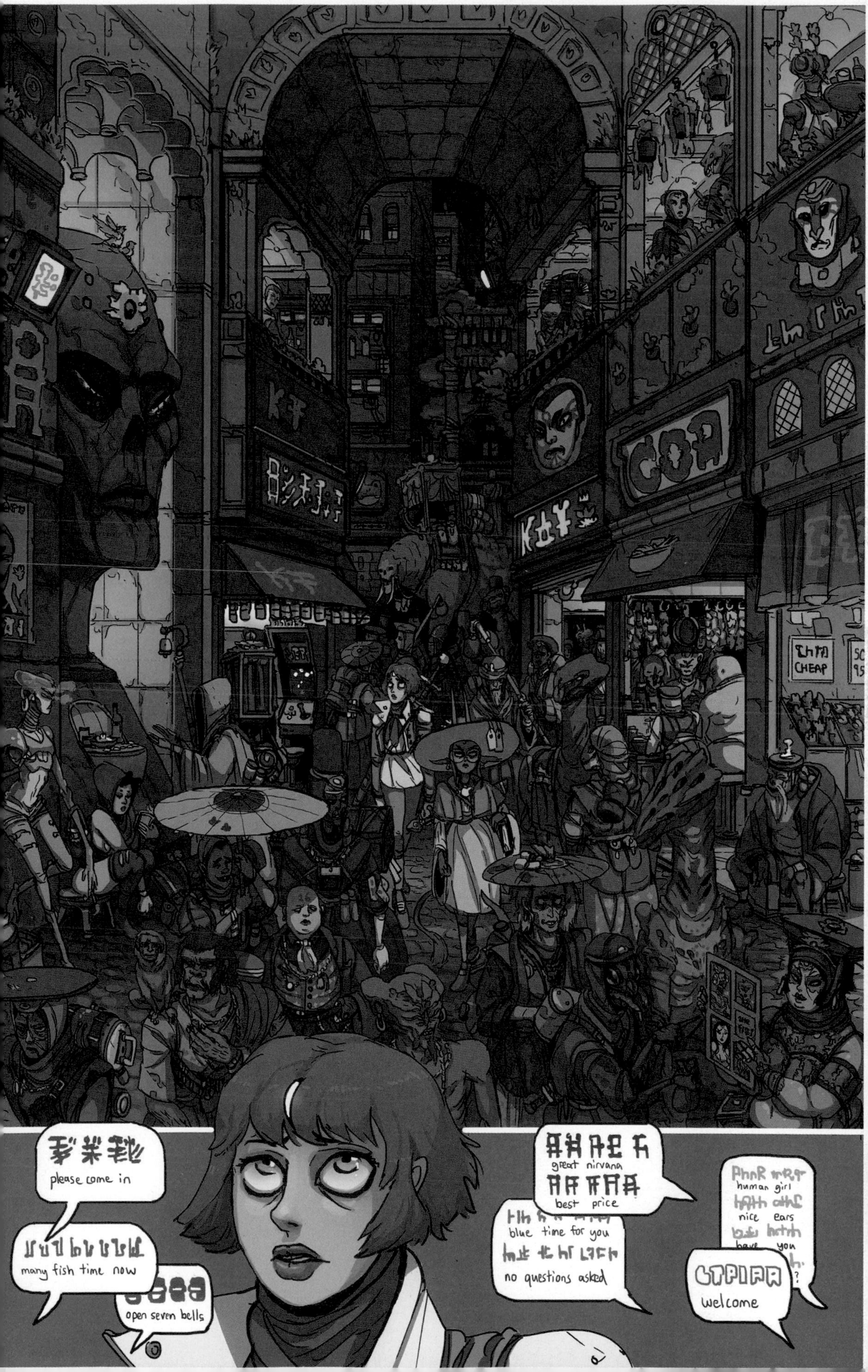

CHEAP
please come in
many fish time now
open seven bells
great nirvana
best price
blue time for you
no questions asked
human girl
nice ears
have you
?
welcome

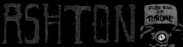

ASHTON

FIRST RING OF THRONE

NAMED FOR THE DUST FROM THE MILLIONS OF BOOTS THAT PASS THROUGH ITS STREETS, ASHTON, OR ASH TOWN, IS THE LOWEST POINT OF THE RED CITY OF THRONE - FILLING ITS FIRST CIRCLE AND SPILLING OUT THROUGH ITS GREAT BRIDGES INTO THE WATERS BELOW. IT IS THE FIRST POINT OF ENTRY FOR ALL TRAVELING THROUGH THRONE, FILLED WITH THE TEEMING POPULACE OF HUNDREDS OF THOUSANDS OF WORLDS. MOST OF THE POPULATION OF THE RED CITY LIVES, EATS, AND TOILS HERE. PREDICTABLY, IT IS A MASSIVE SLUM, THOUGH THE FOOD IS THE BEST IN THE CITY.

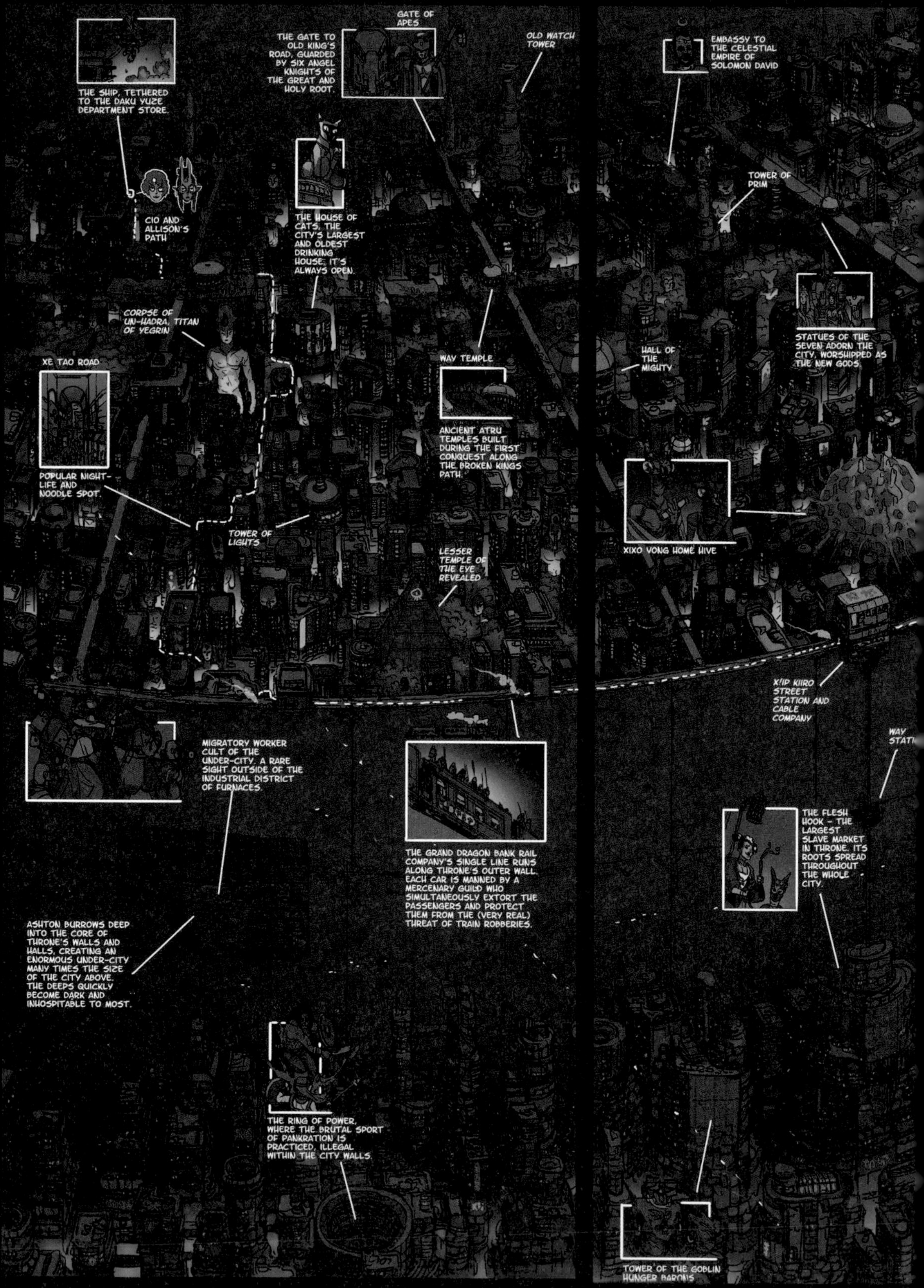

THE SHIP, TETHERED TO THE DAKU YUZE DEPARTMENT STORE.
THE GATE TO OLD KING'S ROAD, GUARDED BY SIX ANGEL KNIGHTS OF THE GREAT AND HOLY ROOT.
GATE OF APES
OLD WATCH TOWER
EMBASSY TO THE CELESTIAL EMPIRE OF SOLOMON DAVID
CIO AND ALLISON'S PATH
THE HOUSE OF CATS, THE CITY'S LARGEST AND OLDEST DRINKING HOUSE. IT'S ALWAYS OPEN.
TOWER OF PRIM
CORPSE OF UN-HADRA, TITAN OF YEGRIN
XE TAO ROAD
WAY TEMPLE
HALL OF THE MIGHTY
STATUES OF THE SEVEN ADORN THE CITY, WORSHIPPED AS THE NEW GODS.
ANCIENT ATRU TEMPLES BUILT DURING THE FIRST CONQUEST ALONG THE BROKEN KINGS PATH.
POPULAR NIGHT-LIFE AND NOODLE SPOT.
TOWER OF LIGHTS
XIXO VONG HOME HIVE
LESSER TEMPLE OF THE EYE REVEALED
X'IP KIIRO STREET STATION AND CABLE COMPANY
MIGRATORY WORKER CULT OF THE UNDER-CITY. A RARE SIGHT OUTSIDE OF THE INDUSTRIAL DISTRICT OF FURNACES.
WAY STATI
THE GRAND DRAGON BANK RAIL COMPANY'S SINGLE LINE RUNS ALONG THRONE'S OUTER WALL. EACH CAR IS MANNED BY A MERCENARY GUILD WHO SIMULTANEOUSLY EXTORT THE PASSENGERS AND PROTECT THEM FROM THE (VERY REAL) THREAT OF TRAIN ROBBERIES.
THE FLESH HOOK - THE LARGEST SLAVE MARKET IN THRONE. ITS ROOTS SPREAD THROUGHOUT THE WHOLE CITY.
ASHTON BURROWS DEEP INTO THE CORE OF THRONE'S WALLS AND HALLS, CREATING AN ENORMOUS UNDER-CITY MANY TIMES THE SIZE OF THE CITY ABOVE. THE DEEPS QUICKLY BECOME DARK AND INHOSPITABLE TO MOST.
THE RING OF POWER, WHERE THE BRUTAL SPORT OF PANKRATION IS PRACTICED, ILLEGAL WITHIN THE CITY WALLS.
TOWER OF THE GOBLIN HUNGER BARONS

OUTER ASHTON

A SHANTYTOWN LARGER THAN MOST NATIONS, OUTER ASHTON IS THE HOLDING PLACE FOR THOSE TOO POOR OR NOT LUCKY ENOUGH TO LIVE WITHIN THE CITY WALLS PROPER. THE LAW HOLDS A MEAGRE GRASP HERE, AND LIFE IS TENUOUS AND HARSH. OUTER ASHTON IS CONSTANTLY GROWING, AND MANY SAY IT WILL SPILL OVER THE WALLS INTO THE CITY EVENTUALLY.

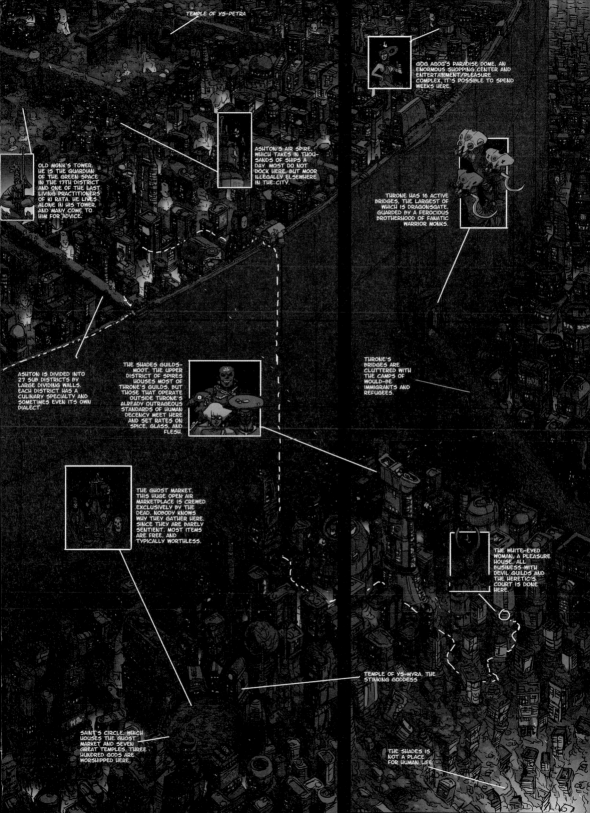

TEMPLE OF YS-PETRA

GOG AGOG'S PARADISE DOME, AN ENORMOUS SHOPPING CENTER AND ENTERTAINMENT/PLEASURE COMPLEX. IT'S POSSIBLE TO SPEND WEEKS HERE.

OLD MONK'S TOWER. HE IS THE GUARDIAN OF THE GREEN SPACE IN THE 17TH DISTRICT AND ONE OF THE LAST LIVING PRACTITIONERS OF KI RATA. HE LIVES ALONE IN HIS TOWER, AND MANY COME TO HIM FOR ADVICE.

ASHTON'S AIR SPIRE, WHICH TAKES IN THOU-SANDS OF SHIPS A DAY. MOST DO NOT DOCK HERE, BUT MOOR ILLEGALLY ELSEWHERE IN THE CITY.

THRONE HAS 16 ACTIVE BRIDGES, THE LARGEST OF WHICH IS DRAGON'SGATE, GUARDED BY A FEROCIOUS BROTHERHOOD OF FANATIC WARRIOR MONKS.

ASHTON IS DIVIDED INTO 27 SUB DISTRICTS BY LARGE DIVIDING WALLS. EACH DISTRICT HAS A CULINARY SPECIALTY AND SOMETIMES EVEN IT'S OWN DIALECT.

THE SHADES GUILDS-MOOT. THE UPPER DISTRICT OF SPIRES HOUSES MOST OF THRONE'S GUILDS, BUT THOSE THAT OPERATE OUTSIDE THRONE'S ALREADY OUTRAGEOUS STANDARDS OF HUMAN DECENCY MEET HERE AND SET RATES ON SPICE, GLASS, AND FLESH.

THRONE'S BRIDGES ARE CLUTTERED WITH THE CAMPS OF WOULD-BE IMMIGRANTS AND REFUGEES.

THE GHOST MARKET. THIS HUGE OPEN AIR MARKETPLACE IS CREWED EXCLUSIVELY BY THE DEAD. NOBODY KNOWS WHY THEY GATHER HERE, SINCE THEY ARE BARELY SENTIENT. MOST ITEMS ARE FREE, AND TYPICALLY WORTHLESS.

THE WHITE-EYED WOMAN, A PLEASURE HOUSE. ALL BUSINESS-WITH DEVIL GUILDS AND THE HERETIC'S COURT IS DONE HERE.

TEMPLE OF YS-MYRA, THE STINKING GODDESS

SAINT'S CIRCLE, WHICH HOUSES THE GHOST MARKET AND SEVEN GREAT TEMPLES. THREE HUNDRED GODS ARE WORSHIPPED HERE.

THE SHADES IS NOT A PLACE FOR HUMAN LIFE

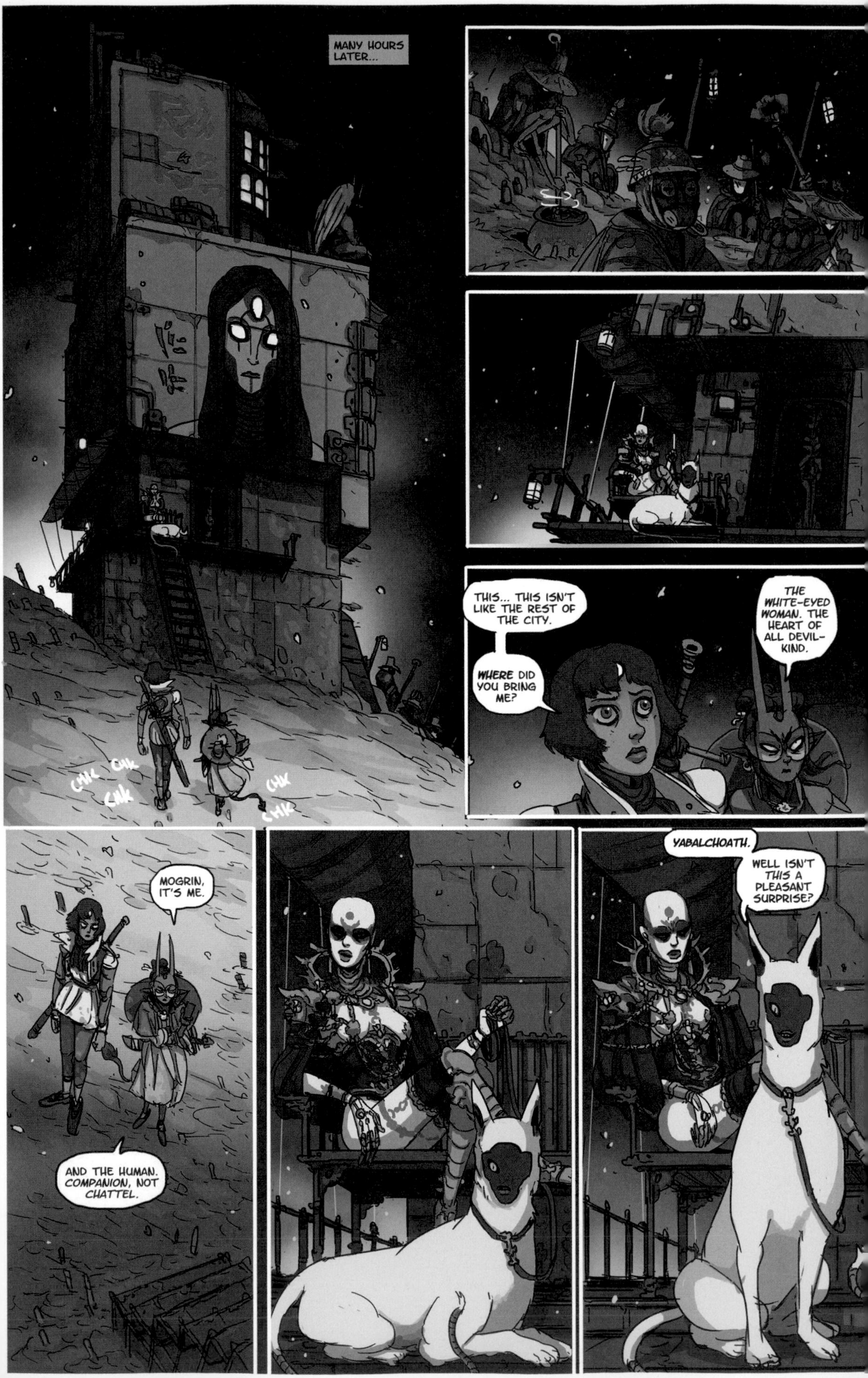
MANY HOURS LATER...
CHK CHK
CHK
CHK
CHK
THIS... THIS ISN'T LIKE THE REST OF THE CITY.
WHERE DID YOU BRING ME?
THE WHITE-EYED WOMAN. THE HEART OF ALL DEVIL-KIND.
MOGRIN, IT'S ME.
AND THE HUMAN. COMPANION, NOT CHATTEL.
YABALCHOATH.
WELL ISN'T THIS A PLEASANT SURPRISE?

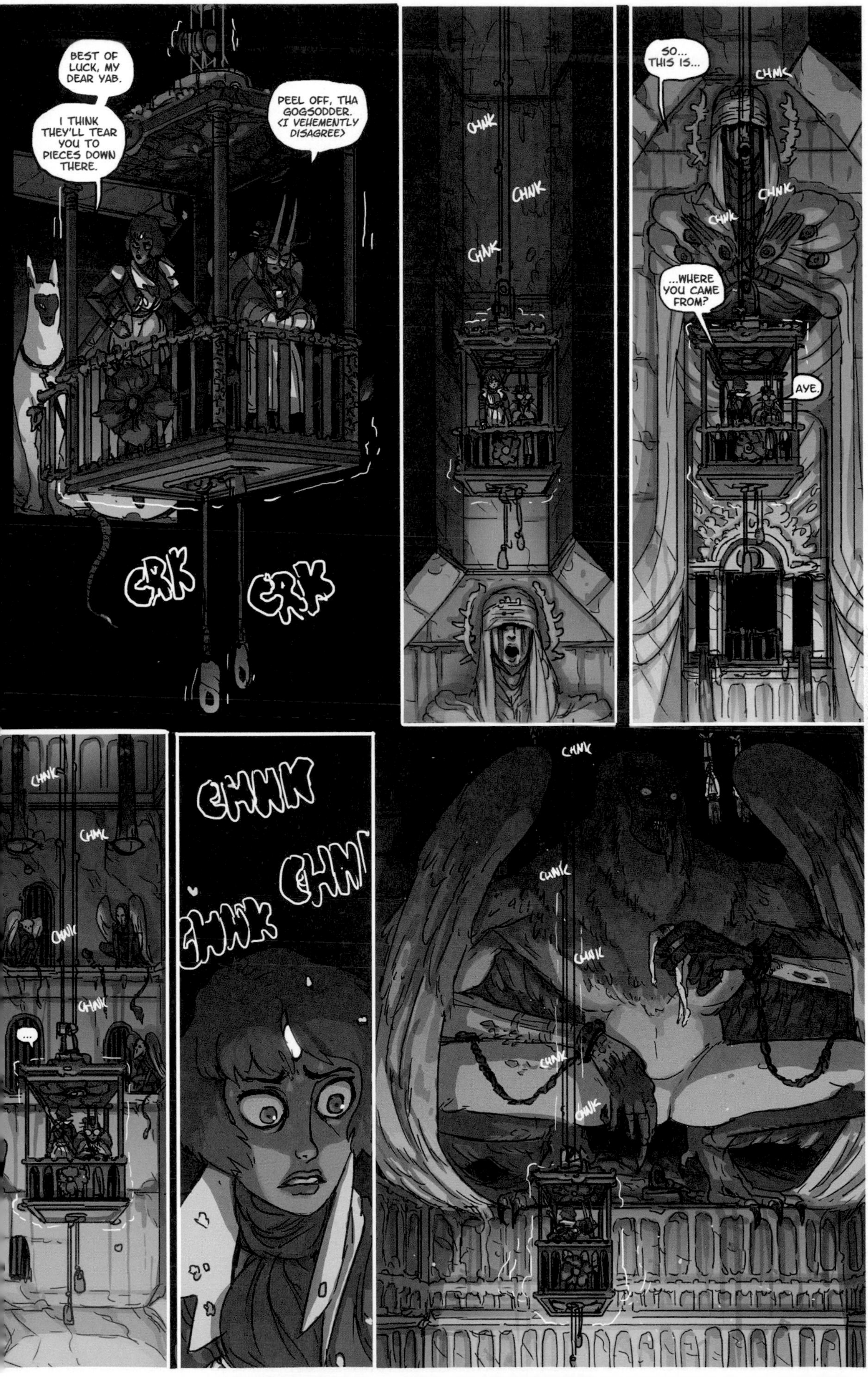
BEST OF LUCK, MY DEAR YAB.
I THINK THEY'LL TEAR YOU TO PIECES DOWN THERE.
PEEL OFF, THA GOGSODDER. <I VEHEMENTLY DISAGREE>
CRK
CRK
CHNK
CHNK
CHNK
SO... THIS IS...
CHNK
CHNK
CHNK
...WHERE YOU CAME FROM?
AYE.
CHNK
CHNK
CHNK
CHNK
...
CHNK
CHNK
CHNK
CHNK
CHNK
CHNK
CHNK
CHNK

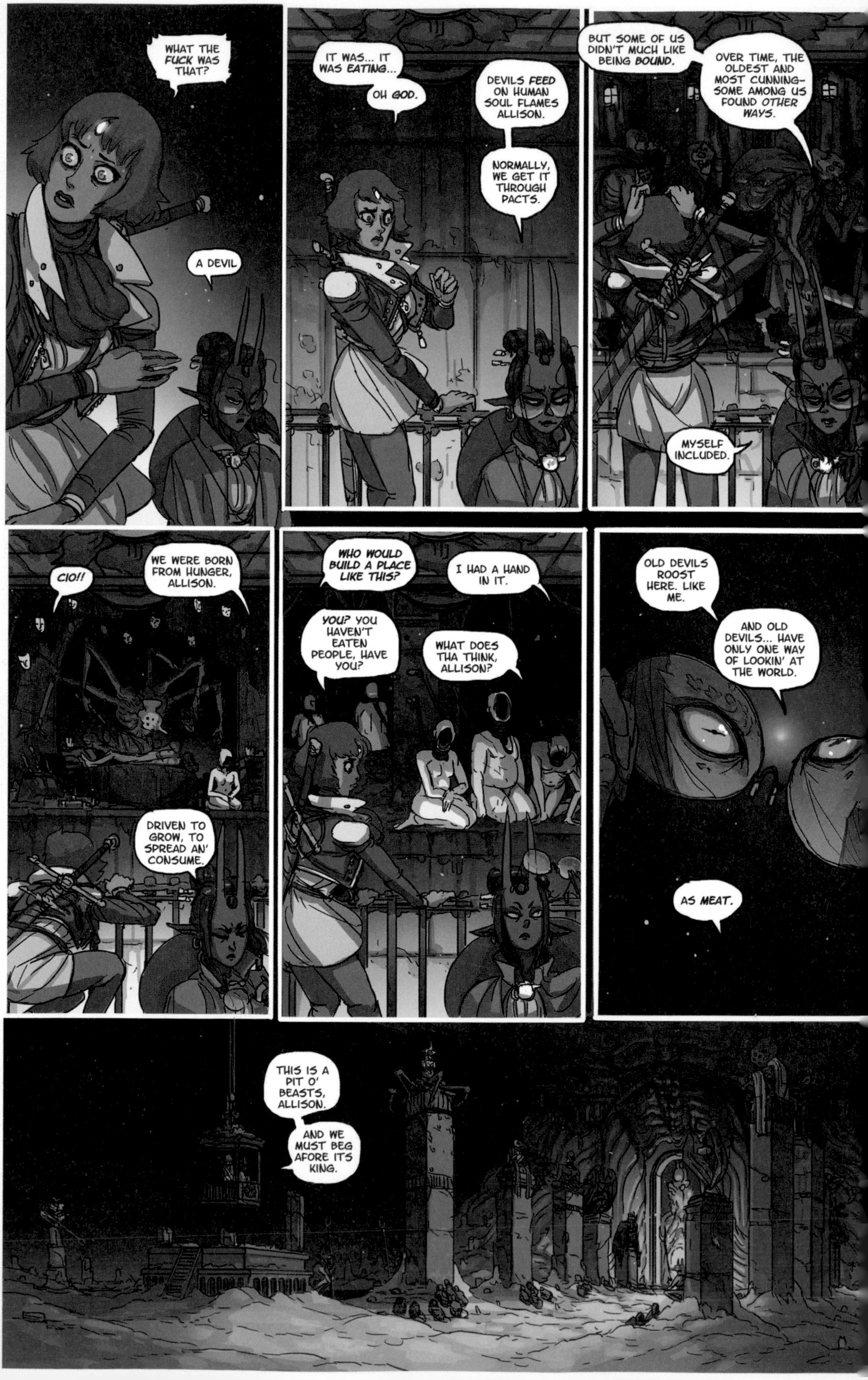
WHAT THE *FUCK* WAS THAT?
A DEVIL
IT WAS... IT WAS *EATING*...
OH *GOD*.
DEVILS *FEED* ON HUMAN SOUL FLAMES ALLISON.
NORMALLY, WE GET IT THROUGH PACTS.
BUT SOME OF US DIDN'T MUCH LIKE BEING *BOUND*.
OVER TIME, THE OLDEST AND MOST CUNNING-SOME AMONG US FOUND *OTHER* WAYS.
MYSELF INCLUDED.
CIO!!
WE WERE BORN FROM HUNGER, ALLISON.
DRIVEN TO GROW, TO SPREAD AN' CONSUME.
WHO WOULD BUILD A PLACE LIKE THIS?
I HAD A HAND IN IT.
YOU? YOU HAVEN'T EATEN PEOPLE, HAVE YOU?
WHAT DOES THA THINK, ALLISON?
OLD DEVILS ROOST HERE. LIKE ME.
AND OLD DEVILS... HAVE ONLY ONE WAY OF LOOKIN' AT THE WORLD.
AS *MEAT*.
THIS IS A PIT O' BEASTS, ALLISON.
AND WE MUST BEG AFORE ITS KING.

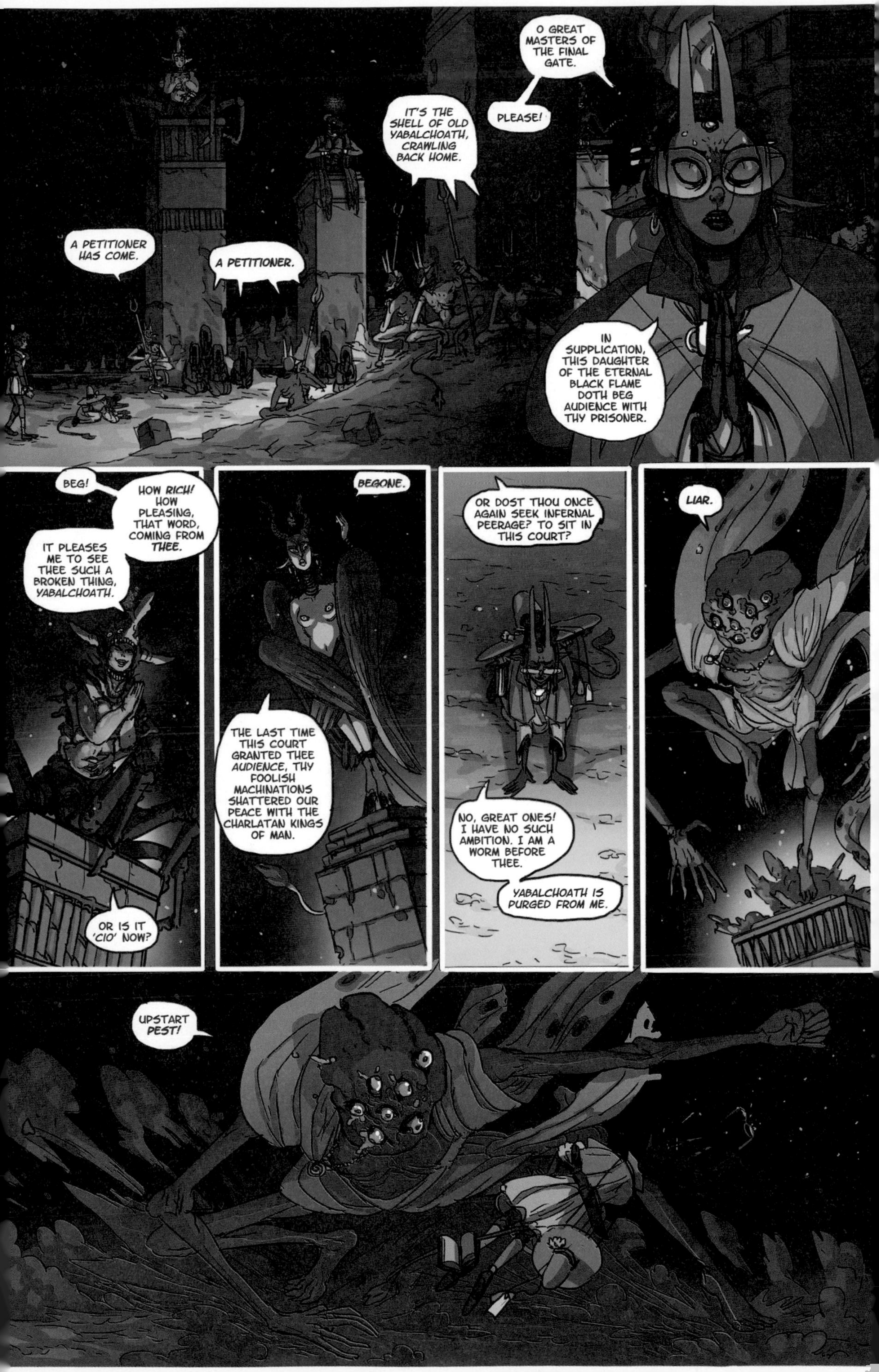
A PETITIONER HAS COME.
A PETITIONER.
IT'S THE SHELL OF OLD YABALCHOATH, CRAWLING BACK HOME.
O GREAT MASTERS OF THE FINAL GATE.
PLEASE!
IN SUPPLICATION, THIS DAUGHTER OF THE ETERNAL BLACK FLAME DOTH BEG AUDIENCE WITH THY PRISONER.
BEG!
HOW RICH! HOW PLEASING, THAT WORD, COMING FROM THEE.
IT PLEASES ME TO SEE THEE SUCH A BROKEN THING, YABALCHOATH.
OR IS IT 'CIO' NOW?
BEGONE.
THE LAST TIME THIS COURT GRANTED THEE AUDIENCE, THY FOOLISH MACHINATIONS SHATTERED OUR PEACE WITH THE CHARLATAN KINGS OF MAN.
OR DOST THOU ONCE AGAIN SEEK INFERNAL PEERAGE? TO SIT IN THIS COURT?
NO, GREAT ONES! I HAVE NO SUCH AMBITION. I AM A WORM BEFORE THEE.
YABALCHOATH IS PURGED FROM ME.
LIAR.
UPSTART PEST!

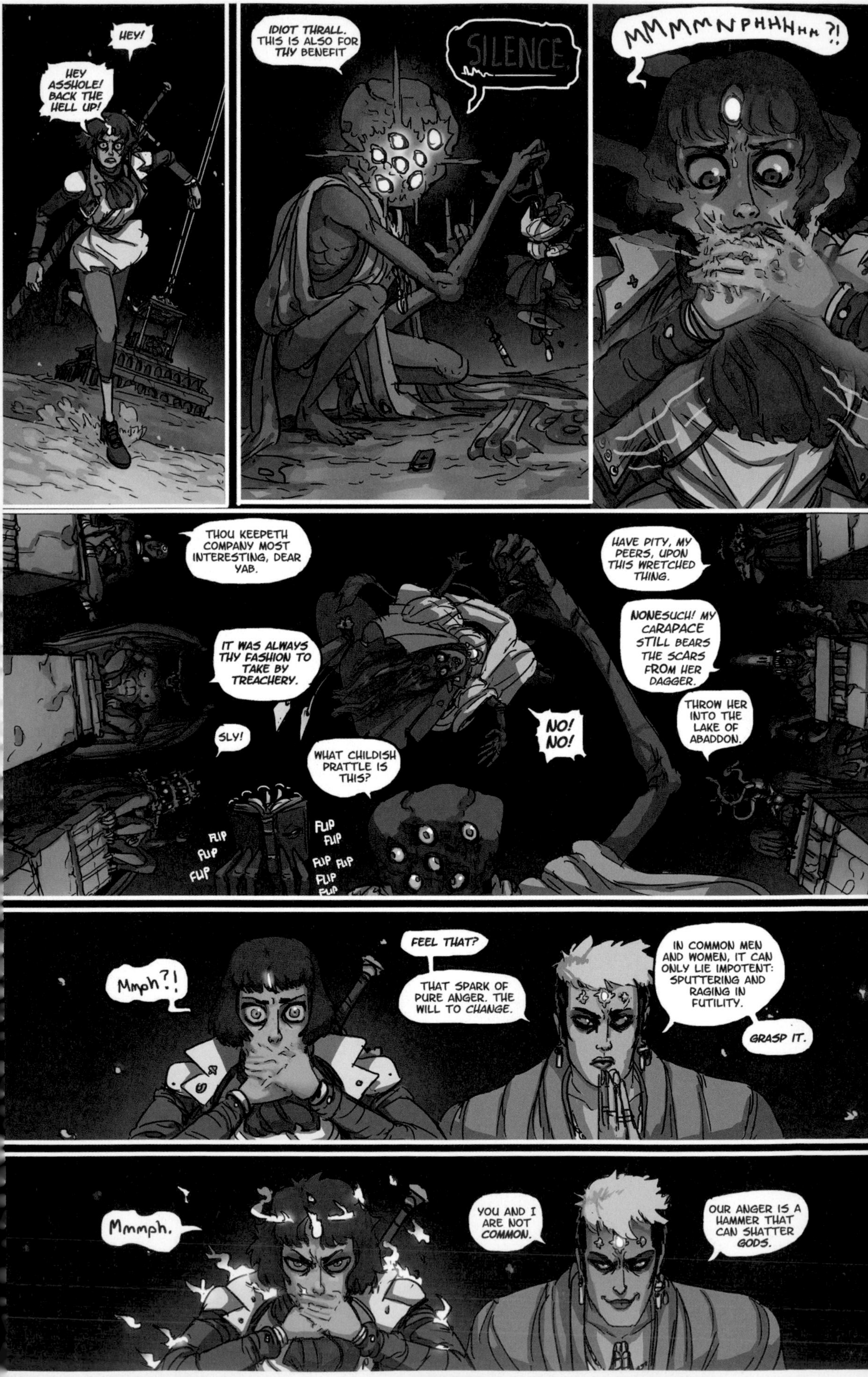
HEY!
HEY ASSHOLE! BACK THE HELL UP!
IDIOT THRALL. THIS IS ALSO FOR THY BENEFIT
SILENCE.
MMMMNPHHHhh?!
THOU KEEPETH COMPANY MOST INTERESTING, DEAR YAB.
IT WAS ALWAYS THY FASHION TO TAKE BY TREACHERY.
SLY!
WHAT CHILDISH PRATTLE IS THIS?
HAVE PITY, MY PEERS, UPON THIS WRETCHED THING.
NONESUCH! MY CARAPACE STILL BEARS THE SCARS FROM HER DAGGER.
NO! NO!
THROW HER INTO THE LAKE OF ABADDON.
FLIP FLIP FLIP
FLIP FLIP FLIP FLIP FLIP
Mmph?!
FEEL THAT?
THAT SPARK OF PURE ANGER. THE WILL TO CHANGE.
IN COMMON MEN AND WOMEN, IT CAN ONLY LIE IMPOTENT: SPUTTERING AND RAGING IN FUTILITY.
GRASP IT.
Mmmph.
YOU AND I ARE NOT COMMON.
OUR ANGER IS A HAMMER THAT CAN SHATTER GODS.

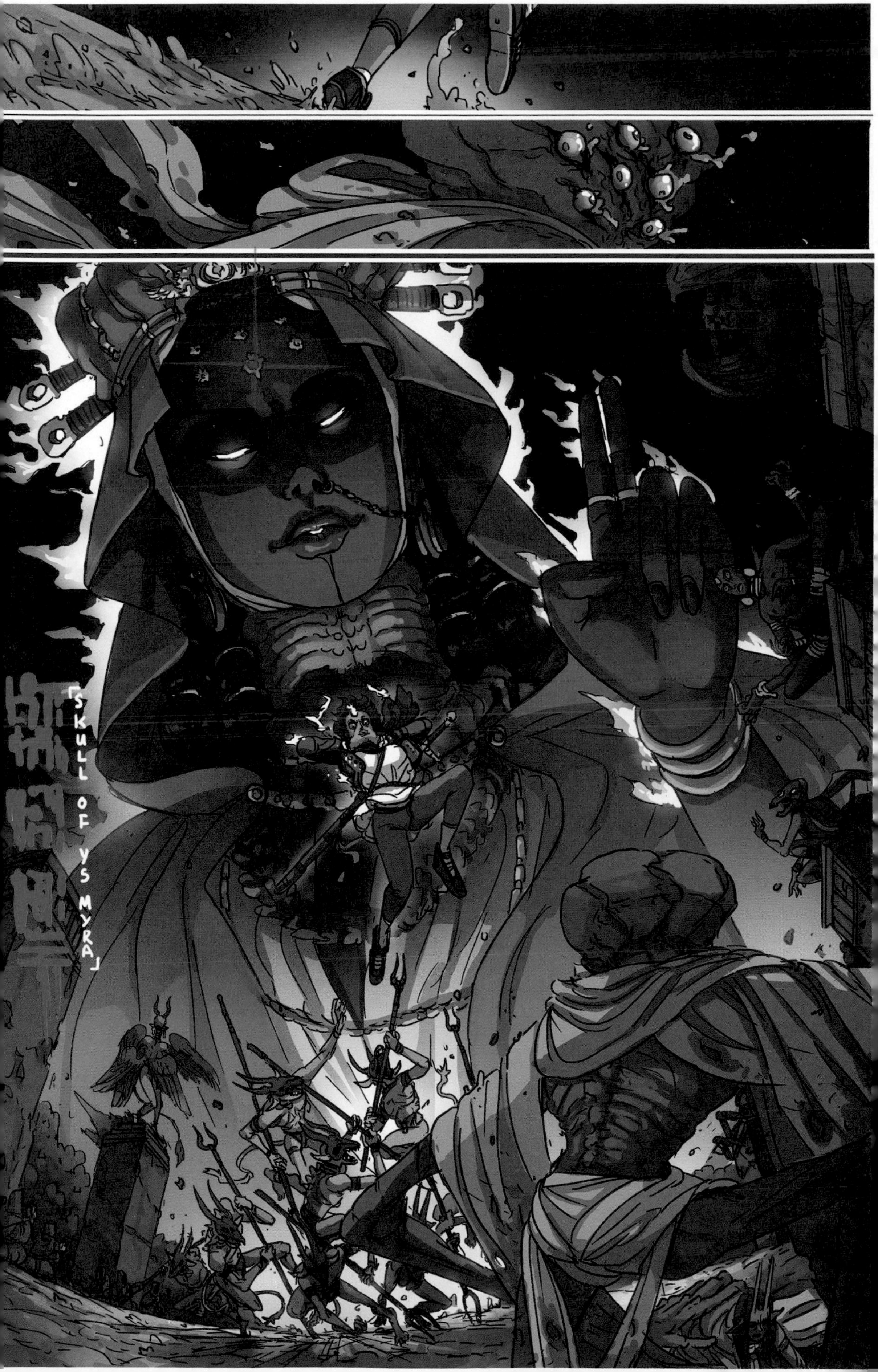
SKULL OF YS MYRA

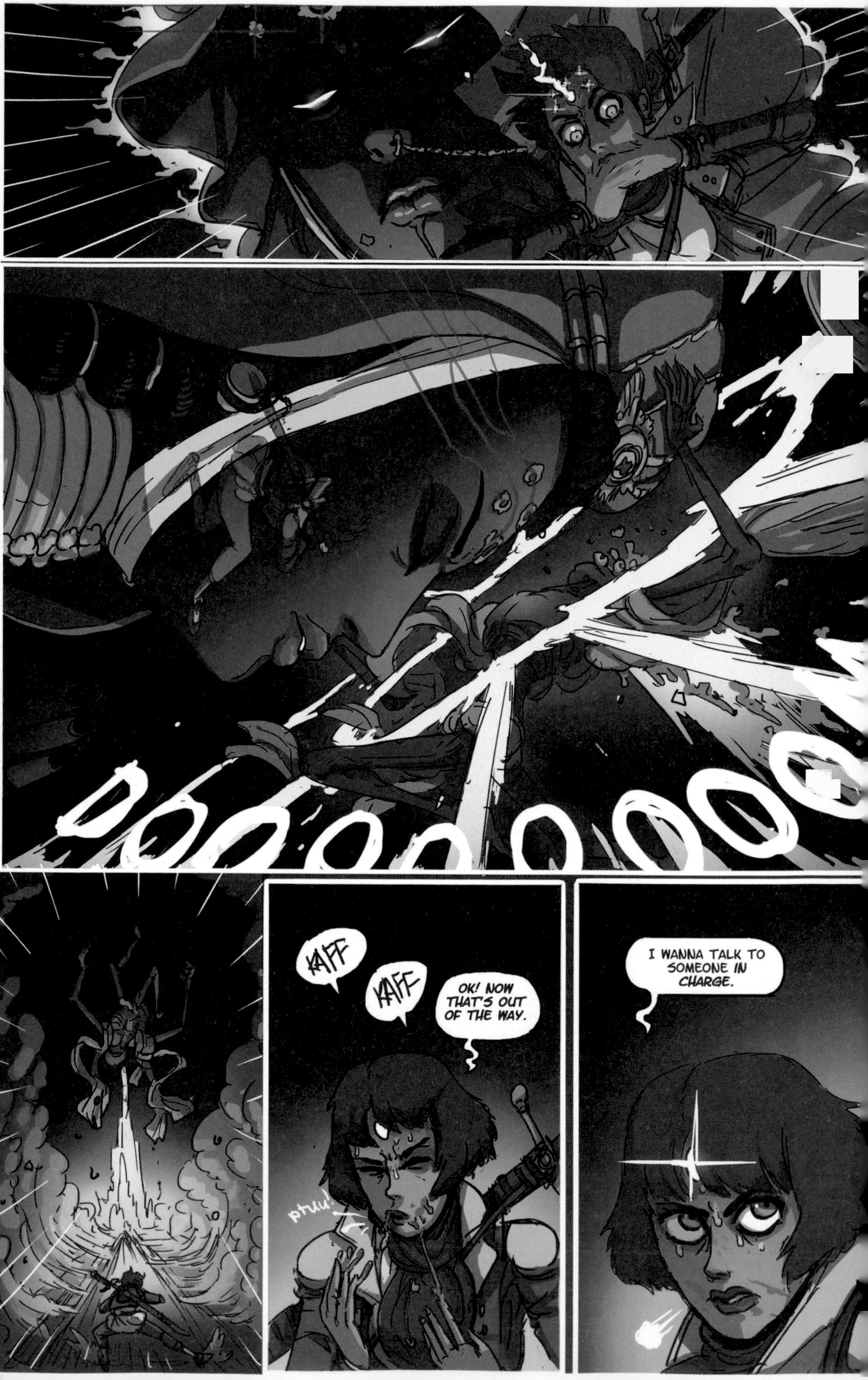
POOOOOOOOM
KAFF
KAFF
OK! NOW THAT'S OUT OF THE WAY.
ptuu!
I WANNA TALK TO SOMEONE IN CHARGE.

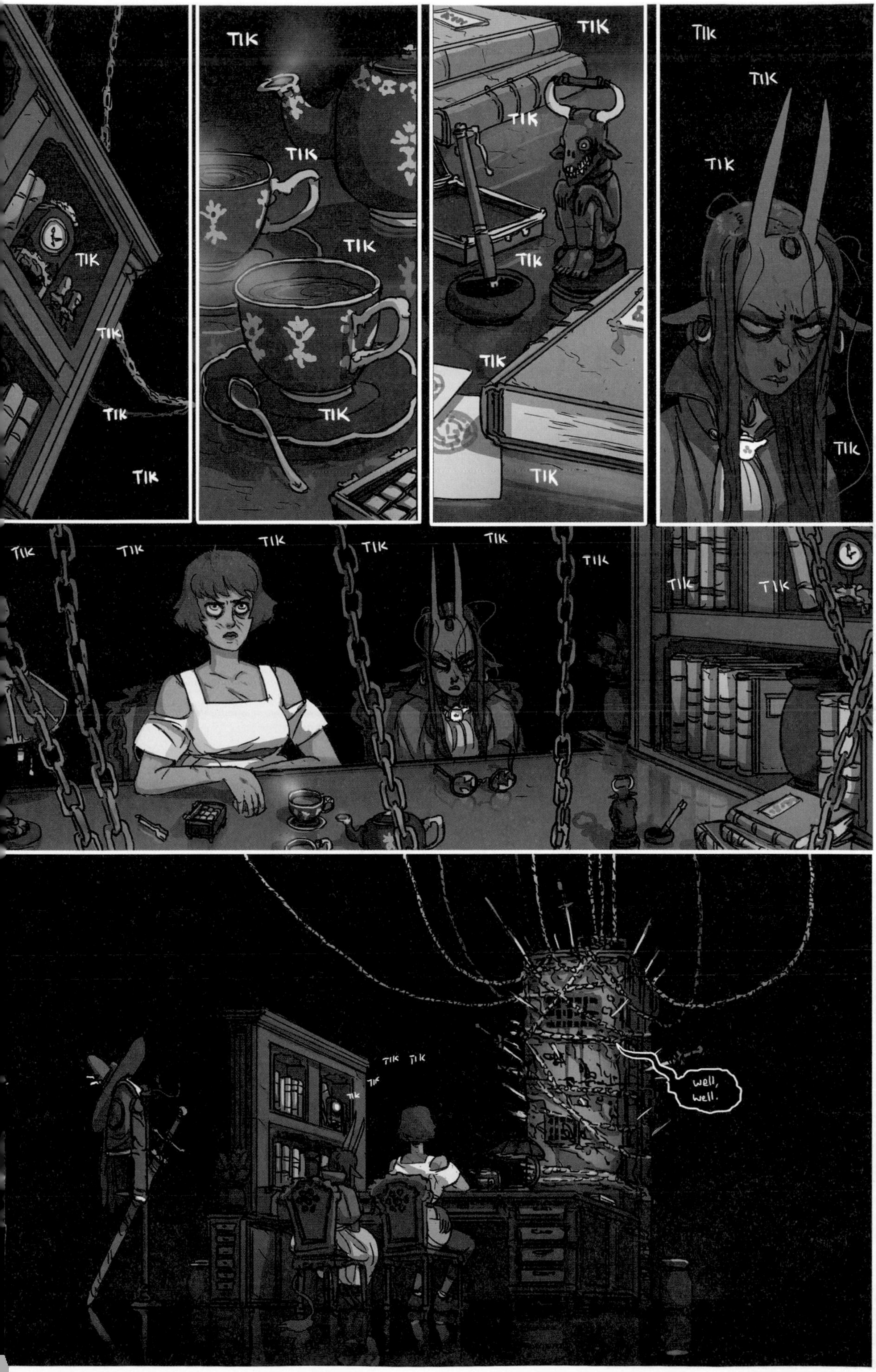
TIK
TIK
TIK
TIK
TIK
TIK
TIK
TIK
TIK
TIK
TIK
TIK
TIK
TIK
TIK
TIK
TIK
TIK
TIK
TIK
TIK
TIK
TIK
TIK
TIK
TIK
TIK
TIK
TIK
TIK
TIK TIK
TIK
TIK
well, well.

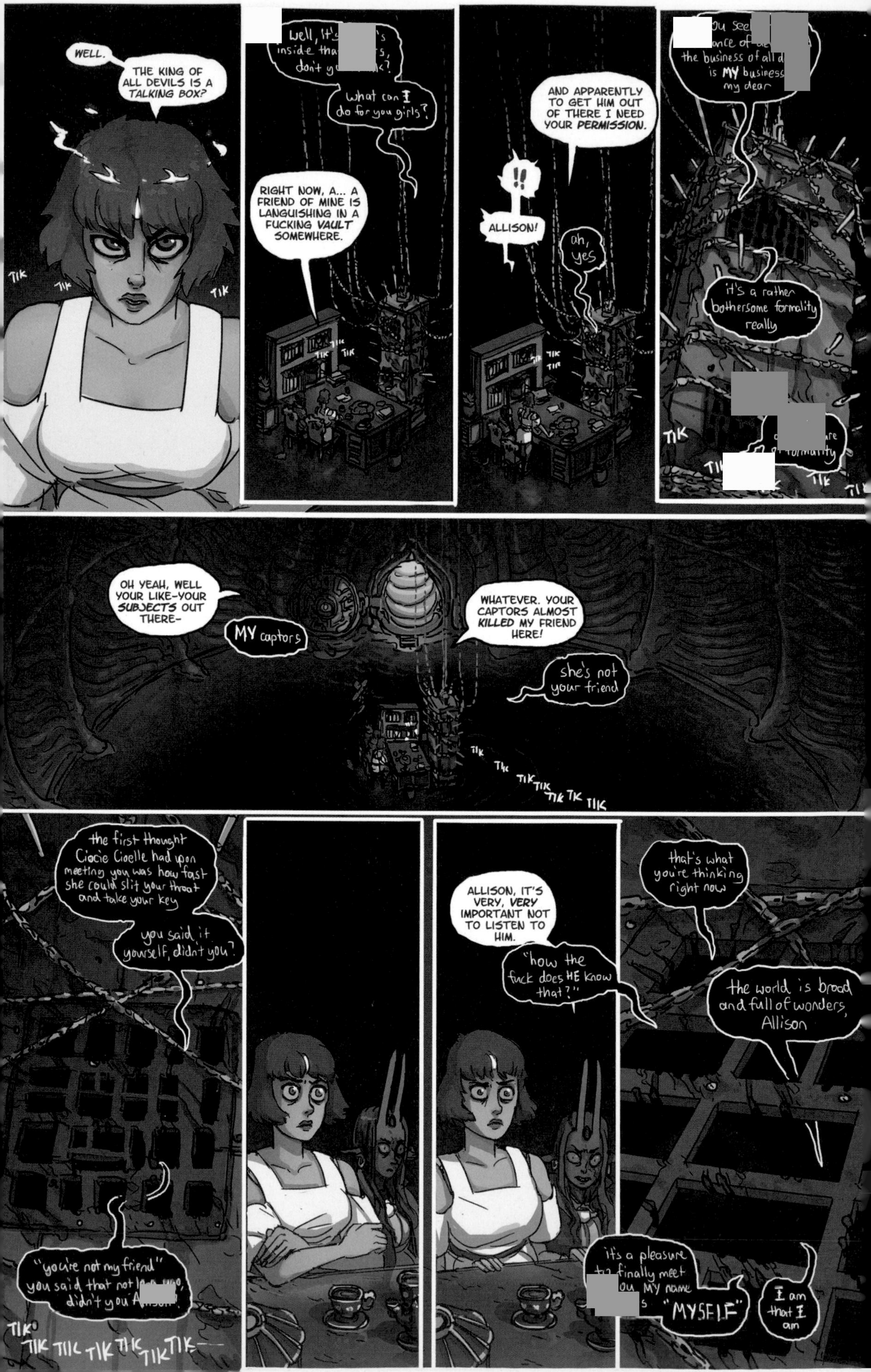

WELL.
THE KING OF ALL DEVILS IS A TALKING BOX?
TIK TIK TIK
Well, it's [redacted]s inside tha[redacted]s, don't y[redacted]k?
what can I do for you girls?
RIGHT NOW, A... A FRIEND OF MINE IS LANGUISHING IN A FUCKING VAULT SOMEWHERE.
TIK TIK TIK
AND APPARENTLY TO GET HIM OUT OF THERE I NEED YOUR PERMISSION.
!!
ALLISON!
ah, yes
TIK TIK
[redacted]ou see[redacted]ance of a[redacted] the business of all d[redacted] is MY business[redacted] my dear
it's a rather bothersome formality really
[redacted] a[redacted]re a formality
TIK TIK TIK TIK
OH YEAH, WELL YOUR LIKE-YOUR SUBJECTS OUT THERE-
MY captors
WHATEVER. YOUR CAPTORS ALMOST KILLED MY FRIEND HERE!
she's not your friend
TIK TIK TIK TIK TIK TIK TIK
the first thought Cicie Cielle had upon meeting you was how fast she could slit your throat and take your key
you said it yourself, didn't you?
"you're not my friend" you said that not lo[redacted] ago, didn't you A[redacted]
TIK TIK TIK TIK TIK TIK TIK—
ALLISON, IT'S VERY, VERY IMPORTANT NOT TO LISTEN TO HIM.
"how the fuck does HE know that?"
that's what you're thinking right now
the world is broad and full of wonders, Allison
it's a pleasure to finally meet [redacted]ou. My name [redacted]s "MYSELF"
I am that I am

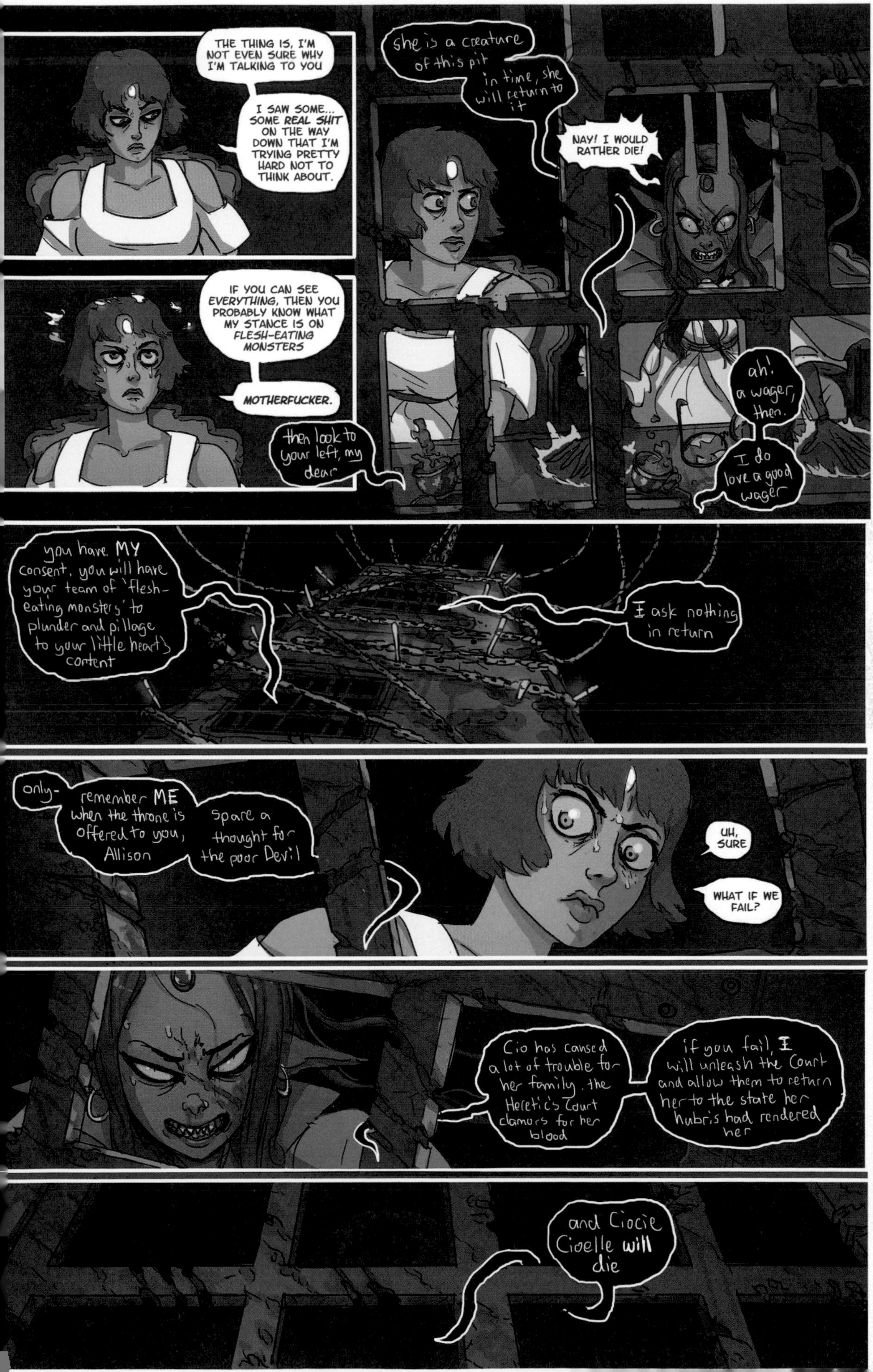
THE THING IS, I'M NOT EVEN SURE WHY I'M TALKING TO YOU
I SAW SOME... SOME REAL SHIT ON THE WAY DOWN THAT I'M TRYING PRETTY HARD NOT TO THINK ABOUT.
IF YOU CAN SEE EVERYTHING, THEN YOU PROBABLY KNOW WHAT MY STANCE IS ON FLESH-EATING MONSTERS
MOTHERFUCKER.
then look to your left, my dear
she is a creature of this pit
in time, she will return to it
NAY! I WOULD RATHER DIE!
ah! a wager, then.
I do love a good wager
you have MY consent. you will have your team of 'flesh-eating monsters' to plunder and pillage to your little heart's content
I ask nothing in return
only-
remember ME when the throne is offered to you, Allison
spare a thought for the poor Devil
UH, SURE
WHAT IF WE FAIL?
Cio has caused a lot of trouble for her family. the Heretic's Court clamors for her blood
if you fail, I will unleash the Court and allow them to return her to the state her hubris had rendered her
and Ciocie Cioelle will die

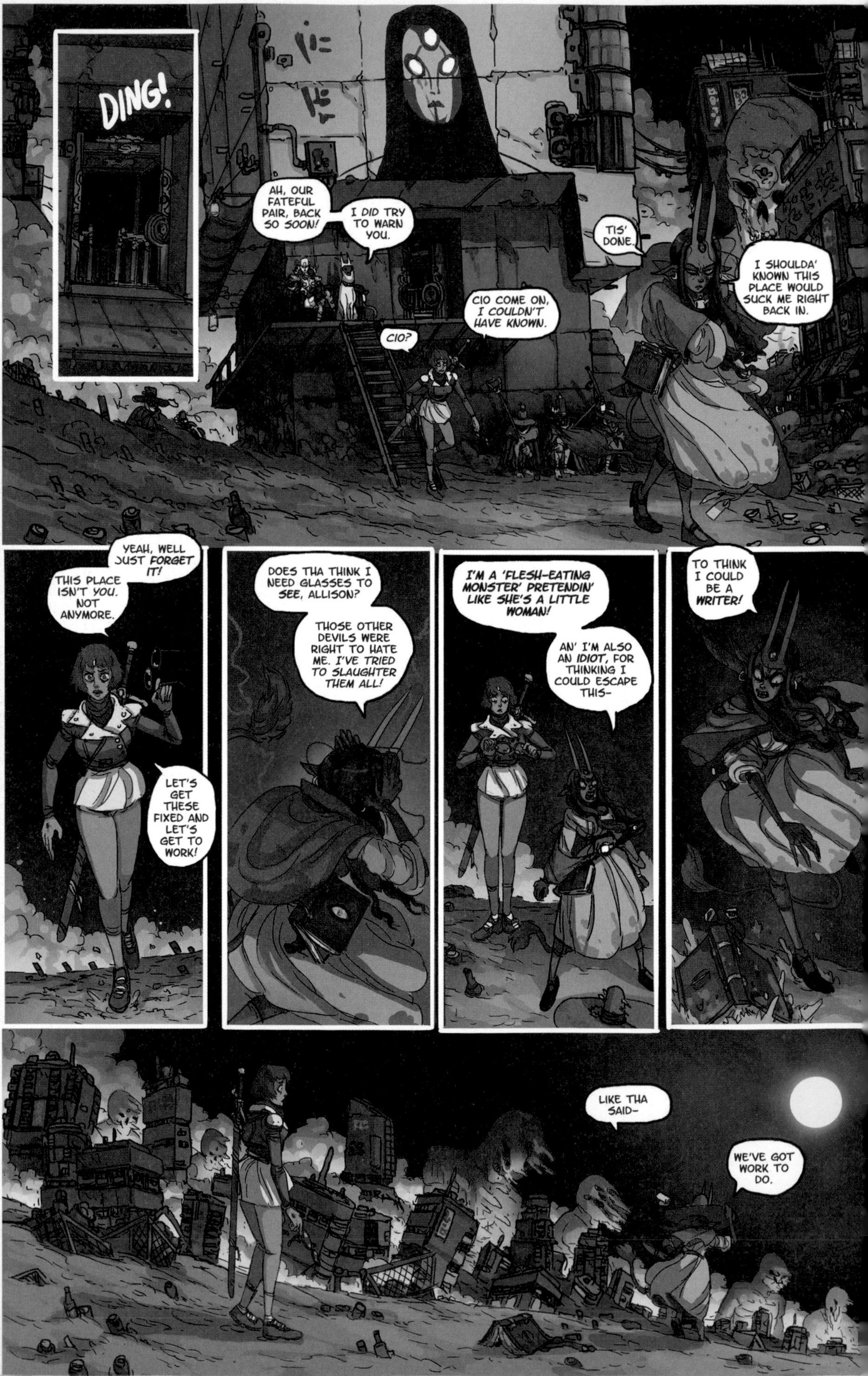

DING!
AH, OUR FATEFUL PAIR, BACK SO SOON!
I DID TRY TO WARN YOU.
TIS' DONE.
I SHOULDA' KNOWN THIS PLACE WOULD SUCK ME RIGHT BACK IN.
CIO COME ON, I COULDN'T HAVE KNOWN.
CIO?
YEAH, WELL JUST FORGET IT!
THIS PLACE ISN'T YOU. NOT ANYMORE.
LET'S GET THESE FIXED AND LET'S GET TO WORK!
DOES THA THINK I NEED GLASSES TO SEE, ALLISON?
THOSE OTHER DEVILS WERE RIGHT TO HATE ME. I'VE TRIED TO SLAUGHTER THEM ALL!
I'M A 'FLESH-EATING MONSTER' PRETENDIN' LIKE SHE'S A LITTLE WOMAN!
AN' I'M ALSO AN IDIOT, FOR THINKING I COULD ESCAPE THIS-
TO THINK I COULD BE A WRITER!
LIKE THA SAID-
WE'VE GOT WORK TO DO.

Vastoki was Prince Kassardi's first wife, and the youngest. She wore only one ring and kept her fingernails expertly trimmed. Her dress was a short cut, her vela plain and good for traveling, and she wore eye glasses. Her teeth were filed to points, and she kept sparrow feathers tucked behind her ear. She was a master markswoman with the long rifle, with which she had trained her whole life, so that on her wedding day she could swiftly assassinate her rivals. By the time it had reached her wedding day she had hunted five men in practice and was thirsty for blood.

It was for this reason she was the first to set out in search when the prince was found missing.

Littari was Prince Kassardis' second wife, and though she was not quite as young and vigorous as his wife Vastoki, nor as patient and wise as his wife Ipreski, her bloodlust was the strongest by far. Where Vastoki was thin and lithe, and favored traveling clothes, Littari wore a full set of eidolon-wrought armor, which she cleaned and polished constantly, and gave her the appearance of a gargantuan demon. She was twelve spans tall, and had enormous teeth. Her bulging muscles meant tailoring for her was a nightmare for her maids, so she spurned their service, and preferred to travel with her cook, sandal bearer, and sword-master only.

Littari was far too strong to use a sword, for any normal weapon would break and shatter with the immense force she put upon it. Instead, she dragged around with her a great and heavy iron cauldron, with which she would beat opponents to death quite savagely. It was to this pot which the prince's other wives had promised to chain her and force her to serve as a scullery slave, and so she had taken an oath of revenge to pulp, cook, and eat them.

Littari was by far the least popular of the prince's three wives, and so she only learned of his escape after the young Vastoki had started her pursuit. Nevertheless, by the second day, she was not far behind her quarry, and her steps shook the dust from the eaves of peasant homes as she passed.

Ipreski was Prince Kassardis' last and oldest wife, though barely by a few years. Despite her relative youth, however, her hair had already become white as snow. Some gossiped about how it was a curse from a vengeful sorcerer, for the offenses of the princess Ipreski's family were broad, and no less horrible for their breadth.

Ipreski kept her white hair long, and bound up in coils that wrapped around her waist five times. She was exceedingly lazy, and would rather order one of her numerous and weary servants to fetch something than walk a mere five paces. She was pampered and fond of food and wine, and complained loudly if there was no place for her to lounge about.

This laziness of hers was a clever mask, for Ipreski kept all her energy coiled up inside of her like a spring. She was a master swordswoman, in the old tradition of her family, and her muscles were like steel cables. Such was her skill that she could kill a man and sheathe her sword before the first drop of his blood hit the ground. She had no need to pursue her opponents, for they could not touch her, and was instead content to wait until they came to their slaughter. This was the source and secret of her arrogance. She loudly mocked Kassardis' other wives, especially the large and slow Littari, for she believed there was no chance they could beat her in open combat – and it was true.

It was only fitting, therefore, that the languid Ipreski was the last to set out in pursuit of the young prince in her palanquin, with her full retinue trailing after her."

– TALES OF THE SILVER PRINCE

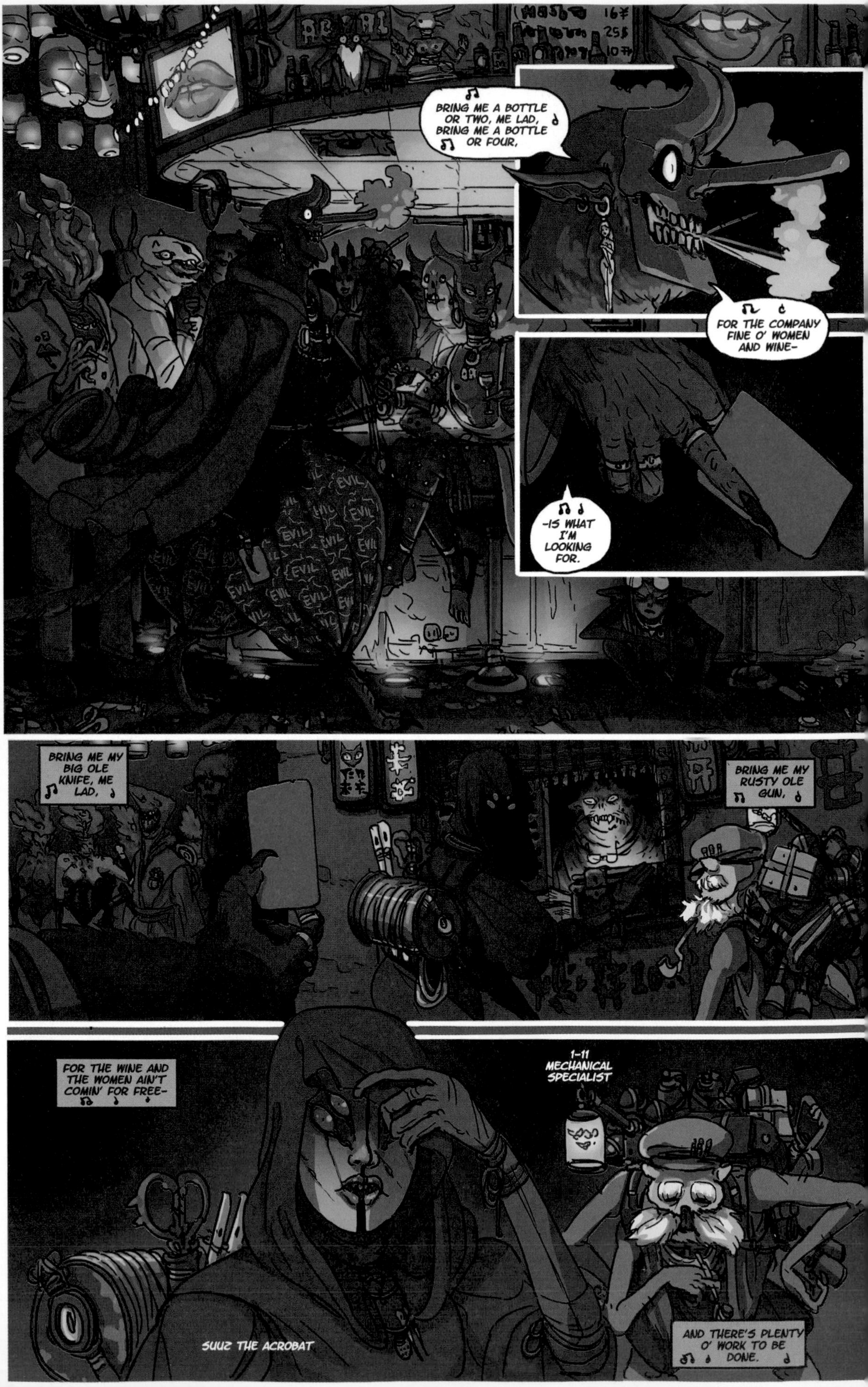
BRING ME A BOTTLE OR TWO, ME LAD, BRING ME A BOTTLE OR FOUR,
FOR THE COMPANY FINE O' WOMEN AND WINE-
-IS WHAT I'M LOOKING FOR.
BRING ME MY BIG OLE KNIFE, ME LAD,
BRING ME MY RUSTY OLE GUN,
FOR THE WINE AND THE WOMEN AIN'T COMIN' FOR FREE-
1-11 MECHANICAL SPECIALIST
SUUZ THE ACROBAT
AND THERE'S PLENTY O' WORK TO BE DONE.

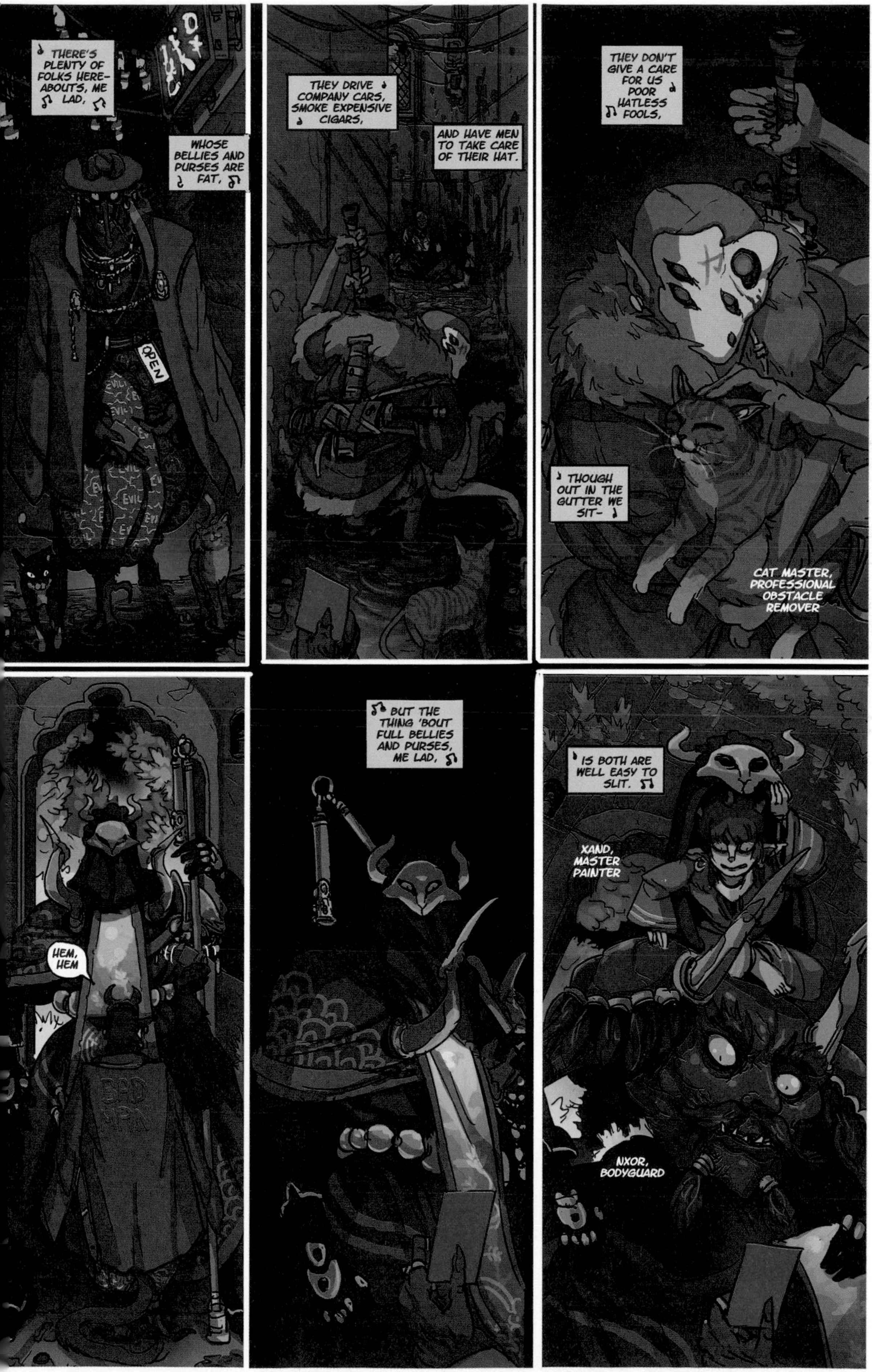

THERE'S PLENTY OF FOLKS HERE-ABOUTS, ME LAD,
WHOSE BELLIES AND PURSES ARE FAT,
OPEN
THEY DRIVE COMPANY CARS, SMOKE EXPENSIVE CIGARS,
AND HAVE MEN TO TAKE CARE OF THEIR HAT.
THEY DON'T GIVE A CARE FOR US POOR HATLESS FOOLS,
THOUGH OUT IN THE GUTTER WE SIT-
CAT MASTER, PROFESSIONAL OBSTACLE REMOVER
HEM, HEM
BUT THE THING 'BOUT FULL BELLIES AND PURSES, ME LAD,
IS BOTH ARE WELL EASY TO SLIT.
XAND, MASTER PAINTER
NXOR, BODYGUARD

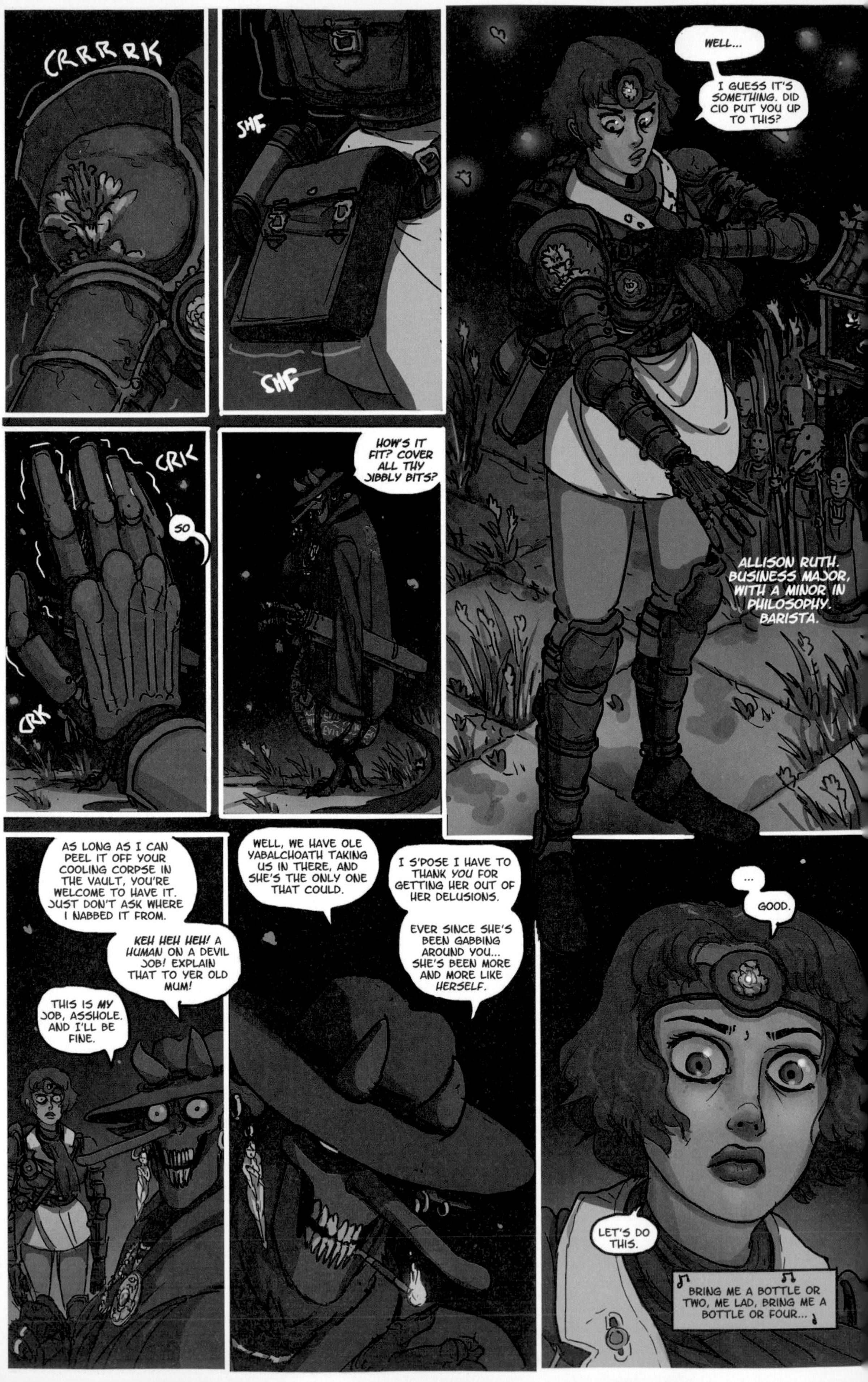
CRRRRK
SHF
SHF
WELL...
I GUESS IT'S SOMETHING. DID CIO PUT YOU UP TO THIS?
CRIK
SO
CRK
HOW'S IT FIT? COVER ALL THY JIBBLY BITS?
ALLISON RUTH. BUSINESS MAJOR, WITH A MINOR IN PHILOSOPHY. BARISTA.
AS LONG AS I CAN PEEL IT OFF YOUR COOLING CORPSE IN THE VAULT, YOU'RE WELCOME TO HAVE IT. JUST DON'T ASK WHERE I NABBED IT FROM.
KEH HEH HEH! A HUMAN ON A DEVIL JOB! EXPLAIN THAT TO YER OLD MUM!
THIS IS MY JOB, ASSHOLE. AND I'LL BE FINE.
WELL, WE HAVE OLE YABALCHOATH TAKING US IN THERE, AND SHE'S THE ONLY ONE THAT COULD.
I S'POSE I HAVE TO THANK YOU FOR GETTING HER OUT OF HER DELUSIONS.
EVER SINCE SHE'S BEEN GABBING AROUND YOU... SHE'S BEEN MORE AND MORE LIKE HERSELF.
...
GOOD.
LET'S DO THIS.
BRING ME A BOTTLE OR TWO, ME LAD, BRING ME A BOTTLE OR FOUR...

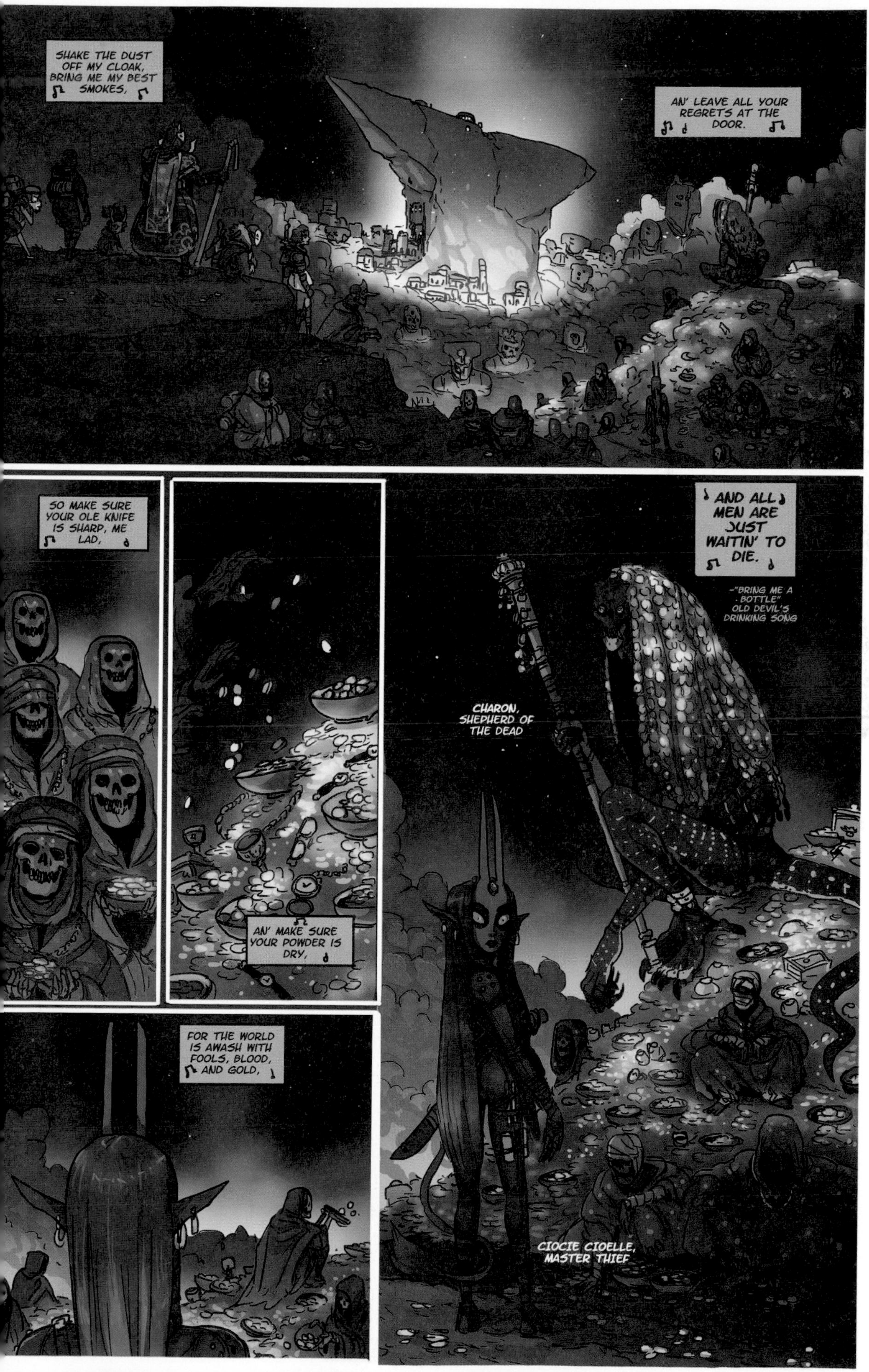
SHAKE THE DUST OFF MY CLOAK, BRING ME MY BEST SMOKES,
AN' LEAVE ALL YOUR REGRETS AT THE DOOR.
SO MAKE SURE YOUR OLE KNIFE IS SHARP, ME LAD,
AN' MAKE SURE YOUR POWDER IS DRY,
FOR THE WORLD IS AWASH WITH FOOLS, BLOOD, AND GOLD,
AND ALL MEN ARE JUST WAITIN' TO DIE.
-"BRING ME A BOTTLE" OLD DEVIL'S DRINKING SONG
CHARON, SHEPHERD OF THE DEAD
CIOCIE CIOELLE, MASTER THIEF

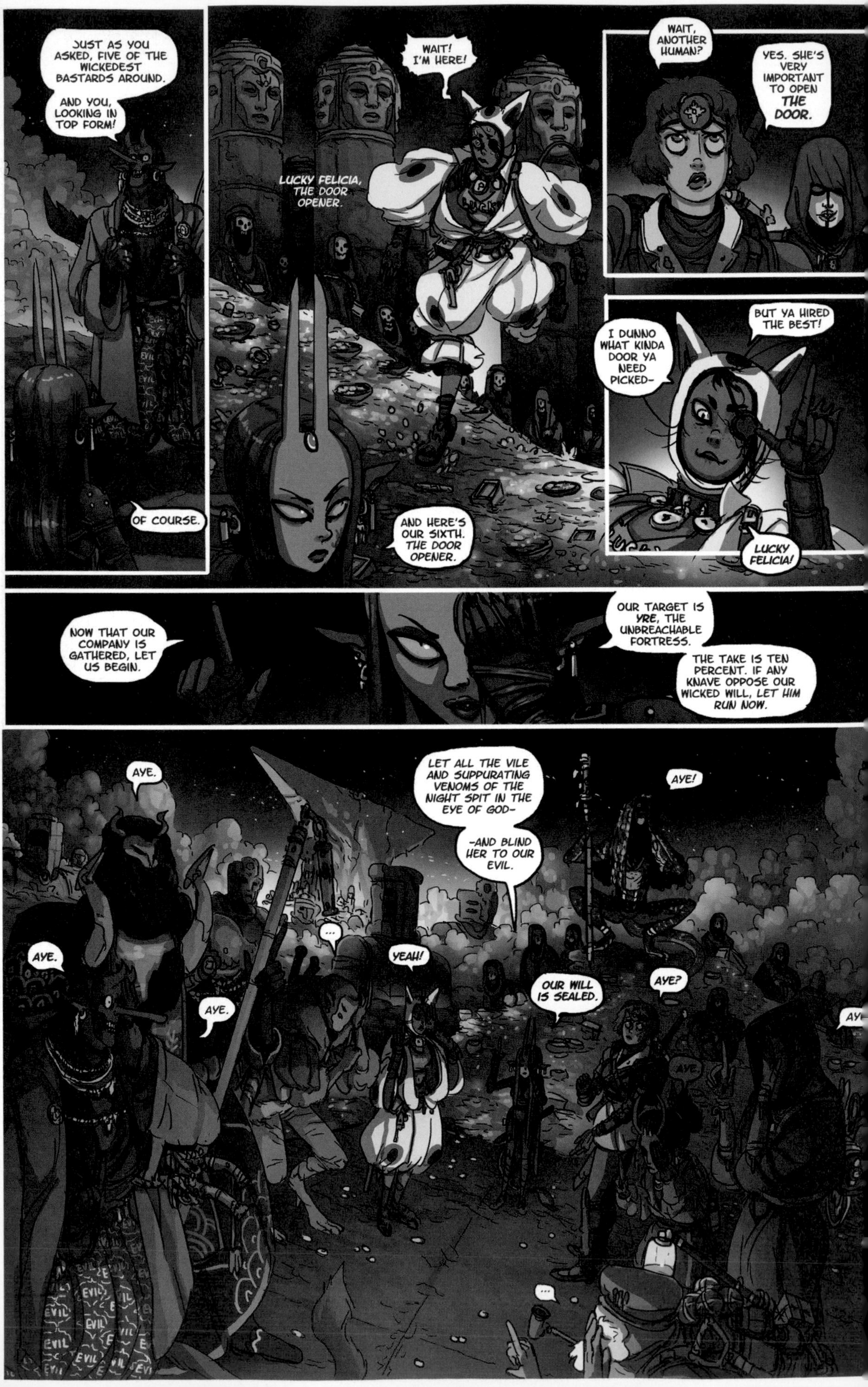

JUST AS YOU ASKED, FIVE OF THE WICKEDEST BASTARDS AROUND.
AND YOU, LOOKING IN TOP FORM!
OF COURSE.
WAIT! I'M HERE!
LUCKY FELICIA, THE DOOR OPENER.
AND HERE'S OUR SIXTH. THE DOOR OPENER.
WAIT, ANOTHER HUMAN?
YES. SHE'S VERY IMPORTANT TO OPEN THE DOOR.
I DUNNO WHAT KINDA DOOR YA NEED PICKED-
BUT YA HIRED THE BEST!
LUCKY FELICIA!
NOW THAT OUR COMPANY IS GATHERED, LET US BEGIN.
OUR TARGET IS YRE, THE UNBREACHABLE FORTRESS.
THE TAKE IS TEN PERCENT. IF ANY KNAVE OPPOSE OUR WICKED WILL, LET HIM RUN NOW.
AYE.
LET ALL THE VILE AND SUPPURATING VENOMS OF THE NIGHT SPIT IN THE EYE OF GOD-
-AND BLIND HER TO OUR EVIL.
AYE!
AYE.
...
YEAH!
AYE.
OUR WILL IS SEALED.
AYE?
AYE.
...

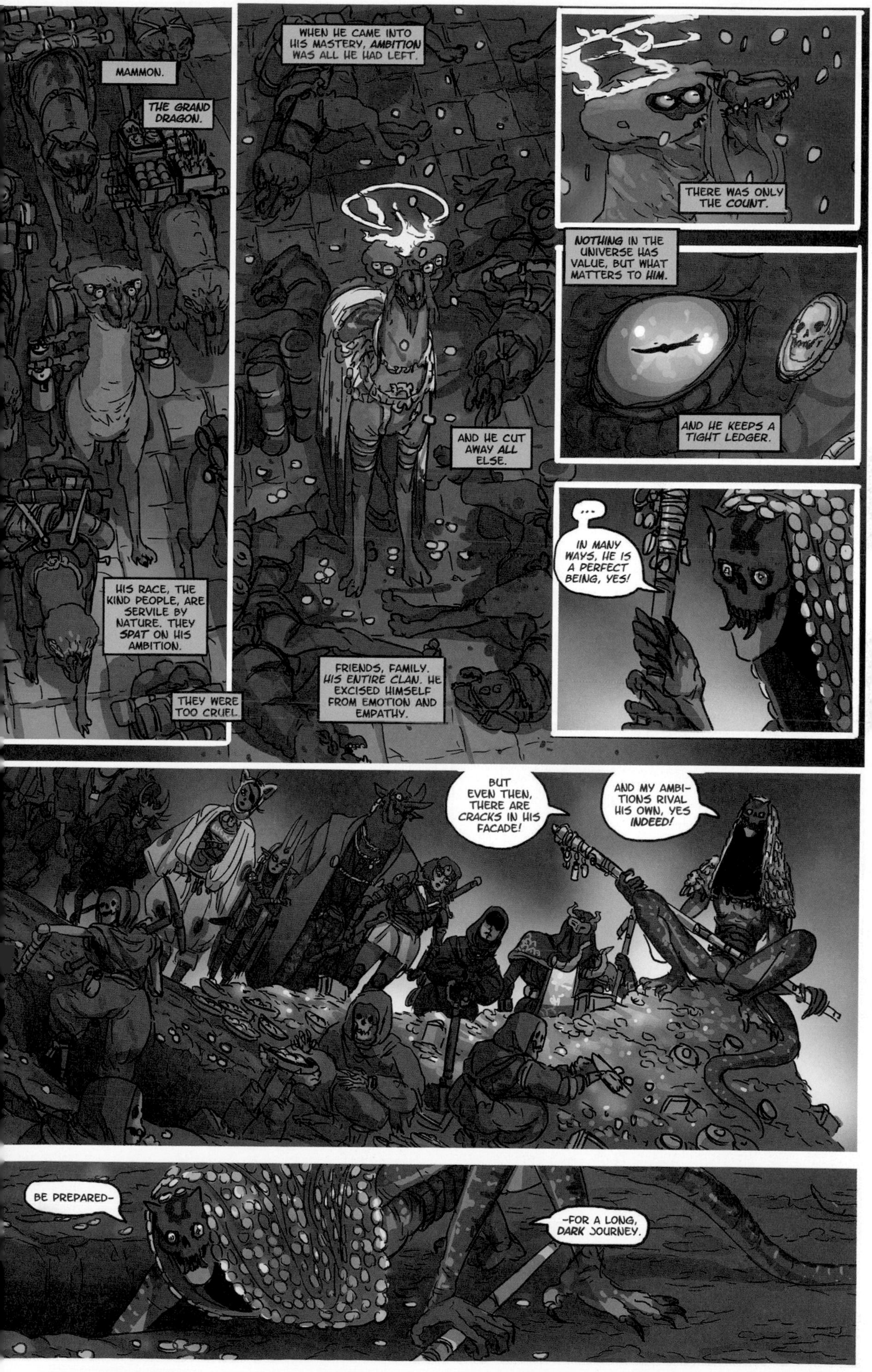

MAMMON.
THE GRAND DRAGON.
HIS RACE, THE KIND PEOPLE, ARE SERVILE BY NATURE. THEY SPAT ON HIS AMBITION.
THEY WERE TOO CRUEL.
WHEN HE CAME INTO HIS MASTERY, AMBITION WAS ALL HE HAD LEFT.
AND HE CUT AWAY ALL ELSE.
FRIENDS, FAMILY. HIS ENTIRE CLAN. HE EXCISED HIMSELF FROM EMOTION AND EMPATHY.
THERE WAS ONLY THE COUNT.
NOTHING IN THE UNIVERSE HAS VALUE, BUT WHAT MATTERS TO HIM.
AND HE KEEPS A TIGHT LEDGER.
...
IN MANY WAYS, HE IS A PERFECT BEING, YES!
BUT EVEN THEN, THERE ARE CRACKS IN HIS FACADE!
AND MY AMBITIONS RIVAL HIS OWN, YES INDEED!
BE PREPARED-
-FOR A LONG, DARK JOURNEY.

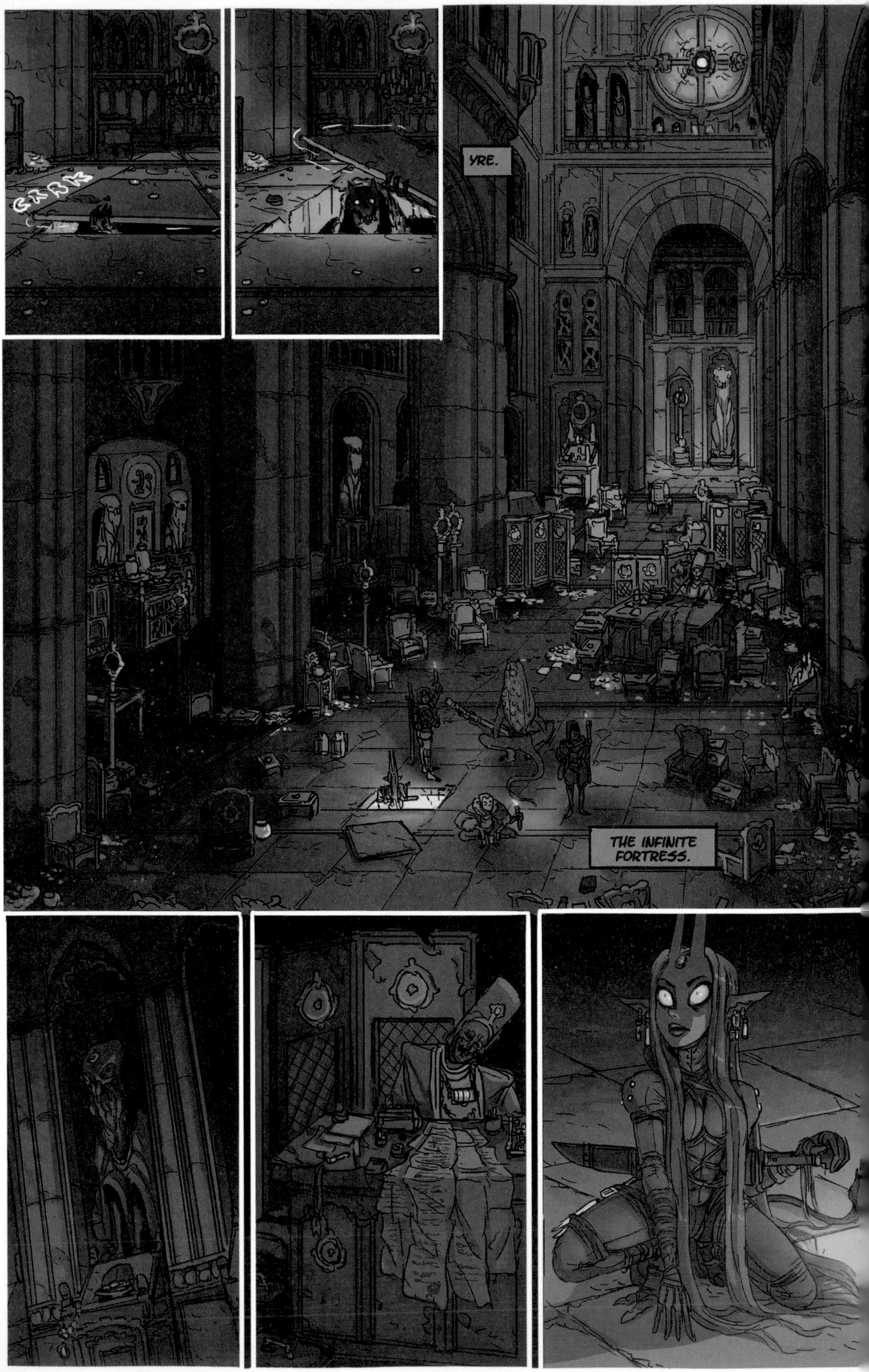
GRRK
YRE.
THE INFINITE FORTRESS.

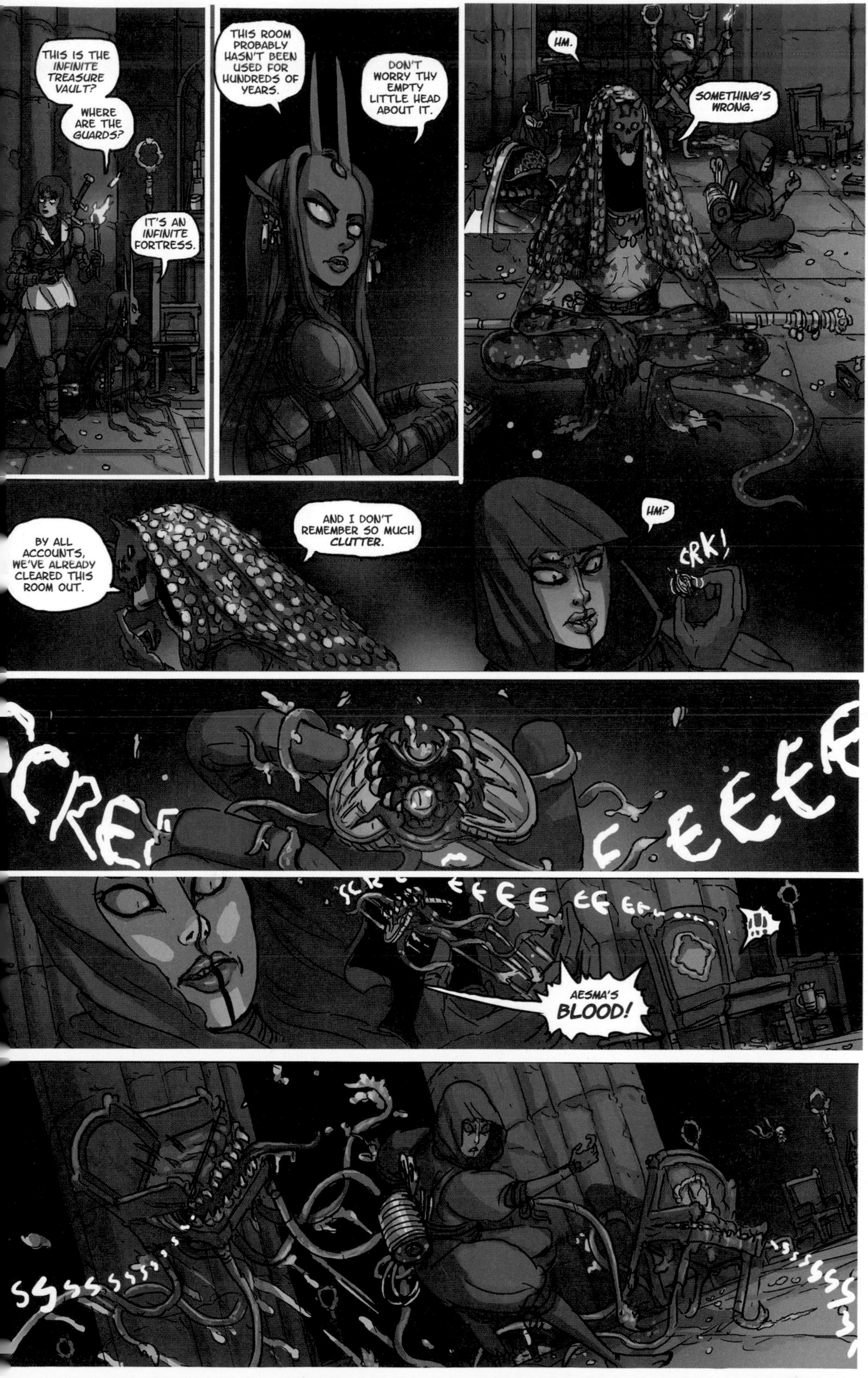
THIS IS THE INFINITE TREASURE VAULT?
WHERE ARE THE GUARDS?
IT'S AN INFINITE FORTRESS.
THIS ROOM PROBABLY HASN'T BEEN USED FOR HUNDREDS OF YEARS.
DON'T WORRY THY EMPTY LITTLE HEAD ABOUT IT.
HM.
SOMETHING'S WRONG.
BY ALL ACCOUNTS, WE'VE ALREADY CLEARED THIS ROOM OUT.
AND I DON'T REMEMBER SO MUCH CLUTTER.
HM?
CRK!
SCREEEEEE
AESMA'S BLOOD!
SSSSSSSSS
SSSSSS

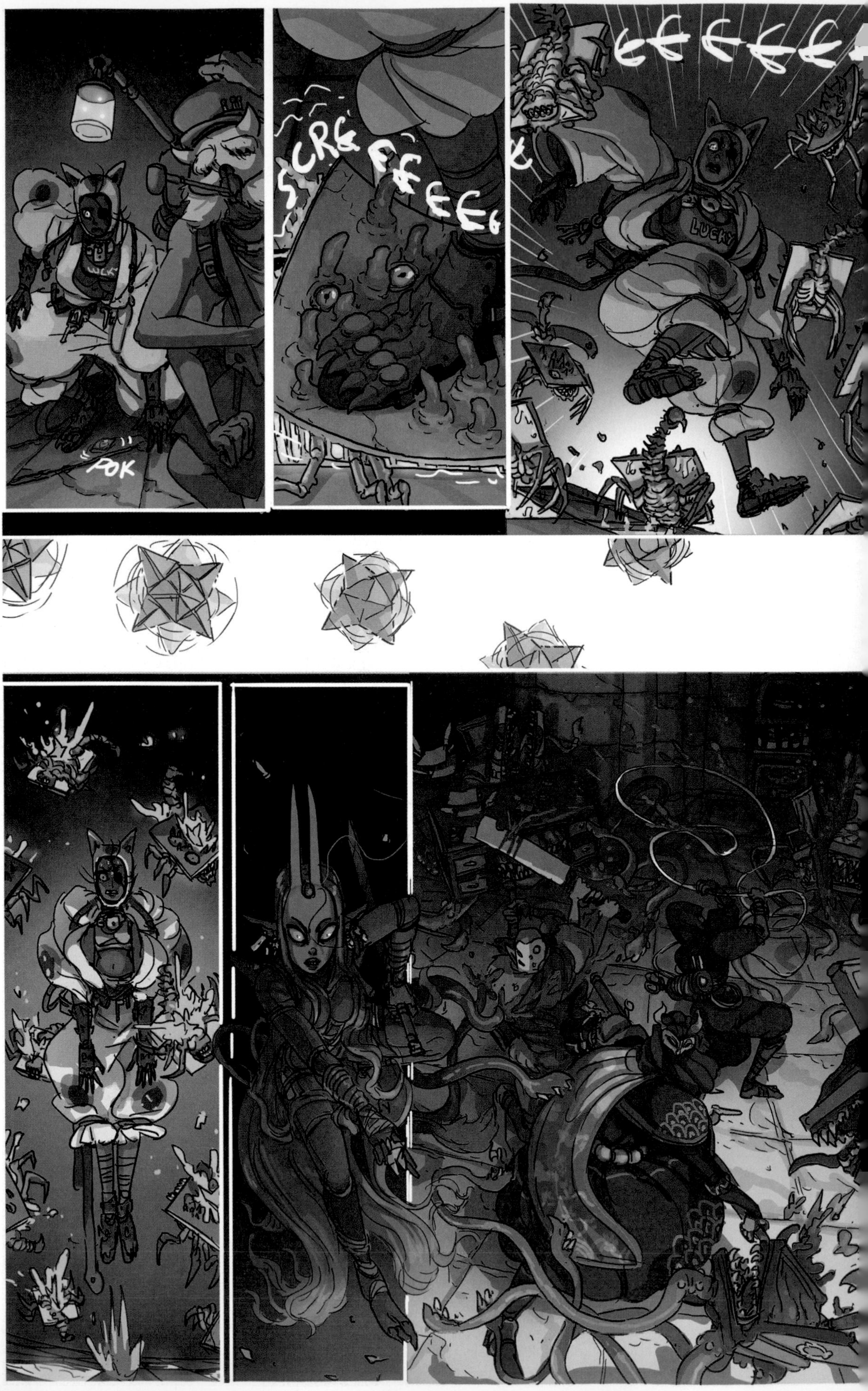
LUCKY
POK
SCREEEEEEE
LUCKY

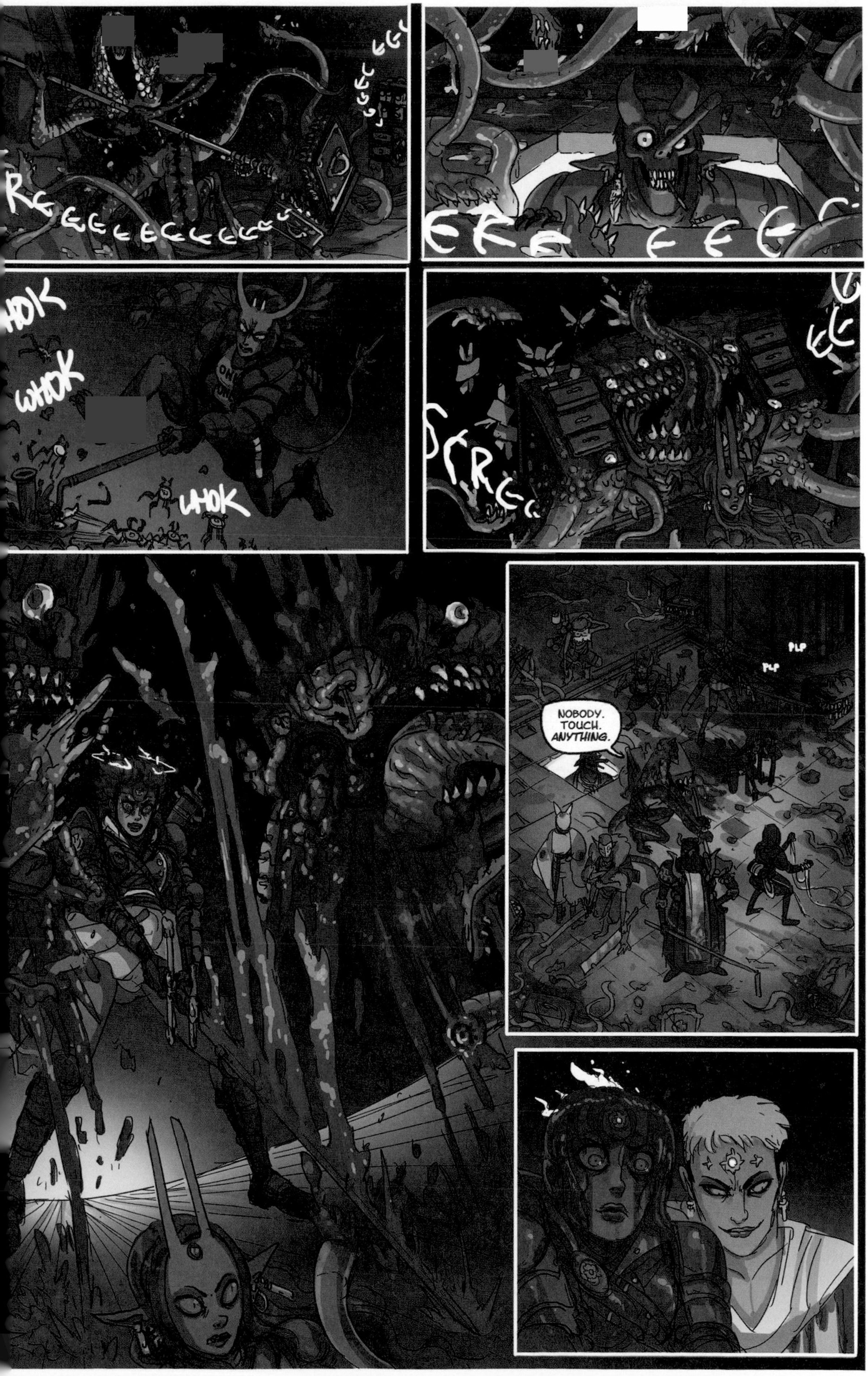
WHOK
WHOK
NOBODY. TOUCH. ANYTHING.
PLP
PLP

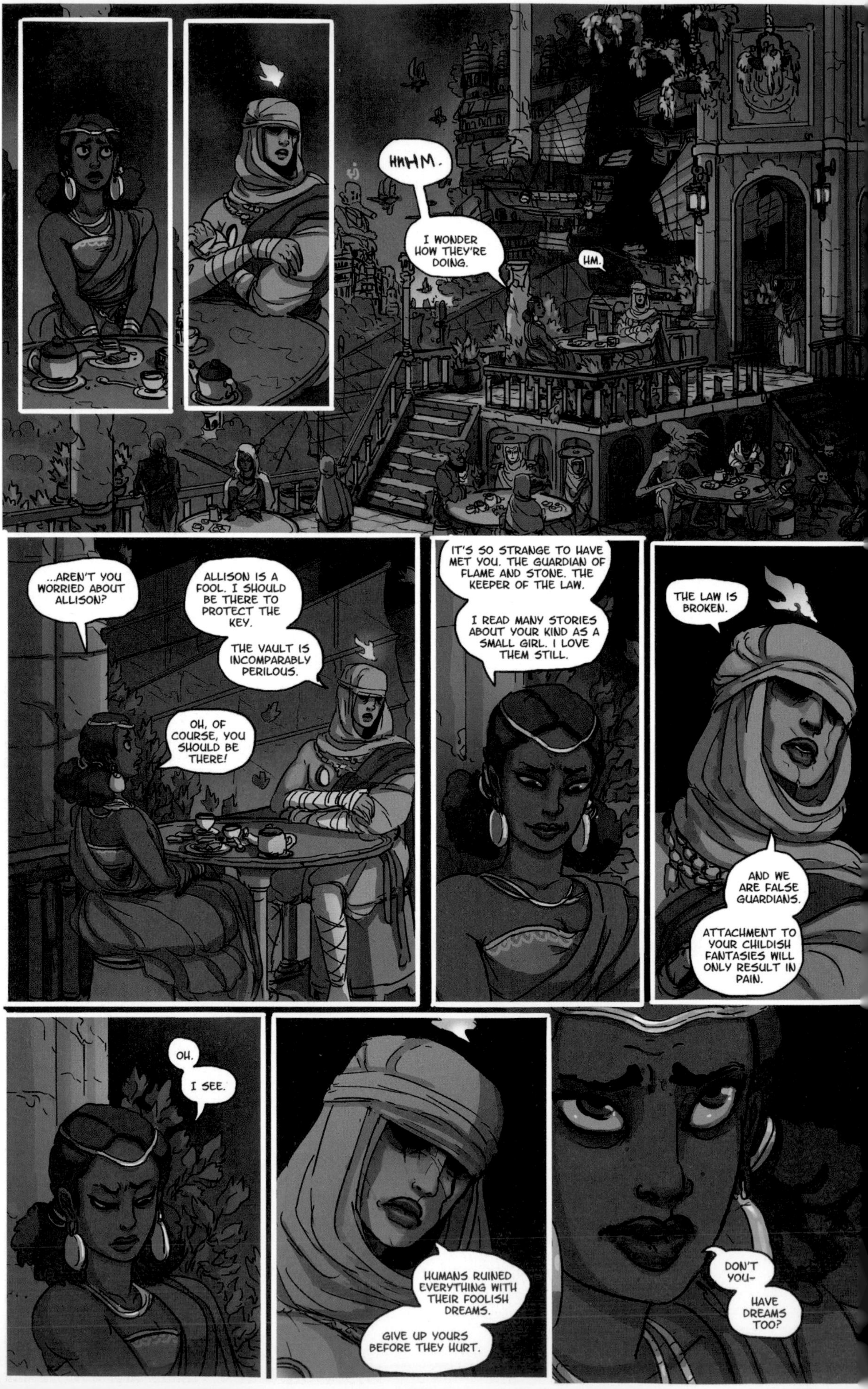
HmHM.
I WONDER HOW THEY'RE DOING.
HM.
...AREN'T YOU WORRIED ABOUT ALLISON?
ALLISON IS A FOOL. I SHOULD BE THERE TO PROTECT THE KEY.
THE VAULT IS INCOMPARABLY PERILOUS.
OH, OF COURSE, YOU SHOULD BE THERE!
IT'S SO STRANGE TO HAVE MET YOU. THE GUARDIAN OF FLAME AND STONE. THE KEEPER OF THE LAW.
I READ MANY STORIES ABOUT YOUR KIND AS A SMALL GIRL. I LOVE THEM STILL.
THE LAW IS BROKEN.
AND WE ARE FALSE GUARDIANS.
ATTACHMENT TO YOUR CHILDISH FANTASIES WILL ONLY RESULT IN PAIN.
OH.
I SEE.
HUMANS RUINED EVERYTHING WITH THEIR FOOLISH DREAMS.
GIVE UP YOURS BEFORE THEY HURT.
DON'T YOU-
HAVE DREAMS TOO?

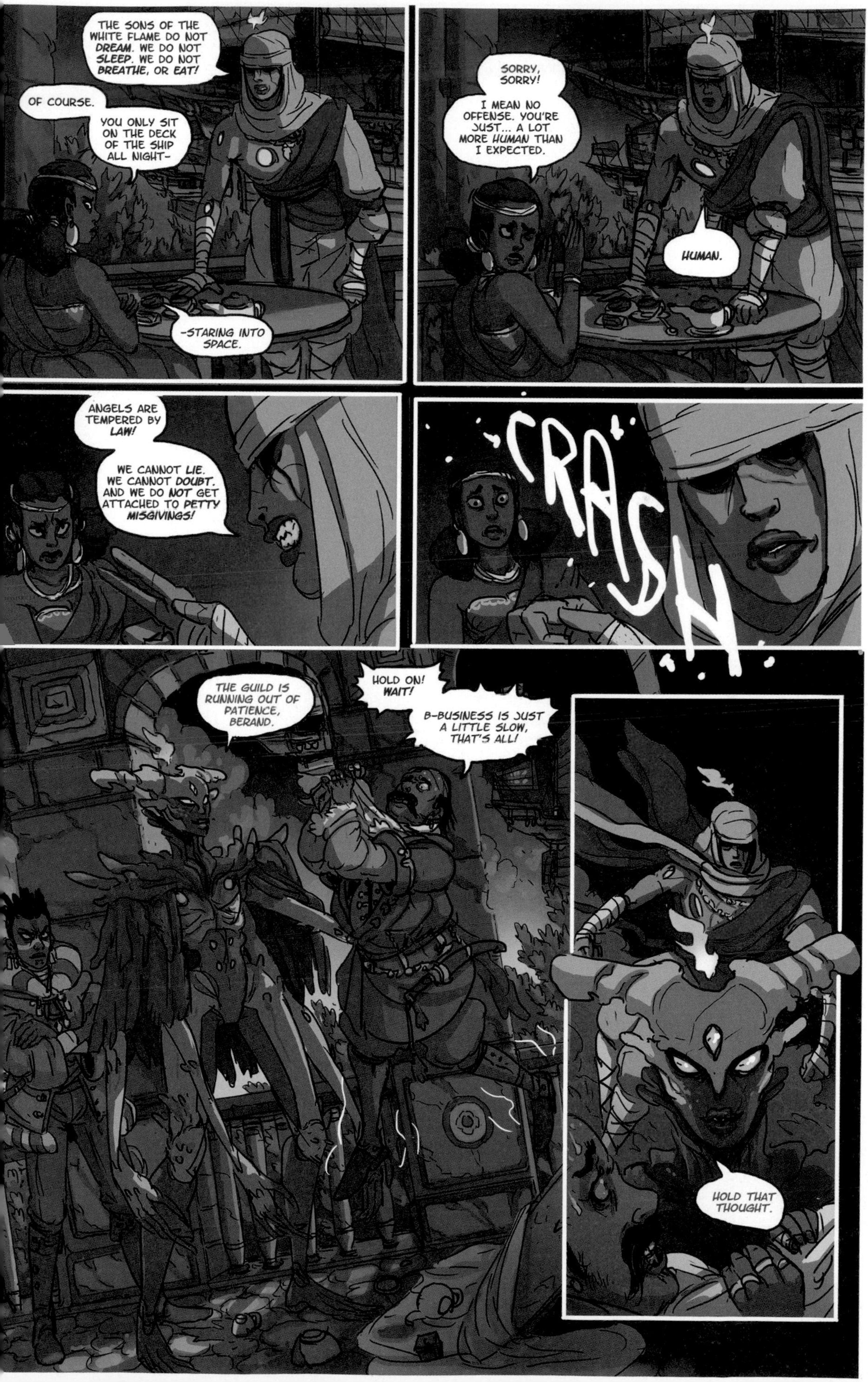
THE SONS OF THE WHITE FLAME DO NOT DREAM. WE DO NOT SLEEP. WE DO NOT BREATHE, OR EAT!
OF COURSE.
YOU ONLY SIT ON THE DECK OF THE SHIP ALL NIGHT-
-STARING INTO SPACE.
SORRY, SORRY!
I MEAN NO OFFENSE. YOU'RE JUST... A LOT MORE HUMAN THAN I EXPECTED.
HUMAN.
ANGELS ARE TEMPERED BY LAW!
WE CANNOT LIE. WE CANNOT DOUBT. AND WE DO NOT GET ATTACHED TO PETTY MISGIVINGS!
CRASH
THE GUILD IS RUNNING OUT OF PATIENCE, BERAND.
HOLD ON! WAIT!
B-BUSINESS IS JUST A LITTLE SLOW, THAT'S ALL!
HOLD THAT THOUGHT.

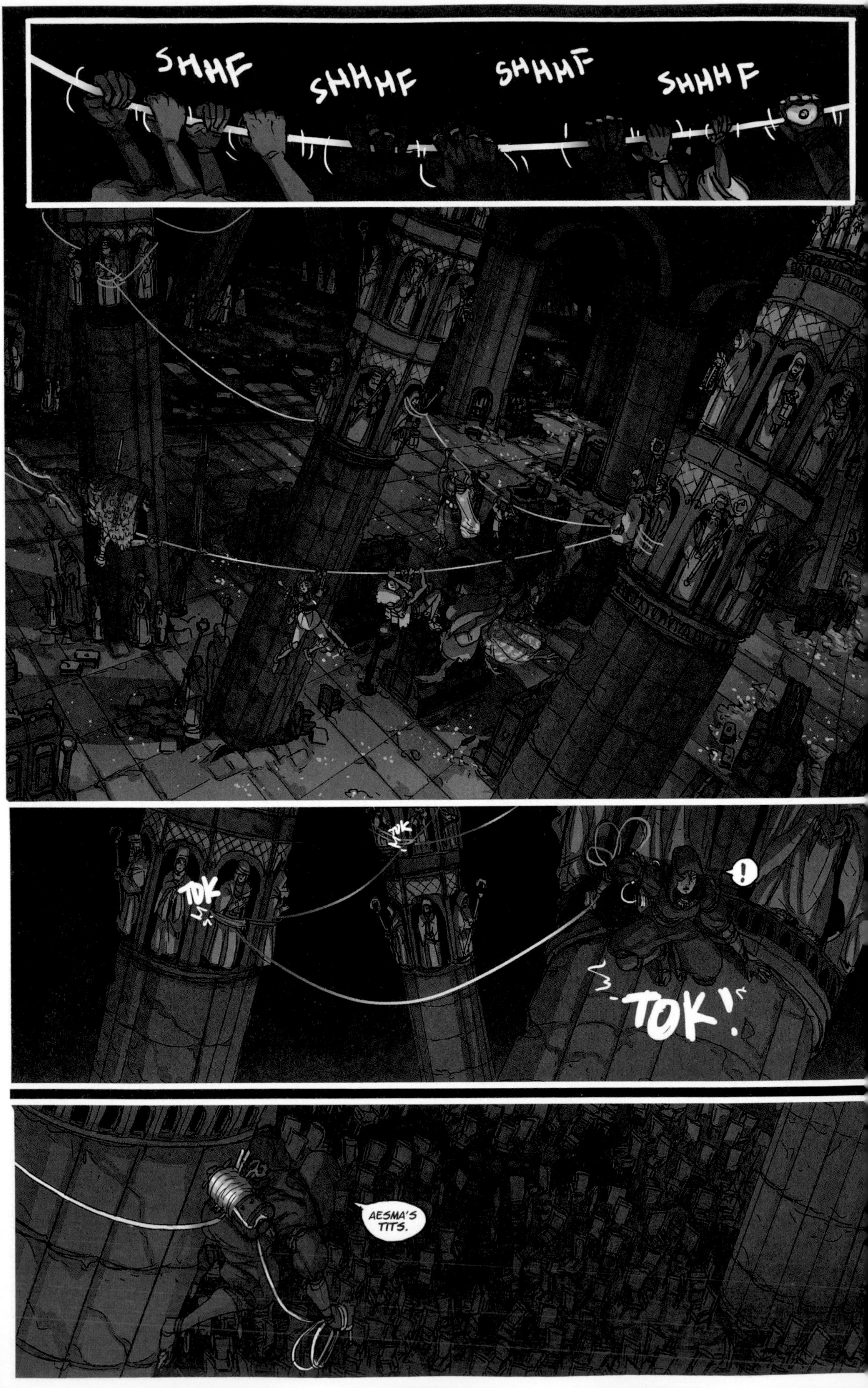
SHHF
SHHHF
SHHMF
SHHHF
TOK
TOK
!
TOK!
AESMA'S TITS.

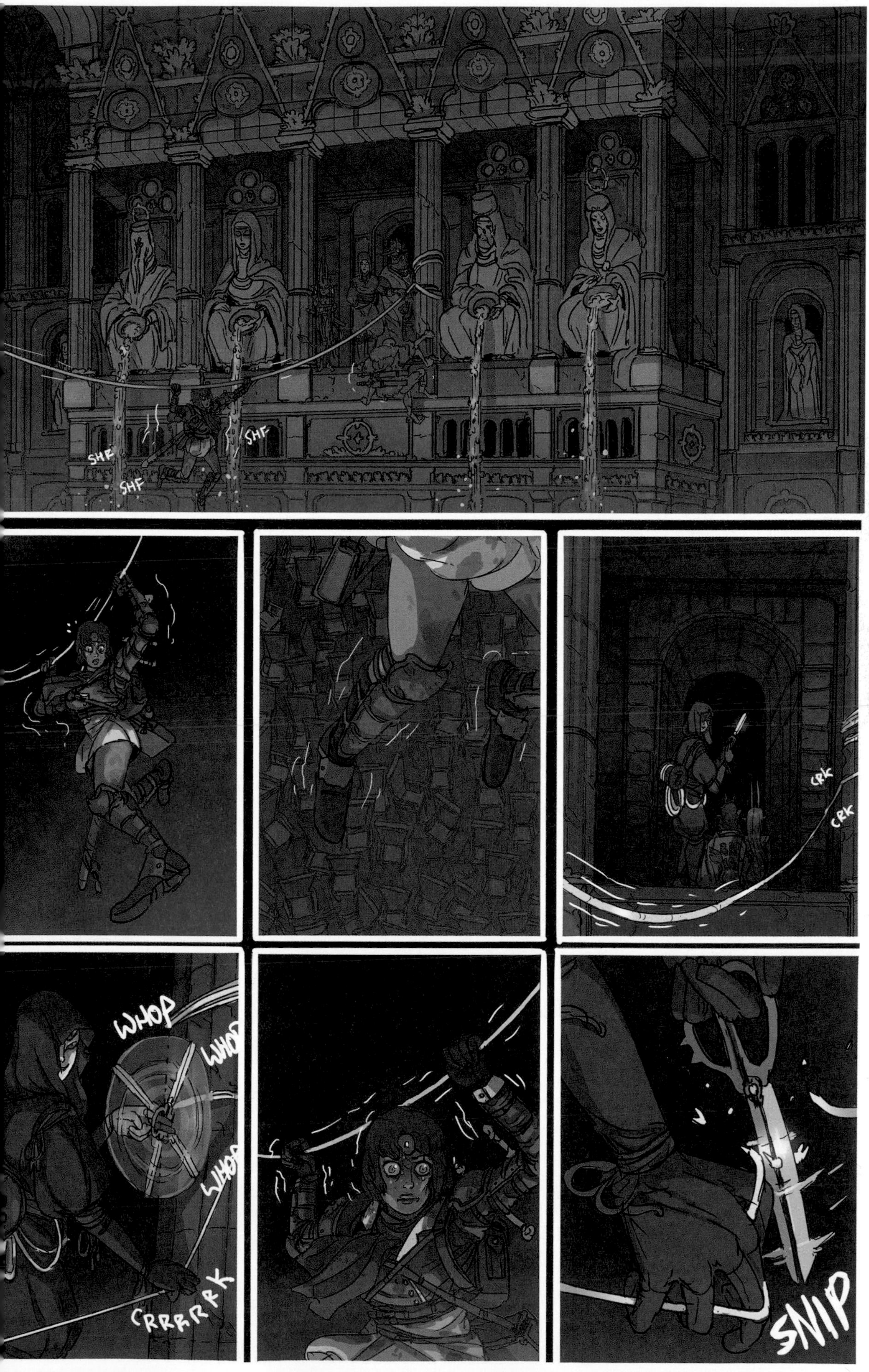
SHF
SHF
SHF
CRK
CRK
WHOP
WHOP
WHOP
CRRRRK
SNIP

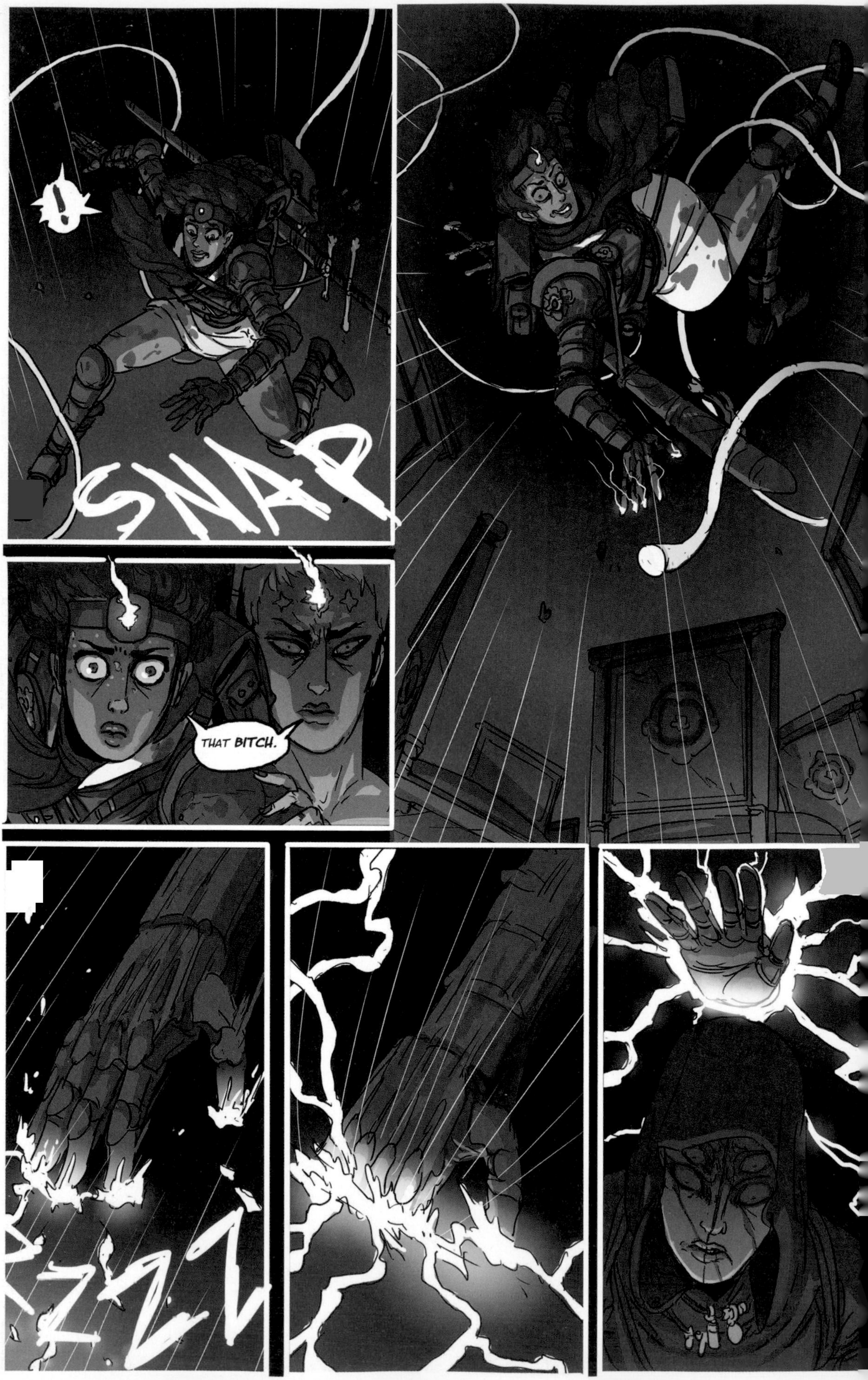
!
SNAP
THAT BITCH.
ZZZZ

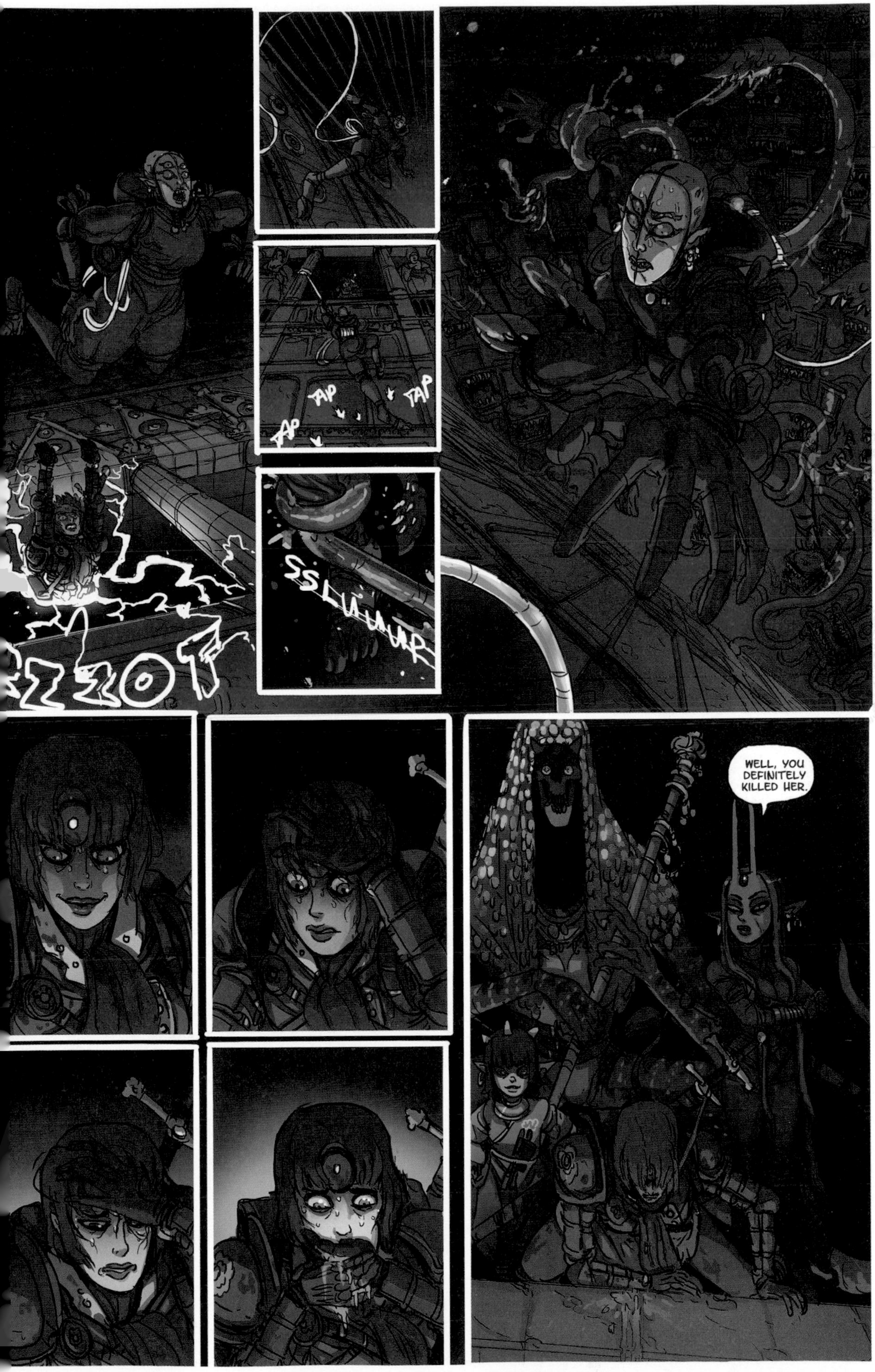
TAP
TAP
TAP
SSLUUUR
ZZZOT
WELL, YOU DEFINITELY KILLED HER.

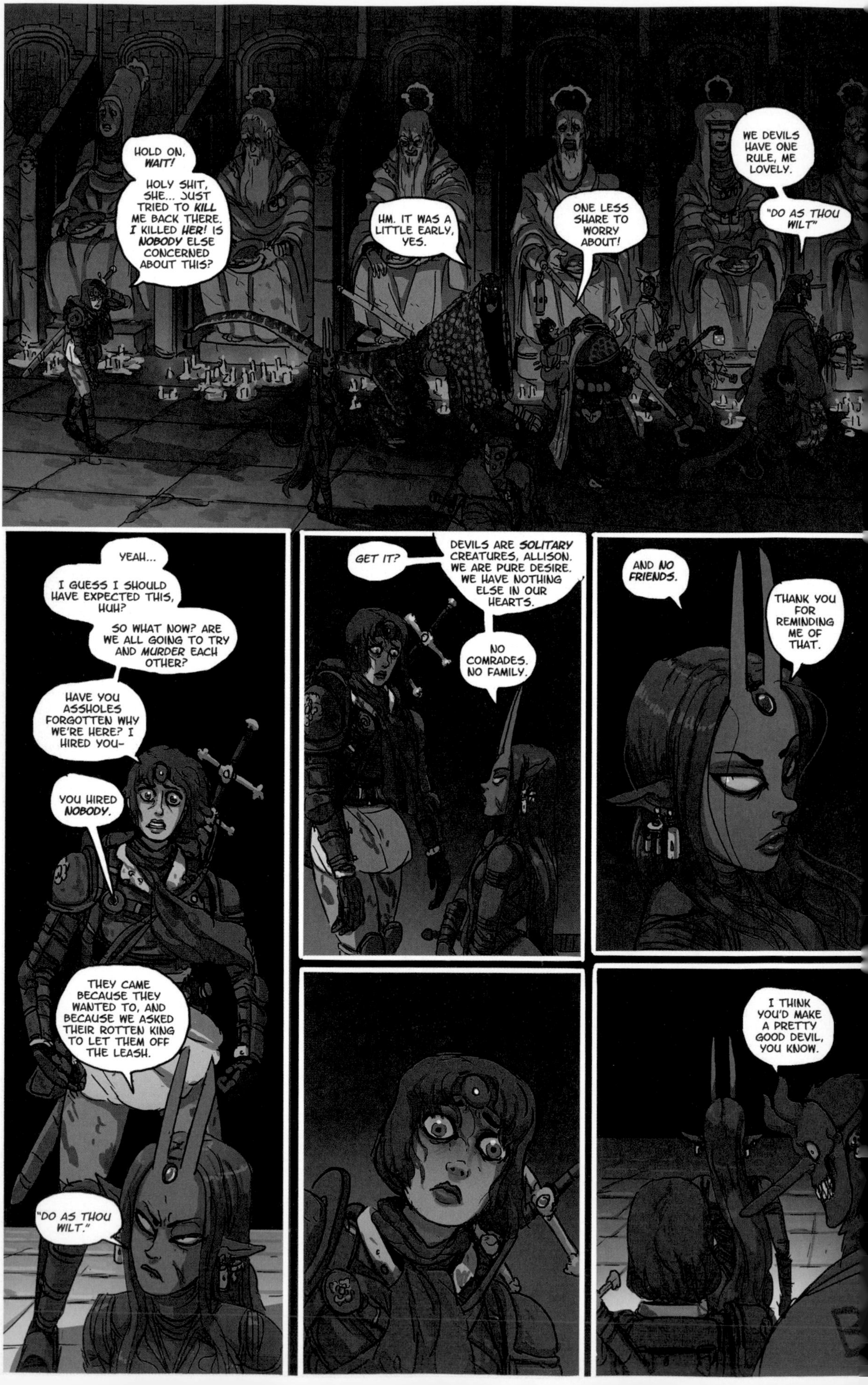
HOLD ON, WAIT!
HOLY SHIT, SHE... JUST TRIED TO KILL ME BACK THERE. I KILLED HER! IS NOBODY ELSE CONCERNED ABOUT THIS?
HM. IT WAS A LITTLE EARLY, YES.
ONE LESS SHARE TO WORRY ABOUT!
WE DEVILS HAVE ONE RULE, ME LOVELY.
"DO AS THOU WILT"
YEAH...
I GUESS I SHOULD HAVE EXPECTED THIS, HUH?
SO WHAT NOW? ARE WE ALL GOING TO TRY AND MURDER EACH OTHER?
HAVE YOU ASSHOLES FORGOTTEN WHY WE'RE HERE? I HIRED YOU-
YOU HIRED NOBODY.
THEY CAME BECAUSE THEY WANTED TO, AND BECAUSE WE ASKED THEIR ROTTEN KING TO LET THEM OFF THE LEASH.
"DO AS THOU WILT."
GET IT?
DEVILS ARE SOLITARY CREATURES, ALLISON. WE ARE PURE DESIRE. WE HAVE NOTHING ELSE IN OUR HEARTS.
NO COMRADES. NO FAMILY.
AND NO FRIENDS.
THANK YOU FOR REMINDING ME OF THAT.
I THINK YOU'D MAKE A PRETTY GOOD DEVIL, YOU KNOW.

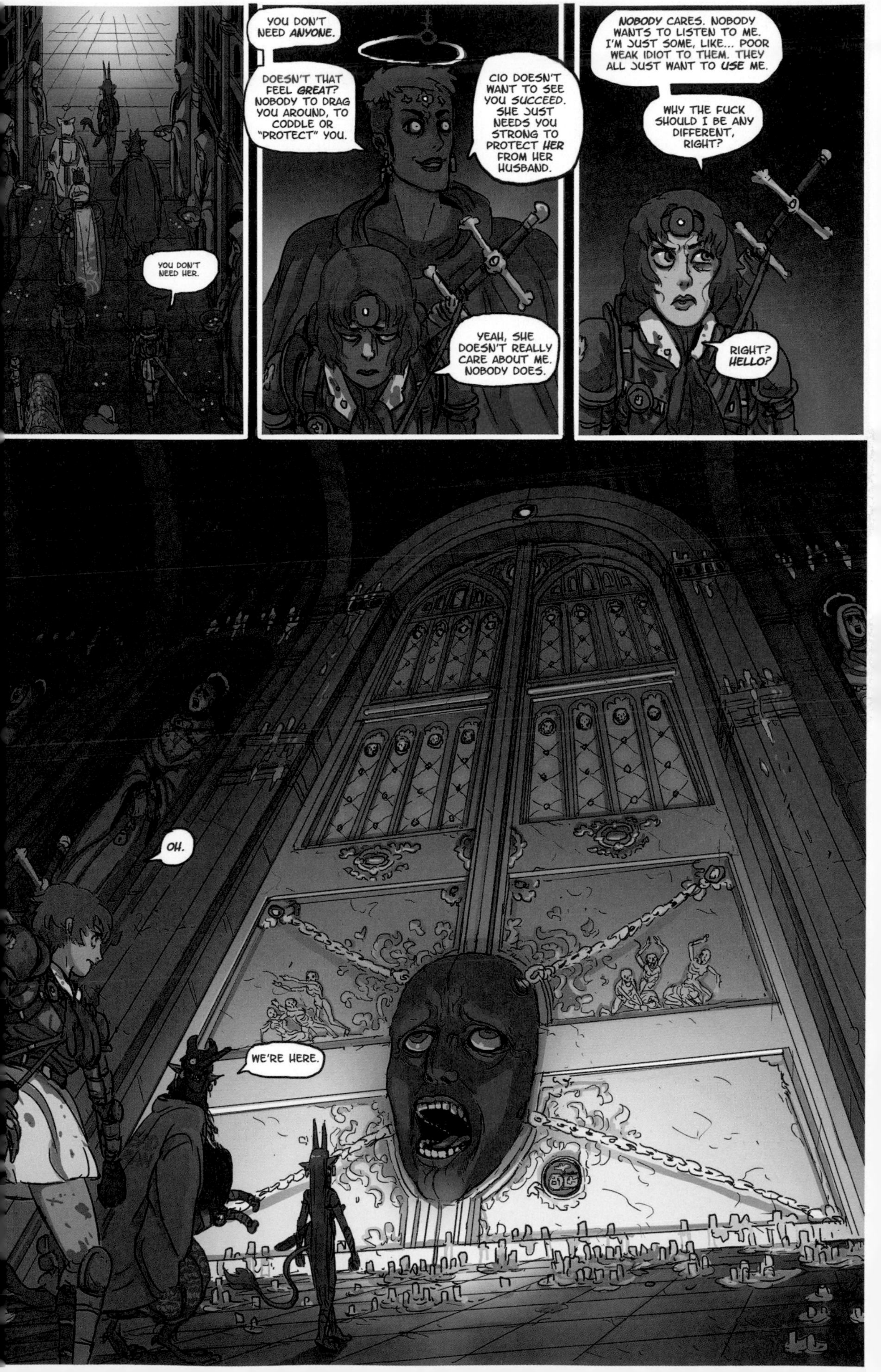
YOU DON'T NEED HER.
YOU DON'T NEED ANYONE.
DOESN'T THAT FEEL GREAT? NOBODY TO DRAG YOU AROUND, TO CODDLE OR "PROTECT" YOU.
CIO DOESN'T WANT TO SEE YOU SUCCEED. SHE JUST NEEDS YOU STRONG TO PROTECT HER FROM HER HUSBAND.
YEAH, SHE DOESN'T REALLY CARE ABOUT ME. NOBODY DOES.
NOBODY CARES. NOBODY WANTS TO LISTEN TO ME. I'M JUST SOME, LIKE... POOR WEAK IDIOT TO THEM. THEY ALL JUST WANT TO USE ME.
WHY THE FUCK SHOULD I BE ANY DIFFERENT, RIGHT?
RIGHT? HELLO?
OH.
WE'RE HERE.

"Prince Kassardis knew his three wives were cunning and vicious in equal measure, and the journey ahead would be hard and grueling. Therefore the very first thing he did was to seek out the Very Wise Frog, which lived on a nearby hill known as King's Rock. The road to the Frog was well worn by pilgrims, so it was not a hard climb for Kassardis, who wore his fine leather boots, but it was steep.

'Very Wise Frog,' said Kassardis, when he reached the summit, 'This brutal life is like a steel cage. My father's kingdom is built on the stacked bodies of his officers. He sups on blood. His surviving wife picks his gray hairs and pushes toy soldiers around from her sedan.'

'Your father's kingdom is very large,' said the Very Wise Frog.

'I will escape my own blood,' said the resolute Kassardis, 'And flee to the land of Samura, where their cities are built on covenants of peace and no blood is shed unjustly. The journey is long and hard, so please give me some advice, as my family has treated you well.'

'Samura is a myth told to small children to comfort them,' said the Very Wise Frog, 'Your wives are much faster than you and will catch up to you, then beat you savagely before returning to the time-honored ritual of trying to murder each other.'

The Prince was aghast. 'I refuse this life of violence!' he said.

'Violence is inescapable,' said the Very Wise Frog.

'Don't gloat at me, Frog!' said the Prince, 'My trial is only just beginning. Surely you have some other advice for me?'

'No,' said the Very Wise Frog.

'Frog!' said Kassardis, growing panicked, 'What do you mean by 'violence is inescapable'?'

'It is,' said the Frog.

'You're a liar!' said Kassardis.

'No, I am not,' said the Frog, 'Nor have I ever been. Violence is inescapable. Inseparable from life itself. Permanent. It is fixed in your cosmology. Forever. I could go on, but that's besides the point.'

At this Kassardis was so enraged that he threw the Frog off the summit of the mountain. It bounced off a cliff and split like a wet melon, dying instantly, and posthumously proving its point to Kassardis.

Kassardis, for his part, wept."

- TALES OF THE SILVER PRINCE

FELICIA.

YEAH, YEAH

HEY, CHEER UP KID!

WE'LL GET YOUR GUY OUT, I PROMISE.

NOW WATCH THIS!

...WELL?

SO, THIS IS THE LOCK, JUST TO BE SURE?

PURELY DECORATIVE SCREAMING HEAD?

...

THERE'S A REASON THEY CALL ME LUCKY FELICIA!

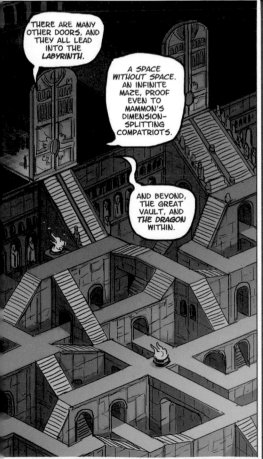

THERE ARE MANY OTHER DOORS, AND THEY ALL LEAD INTO THE LABYRINTH.

A SPACE WITHOUT SPACE. AN INFINITE MAZE, PROOF EVEN TO MAMMON'S DIMENSION-SPLITTING COMPATRIOTS.

AND BEYOND, THE GREAT VAULT, AND THE DRAGON WITHIN.

THIS DOOR IS A CLEVERLY DESIGNED PIECE OF UNIMAGINABLE CRUELTY.

IT'S TOUGH, BUT NOT TOO TOUGH FOR ME.

FIVE HOURS.

I'LL MAKE IT FOUR.

THAT'S NOT THE PROBLEM.

THE PROBLEM IS THE ALARM WILL GO OFF IN ABOUT FIVE SECONDS.

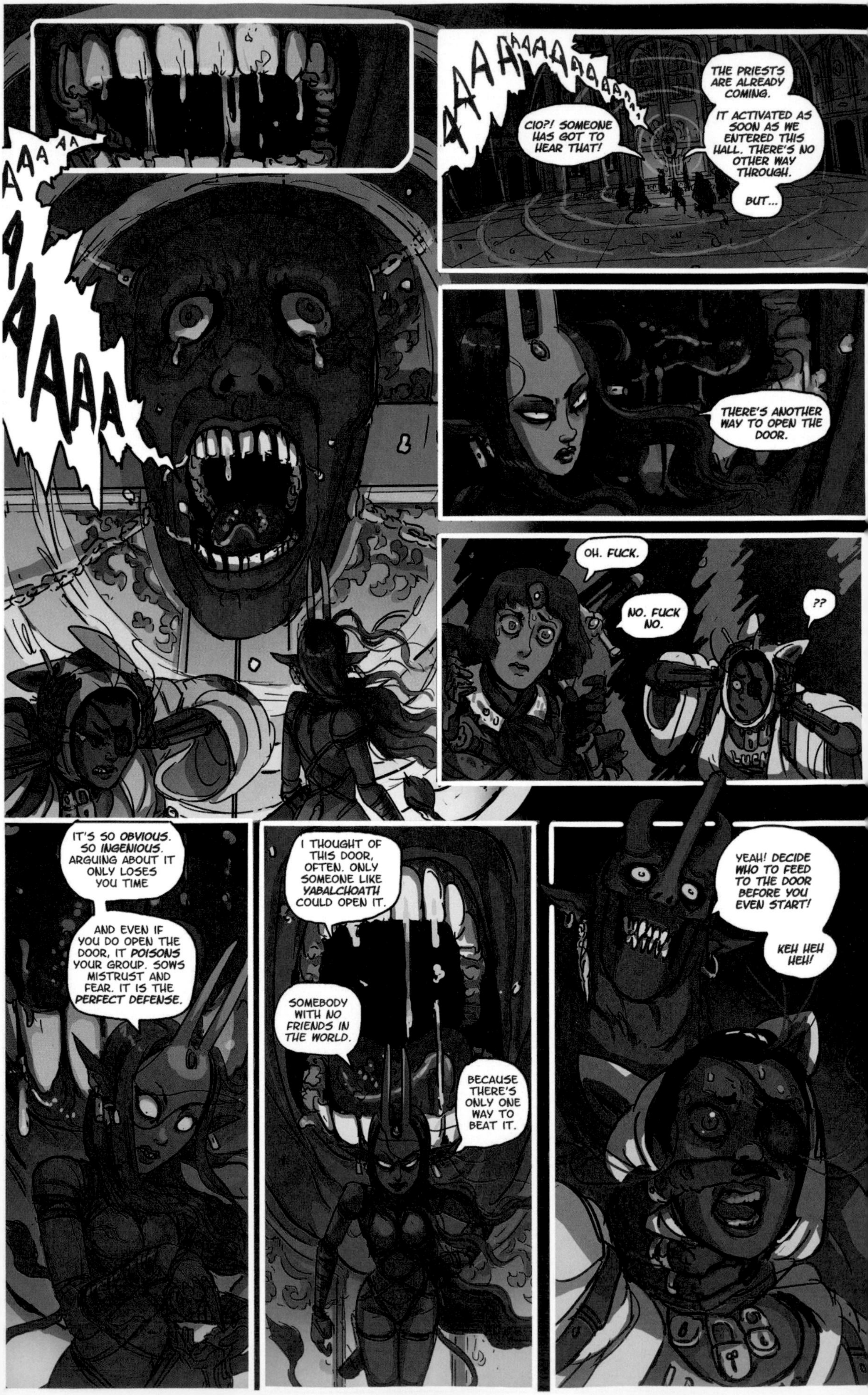
AAAAAAAAAAAA
AAAAAAAAAAAAA
CIO?! SOMEONE HAS GOT TO HEAR THAT!
THE PRIESTS ARE ALREADY COMING.
IT ACTIVATED AS SOON AS WE ENTERED THIS HALL. THERE'S NO OTHER WAY THROUGH.
BUT...
THERE'S ANOTHER WAY TO OPEN THE DOOR.
OH. FUCK.
NO. FUCK NO.
??
IT'S SO OBVIOUS. SO INGENIOUS. ARGUING ABOUT IT ONLY LOSES YOU TIME
AND EVEN IF YOU DO OPEN THE DOOR, IT POISONS YOUR GROUP. SOWS MISTRUST AND FEAR. IT IS THE PERFECT DEFENSE.
I THOUGHT OF THIS DOOR, OFTEN. ONLY SOMEONE LIKE YABALCHOATH COULD OPEN IT.
SOMEBODY WITH NO FRIENDS IN THE WORLD.
BECAUSE THERE'S ONLY ONE WAY TO BEAT IT.
YEAH! DECIDE WHO TO FEED TO THE DOOR BEFORE YOU EVEN START!
KEH HEH HEH!

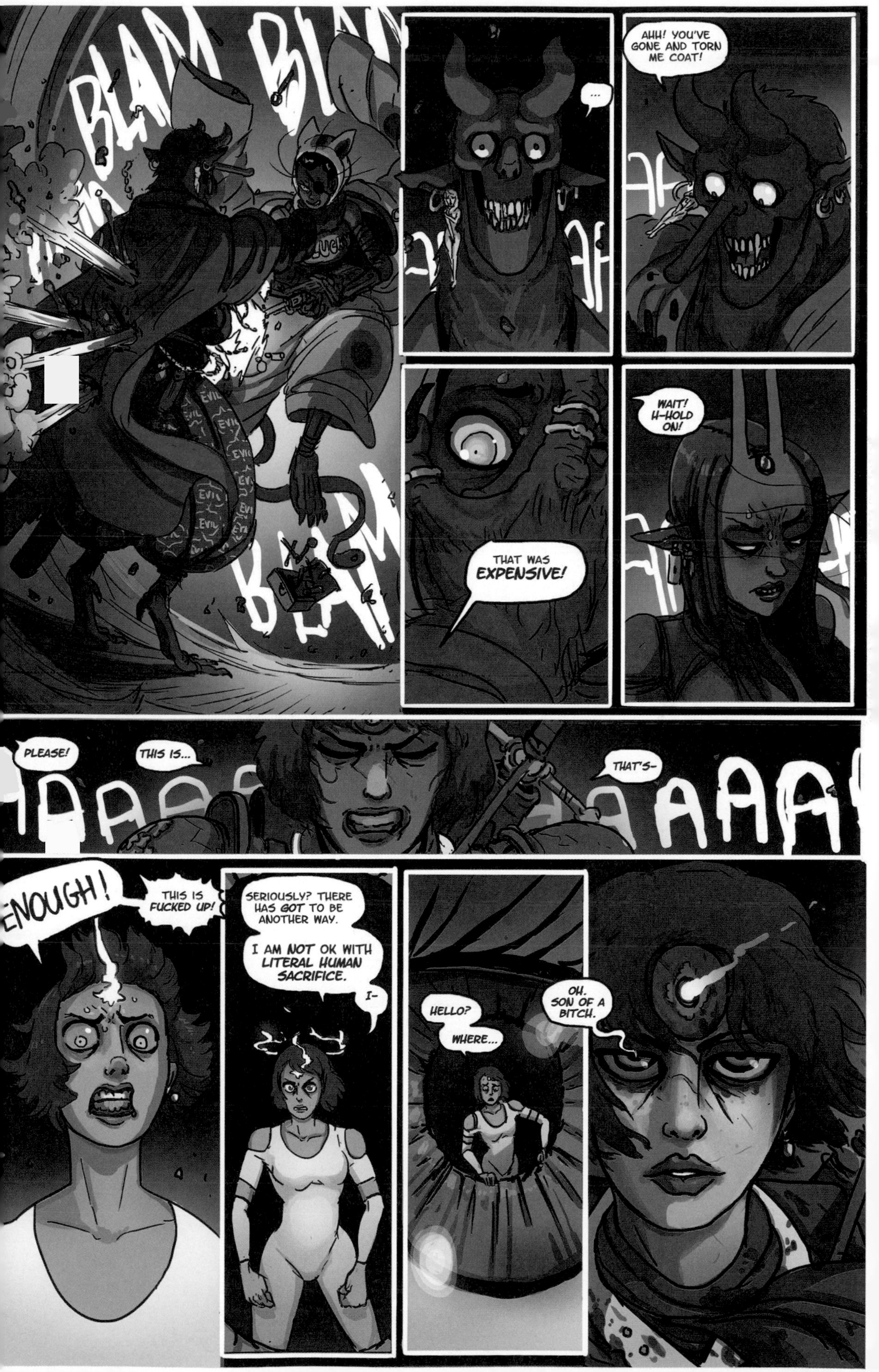
BLAM BLAM
BLAM
...
AHH! YOU'VE GONE AND TORN ME COAT!
THAT WAS **EXPENSIVE!**
WAIT! H-HOLD ON!
PLEASE!
THIS IS...
THAT'S-
AAAA
ENOUGH!
THIS IS FUCKED UP!
SERIOUSLY? THERE HAS *GOT* TO BE ANOTHER WAY.
I AM *NOT* OK WITH ***LITERAL HUMAN SACRIFICE.***
I-
HELLO?
WHERE...
OH. SON OF A BITCH.

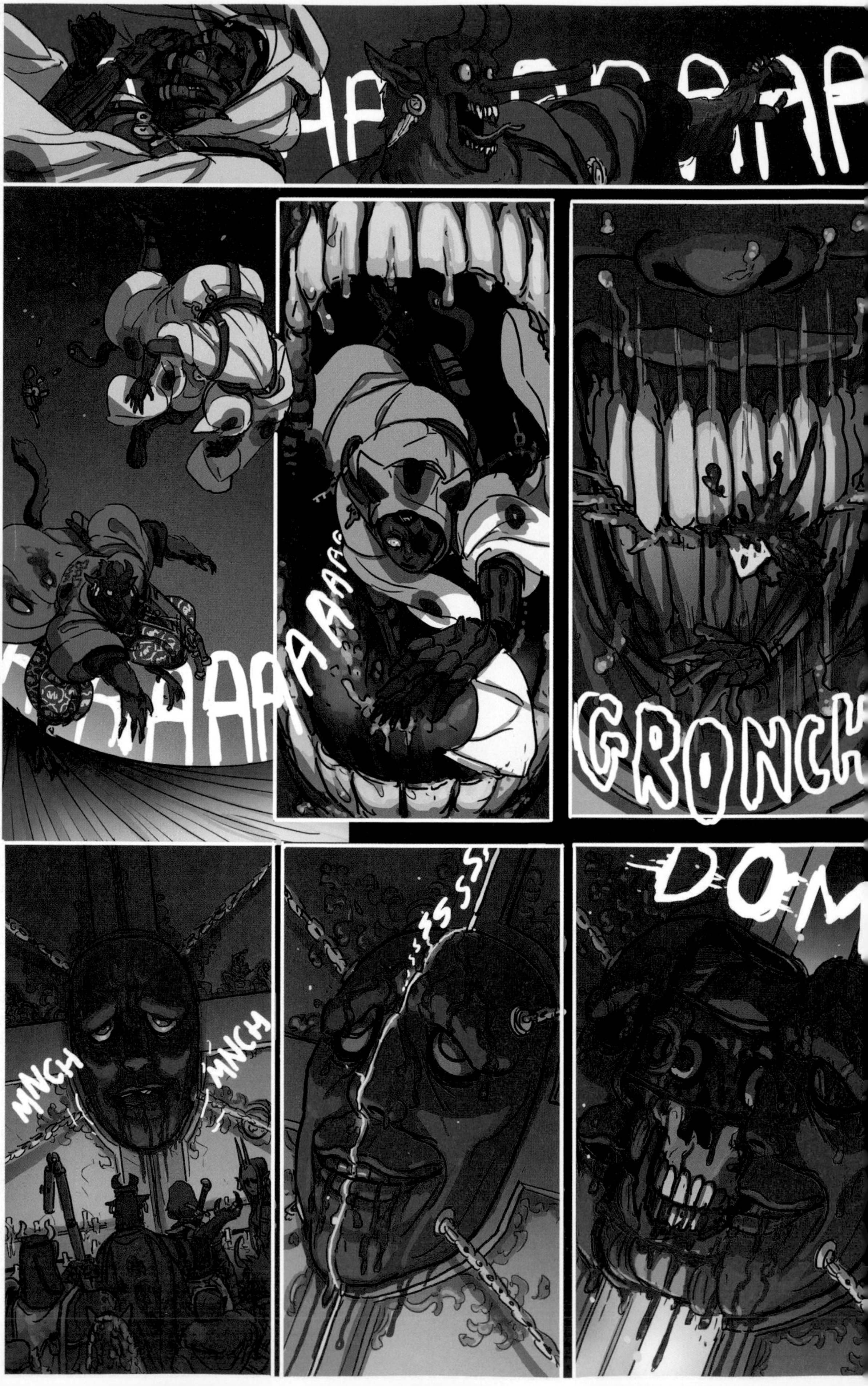
GRONCH
MNCH
MNCH
DOM

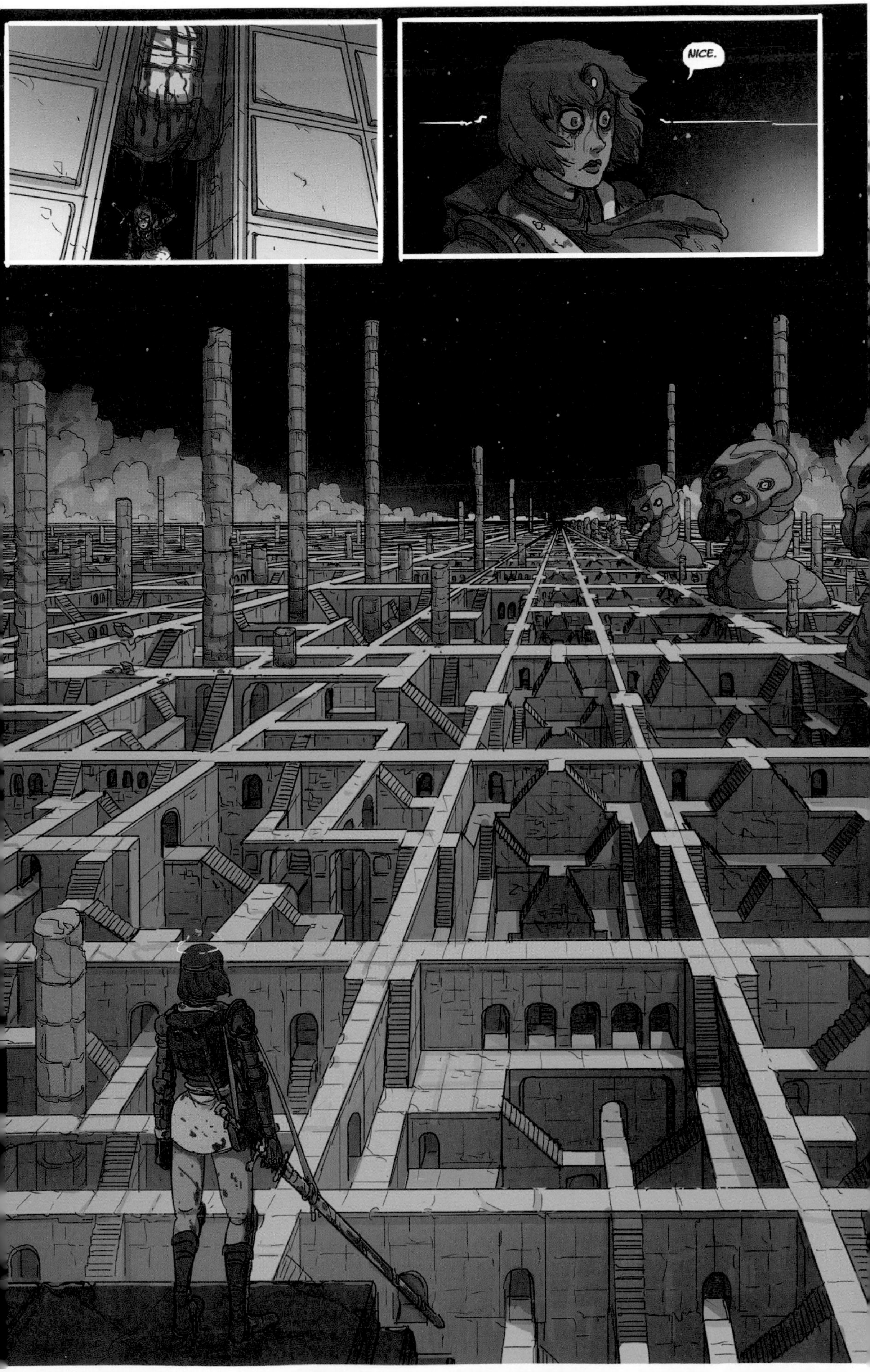
NICE.

"Prince Kassardis was swift, and he was young and his mind was honed. The land about his kingdom was barren but not fierce, and the roads were well kept. Even so, the sun had barely dipped below the horizon before he knew he would soon be caught. For as he glanced back over his shoulder, he saw the cruel glint on Vastoki's eyeglasses as she traversed the bluffs behind him. And a little further back than that, even for all this distance, he thought he could hear the awful grinding of Littari's cauldron as she dragged it across the bare earth. And even further back, just cresting the horizon, were the bright and lazy banners of Ipreski as her palanquin was borne along into the desert.

Prince Kassardis struggled mightily to rid himself of his pursuers, for despite what the Very Wise Frog had told him, he still held within his heart the vain hope that the peaceful land of Samura existed and he would someday find himself upon its gleaming shores, free of his wives and throne.

First, he fled the road, and spying a low and reeking gully hurled himself therein. There, the mud and brambles were so thick that he could barely move, and the fetid water was choked with the corpses of animals that had become trapped in the muck. Thick clouds of flies bit at Kassardis as he struggled heroically onward, until at last he heaved himself from the mud, his trail almost completely invisible, and made for higher ground.

Indeed, when the clever and keen Vastoki came upon Kassardis' trail disappearing into the gully, she was taken aback by his cleverness. But with her specially made eyeglasses, Vastoki's eyesight was keener than a hawk's. She picked out the shining pieces of thread from Kassardi's silver waist-coat clinging to the brambles, and was back on his trail in scarcely an hour, her fellow wives close behind.

Seeing his three wives draw ever closer and that his first plot to foil them had failed miserably, Prince Kassardis doubled his pace. Knowing he would never outrun the cruel Vastoki on open ground, he hurled himself into a sea of dead grass, and used up all his water trying to escape her grasp. A night and a day later, he emerged on the shores of the river Dal, and spent the last of his money hiring a fisherman to take him downriver.

The fisherman's boat overturned in the town of Kol Varas, and there Kassardis did a very shameful thing. He sold to the first rich man he could find his fine silk headwrap, and his father's silver dagger, and his waistcoat lined with sparrow feathers, which were marks of his lineage. With his sack of foreign coin he hired six strong men, belligerent knights from the wars of conquest, and hid himself in a wheelbarrow, hoping against hope that his ploy would be enough.

Vastoki arrived in the dusty town not hours later, and she was almost immediately set upon by the mercenaries that Kassardis had hired. From his hiding place, the young prince watched as Vastoki was caught in their ambush and fought desperately against stave and sword.

Vastoki was very fast, but also very slight, and no match against the six knights in close combat. Though beaten, she merely retreated to lick her wounds and set camp outside of town. One of the knights nearly lost his head to her long rifle when he ventured out to confront her, and that was that for a while.

As night fell, the knights returned to Kassardis. 'Where wandereth thee, young one?' they said in their foreign dialects.

'To the land of Samura, where I may find peace and an escape from violence,' said the exhausted Kassardis, from his hiding place.

'Violence is inescapable,' guffawed the mercenaries, and robbed Kassardis of everything remaining that he owned, for they had seen he was a fool from the start. They threw him naked and beaten into the street, and spent their winnings on drink.

Kassardis, his swollen eyes full of tears and knowing his time was short, stole a woman's garb from a washing line and a small hunk of bread and fled into the desert, the final words of the Very Wise Frog echoing in his ears.

The belligerent knights, for their part, died not hours later when they were squashed into a pulp by Littari's iron cauldron."

– TALES OF THE SILVER PRINCE

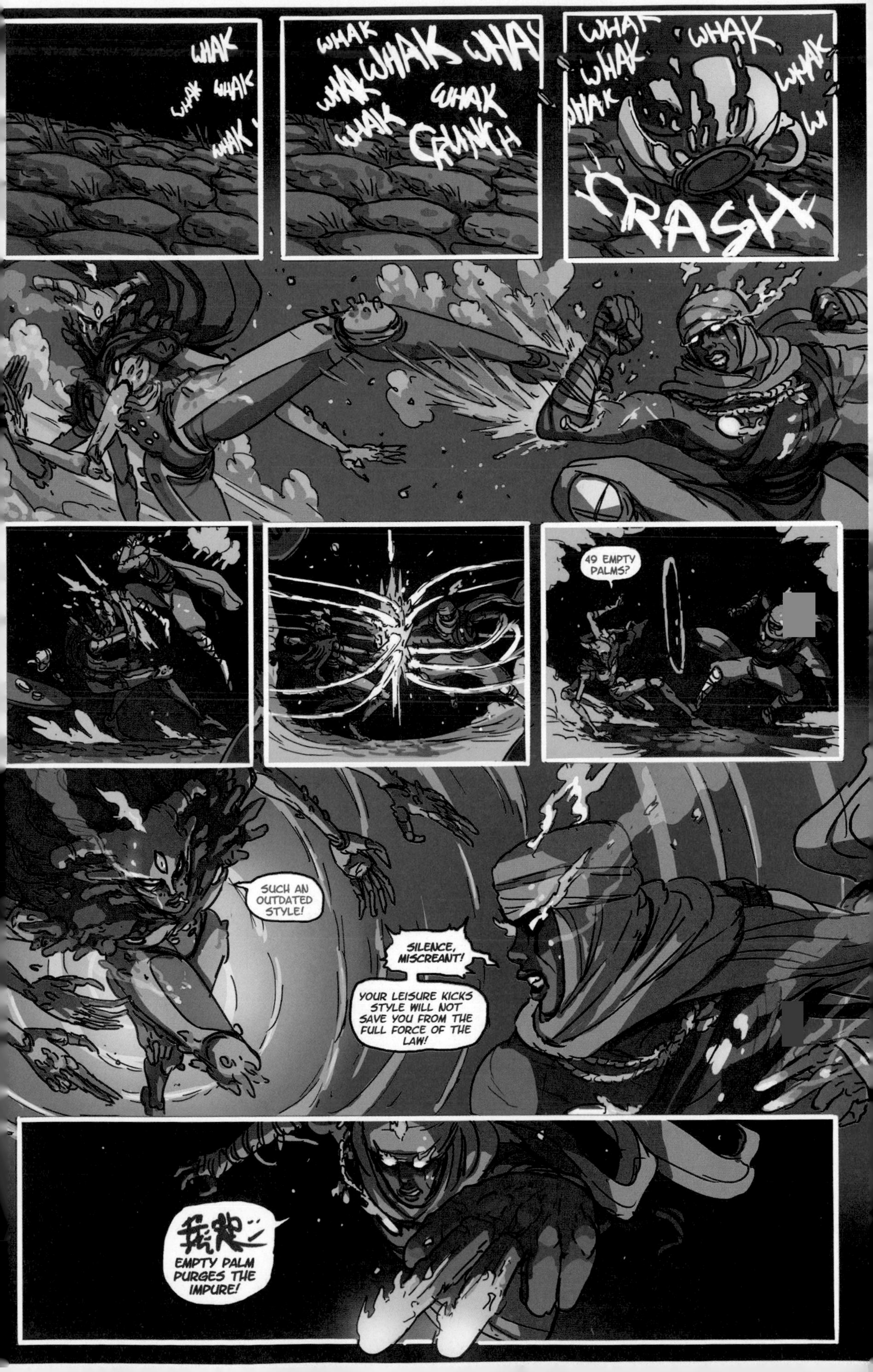

WHAK
WHAK WHAK
WHAK
WHAK WHAK WHAK WHAK
WHAK WHAK
CRUNCH
WHAK WHAK
WHAK WHAK
CRASH
49 EMPTY PALMS?
SUCH AN OUTDATED STYLE!
SILENCE, MISCREANT!
YOUR LEISURE KICKS STYLE WILL NOT SAVE YOU FROM THE FULL FORCE OF THE LAW!
EMPTY PALM PURGES THE IMPURE!

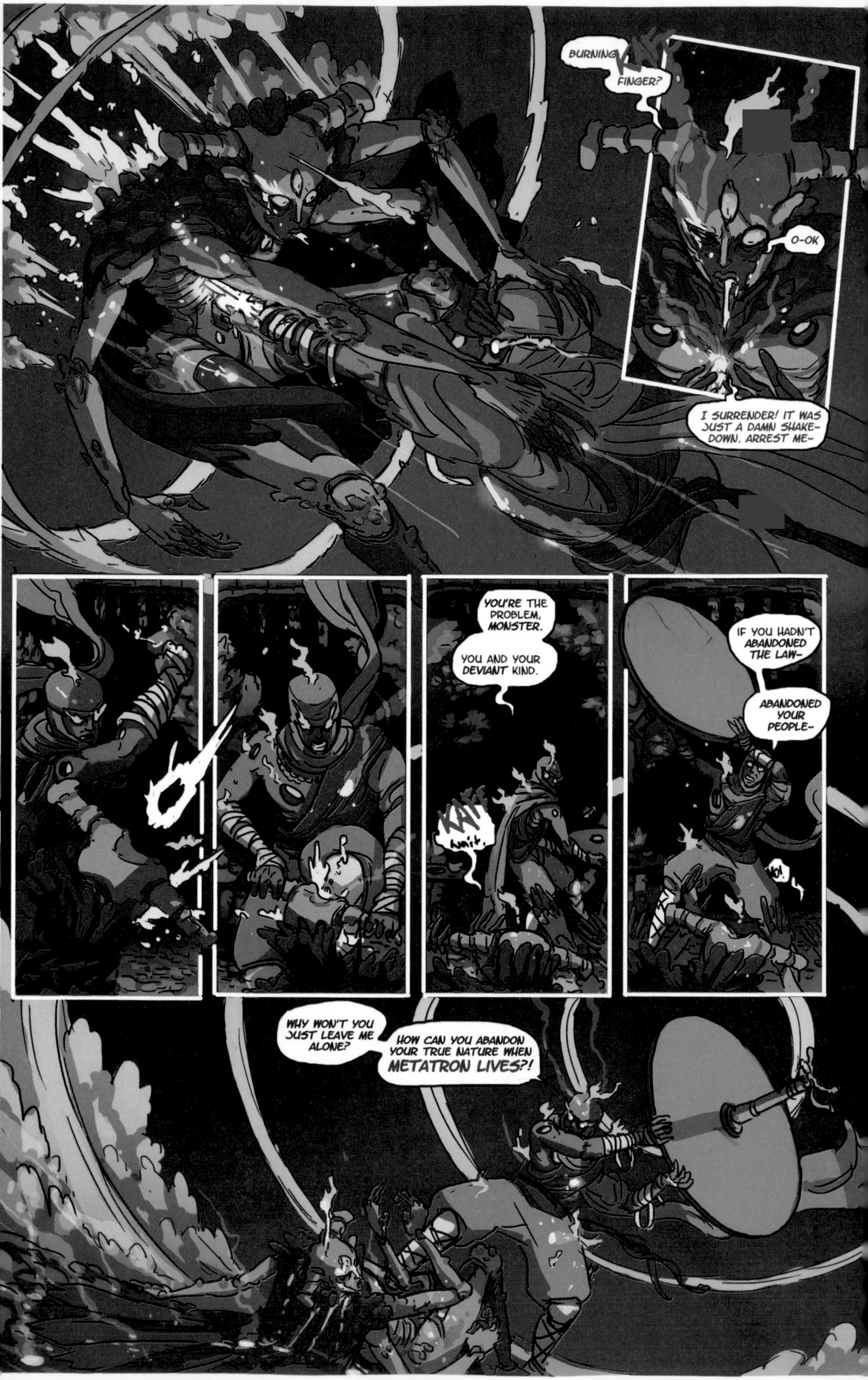
BURNING
FINGER?
O-OK
I SURRENDER! IT WAS JUST A DAMN SHAKE-DOWN. ARREST ME-
YOU'RE THE PROBLEM, MONSTER.
YOU AND YOUR DEVIANT KIND.
IF YOU HADN'T ABANDONED THE LAW-
ABANDONED YOUR PEOPLE-
WHY WON'T YOU JUST LEAVE ME ALONE?
HOW CAN YOU ABANDON YOUR TRUE NATURE WHEN METATRON LIVES?!

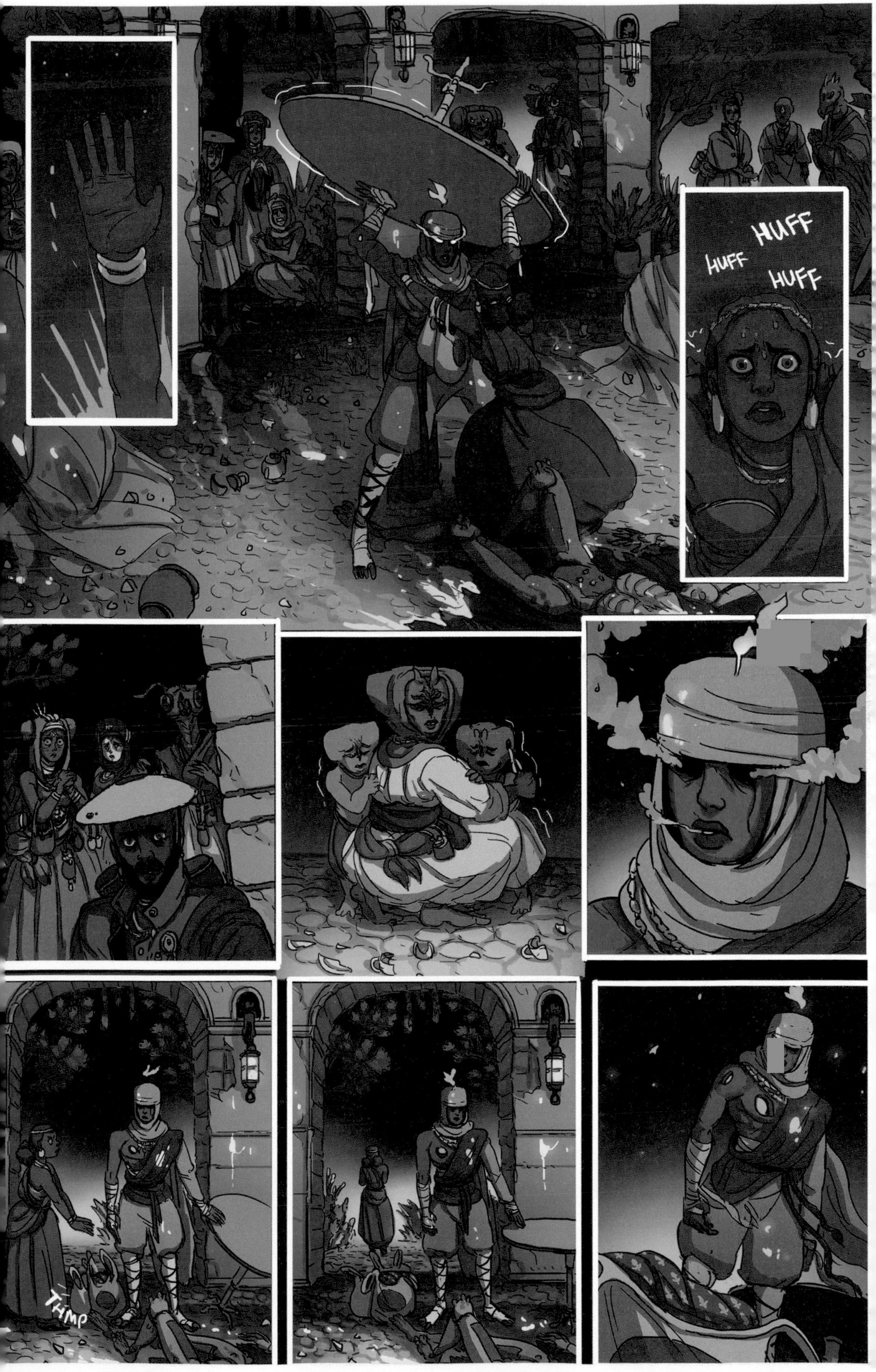
HUFF
HUFF
HUFF
THMP

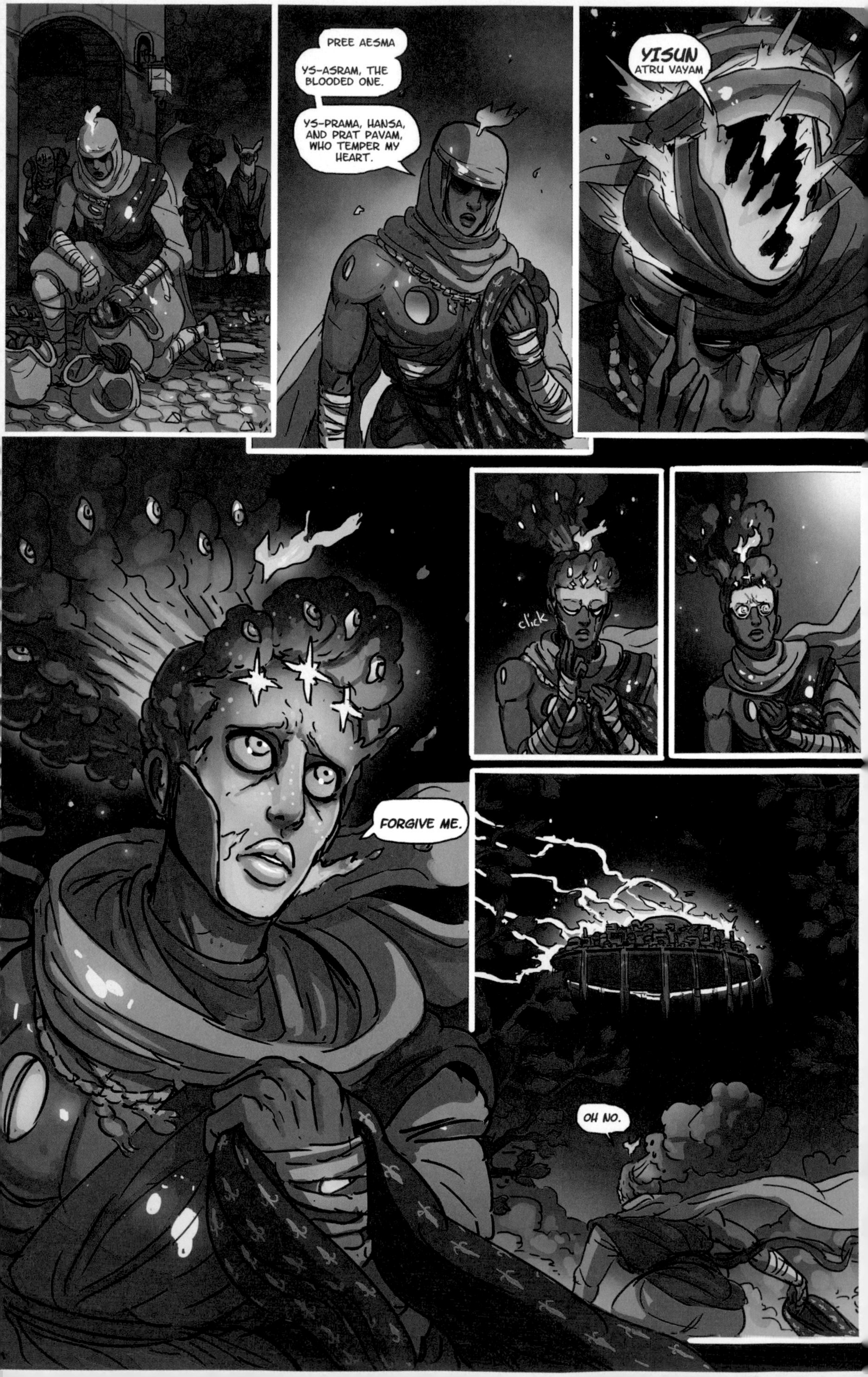
PREE AESMA
YS-ASRAM, THE BLOODED ONE.
YS-PRAMA, HANSA, AND PRAT PAVAM, WHO TEMPER MY HEART.
YISUN ATRU VAYAM
FORGIVE ME.
click
OH NO.

Kassardis knew his time was running short as he fled into the wastes around the town of Kol Varas. Instead of his naming knife, he had a stale hunk of bread, and instead of his prince's garb he had only a stolen woman's garment, thin and nearly useless against the freezing cold of the desert nights. He knew his three wives were not far behind, and despair was his constant companion. But still, he pushed on, wholly consumed with the conviction that he would find the peaceful land of Samura, or die in the process.

"By the third day, when the desperate prince's wives were closing in rapidly, the scorched and tortured soles of Kassardis' feet felt stone and not sand beneath them. Kassardis looked up and saw that he had stumbled upon a mighty road, broad and sweeping, that passed through enormous stone arches into the distance. The road was crumbled with age, but Kassardis recognized at once that it was the famous Arched Road of Samura, and a great burst of hope filled his heart.

"Kassardis followed the road until it was dark, and lightness filled his step, so that he did not even notice when the sun had gone and the nightmare chill of the desert began to grasp at him. All through the night, he followed the road, and the night itself could not touch him. And when the sun grazed his face, Kassardis was still walking, but he still had not found the kingdom of Samura. It remained like this for a day longer, until Kassardis, sustained by hope alone, and dying of thirst, stumbled across a battered old sword master encamped by the side of the road.

"The sword master was aghast at Kassardis' dreadful condition, and at once tended to him, and gave him water. 'Young man,' said the old sword master, 'I am Ket Amonket, the gate keeper of the kingdom of Samura. There is nothing for you here. Turn back.' Kassardis was shocked. 'Uncle!' he gasped, 'If you are indeed the gatekeeper of that mighty kingdom, please take me there at once. I am fleeing from my three wives, who wish to drag me back into a world of bloody tyranny!'

"'You are here already,' said Ket Amonket, and motioned to the desert, 'This is the kingdom of Samura, burned to ashes and ground into dust for decades.'

"'Mortified, Kassardis could only gape at the empty desert. But here and there, the young prince could see what he had been blind to while hope had still filled him up: the corroded remnants of great and stately buildings and fluted columns poking out of the desert like bleached ribs. 'Samura was founded on the principles of peace,' said Ket Amonket, 'So it was sought out by many across all the ten thousand realms. Those that sought to flee from the world of violence.'

"'Violence is inescapable,' moaned Kassardis.'Yes,' said the old man. 'Very wise words indeed. Soon this land contained more people than it could sustain. Violence once again began to grow in the hearts of its people, like a foul disease, until it blossomed into destruction. It was a foolish hope.'

"'Then there is no hope for me,' said Kassardis.

"'There is still yet,' said Ket Amonket, resolute. 'Let me do one favor for you, young man, as one who has already lived too long. You must flee to the canyon south of here and hide yourself there as best as you can, until the sun sets. I will tell your wives you vanished into the desert a day past, and throw them off your trail.'

"'Thank you Uncle,' said Kassardis, 'I will hold on to my hope a little while longer.'

"'Hold on to this,' said Ket Amonket, giving Kassardis his sword, 'It will protect you a lot better than hope.' Kassardis took the weapon very reluctantly, and would have thrown it away at the first chance he had, but the words of the Very Wise Frog continued to tear at his mind, so he clung on to it as he fled for the canyon.

"*At the very least I'll give the boy a good head start,* Ket Amonket assured himself as he watched Kassardis' three wives trek over the dunes a little while later. The sword master was wrong. Ipreski severed his wind pipe before he could get a single word out, and all that passed his lips was a spray of blood. Kassardis got a head start of about ten minutes."

— TALES OF THE SILVER PRINCE

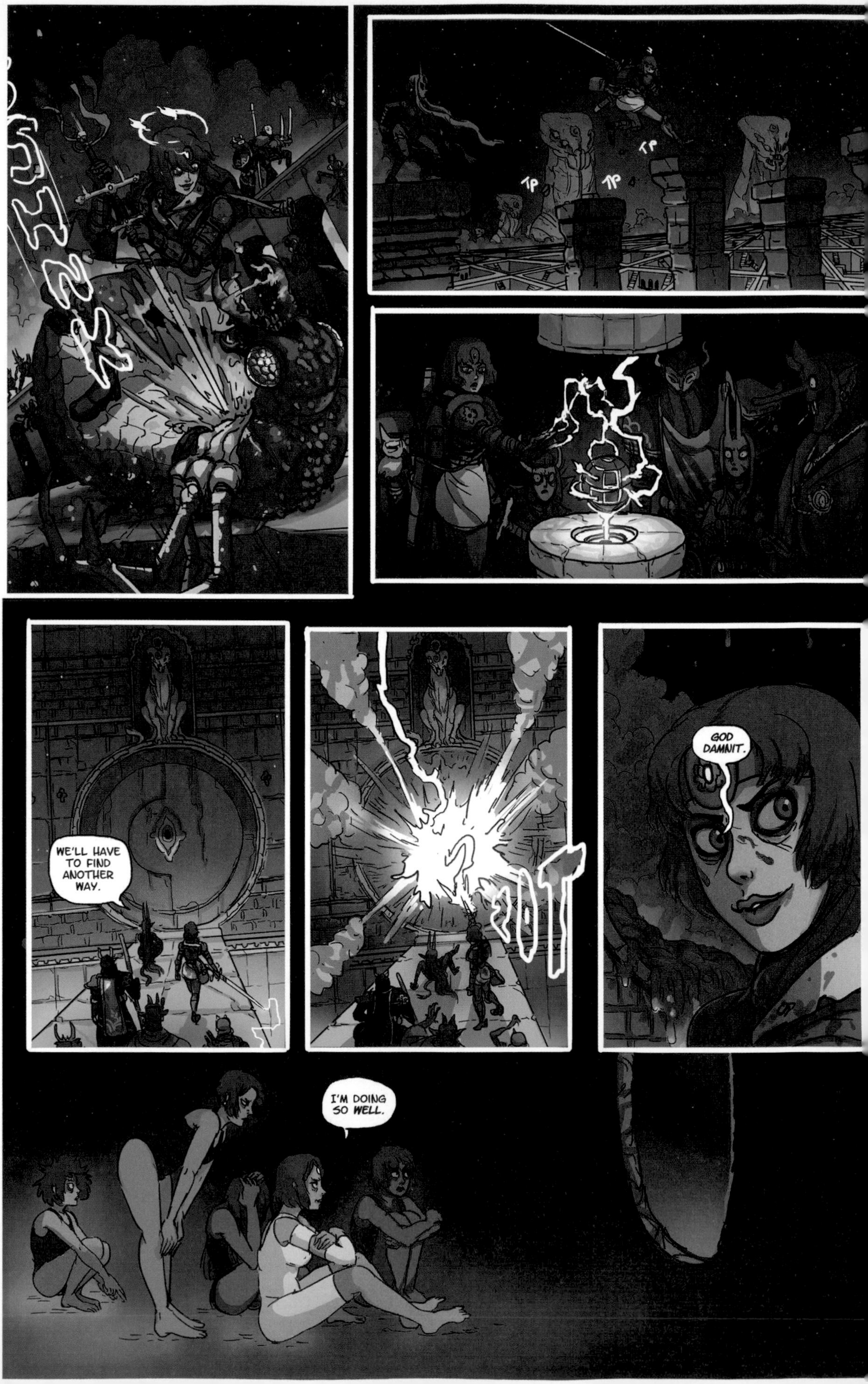
TP
TP
TP
TP
WE'LL HAVE TO FIND ANOTHER WAY.
GOD DAMNIT.
I'M DOING SO *WELL*.

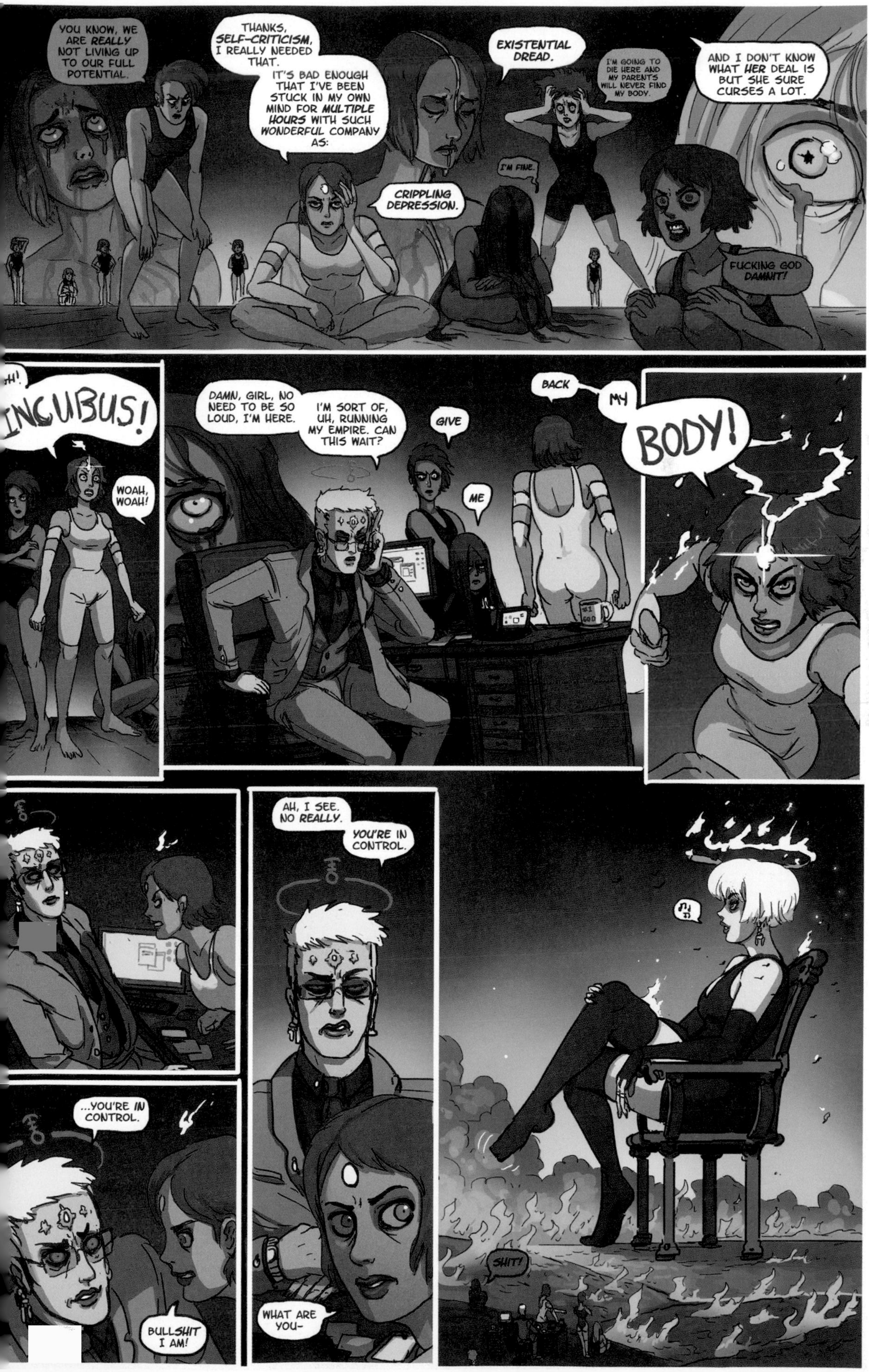

YOU KNOW, WE ARE REALLY NOT LIVING UP TO OUR FULL POTENTIAL.
THANKS, SELF-CRITICISM, I REALLY NEEDED THAT.
IT'S BAD ENOUGH THAT I'VE BEEN STUCK IN MY OWN MIND FOR MULTIPLE HOURS WITH SUCH WONDERFUL COMPANY AS:
CRIPPLING DEPRESSION.
I'M FINE.
EXISTENTIAL DREAD.
I'M GOING TO DIE HERE AND MY PARENTS WILL NEVER FIND MY BODY.
AND I DON'T KNOW WHAT HER DEAL IS BUT SHE SURE CURSES A LOT.
FUCKING GOD DAMNIT!
INCUBUS!
WOAH, WOAH!
DAMN, GIRL, NO NEED TO BE SO LOUD, I'M HERE.
I'M SORT OF, UH, RUNNING MY EMPIRE. CAN THIS WAIT?
GIVE
ME
BACK
MY
BODY!
AH, I SEE. NO REALLY.
YOU'RE IN CONTROL.
...YOU'RE IN CONTROL.
BULLSHIT I AM!
WHAT ARE YOU-
SHIT!

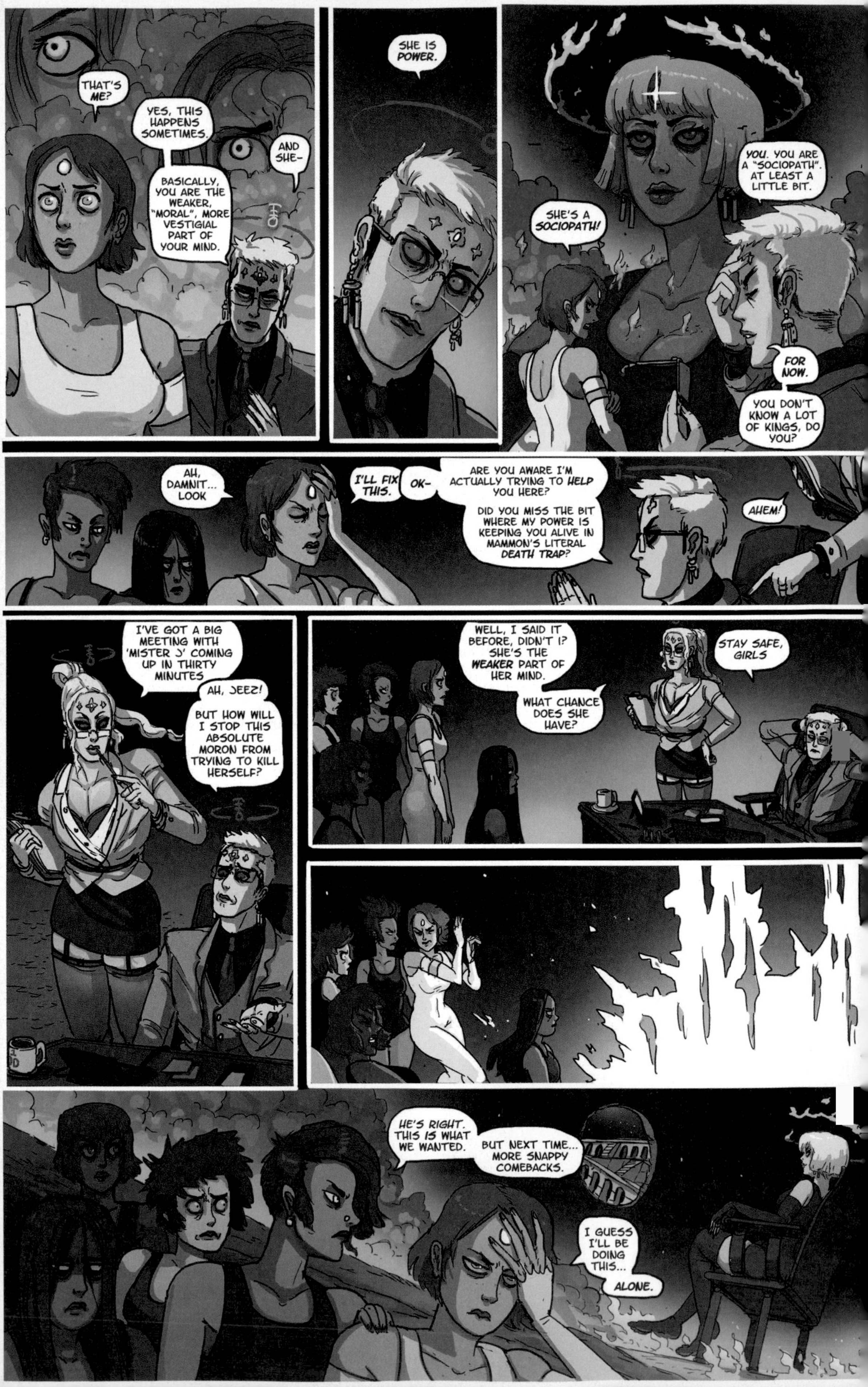
THAT'S ME?
YES, THIS HAPPENS SOMETIMES.
AND SHE-
BASICALLY, YOU ARE THE WEAKER, "MORAL", MORE VESTIGIAL PART OF YOUR MIND.
SHE IS POWER.
SHE'S A SOCIOPATH!
YOU. YOU ARE A "SOCIOPATH". AT LEAST A LITTLE BIT.
FOR NOW.
YOU DON'T KNOW A LOT OF KINGS, DO YOU?
AH, DAMNIT... LOOK
I'LL FIX THIS.
OK-
ARE YOU AWARE I'M ACTUALLY TRYING TO HELP YOU HERE?
DID YOU MISS THE BIT WHERE MY POWER IS KEEPING YOU ALIVE IN MAMMON'S LITERAL DEATH TRAP?
AHEM!
I'VE GOT A BIG MEETING WITH 'MISTER J' COMING UP IN THIRTY MINUTES
AH, JEEZ!
BUT HOW WILL I STOP THIS ABSOLUTE MORON FROM TRYING TO KILL HERSELF?
WELL, I SAID IT BEFORE, DIDN'T I? SHE'S THE WEAKER PART OF HER MIND.
WHAT CHANCE DOES SHE HAVE?
STAY SAFE, GIRLS
HE'S RIGHT. THIS IS WHAT WE WANTED.
BUT NEXT TIME... MORE SNAPPY COMEBACKS.
I GUESS I'LL BE DOING THIS...
ALONE.

Kassardis, for his part, could do little but flee to the canyon, carrying the old swordmaster's weapon and clad in near-rags. Once there, he hid himself among the reeds in a low pool in the bottom of the canyon. It was cool, and shady there, and the coming evening began to wash over the land, and Kassardis felt, for the first time in days, peace enter his heart.

"It was with dread then, that he heard the footfalls of his three wives entering the canyon not an hour later, and knew that his time had run out. Kassardis knew instantaneously that the words of the Very Wise Frog had come true. For the canyon had three entrances, and down each came one of his wives, armed and thirsty for blood. First, small and cunning Vastoki with the glint of her rifle sights, then enormous and brutal Littari, dragging her iron cauldron, and finally the refined Ipreski, languid and resplendent on her palanquin. And one after the other, all three of their cruel and lusty eyes fell upon Kassardis.

"Kassardis tried to pray, but found no sound would come out of his lungs. He tried to hide deeper in the reeds, but he found the mud unyielding. He tried to shut his eyes, but his heartbeat drowned out his thoughts. So instead, he clutched on to the old swordmaster's weapon like a good luck charm, its cruel metal cold against his bare chest. A strange thought entered his mind and gripped his tendons like a vice.

"As this thought gripped Kassardis, it was then that the truth of the Very Wise Frog revealed itself in its full glory. For violence truly was inescapable, and the three wives were inundated with it. They had no other language with which to negotiate their hard-won spoils.
-
"Stand aside," said soft Ipreski, "As oldest wife the Silver Prince is mine by right."

"Move an inch further," said Vastoki, "And I will put a bullet through that milky throat."

Littari, for her part, said nothing, but rather hefted her cauldron into the air with a tremendous roar, and charged. Kassardis watched as a brutal combat unfolded.

"Realizing the danger that Vastoki's rifle presented, Ipreski slid off her palanquin and behind an enormous boulder. But that boulder was shattered a moment later by the tremendous force of Littari's iron cauldron, sending her flying. Ipreski's servants and retainers were pulped a moment later against the heavy bottom of the cauldron and spread across the rock, and Littari advanced on the eldest wife, frothing at the mouth. She would have crushed Ipreski as she had promised, but in a mere second there were three cracks of Vastoki's rifle, and Littari's skull blossomed in gore, her cauldron smashing to the rocks below as she slumped forward. Ipreski sprang to her feet, her fine silks tearing, and drew her blade, dashing at Vastoki before she could reload.

"Vastoki was impossibly agile, and even though her fingers were slick with grit and sweat, she chambered a round and fired it right at the smooth face of the eldest wife. But Ipreski had anticipated this for years, and had practiced a blade art specifically for this purpose, which she called Ego Ballistics. With impossible speed, she cut through possibility and cleft the bullet in two before it could touch her flesh.

"Vastoki was taken aback. Such was her speed, however, that the incoming blow merely severed her nose from her face and cleft her glasses in two, instead of separating her head from her shoulders as was intended. Blinded by gouts of blood and shrieking in pain, she crawled away. But Ipreski, caught in the moment of victory, was blinded in her own way to Littari, who had survived three bullets to the head by the virtue of her enormously thick skull and was now staggering up behind her with cauldron in hand.

"The first blow of the cauldron cracked Ipreski's back and sent her sprawling, the second crushed her shins and feet to splinters. The third did not come, for Vastoki, acting on instinct, loosed three more shots, which blew the throat out from Littari and sent her reeling backwards.

This gory sight, and the ruin of his three wives, Kassardis beheld, and his resolve hardened into ice. He emerged from the pool, his blood cold in his veins, and the old swordmaster's blade clutched tight in his hand."

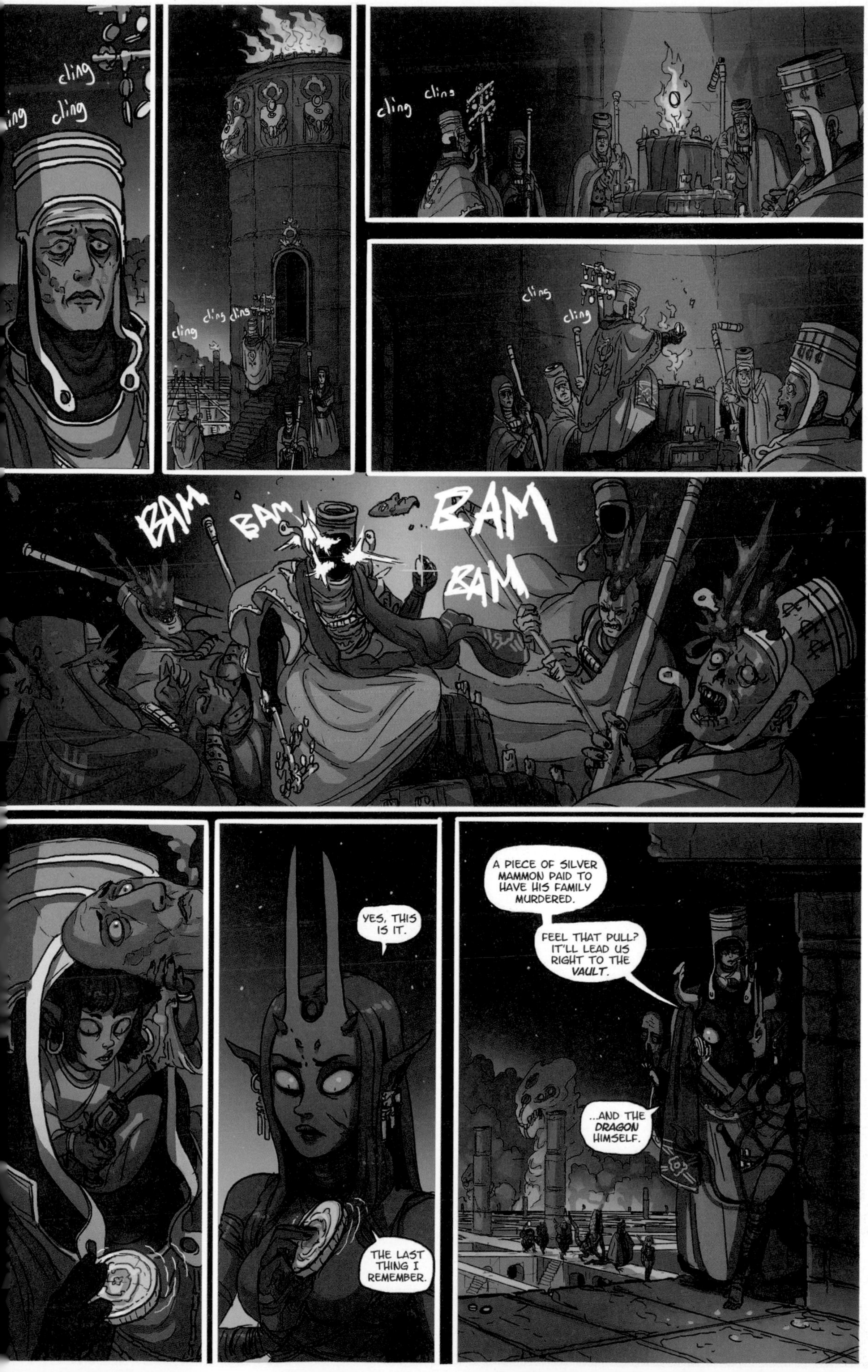
cling
cling cling
cling cling cling
cling
cling cling
cling
cling
BAM
BAM
BAM
BAM
YES, THIS IS IT.
THE LAST THING I REMEMBER.
A PIECE OF SILVER MAMMON PAID TO HAVE HIS FAMILY MURDERED.
FEEL THAT PULL? IT'LL LEAD US RIGHT TO THE *VAULT*.
...AND THE *DRAGON* HIMSELF.

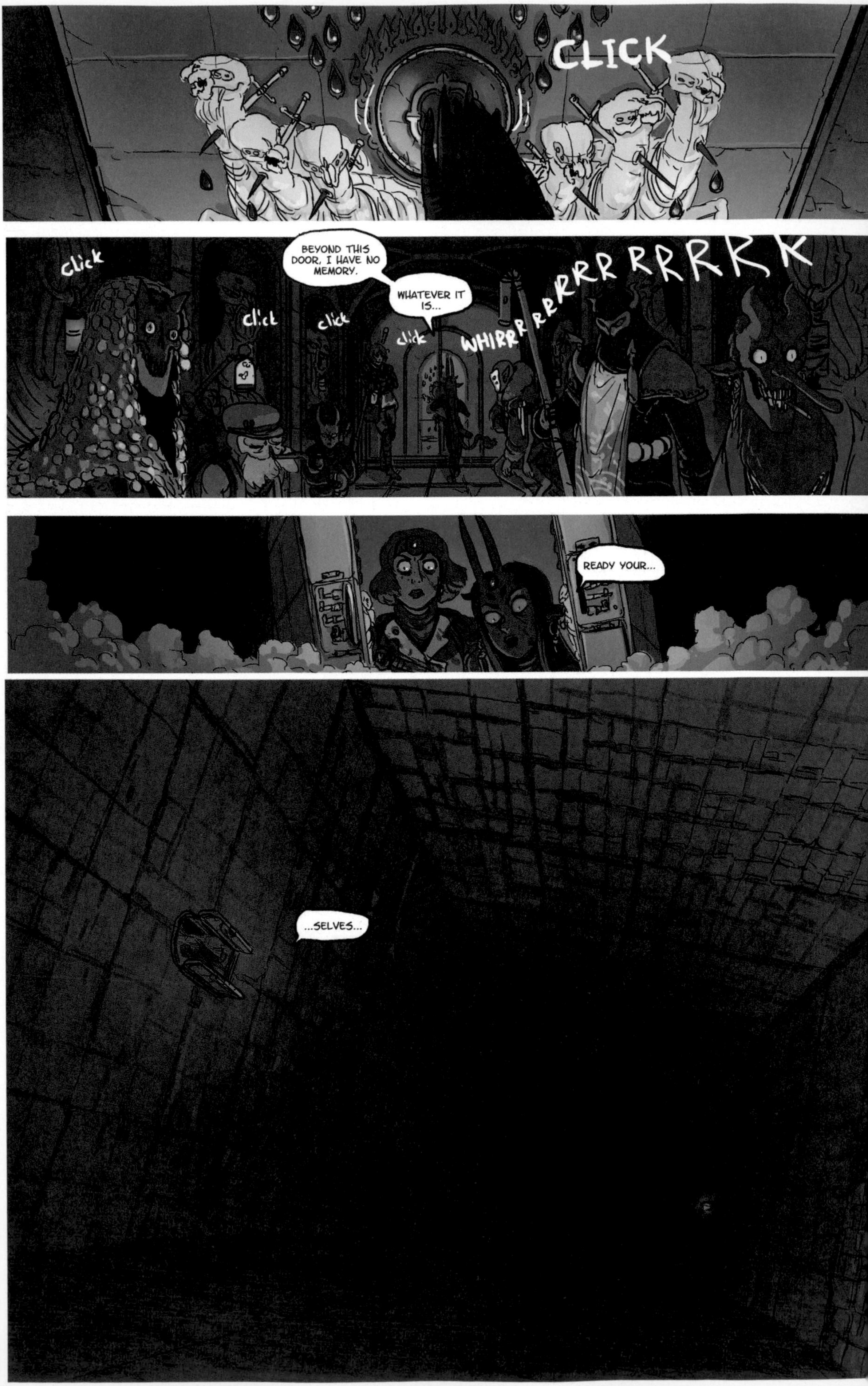
CLICK
click
BEYOND THIS DOOR, I HAVE NO MEMORY.
WHATEVER IT IS...
click
click
click
WHIRRRRRRRRRRRRRK
READY YOUR...
...SELVES...

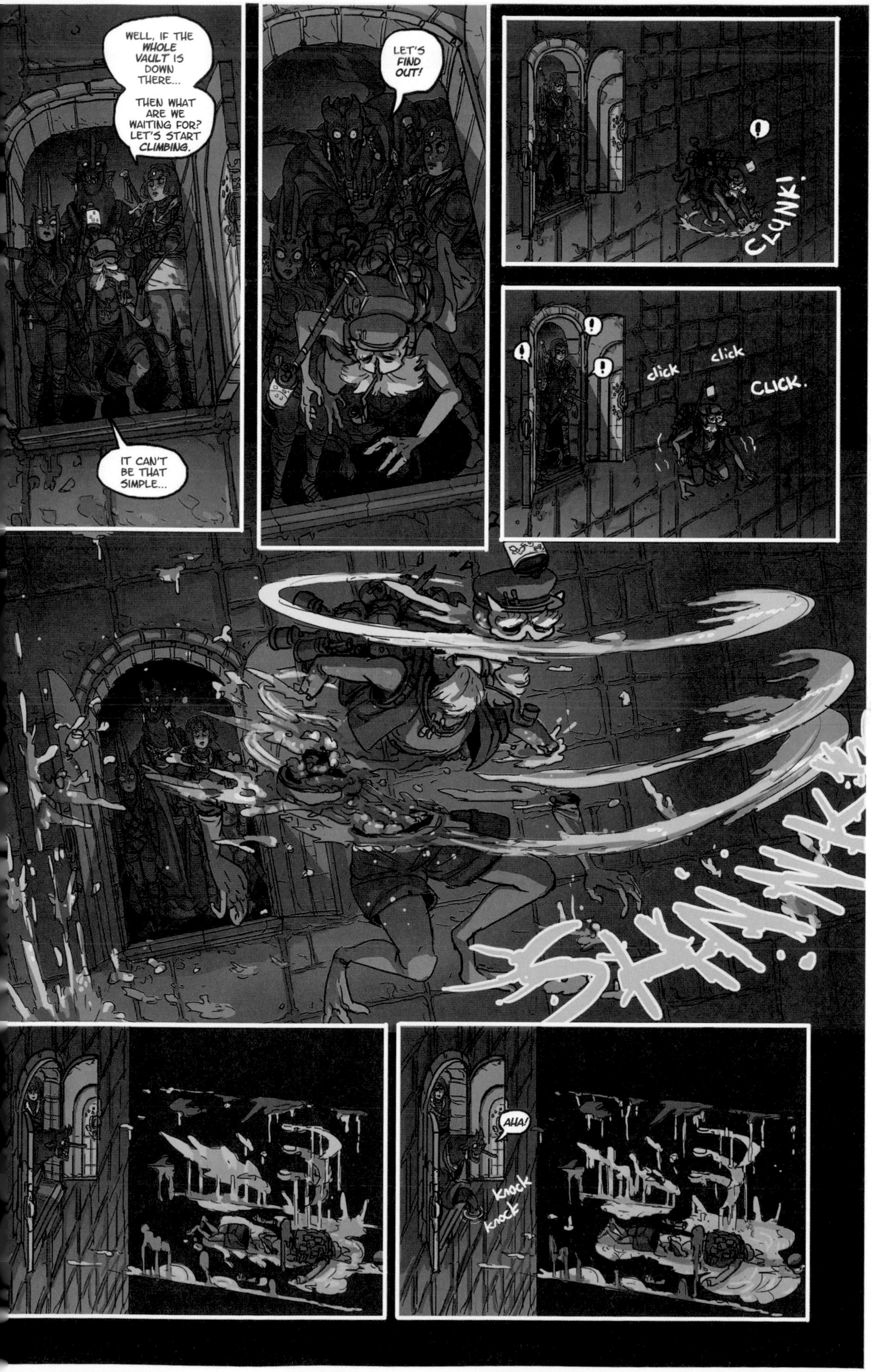

WELL, IF THE *WHOLE VAULT* IS DOWN THERE...
THEN WHAT ARE WE WAITING FOR? LET'S START *CLIMBING*.
IT CAN'T BE THAT SIMPLE...
LET'S *FIND OUT!*
!
CLUNK!
!
!
!
click
click
CLICK.
SHUNK!
AHA!
knock
knock

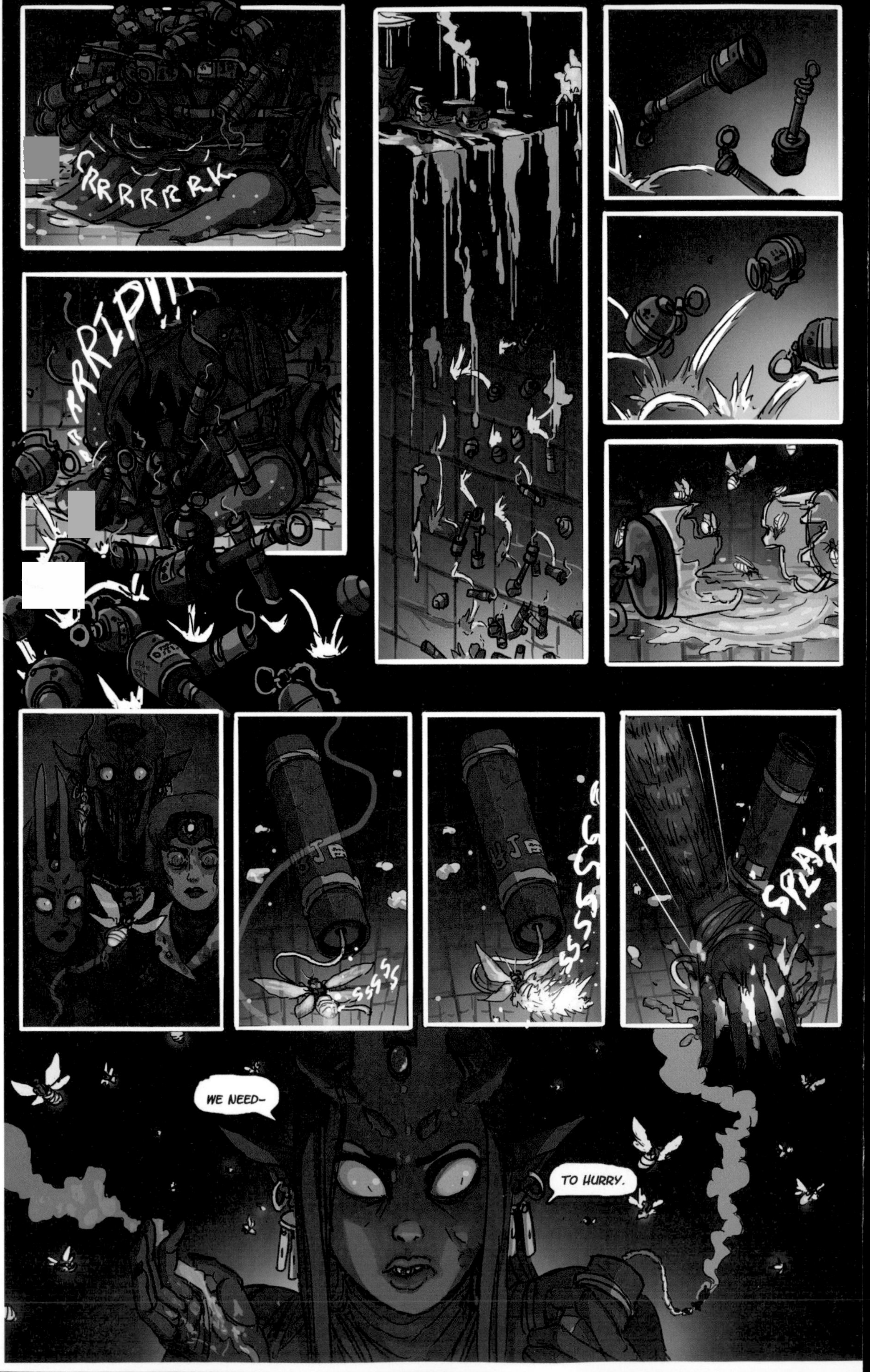
CRRRRRRK
RRRIP!!!
SSSSS
SSSSS
SPLAT
WE NEED-
TO HURRY.

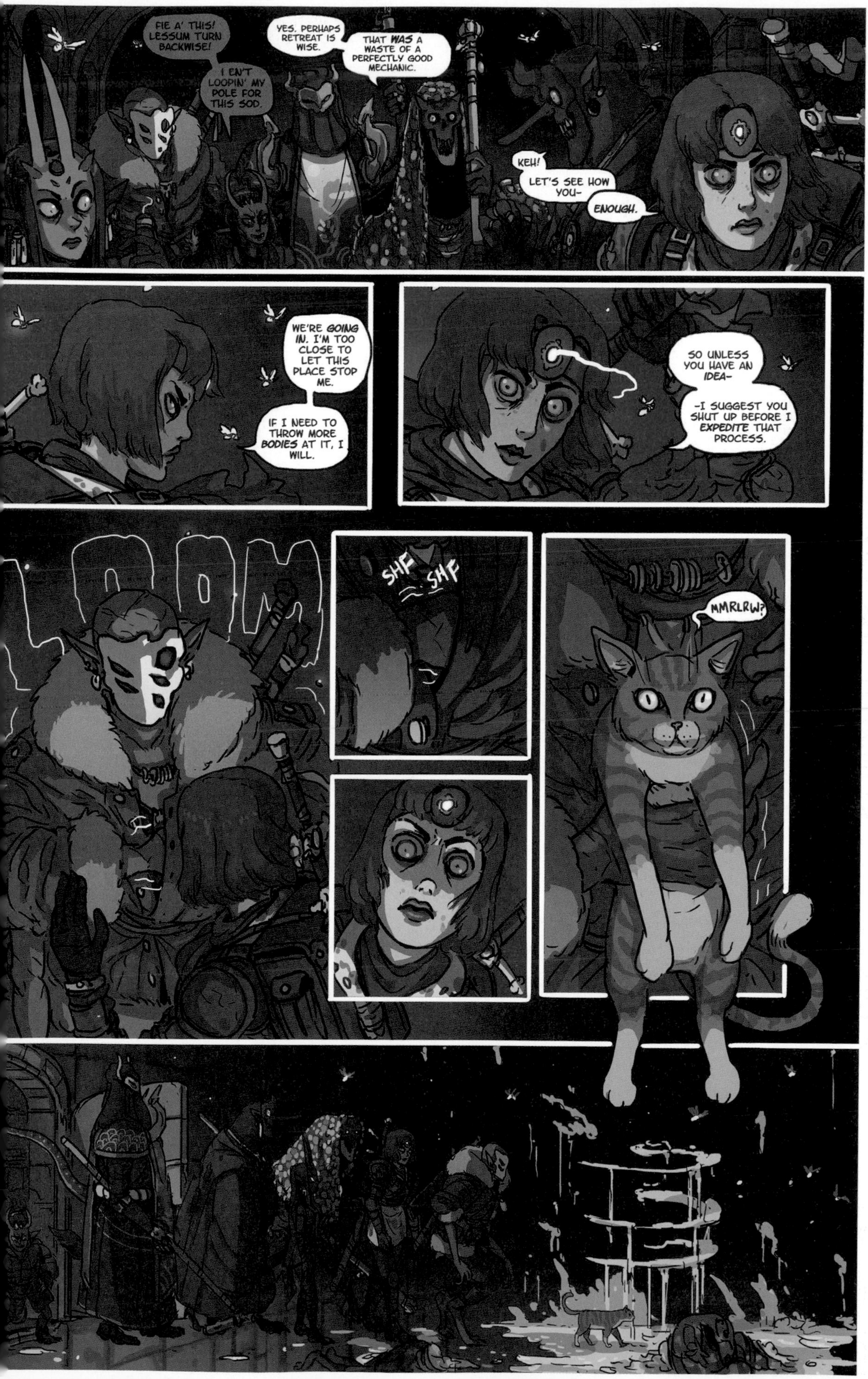
FIE A' THIS! LESSUM TURN BACKWISE!
I EN'T LOOPIN' MY POLE FOR THIS SOD.
YES. PERHAPS RETREAT IS WISE.
THAT WAS A WASTE OF A PERFECTLY GOOD MECHANIC.
KEH!
LET'S SEE HOW YOU-
ENOUGH.
WE'RE GOING IN. I'M TOO CLOSE TO LET THIS PLACE STOP ME.
IF I NEED TO THROW MORE BODIES AT IT, I WILL.
SO UNLESS YOU HAVE AN IDEA-
-I SUGGEST YOU SHUT UP BEFORE I EXPEDITE THAT PROCESS.
SHF SHF
MMRLRW?

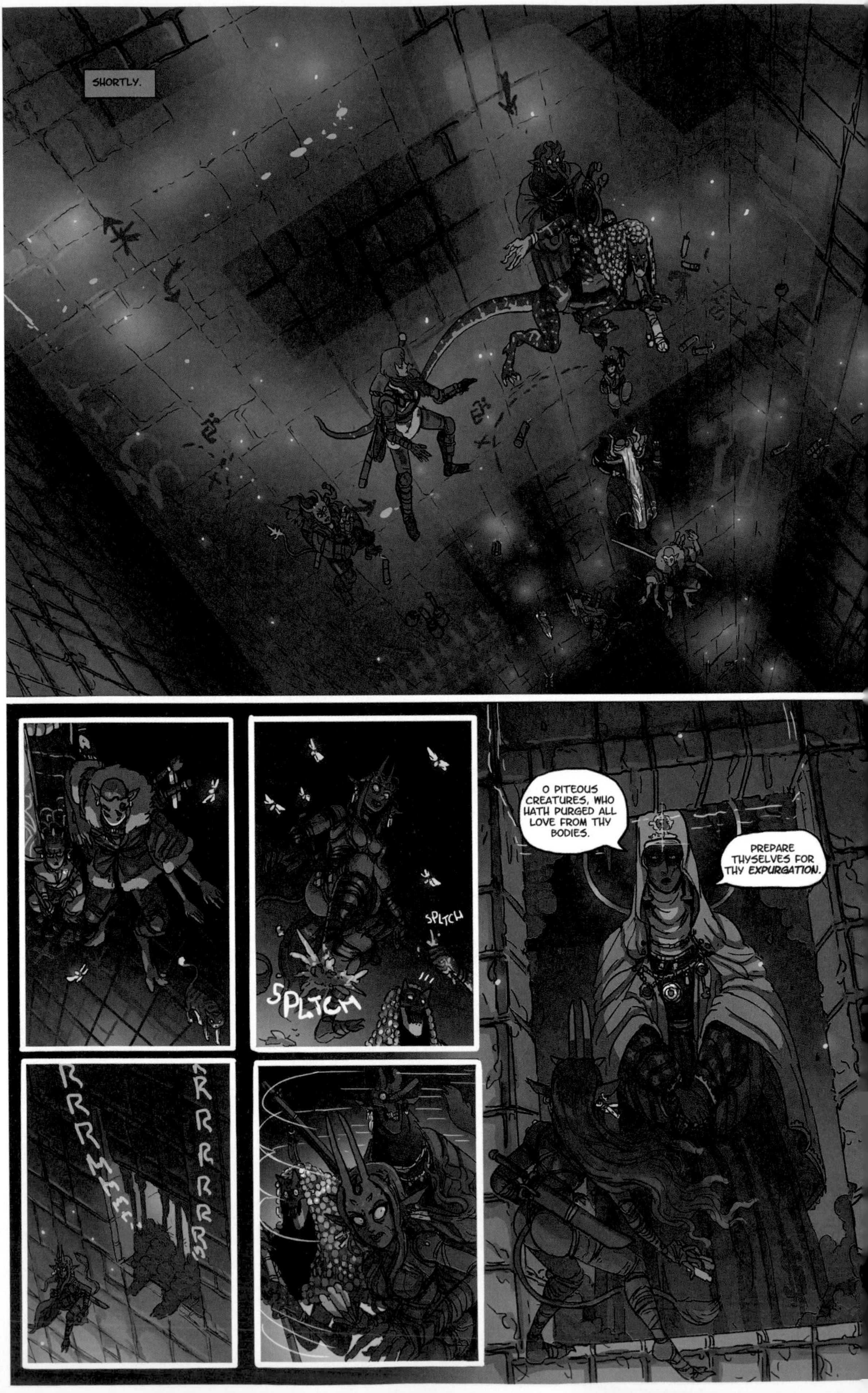
SHORTLY.
SPLTCH
SPLTCH
RRRMMMM
RRRRRRRM
O PITEOUS CREATURES, WHO HATH PURGED ALL LOVE FROM THY BODIES.
PREPARE THYSELVES FOR THY *EXPURGATION*.

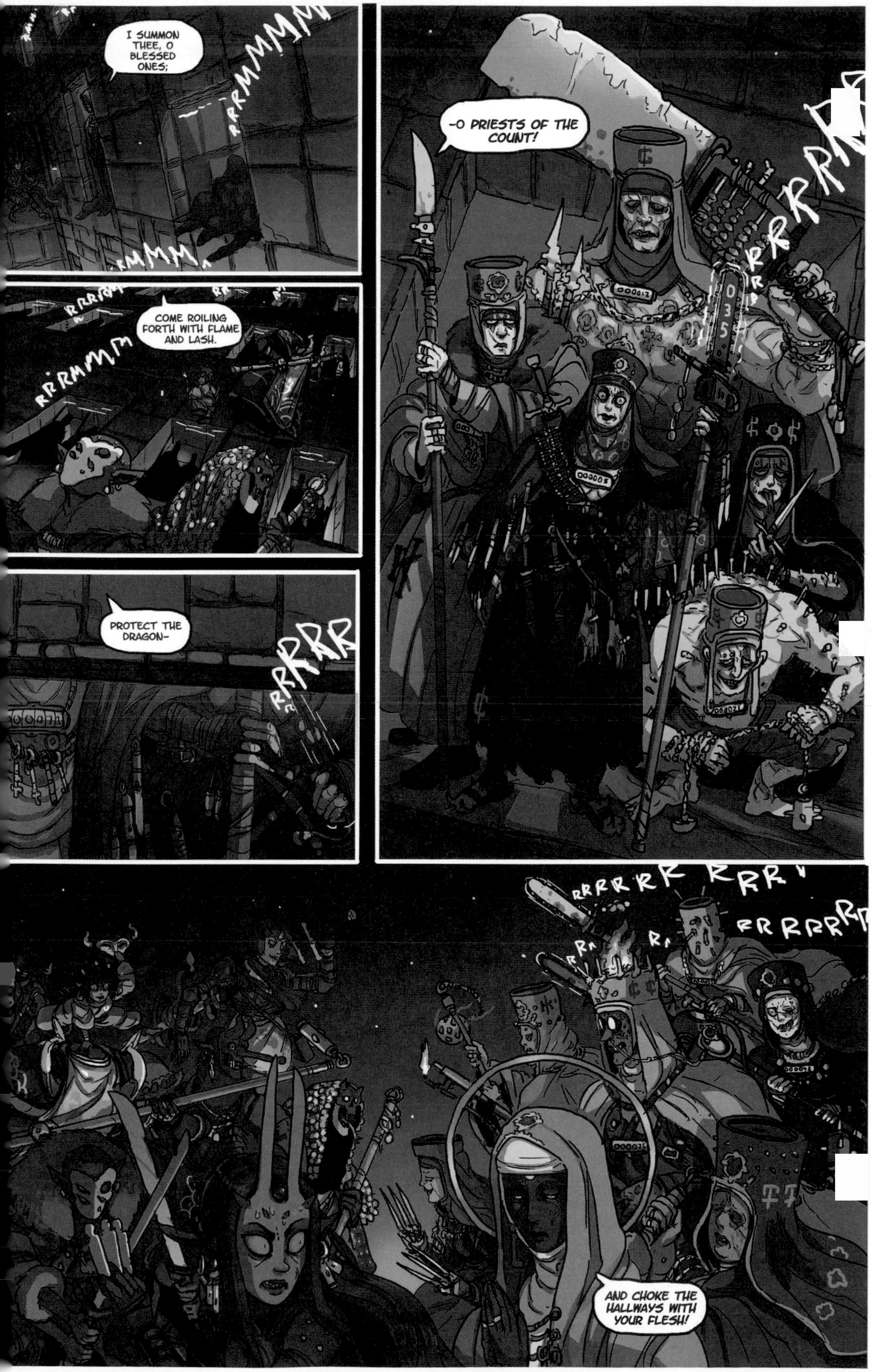
I SUMMON THEE, O BLESSED ONES;
RRRMMMMM
-O PRIESTS OF THE COUNT!
COME ROILING FORTH WITH FLAME AND LASH.
RRRMMM
PROTECT THE DRAGON-
RRRR
AND CHOKE THE HALLWAYS WITH YOUR FLESH!

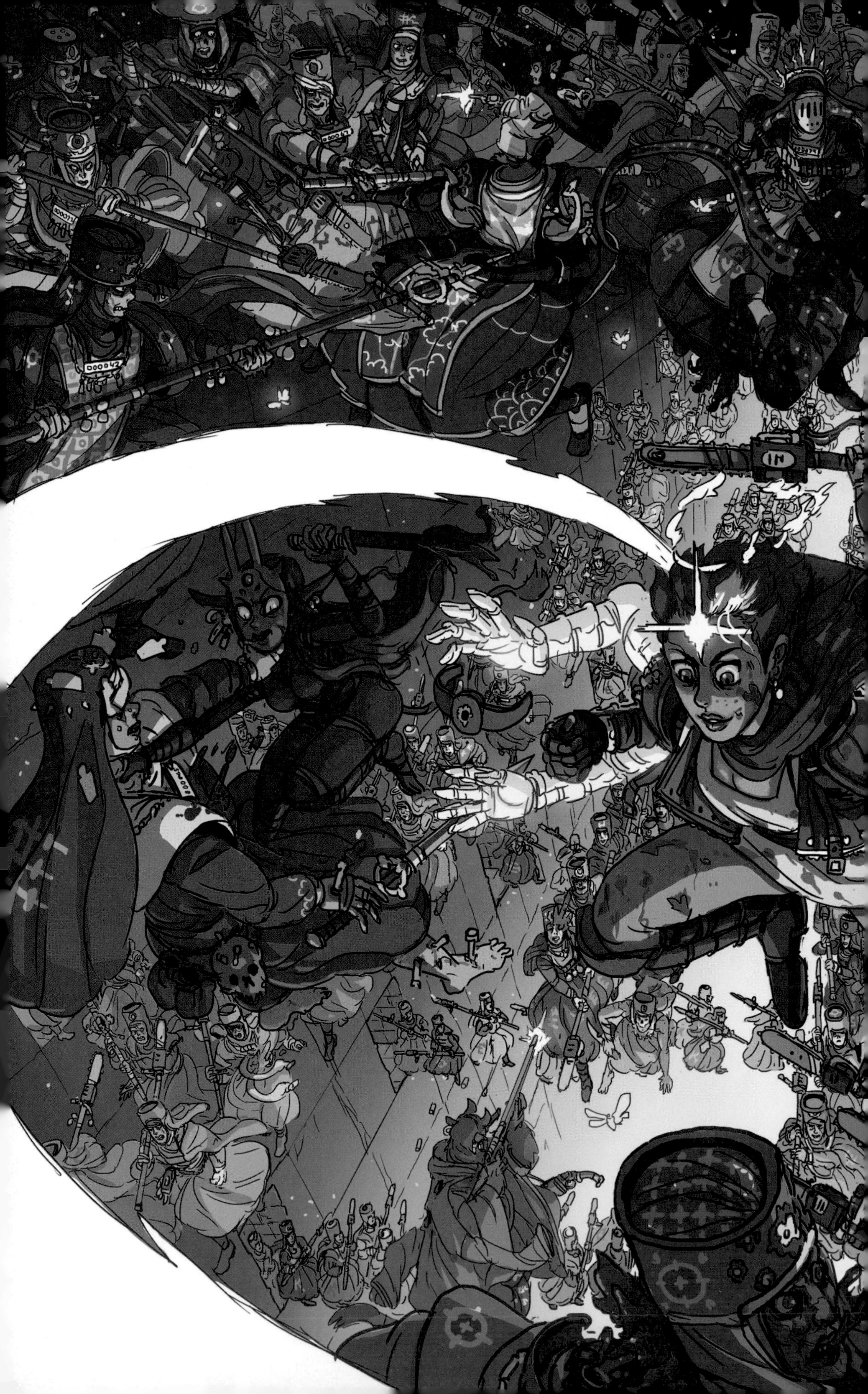

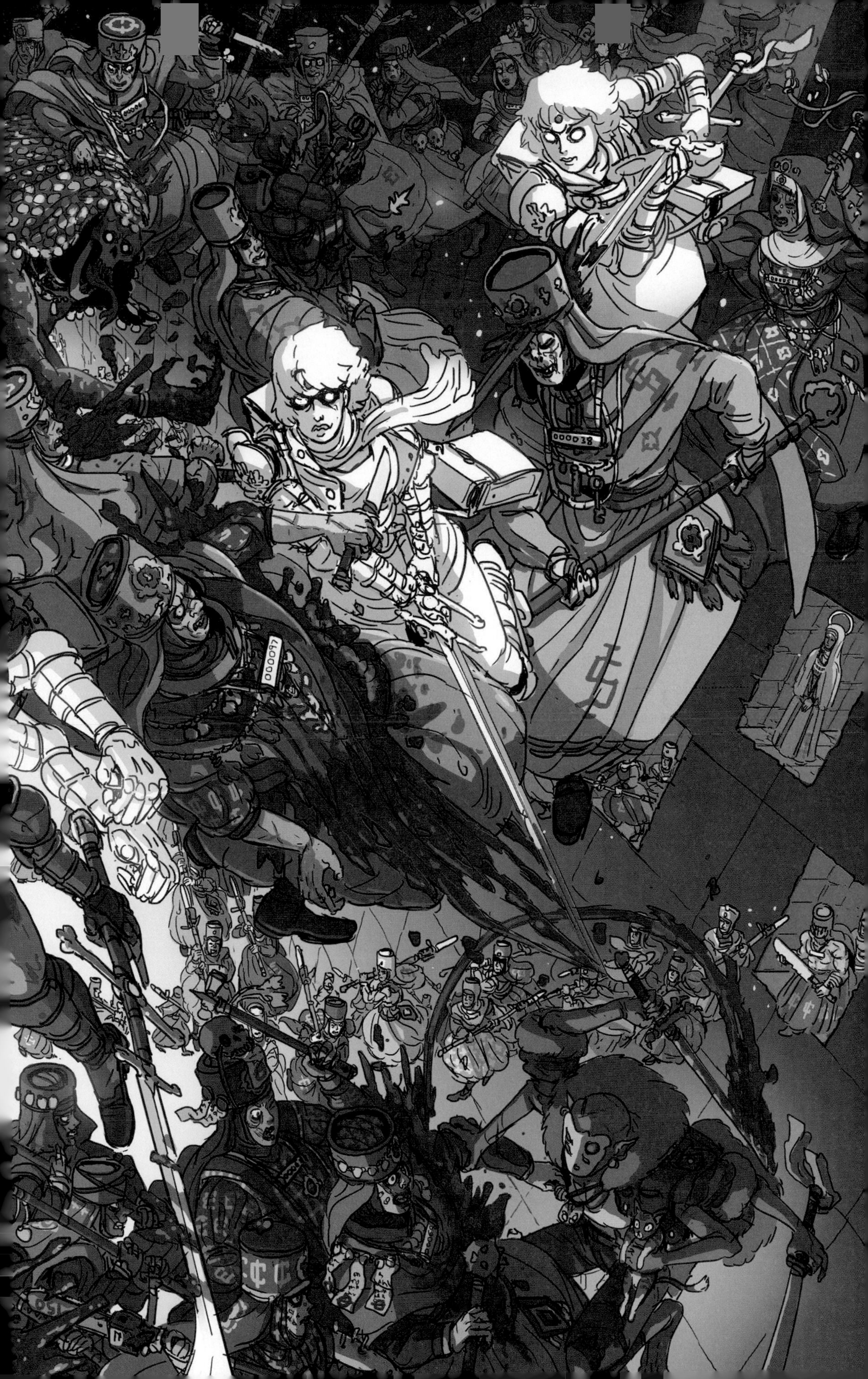
000038

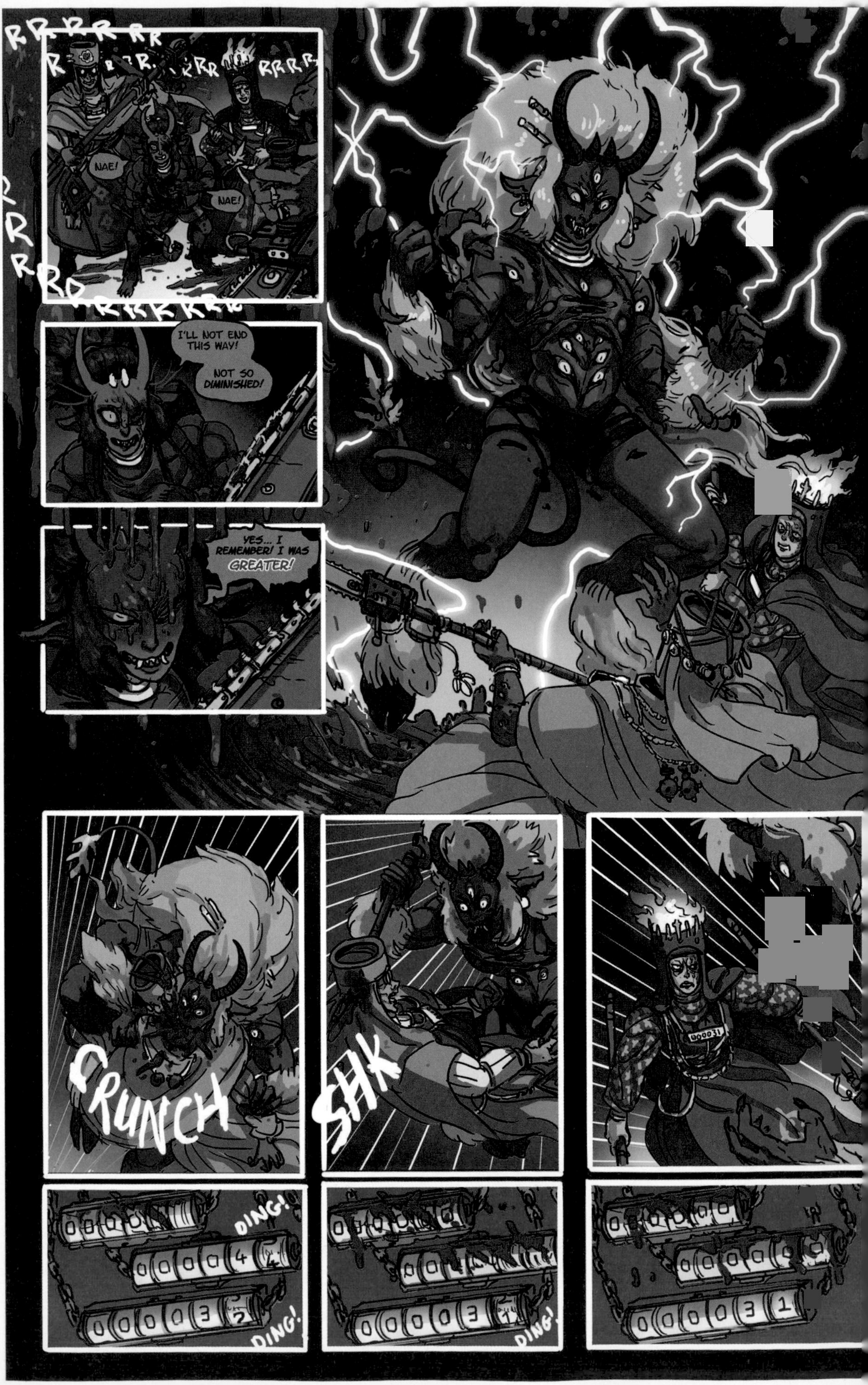
RRRRRR
NAE!
NAE!
I'LL NOT END THIS WAY!
NOT SO DIMINISHED!
YES... I REMEMBER! I WAS GREATER!
CRUNCH
SHK
000031
DING!
DING!
DING!

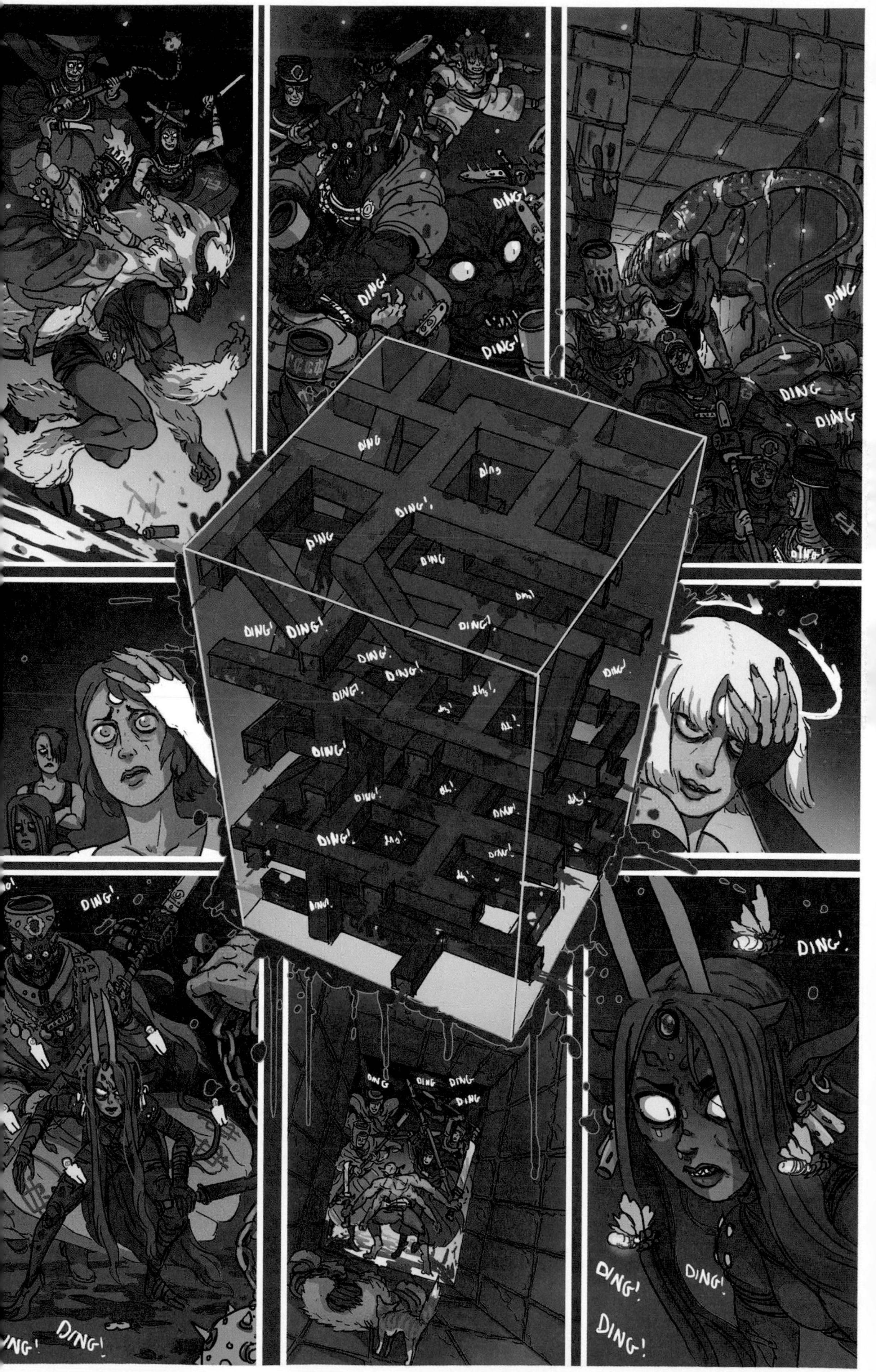
DING!
DING!
DING!
DING
DING
DING
DING
DING
DING
DING!
DING
DING
DING!
DING!
DING!
DING!
DING!
DING!
DING!
DING!
DING!
DING!
DING!
DING!
DING!
DING
DING
DING
DING
DING!
DING!
DING!
DING!
DING!
DING!
DING!

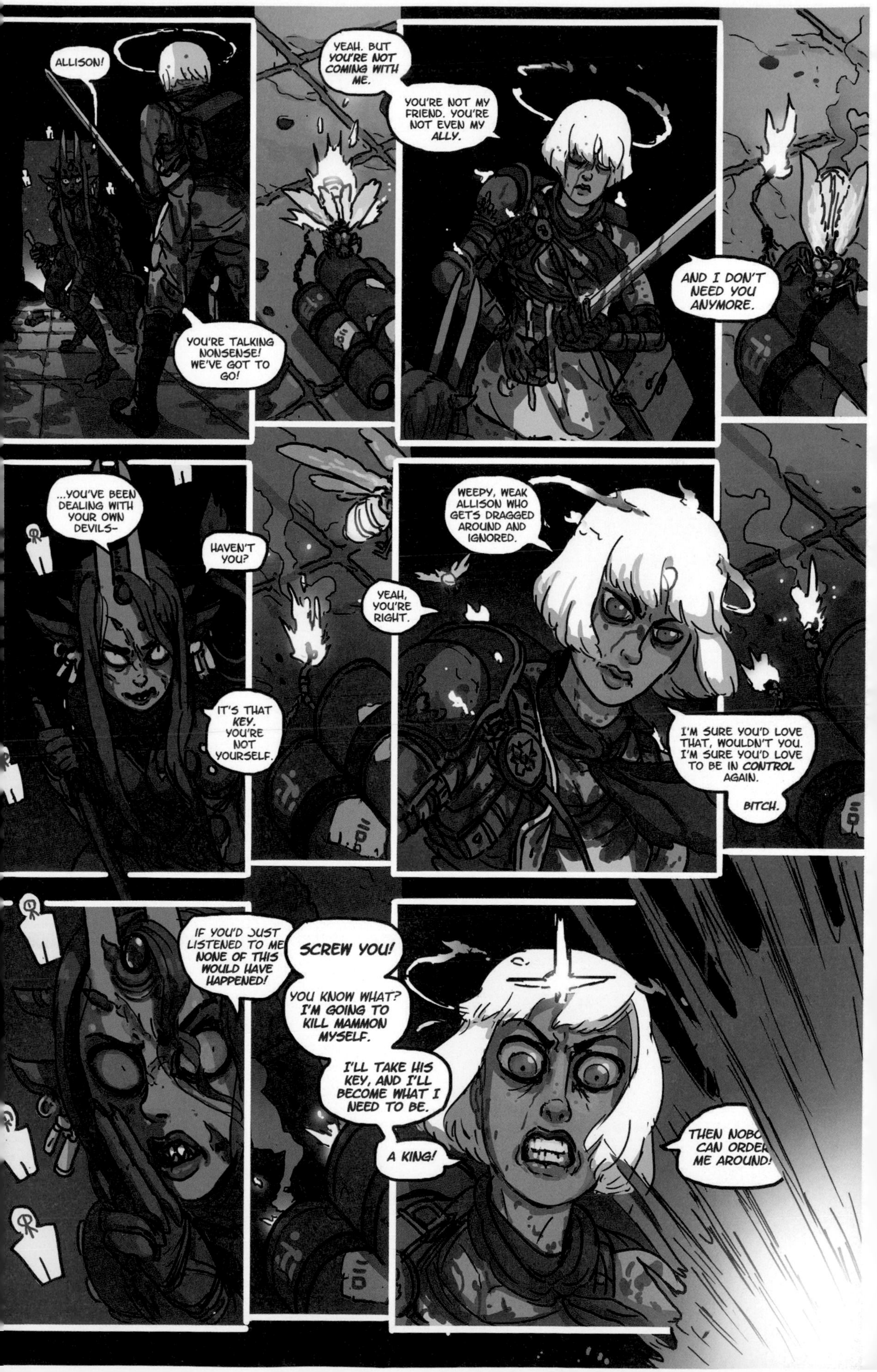
ALLISON!
YOU'RE TALKING NONSENSE! WE'VE GOT TO GO!
YEAH. BUT YOU'RE NOT COMING WITH ME.
YOU'RE NOT MY FRIEND. YOU'RE NOT EVEN MY ALLY.
AND I DON'T NEED YOU ANYMORE.
...YOU'VE BEEN DEALING WITH YOUR OWN DEVILS-
HAVEN'T YOU?
IT'S THAT KEY. YOU'RE NOT YOURSELF.
YEAH, YOU'RE RIGHT.
WEEPY, WEAK ALLISON WHO GETS DRAGGED AROUND AND IGNORED.
I'M SURE YOU'D LOVE THAT, WOULDN'T YOU. I'M SURE YOU'D LOVE TO BE IN CONTROL AGAIN.
BITCH.
IF YOU'D JUST LISTENED TO ME NONE OF THIS WOULD HAVE HAPPENED!
SCREW YOU!
YOU KNOW WHAT? I'M GOING TO KILL MAMMON MYSELF.
I'LL TAKE HIS KEY, AND I'LL BECOME WHAT I NEED TO BE.
A KING!
THEN NOBO CAN ORDER ME AROUND!

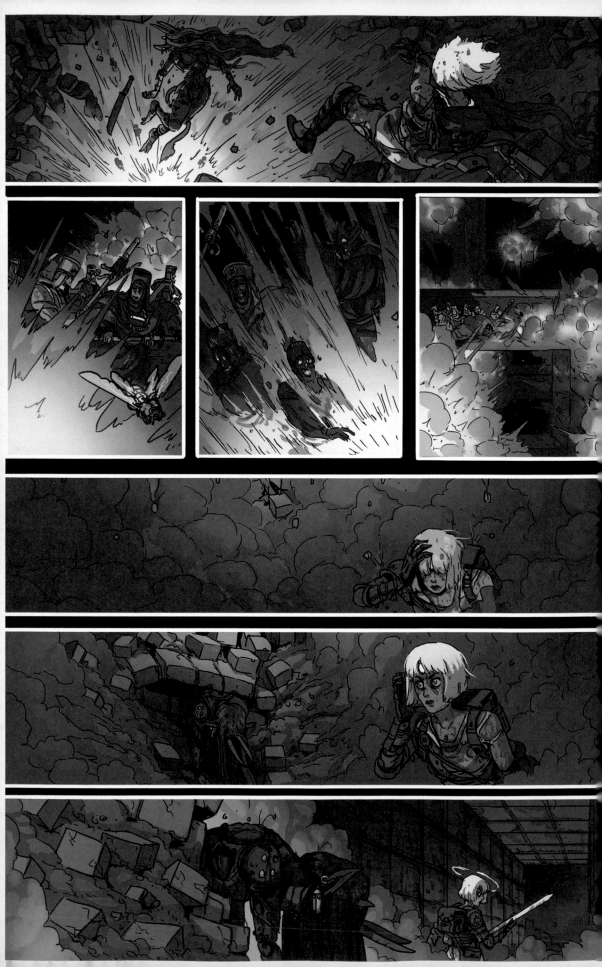

"As Kassardis approached his maimed and mangled wives, they scrabbled for their weapons in whatever way they could, clutching their gory injuries. For Kassardis was a ghastly sight: malnourished, clad only in rags, and with a terrible light in his eyes. They should have known then that the fate Kassardis had chosen for them was far worse than they ever could have expected, but they were fools with little imagination, and so chose to fight anyway.

Kassardis took the pommel of his blade, and with all his strength struck each of the wives across the head, knocking them unconscious. It took four blows from the great enameled hilt of the sword to fell Littari, but eventually the pints of blood she had lost stopped her struggle.

With great fierceness, Kassardis drove off Ipreski's retainers, and tearing scraps of cloth, bound the gushing wounds of his wives however he could. He knew however dire their injuries seemed, they would likely survive, having been bred for generations for thick blood, tough skin, and other valued traits to place them above his other potential wives.

Exhausted, the silver prince finally dragged himself to the road, where he waited for a merchant's cart, and went to a hard-scrabble town to find an apothecary. There, he bartered the remainder of the old swordmaster's belongings for medicine, keeping only the blade and the old man's boots, which he put on.

Finally, there in the gulch, Kassardis made camp, and over the next few days tended to his wives with incredible care. He sewed up gashes, blotted dried blood, and fed them water as they suffered. And though he tried his best, Littari would surely never speak again, Ipreski surely never walk again, and Vastoki's nose had long since disappeared into a pond.

On the third day, Vastoki, the youngest and most calculating, could finally speak, and when she did she was astonished. "You fool!" she croaked, "Do you seek to garner my sympathy? When I am well again, I will subdue you, husband, and take you back to our great kingdom and our rightful throne. This changes nothing!"

"Of course," said Kassardis, "Violence is inescapable. The Very Wise Frog was right."

And to Vastoki, something had changed in Kassardis. He was more relaxed, and more tense at the same time, like flexible steel. A great truth had settled into his flesh, and his calm was a terrible thing to behold. "I came to find the land of Samura, where peace is eternal," said Kassardis, "But instead, I find that I must carry Samura with me." And he grasped the hilt of his sword and stood, and Vastoki finally realized how tall he was.

"None of the three of you will ever agree to share me, and none of the three of you can best the other," said Kassardis, "You are already too poisoned by violence. I will run from you, and you will find me, again and again, and again and again you will destroy yourselves in trying to claim me. And again and again, I will tend to your wounds, and flee, knowing that I will never truly escape."

"Again and again you will destroy yourselves until you are mere hunks of flesh, crippled wrecks of meat. And there will come a day when you have become so ruined that even I will be able to best you in combat, and you will submit to my peace."

Vastoki did not believe Kassardis at first, for she was a fool, but she humored him anyway. "And what then?" she scoffed, "Your kingdom, my silver prince, will ever await you. It is worth a hundred thousand cattle, and half a million sheep. They will send more wives. Ten thousand of them!"

"I will tend to them too," said Kassardis.

It was then that Vastoki knew the truth of Kassardis' words, but she could do nothing about it, for violence was inescapable. She knew she could not turn from her fate, for the vain hope that she would still win grasped her beyond all reason.

"You will never rest!" she spat, and her missing nose wept blood, "You will flee for all eternity!"

"Such is the cost of peace," said Kassardis, "Even if I should care for ten thousand maimed wives."

Then he tightened his wives' bandages, and soothed the struggling Vastoki, and left them ample supplies. And though his wives spat and cursed at him, they could do little but let him leave, his countenance calm and resolute as he said one last thing:

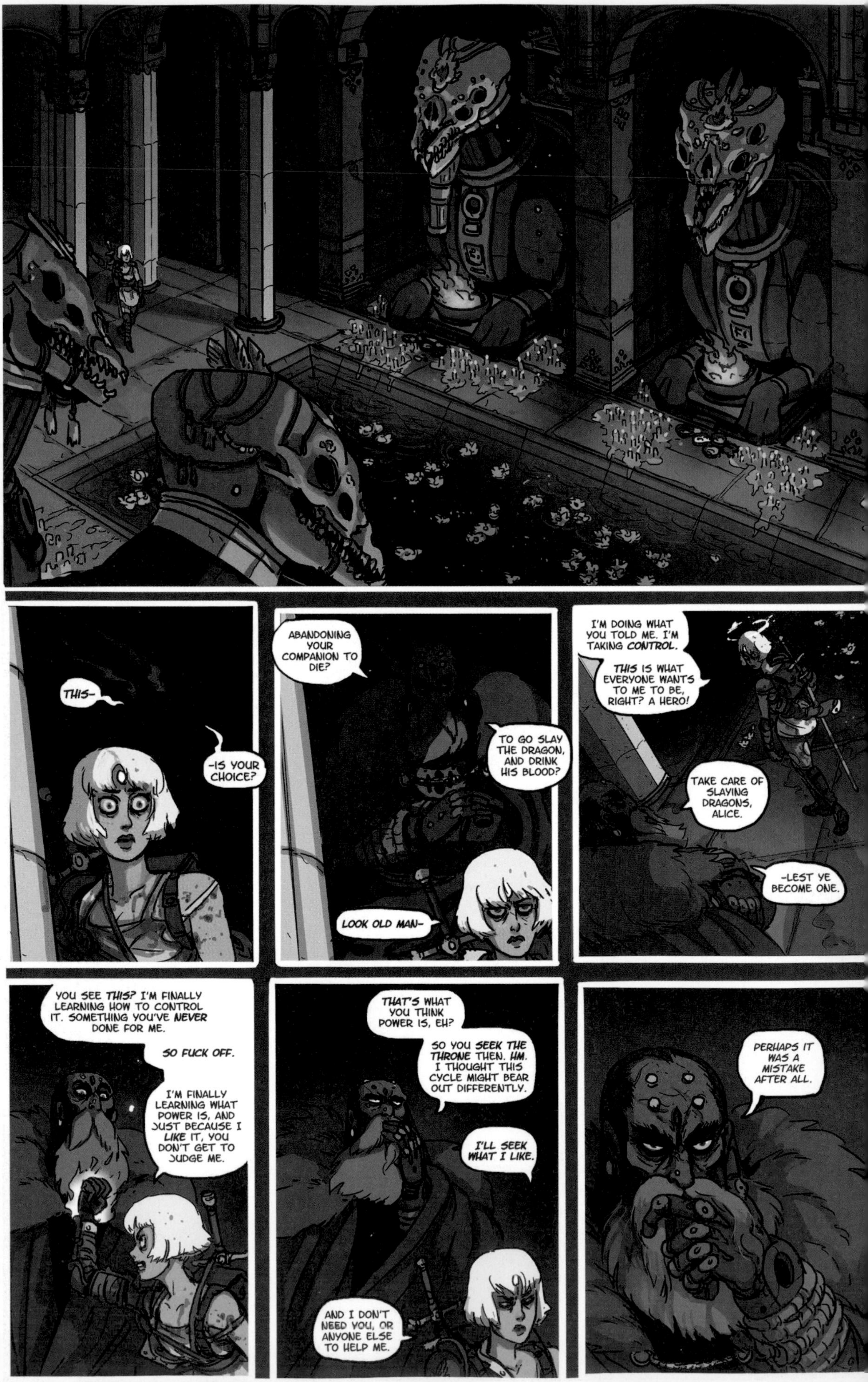
THIS-
-IS YOUR CHOICE?
ABANDONING YOUR COMPANION TO DIE?
TO GO SLAY THE DRAGON, AND DRINK HIS BLOOD?
LOOK OLD MAN-
I'M DOING WHAT YOU TOLD ME. I'M TAKING CONTROL.
THIS IS WHAT EVERYONE WANTS TO ME TO BE, RIGHT? A HERO!
TAKE CARE OF SLAYING DRAGONS, ALICE.
-LEST YE BECOME ONE.
YOU SEE THIS? I'M FINALLY LEARNING HOW TO CONTROL IT. SOMETHING YOU'VE NEVER DONE FOR ME.
SO FUCK OFF.
I'M FINALLY LEARNING WHAT POWER IS, AND JUST BECAUSE I LIKE IT, YOU DON'T GET TO JUDGE ME.
THAT'S WHAT YOU THINK POWER IS, EH?
SO YOU SEEK THE THRONE THEN. HM. I THOUGHT THIS CYCLE MIGHT BEAR OUT DIFFERENTLY.
I'LL SEEK WHAT I LIKE.
AND I DON'T NEED YOU, OR ANYONE ELSE TO HELP ME.
PERHAPS IT WAS A MISTAKE AFTER ALL.

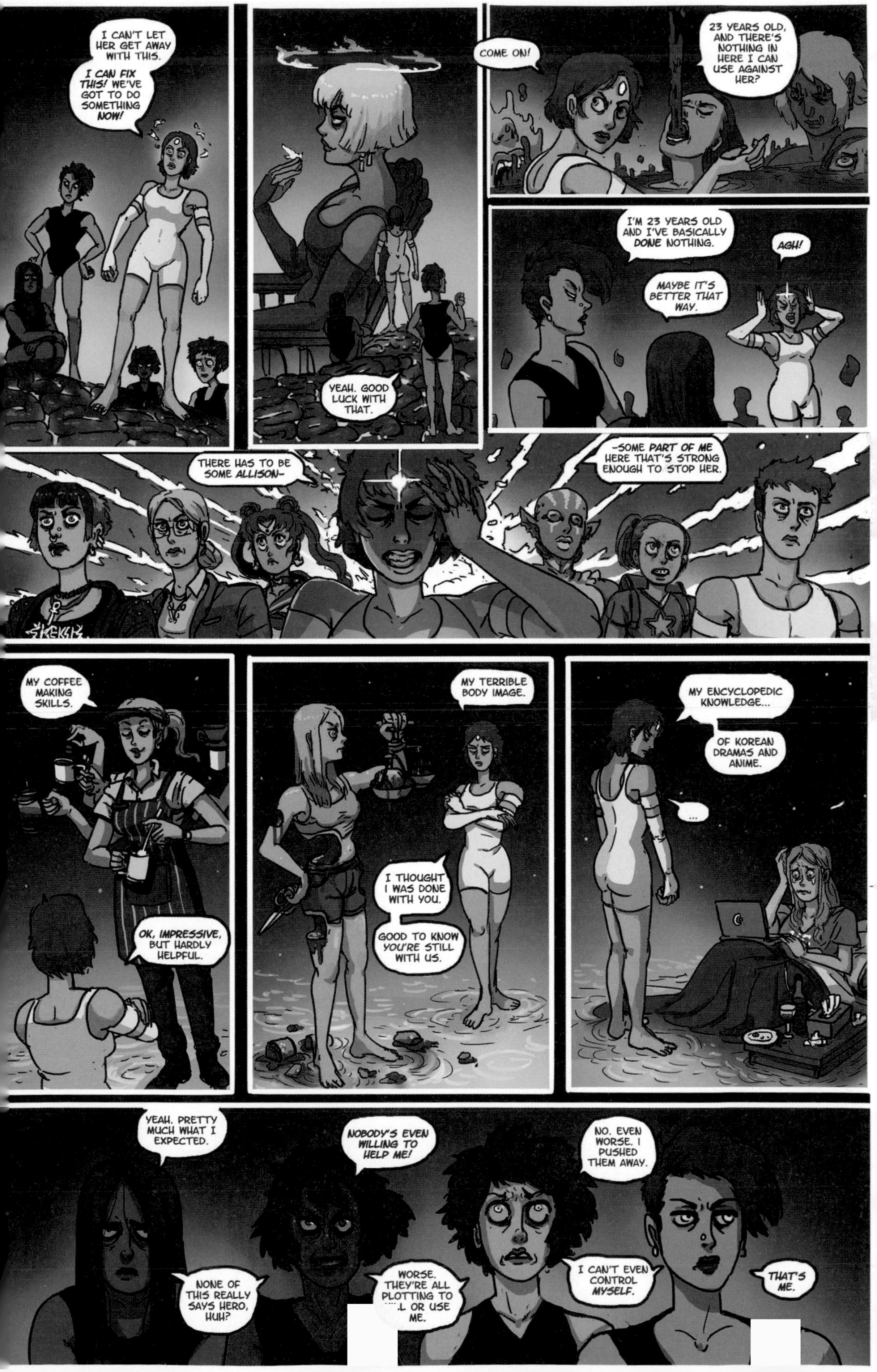
I CAN'T LET HER GET AWAY WITH THIS.
I CAN FIX THIS! WE'VE GOT TO DO SOMETHING NOW!
YEAH. GOOD LUCK WITH THAT.
COME ON!
23 YEARS OLD, AND THERE'S NOTHING IN HERE I CAN USE AGAINST HER?
I'M 23 YEARS OLD AND I'VE BASICALLY DONE NOTHING.
AGH!
MAYBE IT'S BETTER THAT WAY.
THERE HAS TO BE SOME ALLISON-
-SOME PART OF ME HERE THAT'S STRONG ENOUGH TO STOP HER.
MY COFFEE MAKING SKILLS.
OK, IMPRESSIVE, BUT HARDLY HELPFUL.
MY TERRIBLE BODY IMAGE.
I THOUGHT I WAS DONE WITH YOU.
GOOD TO KNOW YOU'RE STILL WITH US.
MY ENCYCLOPEDIC KNOWLEDGE...
OF KOREAN DRAMAS AND ANIME.
...
YEAH. PRETTY MUCH WHAT I EXPECTED.
NONE OF THIS REALLY SAYS HERO, HUH?
NOBODY'S EVEN WILLING TO HELP ME!
WORSE. THEY'RE ALL PLOTTING TO
LL OR USE ME.
NO. EVEN WORSE. I PUSHED THEM AWAY.
I CAN'T EVEN CONTROL MYSELF.
THAT'S ME.

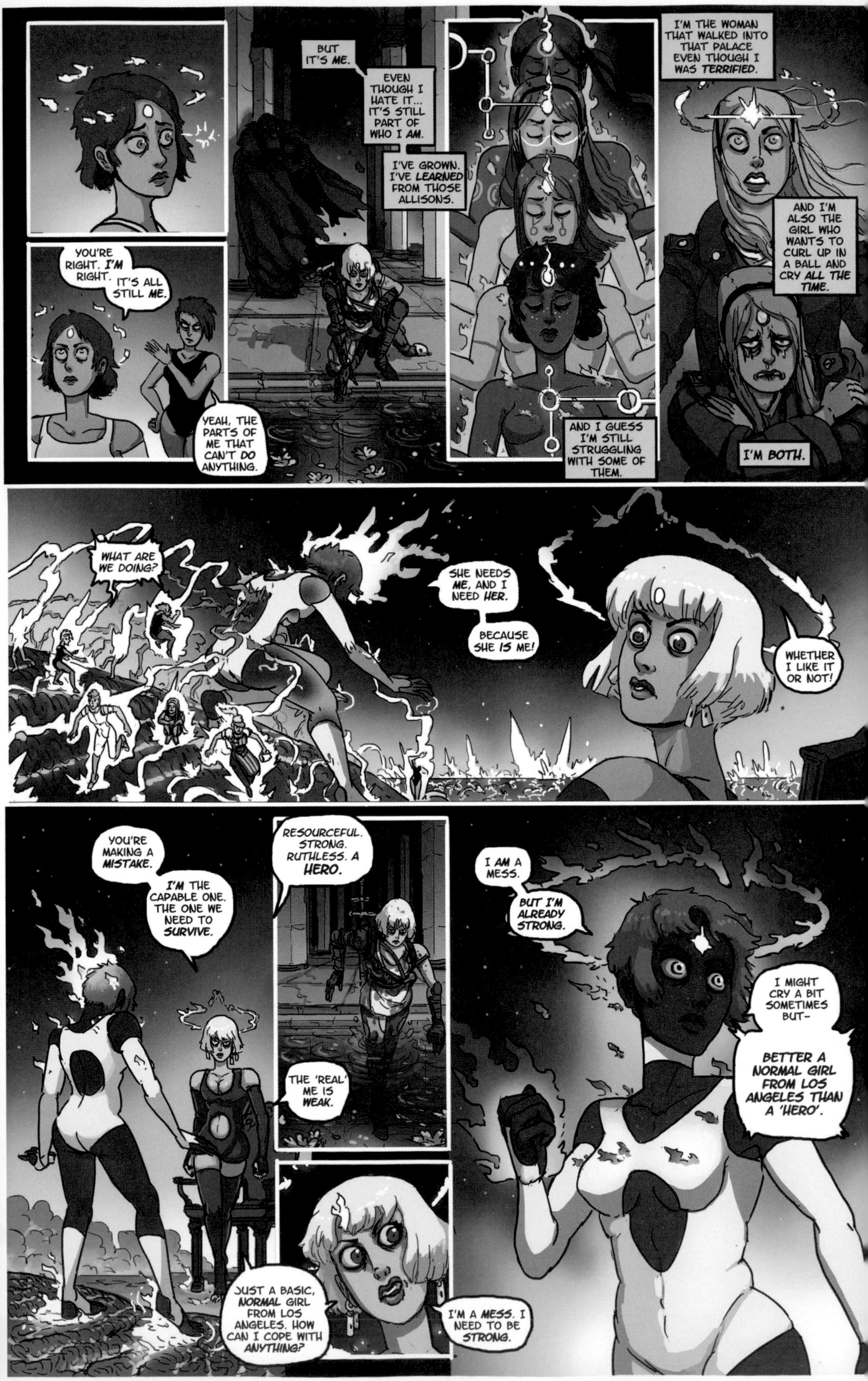

YOU'RE RIGHT. I'M RIGHT.
IT'S ALL STILL ME.
YEAH, THE PARTS OF ME THAT CAN'T DO ANYTHING.
BUT IT'S ME.
EVEN THOUGH I HATE IT... IT'S STILL PART OF WHO I AM.
I'VE GROWN. I'VE LEARNED FROM THOSE ALLISONS.
AND I GUESS I'M STILL STRUGGLING WITH SOME OF THEM.
I'M THE WOMAN THAT WALKED INTO THAT PALACE EVEN THOUGH I WAS TERRIFIED.
AND I'M ALSO THE GIRL WHO WANTS TO CURL UP IN A BALL AND CRY ALL THE TIME.
I'M BOTH.
WHAT ARE WE DOING?
SHE NEEDS ME, AND I NEED HER.
BECAUSE SHE IS ME!
WHETHER I LIKE IT OR NOT!
YOU'RE MAKING A MISTAKE.
I'M THE CAPABLE ONE. THE ONE WE NEED TO SURVIVE.
RESOURCEFUL. STRONG. RUTHLESS. A HERO.
THE 'REAL' ME IS WEAK.
JUST A BASIC, NORMAL GIRL FROM LOS ANGELES. HOW CAN I COPE WITH ANYTHING?
I'M A MESS. I NEED TO BE STRONG.
I AM A MESS.
BUT I'M ALREADY STRONG.
I MIGHT CRY A BIT SOMETIMES BUT–
BETTER A NORMAL GIRL FROM LOS ANGELES THAN A 'HERO'.

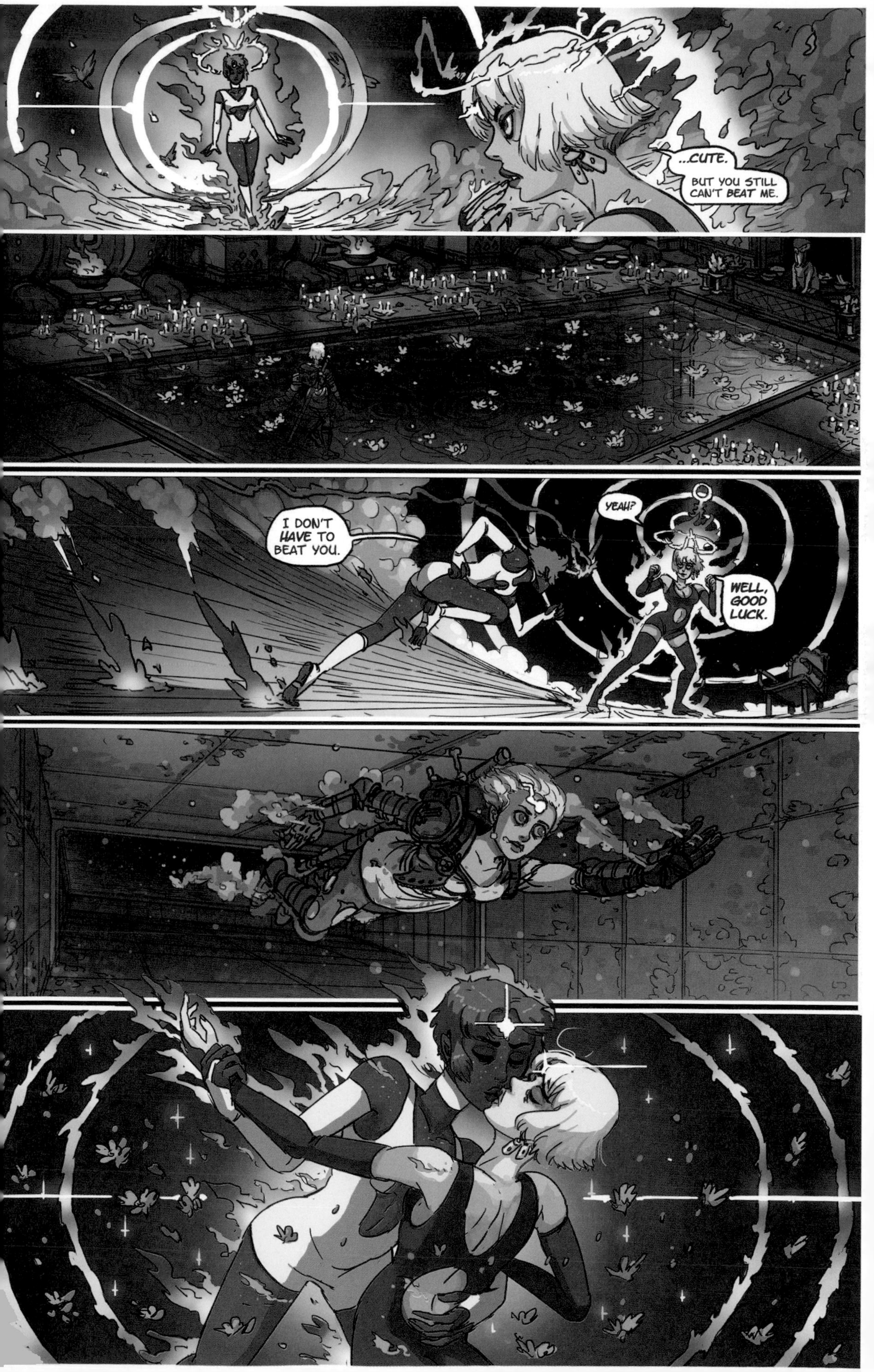

...CUTE.
BUT YOU STILL CAN'T BEAT ME.
I DON'T HAVE TO BEAT YOU.
YEAH?
WELL, GOOD LUCK.

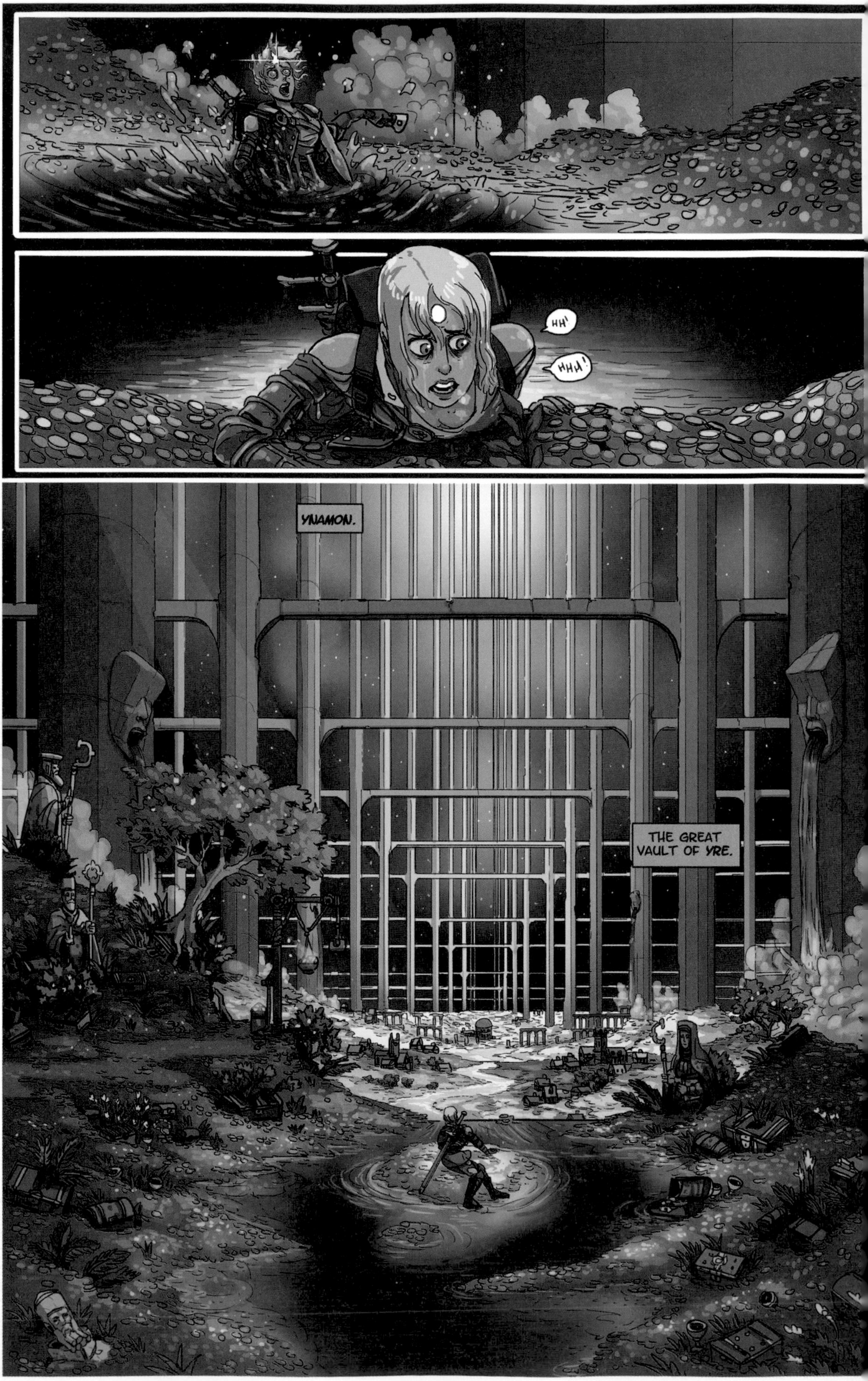
HH'
HHH!
YNAMON.
THE GREAT VAULT OF YRE.

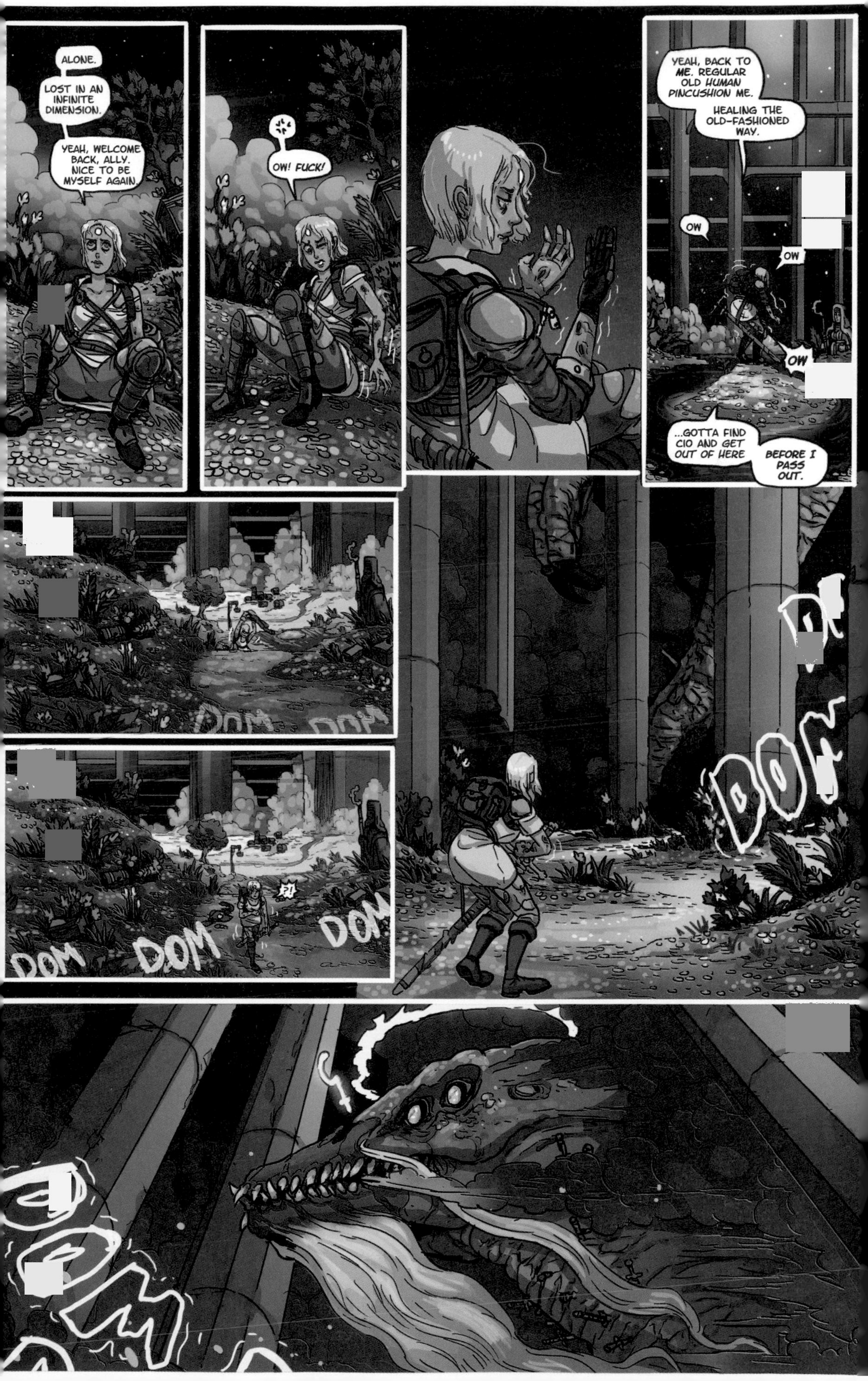
ALONE.
LOST IN AN INFINITE DIMENSION.
YEAH, WELCOME BACK, ALLY. NICE TO BE MYSELF AGAIN.
OW! FUCK!
YEAH, BACK TO ME. REGULAR OLD HUMAN PINCUSHION ME.
HEALING THE OLD-FASHIONED WAY.
OW
OW
OW
...GOTTA FIND CIO AND GET OUT OF HERE
BEFORE I PASS OUT.
DOM
DOM DOM DOM

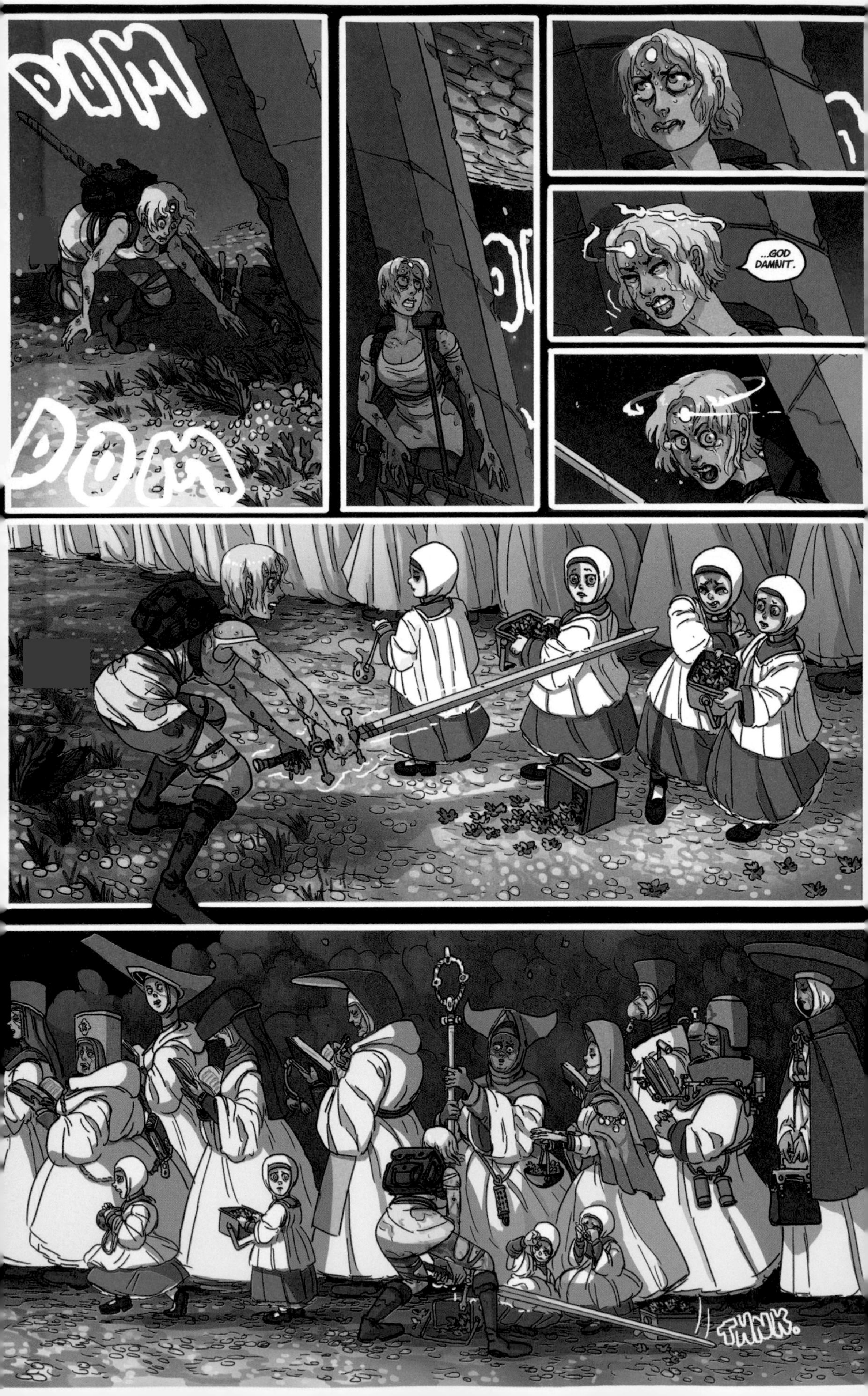
DOM
DOM
...GOD DAMNIT.
THNK.

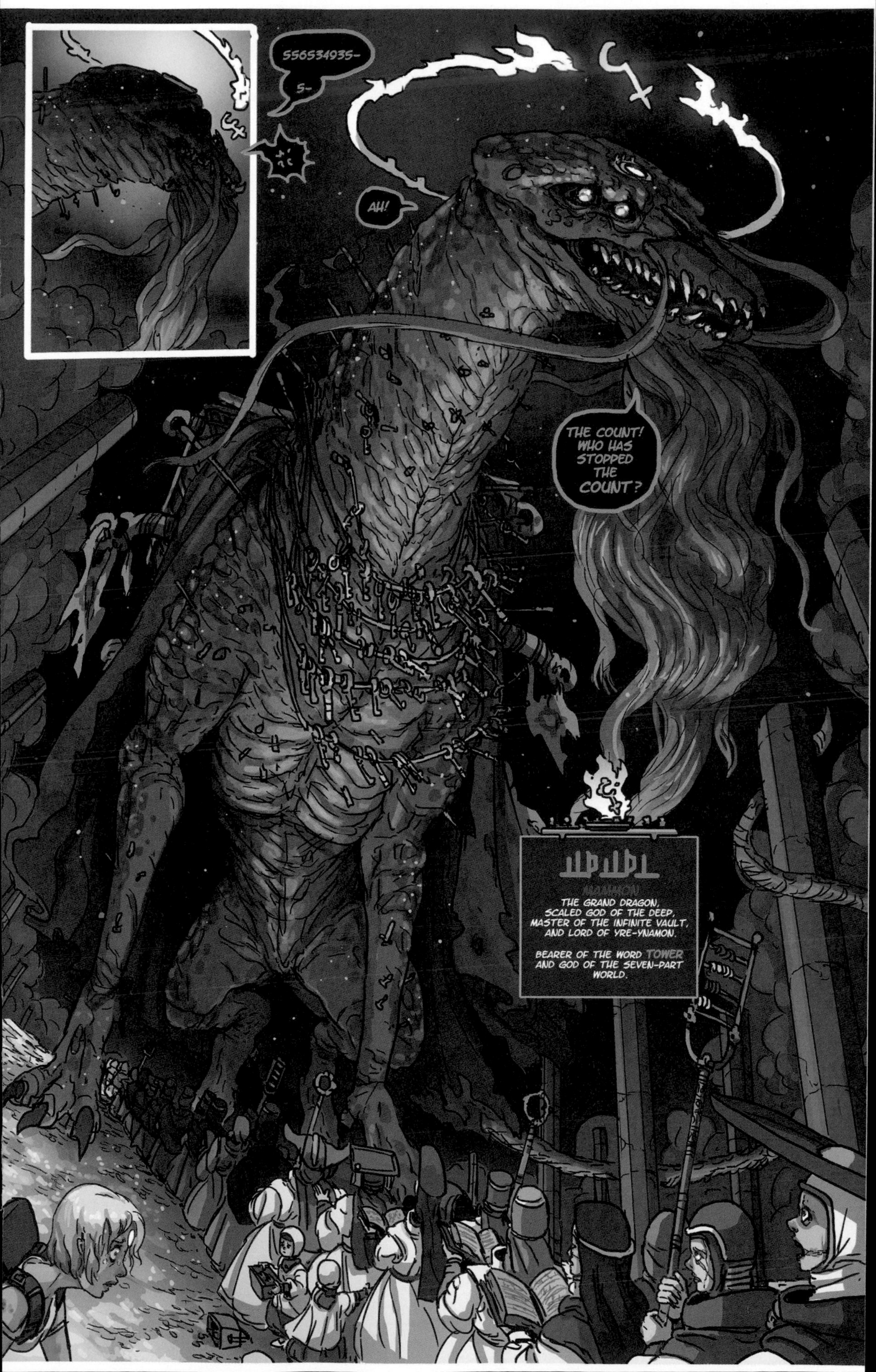
SS6S34935-
S-
AH!
THE COUNT! WHO HAS STOPPED THE COUNT?
MAMMON
THE GRAND DRAGON, SCALED GOD OF THE DEEP, MASTER OF THE INFINITE VAULT, AND LORD OF YRE-YNAMON.
BEARER OF THE WORD TOWER AND GOD OF THE SEVEN-PART WORLD.

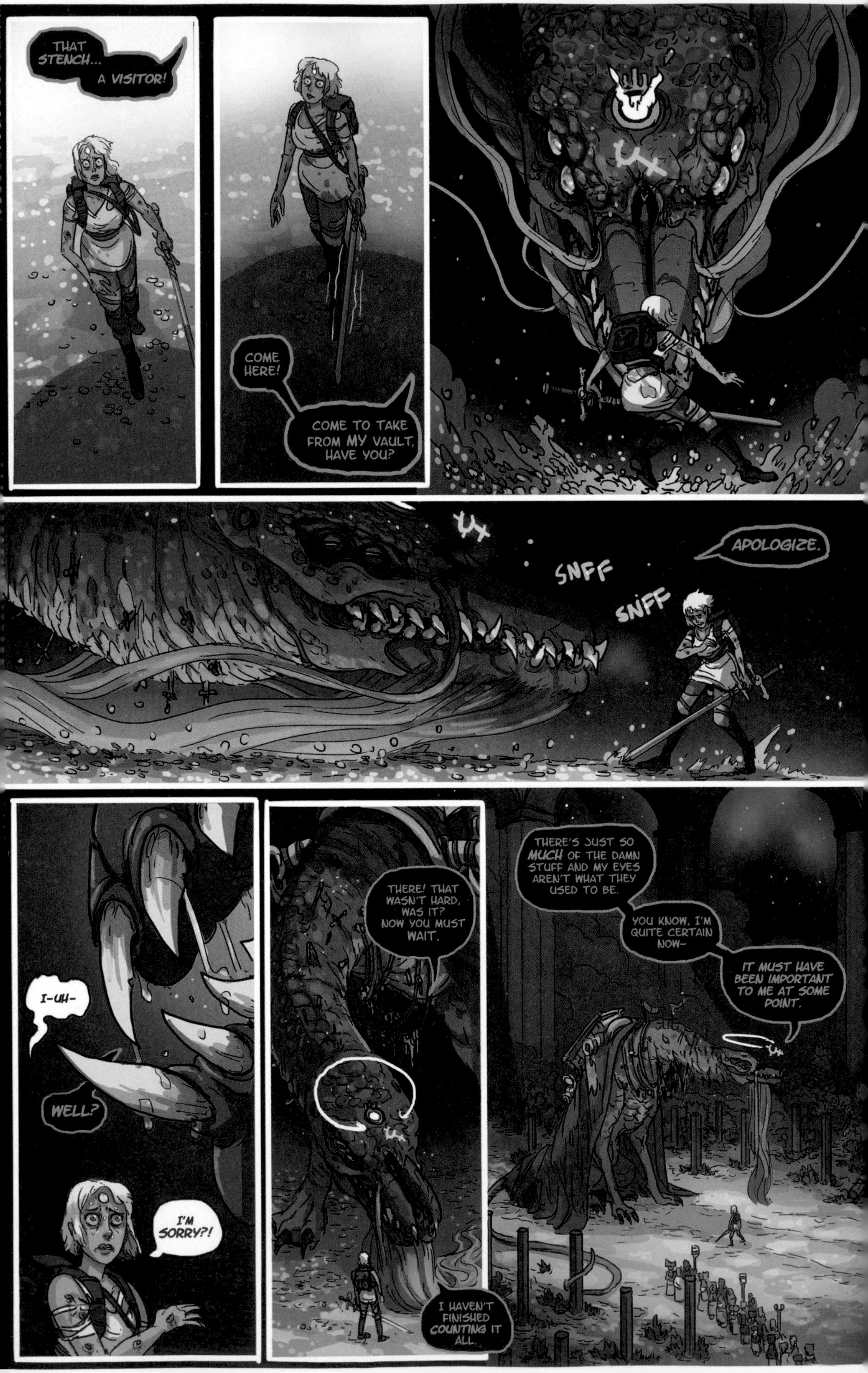
THAT STENCH... A VISITOR!
COME HERE!
COME TO TAKE FROM MY VAULT, HAVE YOU?
SNFF
SNFF
APOLOGIZE.
I-UH-
WELL?
I'M SORRY?!
THERE! THAT WASN'T HARD, WAS IT? NOW YOU MUST WAIT.
I HAVEN'T FINISHED COUNTING IT ALL.
THERE'S JUST SO MUCH OF THE DAMN STUFF AND MY EYES AREN'T WHAT THEY USED TO BE.
YOU KNOW, I'M QUITE CERTAIN NOW-
IT MUST HAVE BEEN IMPORTANT TO ME AT SOME POINT.

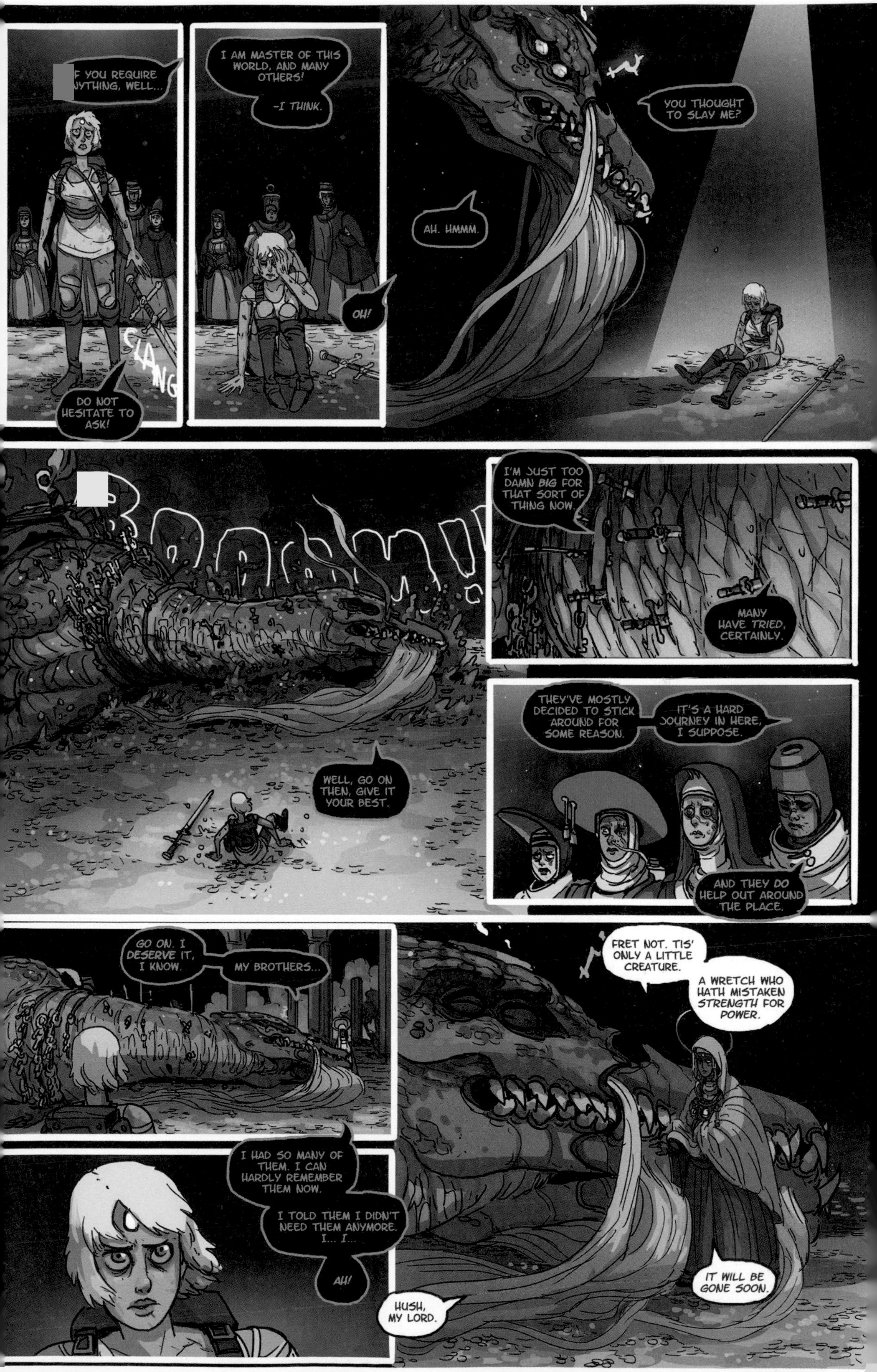

F YOU REQUIRE NYTHING, WELL...
CLANG
DO NOT HESITATE TO ASK!
I AM MASTER OF THIS WORLD, AND MANY OTHERS!
-I THINK.
OH!
AH. HMMM.
YOU THOUGHT TO SLAY ME?
BOOOOM!!
I'M JUST TOO DAMN BIG FOR THAT SORT OF THING NOW.
MANY HAVE TRIED, CERTAINLY.
WELL, GO ON THEN, GIVE IT YOUR BEST.
THEY'VE MOSTLY DECIDED TO STICK AROUND FOR SOME REASON.
IT'S A HARD JOURNEY IN HERE, I SUPPOSE.
AND THEY DO HELP OUT AROUND THE PLACE.
GO ON. I DESERVE IT, I KNOW.
MY BROTHERS...
I HAD SO MANY OF THEM. I CAN HARDLY REMEMBER THEM NOW.
I TOLD THEM I DIDN'T NEED THEM ANYMORE. I... I...
AH!
FRET NOT. TIS' ONLY A LITTLE CREATURE.
A WRETCH WHO HATH MISTAKEN STRENGTH FOR POWER.
HUSH, MY LORD.
IT WILL BE GONE SOON.

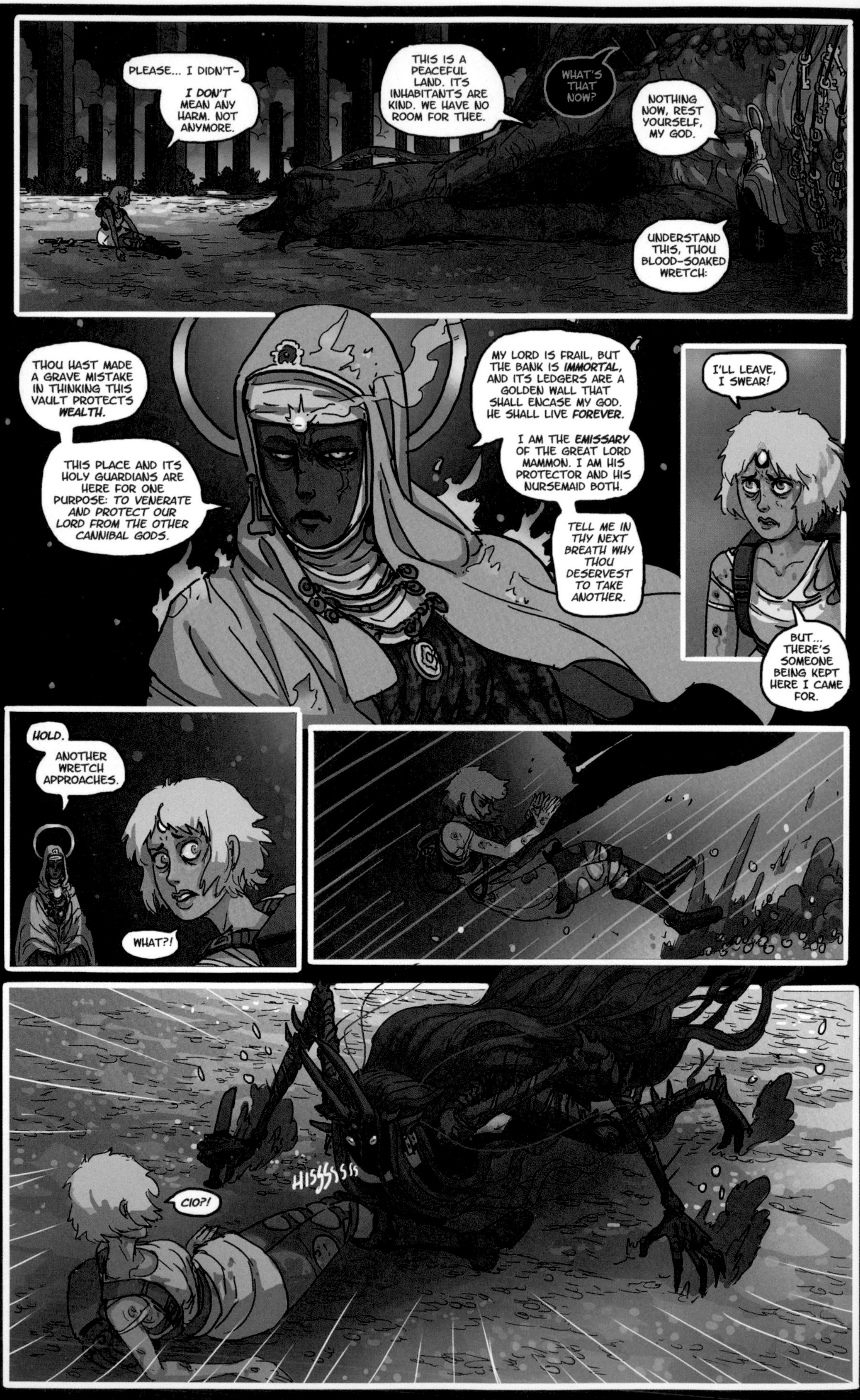

PLEASE... I DIDN'T-
I DON'T MEAN ANY HARM. NOT ANYMORE.
THIS IS A PEACEFUL LAND. ITS INHABITANTS ARE KIND. WE HAVE NO ROOM FOR THEE.
WHAT'S THAT NOW?
NOTHING NOW, REST YOURSELF, MY GOD.
UNDERSTAND THIS, THOU BLOOD-SOAKED WRETCH:
THOU HAST MADE A GRAVE MISTAKE IN THINKING THIS VAULT PROTECTS WEALTH.
THIS PLACE AND ITS HOLY GUARDIANS ARE HERE FOR ONE PURPOSE: TO VENERATE AND PROTECT OUR LORD FROM THE OTHER CANNIBAL GODS.
MY LORD IS FRAIL, BUT THE BANK IS IMMORTAL, AND ITS LEDGERS ARE A GOLDEN WALL THAT SHALL ENCASE MY GOD. HE SHALL LIVE FOREVER.
I AM THE EMISSARY OF THE GREAT LORD MAMMON. I AM HIS PROTECTOR AND HIS NURSEMAID BOTH.
TELL ME IN THY NEXT BREATH WHY THOU DESERVEST TO TAKE ANOTHER.
I'LL LEAVE, I SWEAR!
BUT... THERE'S SOMEONE BEING KEPT HERE I CAME FOR.
HOLD.
ANOTHER WRETCH APPROACHES.
WHAT?!
HISSSSSS
CIO?!

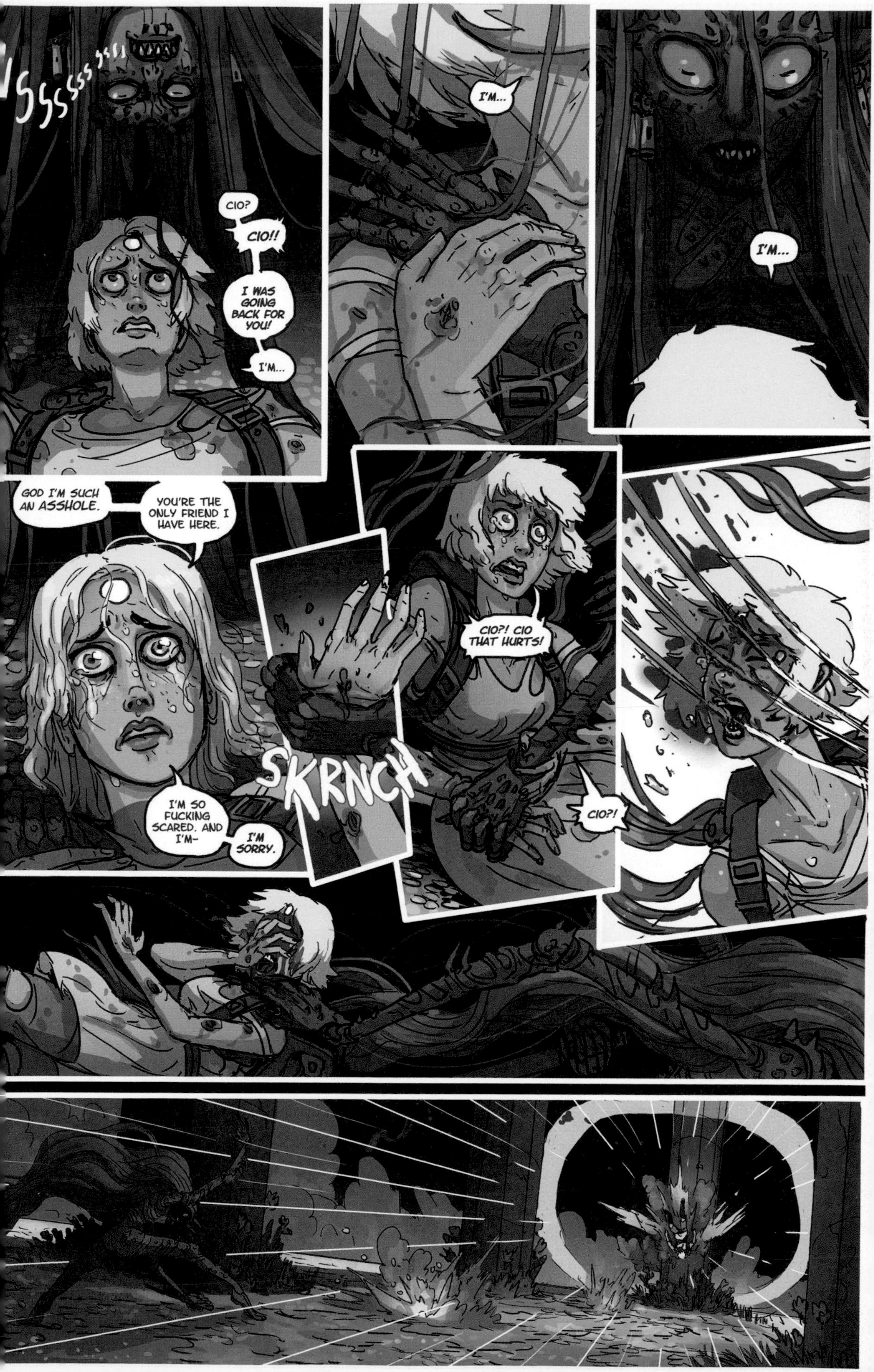

SSSSSSSSSS
CIO?
CIO!!
I WAS GOING BACK FOR YOU!
I'M...
I'M...
I'M...
GOD I'M SUCH AN ASSHOLE.
YOU'RE THE ONLY FRIEND I HAVE HERE.
I'M SO FUCKING SCARED. AND I'M-
I'M SORRY.
SKRNCH
CIO?! CIO THAT HURTS!
CIO?!

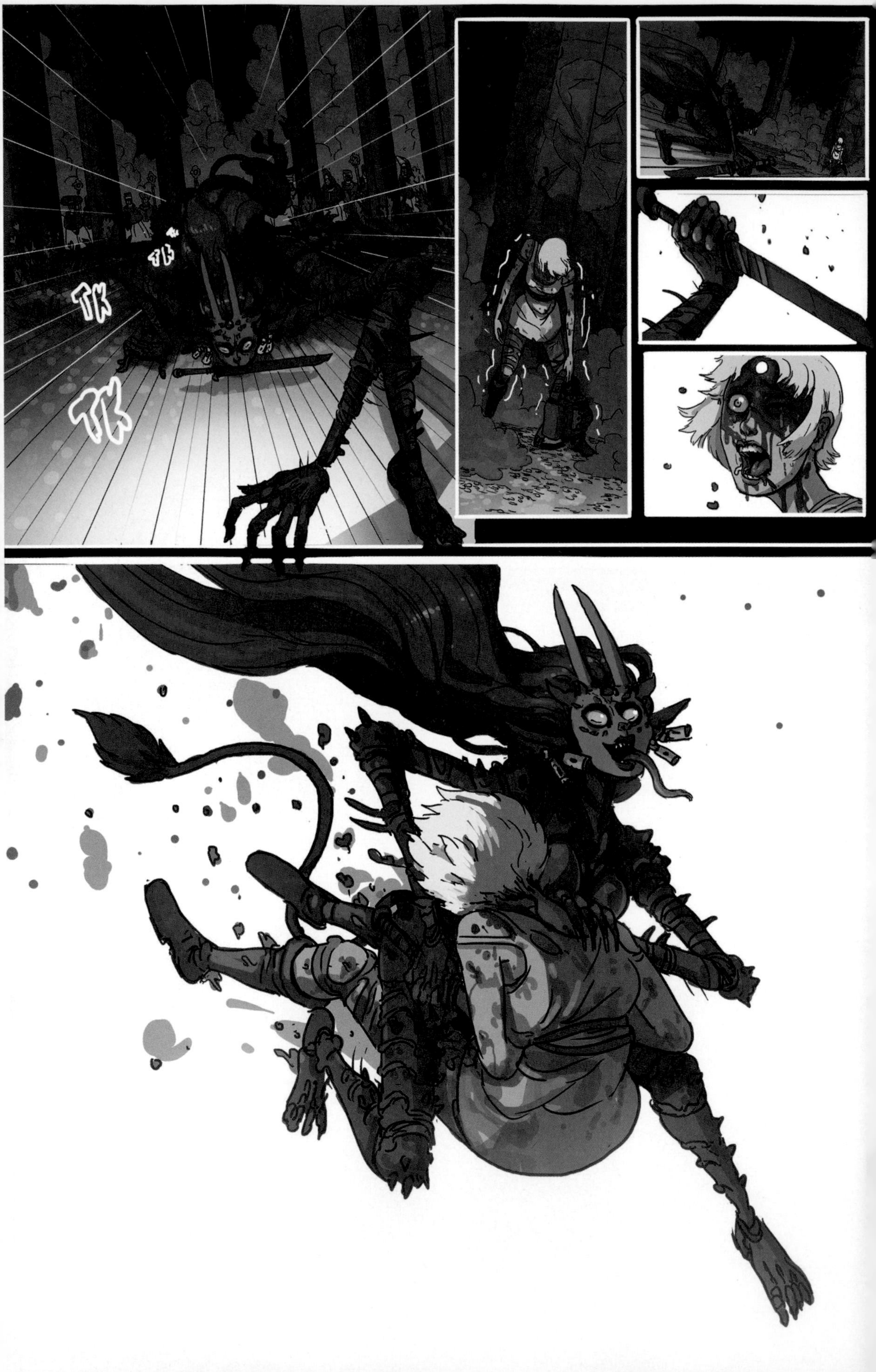
TK
TK
TK
TK

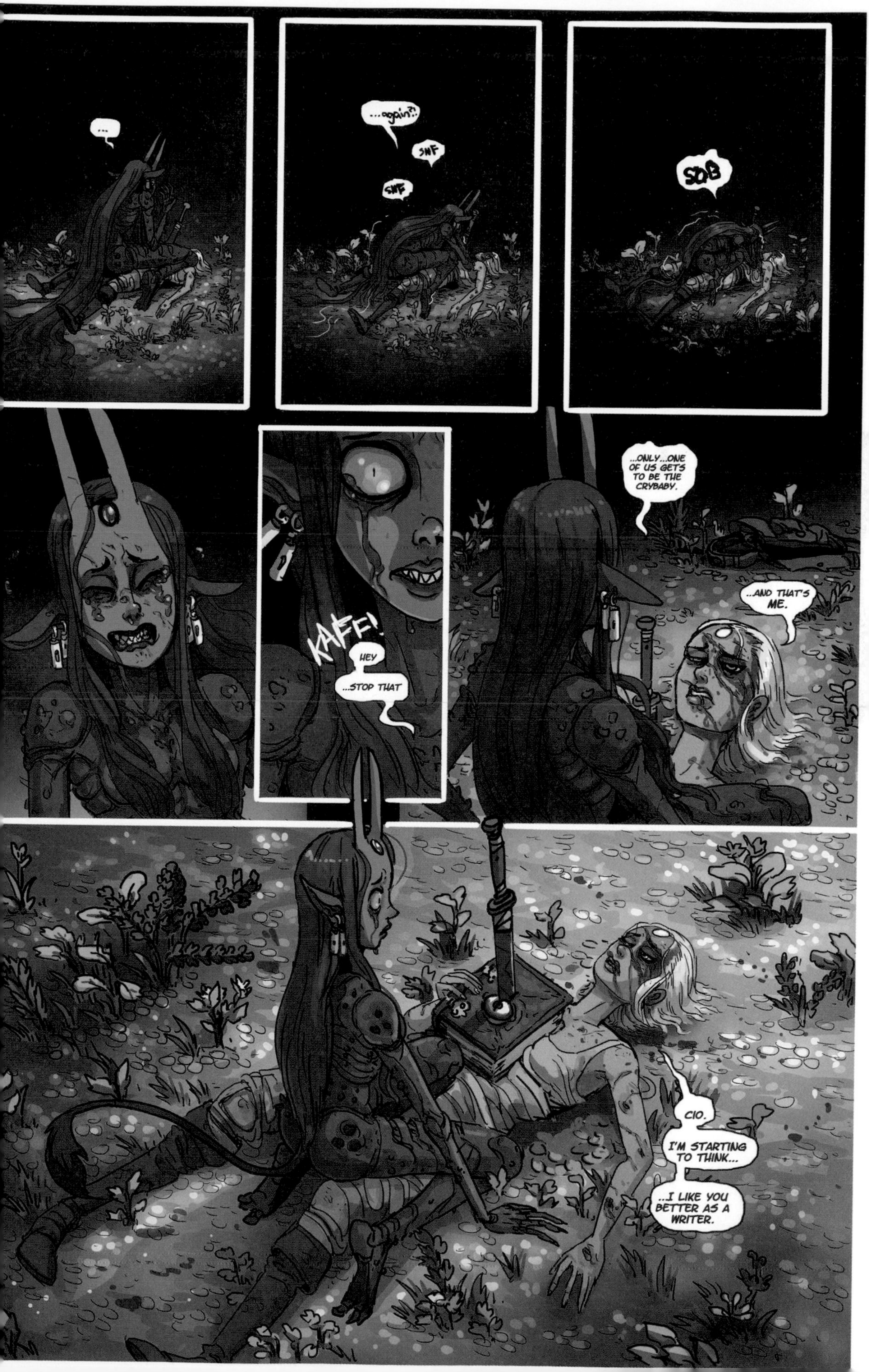
...
...again?!
SNF
SNF
SOB
KAFF!
HEY
...STOP THAT
...ONLY...ONE OF US GETS TO BE THE CRYBABY.
...AND THAT'S ME.
CIO.
I'M STARTING TO THINK...
...I LIKE YOU BETTER AS A WRITER.

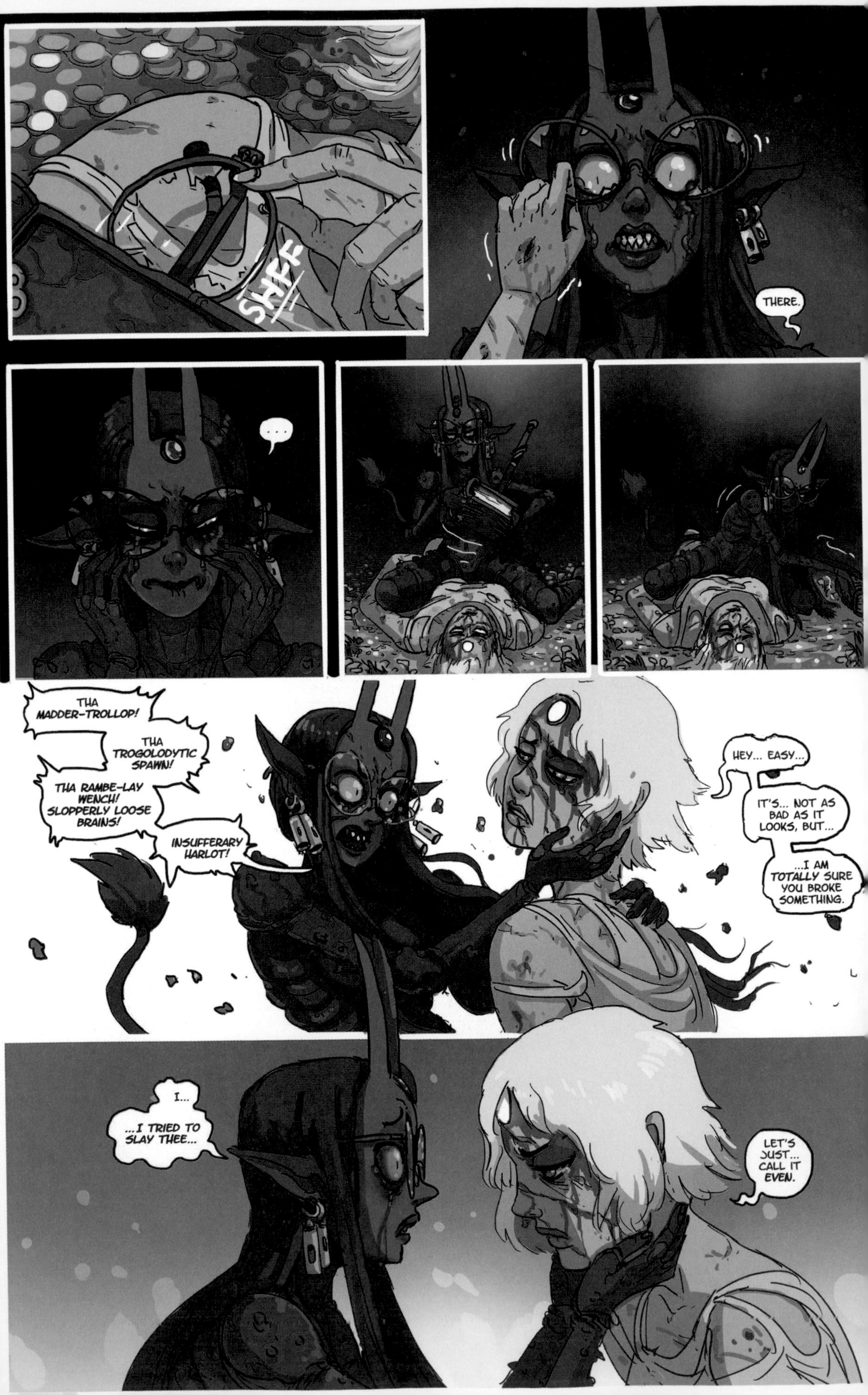
SHFF
THERE.
...
THA MADDER-TROLLOP!
THA TROGOLODYTIC SPAWN!
THA RAMBE-LAY WENCH! SLOPPERLY LOOSE BRAINS!
INSUFFERARY HARLOT!
HEY... EASY...
IT'S... NOT AS BAD AS IT LOOKS, BUT...
...I AM TOTALLY SURE YOU BROKE SOMETHING.
I...
...I TRIED TO SLAY THEE...
LET'S JUST... CALL IT EVEN.

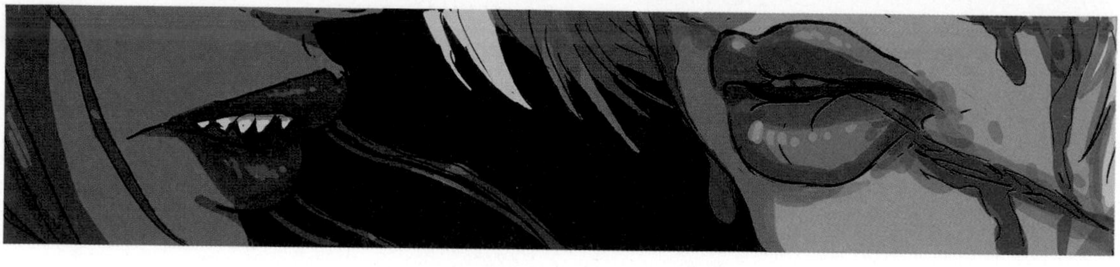
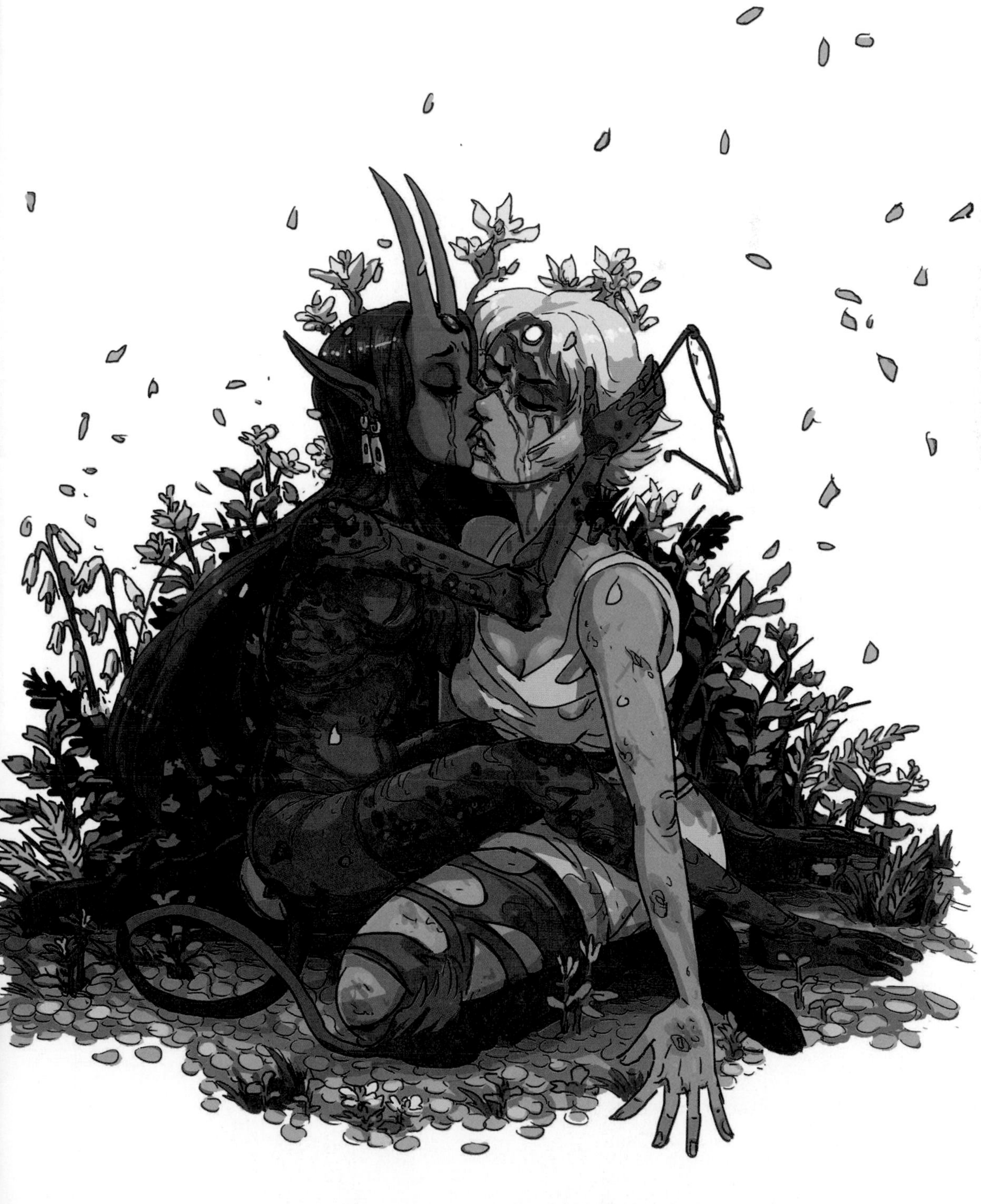

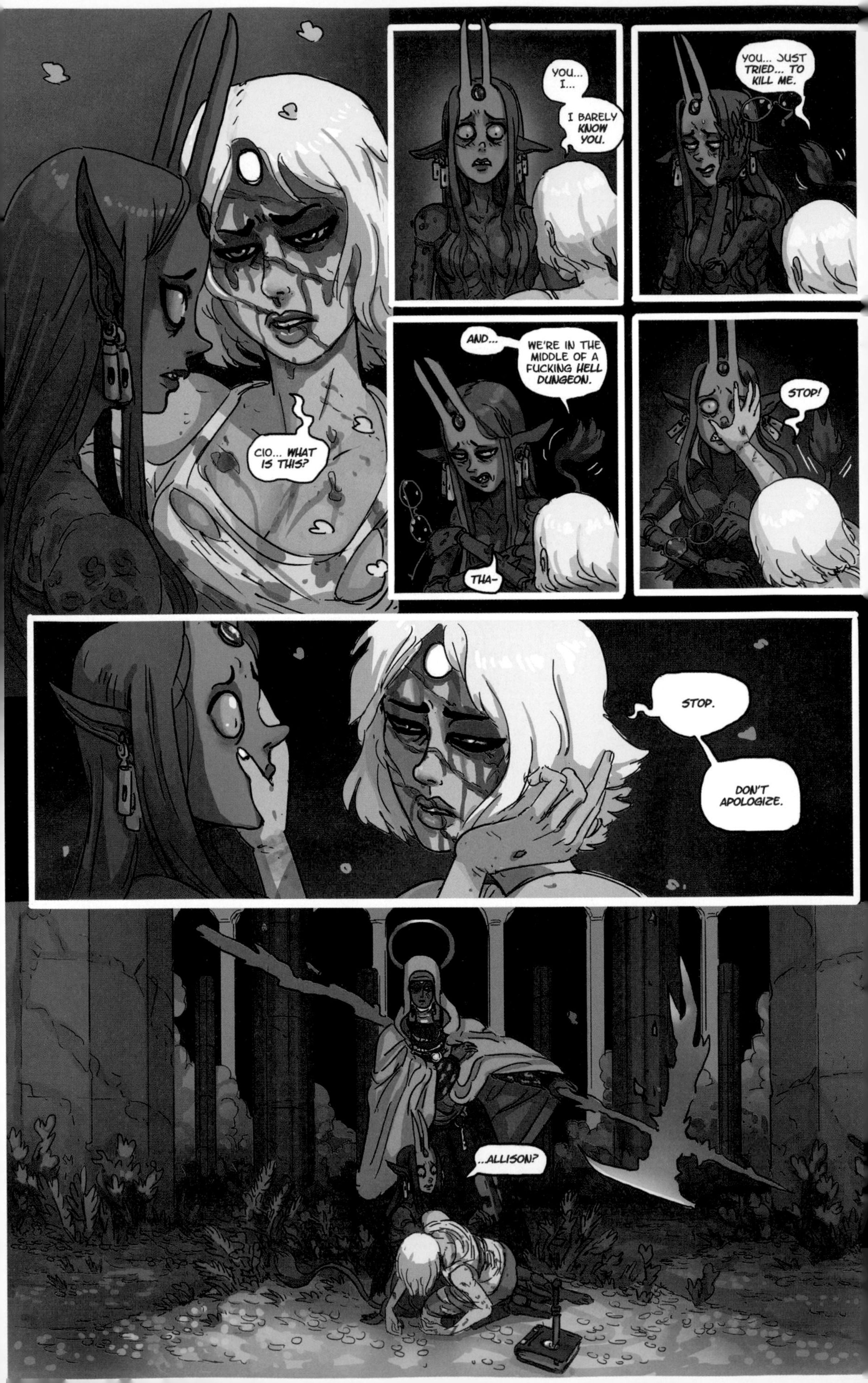
CIO... WHAT IS THIS?
YOU... I...
I BARELY KNOW YOU.
YOU... JUST TRIED... TO KILL ME.
AND...
WE'RE IN THE MIDDLE OF A FUCKING HELL DUNGEON.
THA-
STOP!
STOP.
DON'T APOLOGIZE.
...ALLISON?

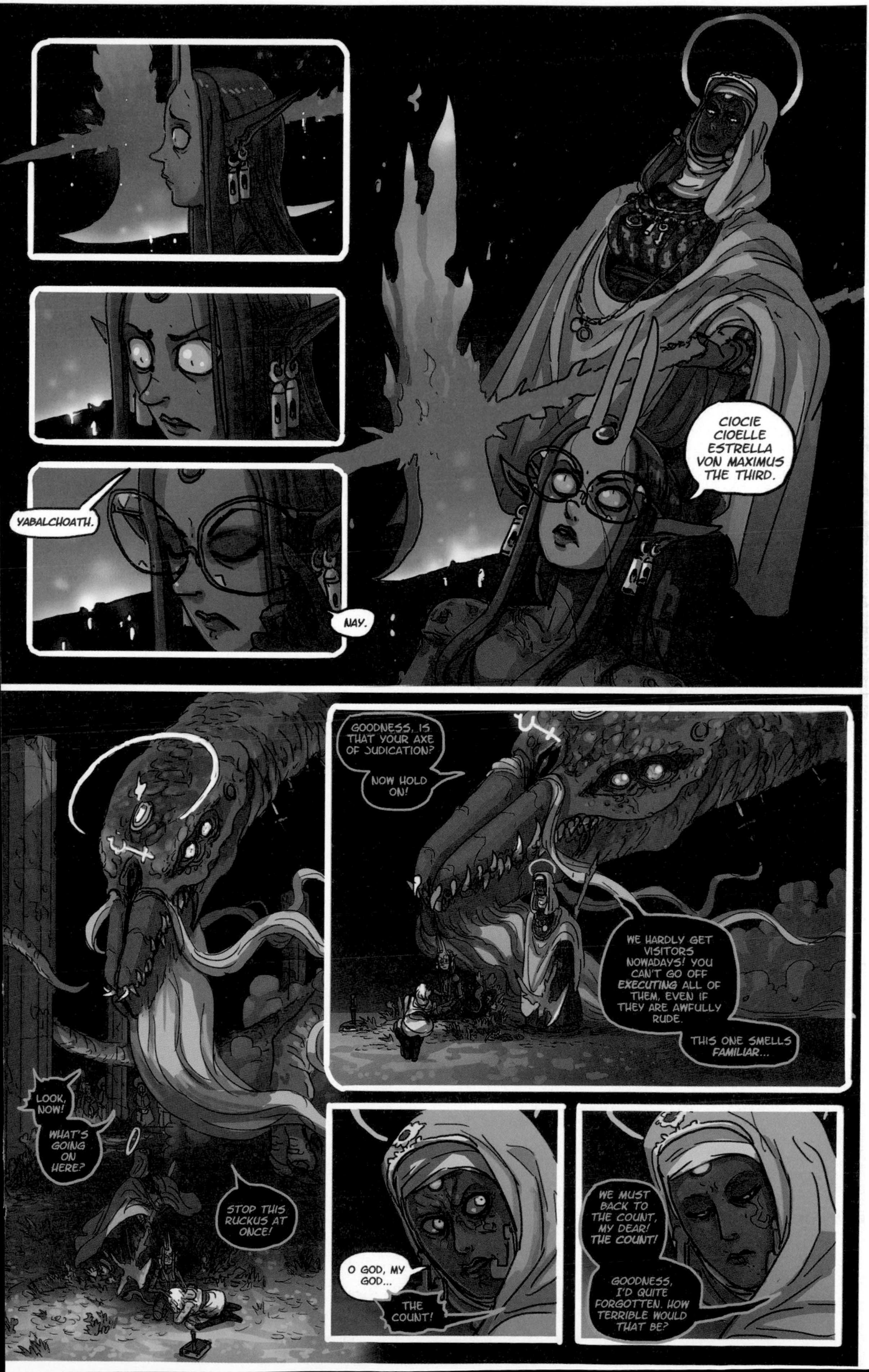
YABALCHOATH.
NAY.
CIOCIE CIOELLE ESTRELLA VON MAXIMUS THE THIRD.
GOODNESS, IS THAT YOUR AXE OF JUDICATION?
NOW HOLD ON!
WE HARDLY GET VISITORS NOWADAYS! YOU CAN'T GO OFF EXECUTING ALL OF THEM, EVEN IF THEY ARE AWFULLY RUDE.
THIS ONE SMELLS FAMILIAR...
LOOK, NOW!
WHAT'S GOING ON HERE?
STOP THIS RUCKUS AT ONCE!
O GOD, MY GOD...
THE COUNT!
WE MUST BACK TO THE COUNT, MY DEAR! THE COUNT!
GOODNESS, I'D QUITE FORGOTTEN. HOW TERRIBLE WOULD THAT BE?

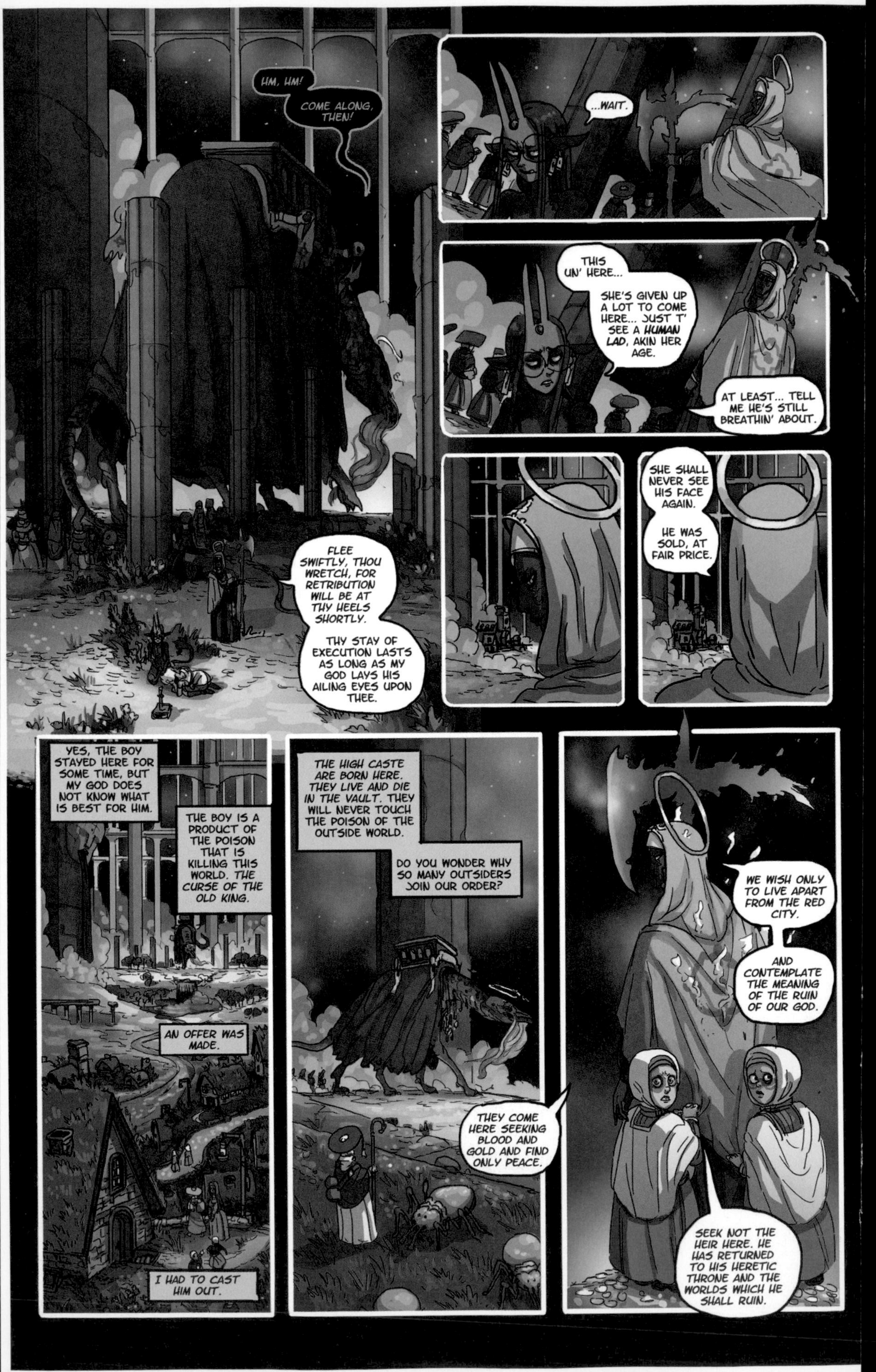
HM, HM!
COME ALONG, THEN!
FLEE SWIFTLY, THOU WRETCH, FOR RETRIBUTION WILL BE AT THY HEELS SHORTLY.
THY STAY OF EXECUTION LASTS AS LONG AS MY GOD LAYS HIS AILING EYES UPON THEE.
...WAIT.
THIS UN' HERE...
SHE'S GIVEN UP A LOT TO COME HERE... JUST T' SEE A HUMAN LAD, AKIN HER AGE.
AT LEAST... TELL ME HE'S STILL BREATHIN' ABOUT.
SHE SHALL NEVER SEE HIS FACE AGAIN.
HE WAS SOLD, AT FAIR PRICE.
YES, THE BOY STAYED HERE FOR SOME TIME, BUT MY GOD DOES NOT KNOW WHAT IS BEST FOR HIM.
THE BOY IS A PRODUCT OF THE POISON THAT IS KILLING THIS WORLD. THE CURSE OF THE OLD KING.
AN OFFER WAS MADE.
I HAD TO CAST HIM OUT.
THE HIGH CASTE ARE BORN HERE. THEY LIVE AND DIE IN THE VAULT. THEY WILL NEVER TOUCH THE POISON OF THE OUTSIDE WORLD.
DO YOU WONDER WHY SO MANY OUTSIDERS JOIN OUR ORDER?
THEY COME HERE SEEKING BLOOD AND GOLD AND FIND ONLY PEACE.
WE WISH ONLY TO LIVE APART FROM THE RED CITY.
AND CONTEMPLATE THE MEANING OF THE RUIN OF OUR GOD.
SEEK NOT THE HEIR HERE. HE HAS RETURNED TO HIS HERETIC THRONE AND THE WORLDS WHICH HE SHALL RUIN.

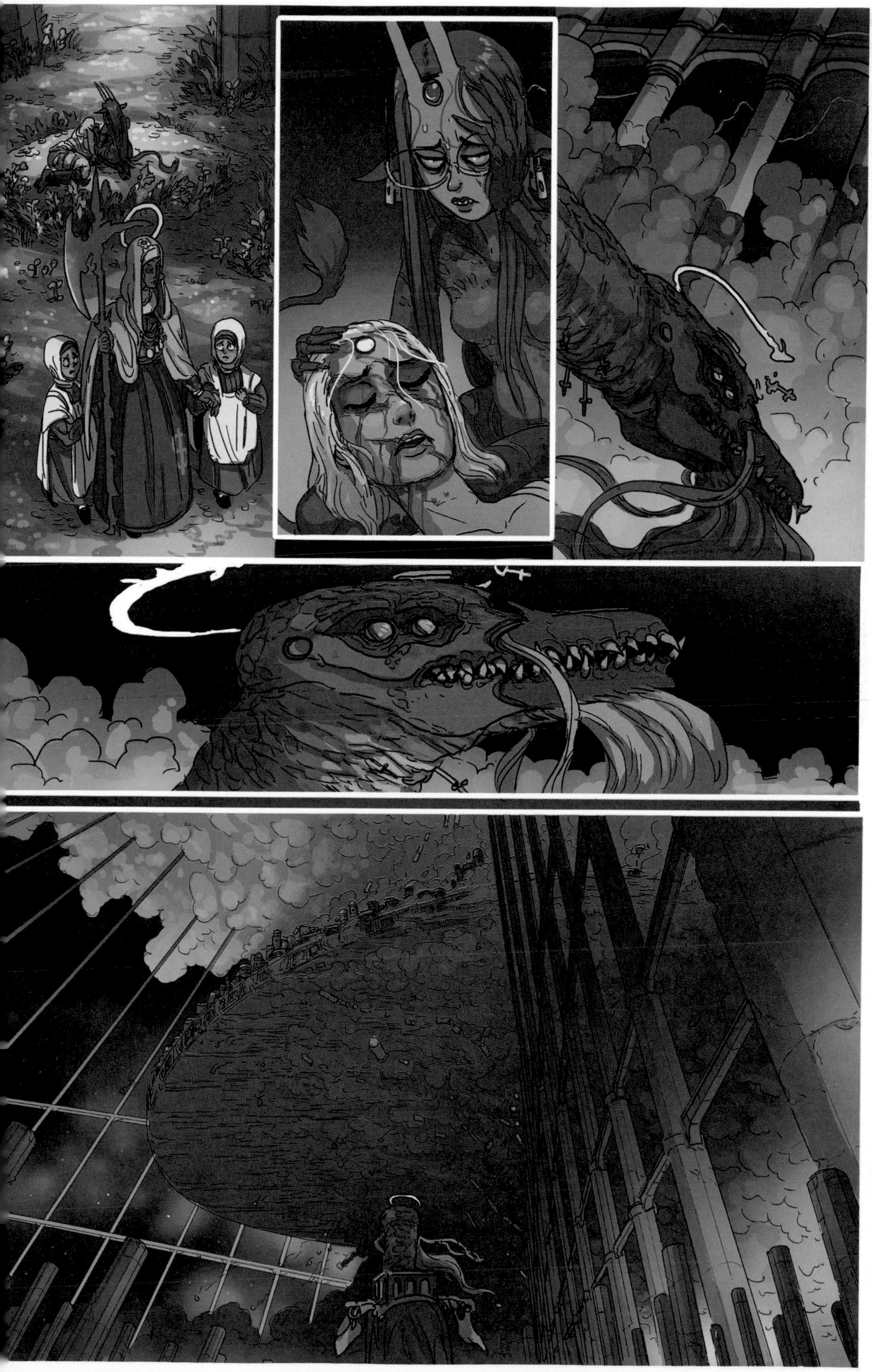

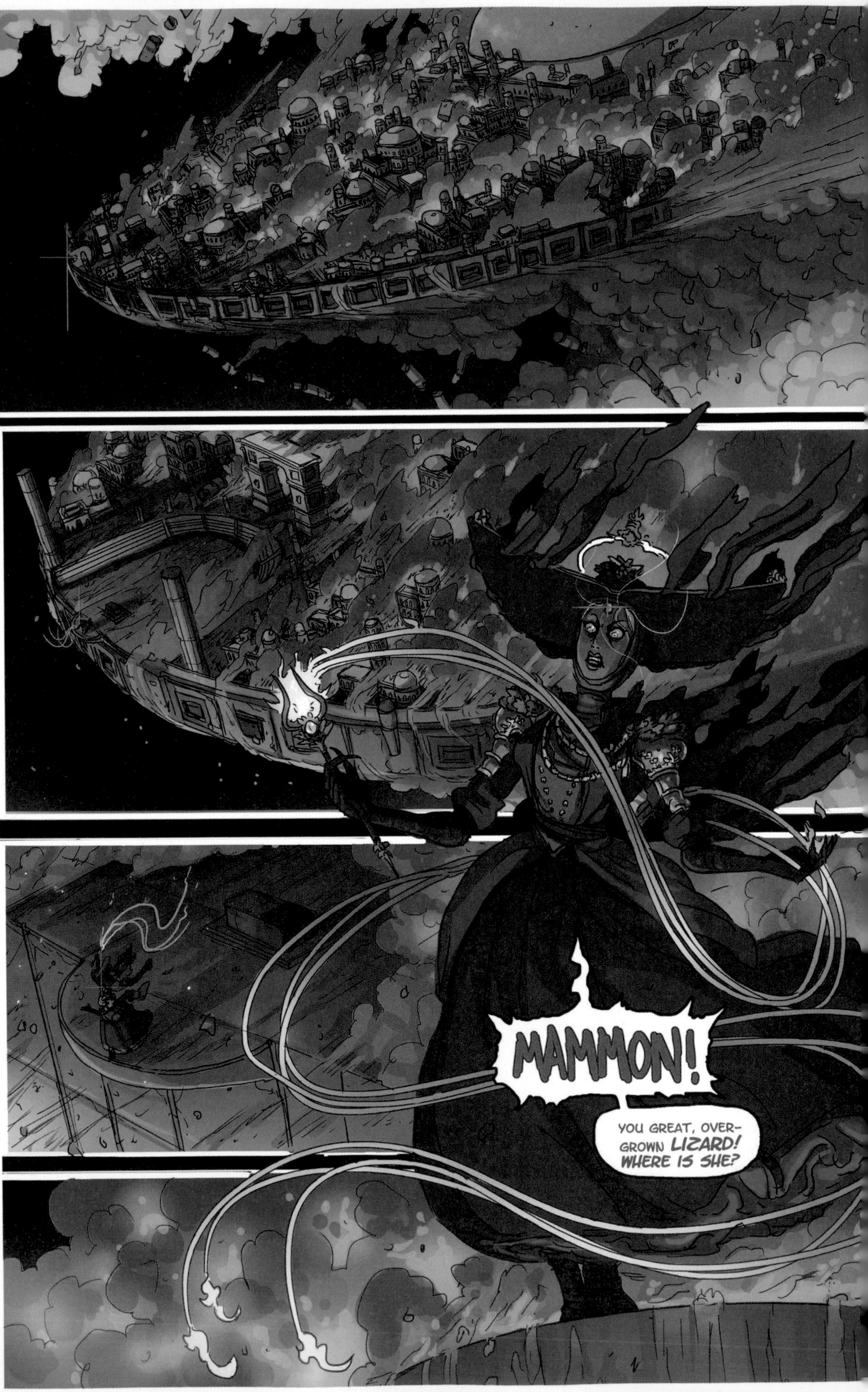
MAMMON!
YOU GREAT, OVER-GROWN LIZARD! WHERE IS SHE?

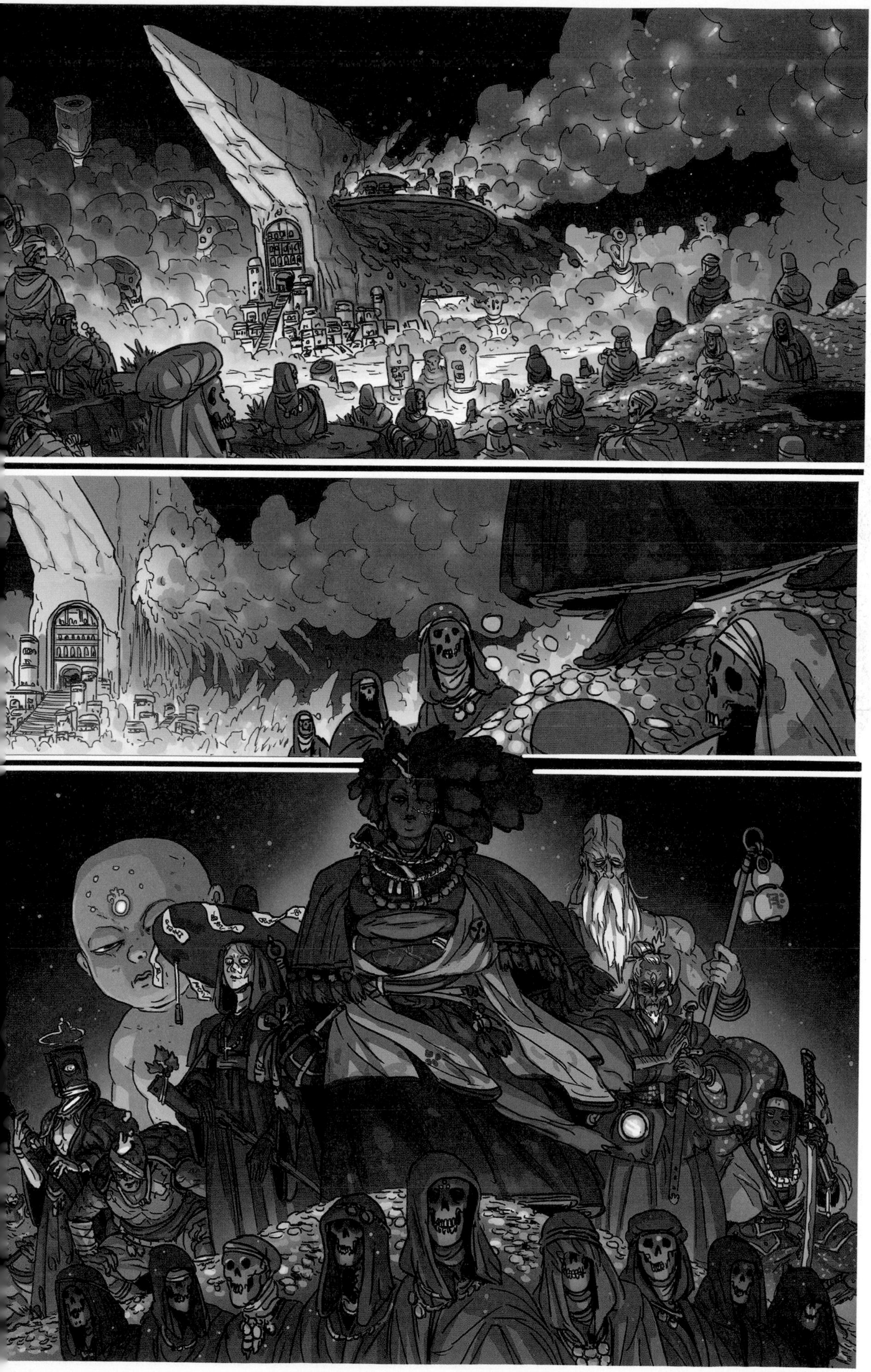

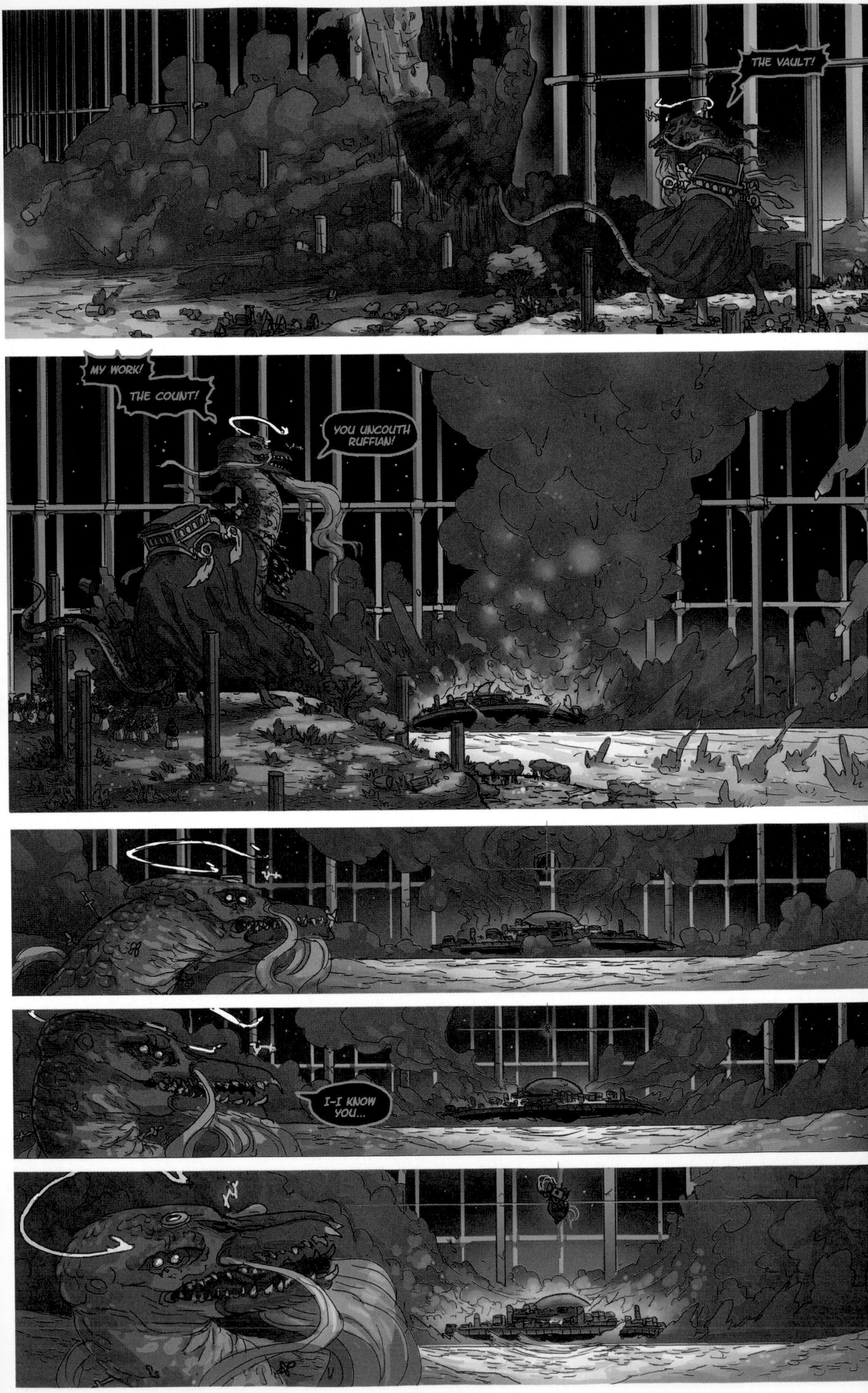
THE VAULT!
MY WORK!
THE COUNT!
YOU UNCOUTH RUFFIAN!
I-I KNOW YOU...

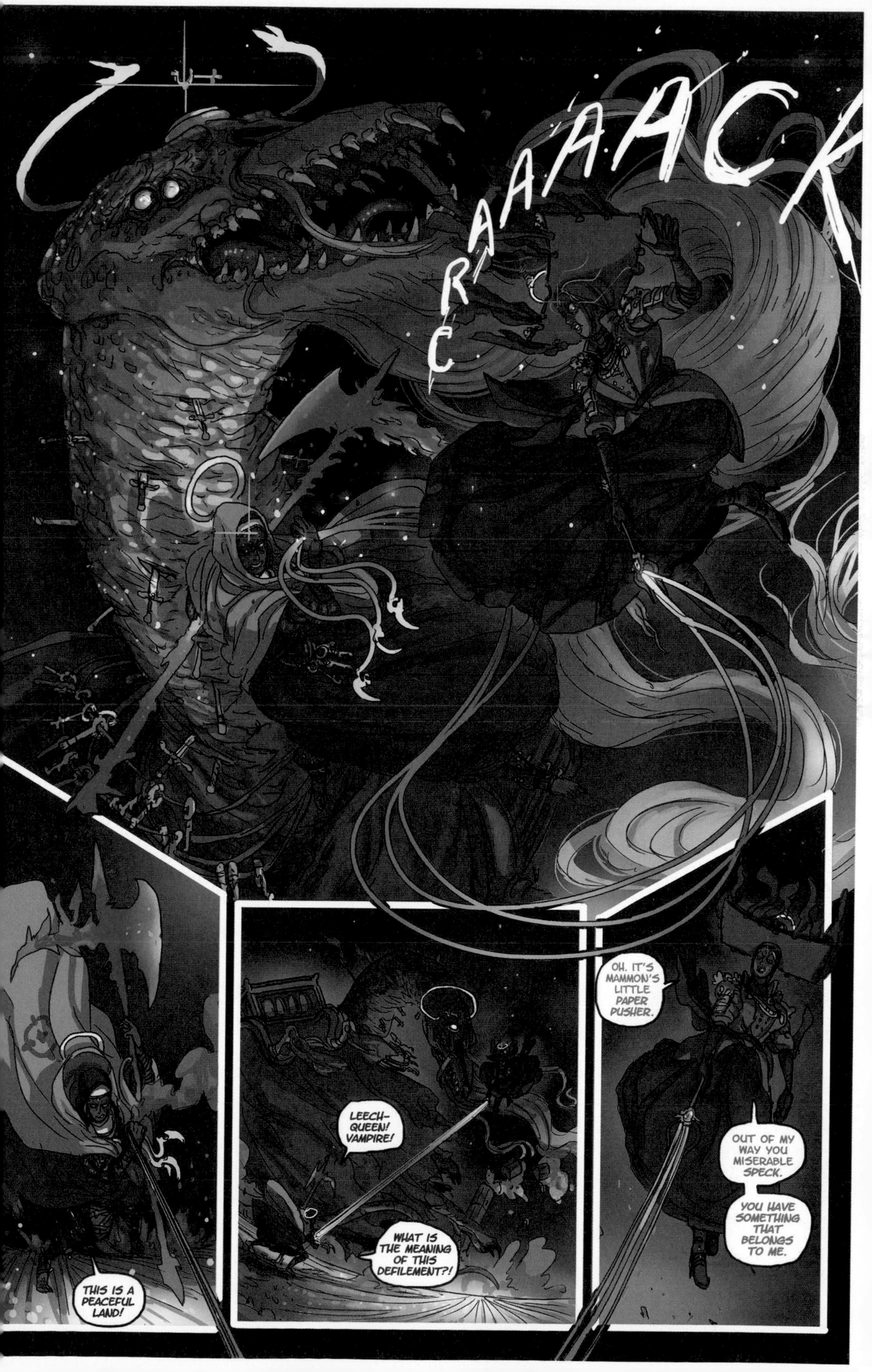
CRAAAAACK
THIS IS A PEACEFUL LAND!
LEECH-QUEEN! VAMPIRE!
WHAT IS THE MEANING OF THIS DEFILEMENT?!
OH. IT'S MAMMON'S LITTLE PAPER PUSHER.
OUT OF MY WAY YOU MISERABLE SPECK.
YOU HAVE SOMETHING THAT BELONGS TO ME.

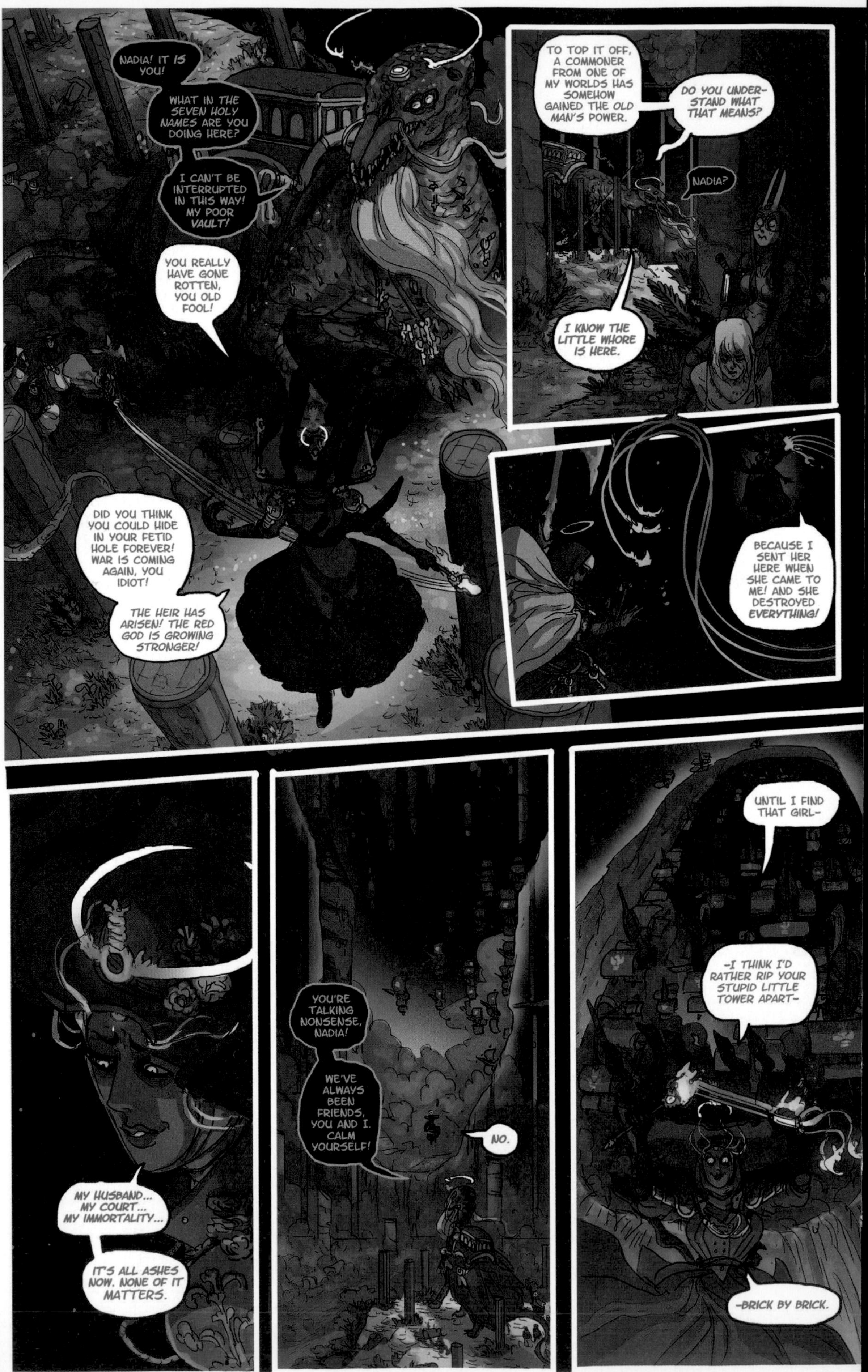
NADIA! IT IS YOU!
WHAT IN THE SEVEN HOLY NAMES ARE YOU DOING HERE?
I CAN'T BE INTERRUPTED IN THIS WAY! MY POOR VAULT!
YOU REALLY HAVE GONE ROTTEN, YOU OLD FOOL!
DID YOU THINK YOU COULD HIDE IN YOUR FETID HOLE FOREVER! WAR IS COMING AGAIN, YOU IDIOT!
THE HEIR HAS ARISEN! THE RED GOD IS GROWING STRONGER!
TO TOP IT OFF, A COMMONER FROM ONE OF MY WORLDS HAS SOMEHOW GAINED THE OLD MAN'S POWER.
DO YOU UNDERSTAND WHAT THAT MEANS?
NADIA?
I KNOW THE LITTLE WHORE IS HERE.
BECAUSE I SENT HER HERE WHEN SHE CAME TO ME! AND SHE DESTROYED EVERYTHING!
MY HUSBAND... MY COURT... MY IMMORTALITY...
IT'S ALL ASHES NOW. NONE OF IT MATTERS.
YOU'RE TALKING NONSENSE, NADIA!
WE'VE ALWAYS BEEN FRIENDS, YOU AND I. CALM YOURSELF!
NO.
UNTIL I FIND THAT GIRL-
-I THINK I'D RATHER RIP YOUR STUPID LITTLE TOWER APART-
-BRICK BY BRICK.

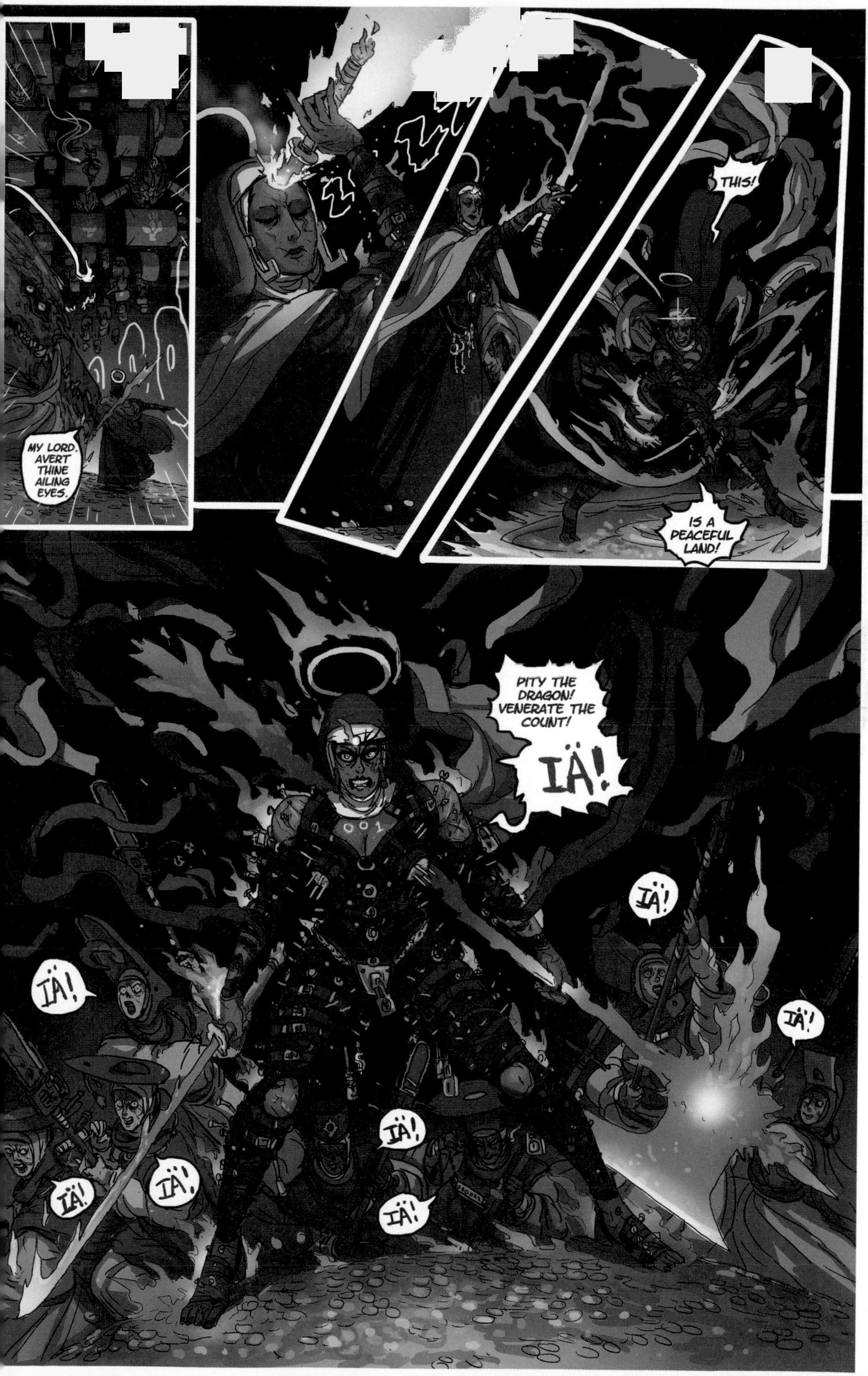
MY LORD. AVERT THINE AILING EYES.
THIS!
IS A PEACEFUL LAND!
PITY THE DRAGON! VENERATE THE COUNT!
IÄ!
IÄ!
IÄ!
IÄ!
IÄ!
IÄ!
IÄ!
IÄ!

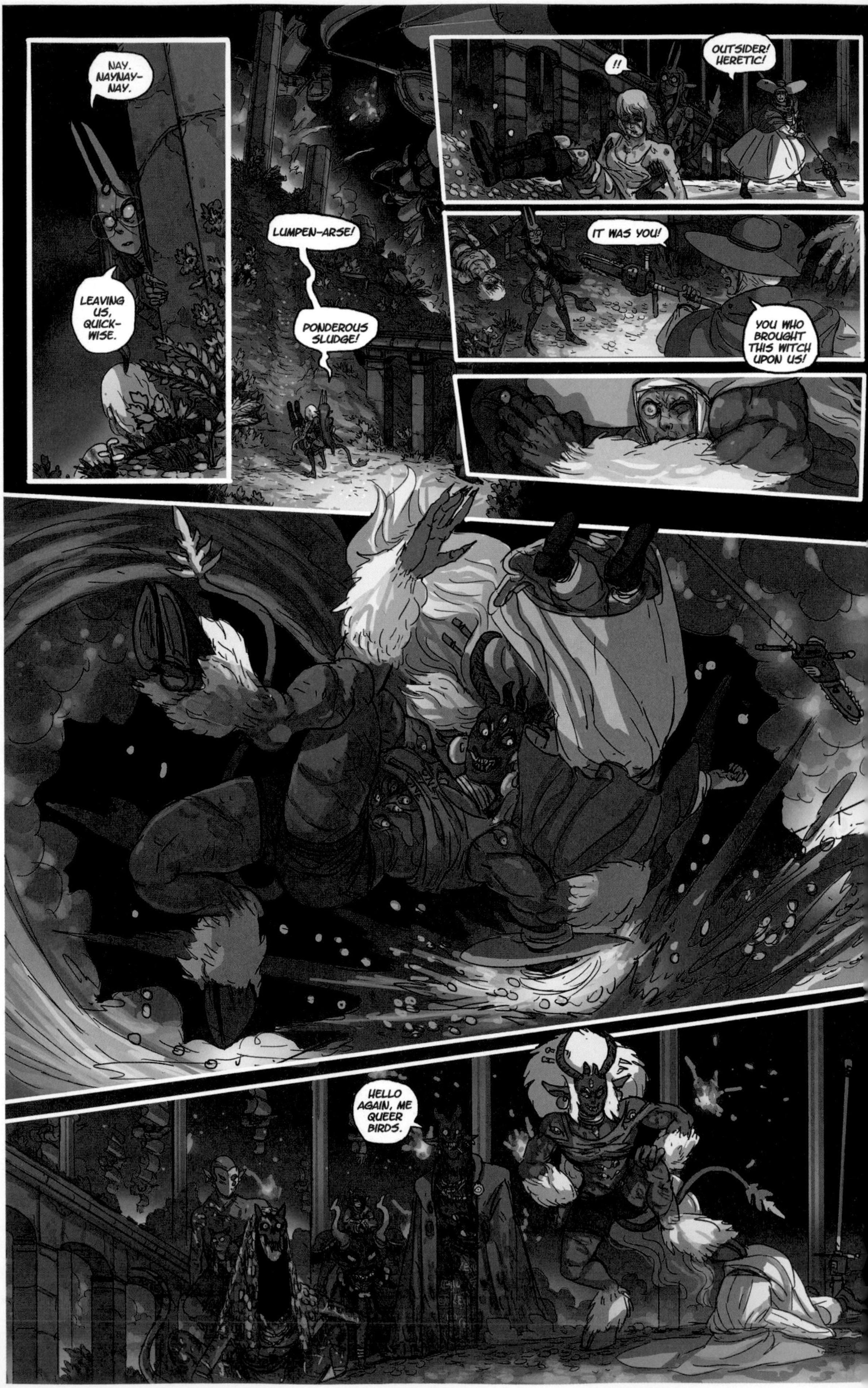
NAY. NAYNAY-NAY.
LEAVING US, QUICK-WISE.
LUMPEN-ARSE!
PONDEROUS SLUDGE!
!!
OUTSIDER! HERETIC!
IT WAS YOU!
YOU WHO BROUGHT THIS WITCH UPON US!
HELLO AGAIN, ME QUEER BIRDS.

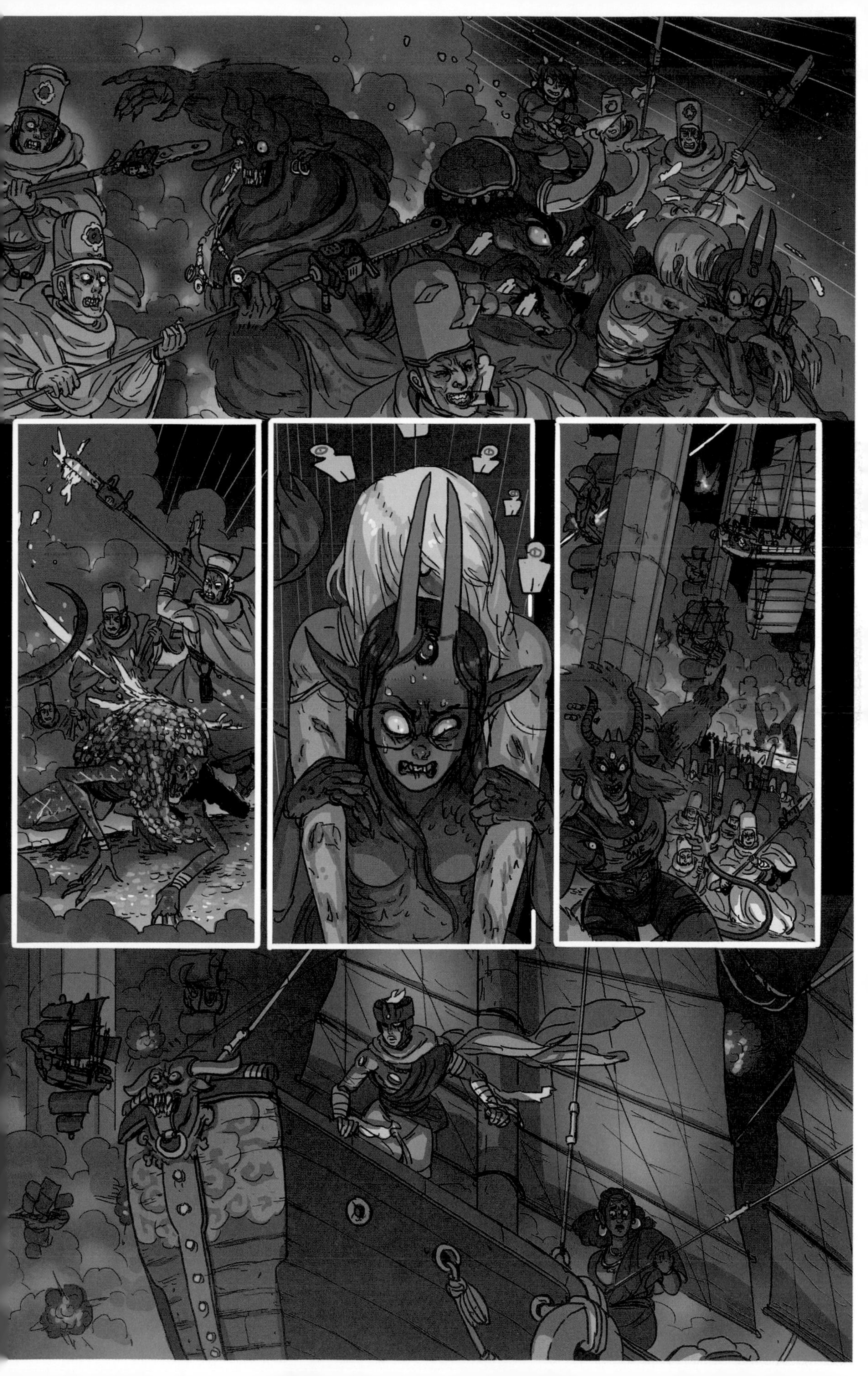

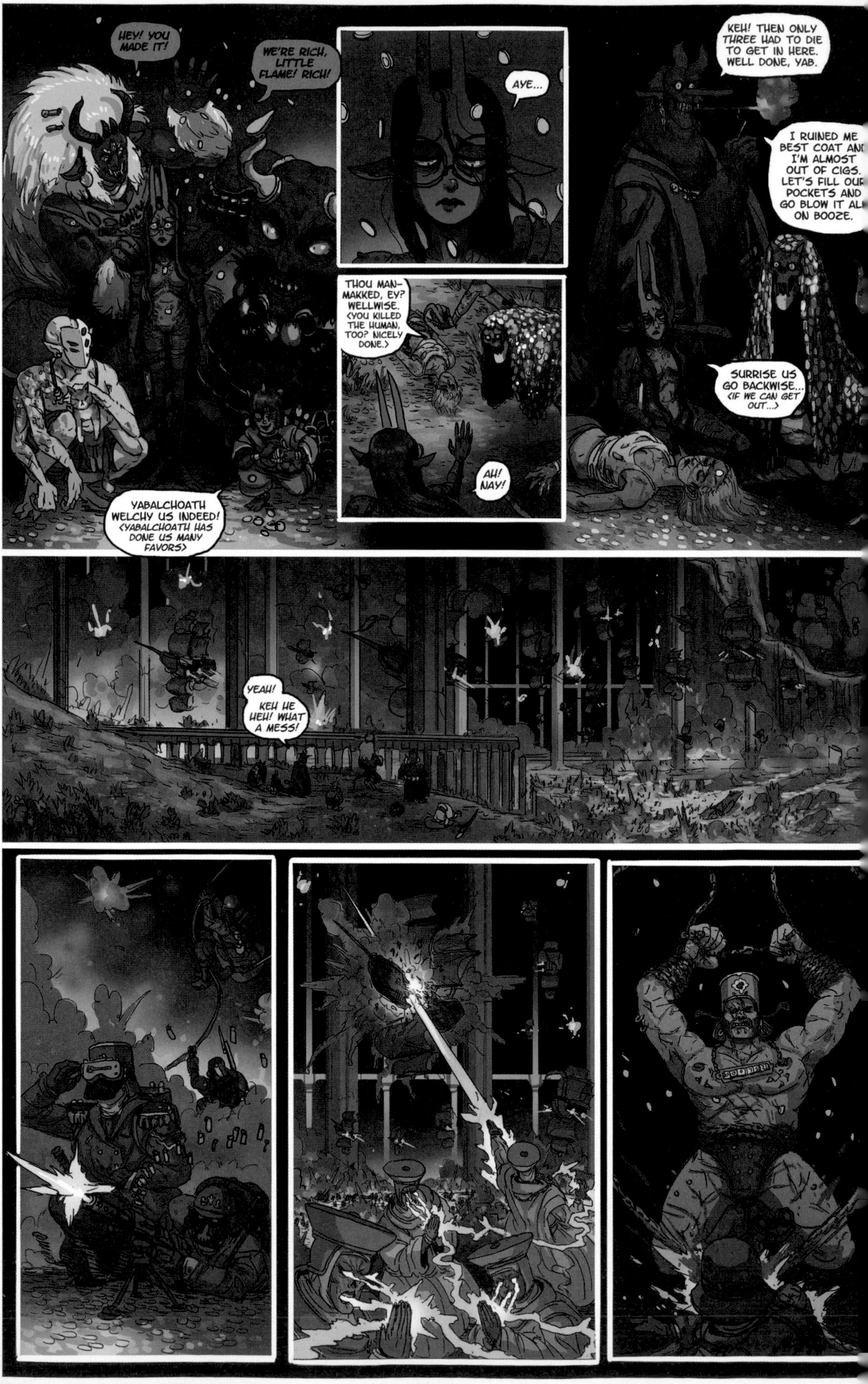
HEY! YOU MADE IT!
WE'RE RICH, LITTLE FLAME! RICH!
YABALCHOATH WELCHY US INDEED! <YABALCHOATH HAS DONE US MANY FAVORS>
AYE...
THOU MAN-MAKKED, EY? WELLWISE. <YOU KILLED THE HUMAN, TOO? NICELY DONE.>
AH! NAY!
KEH! THEN ONLY THREE HAD TO DIE TO GET IN HERE. WELL DONE, YAB.
I RUINED ME BEST COAT AND I'M ALMOST OUT OF CIGS. LET'S FILL OUR POCKETS AND GO BLOW IT ALL ON BOOZE.
SURRISE US GO BACKWISE... <IF WE CAN GET OUT...>
YEAH! KEH HE HEH! WHAT A MESS!

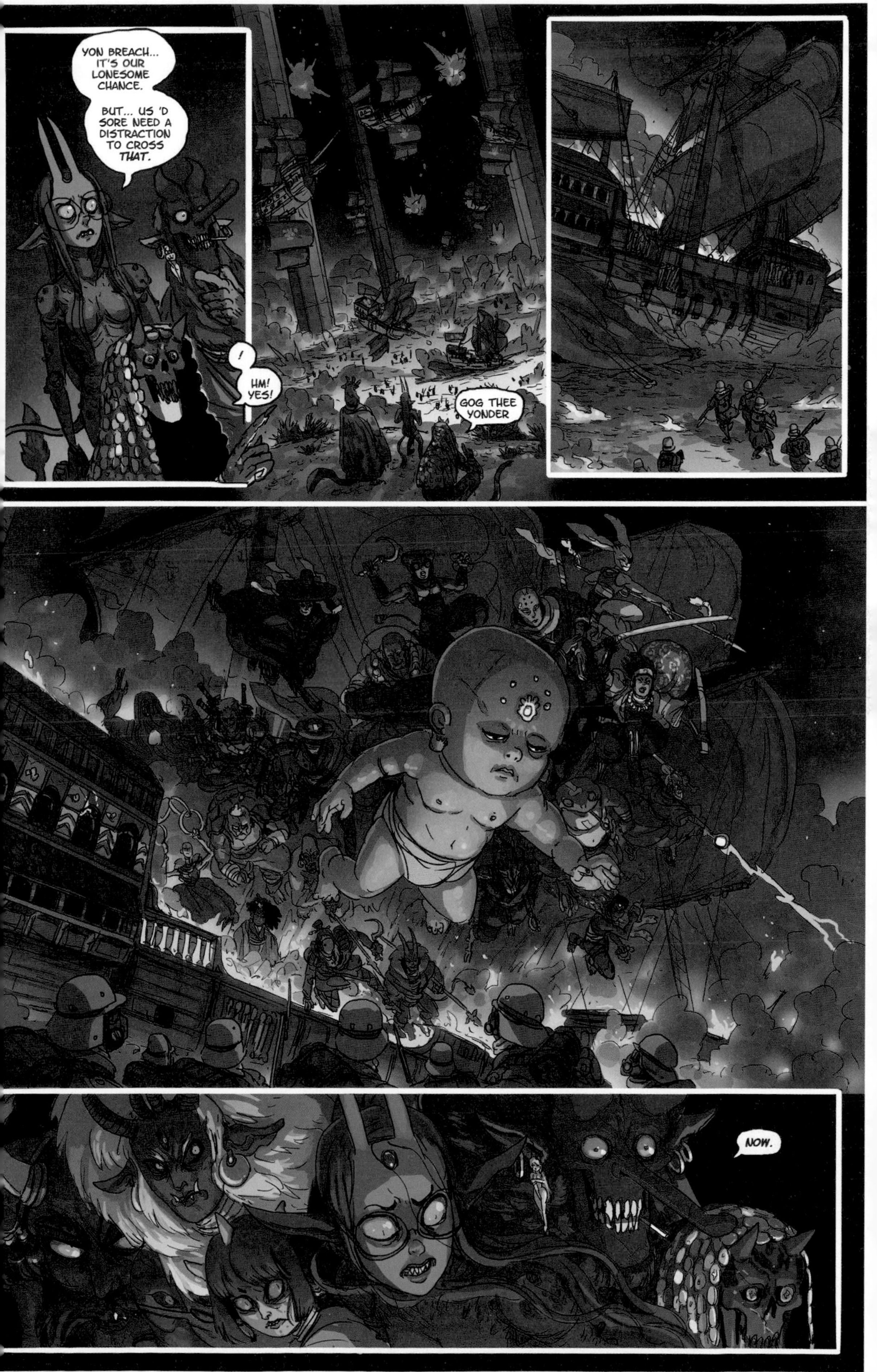
YON BREACH... IT'S OUR LONESOME CHANCE.
BUT... US 'D SORE NEED A DISTRACTION TO CROSS THAT.
!
HM! YES!
GOG THEE YONDER
NOW.

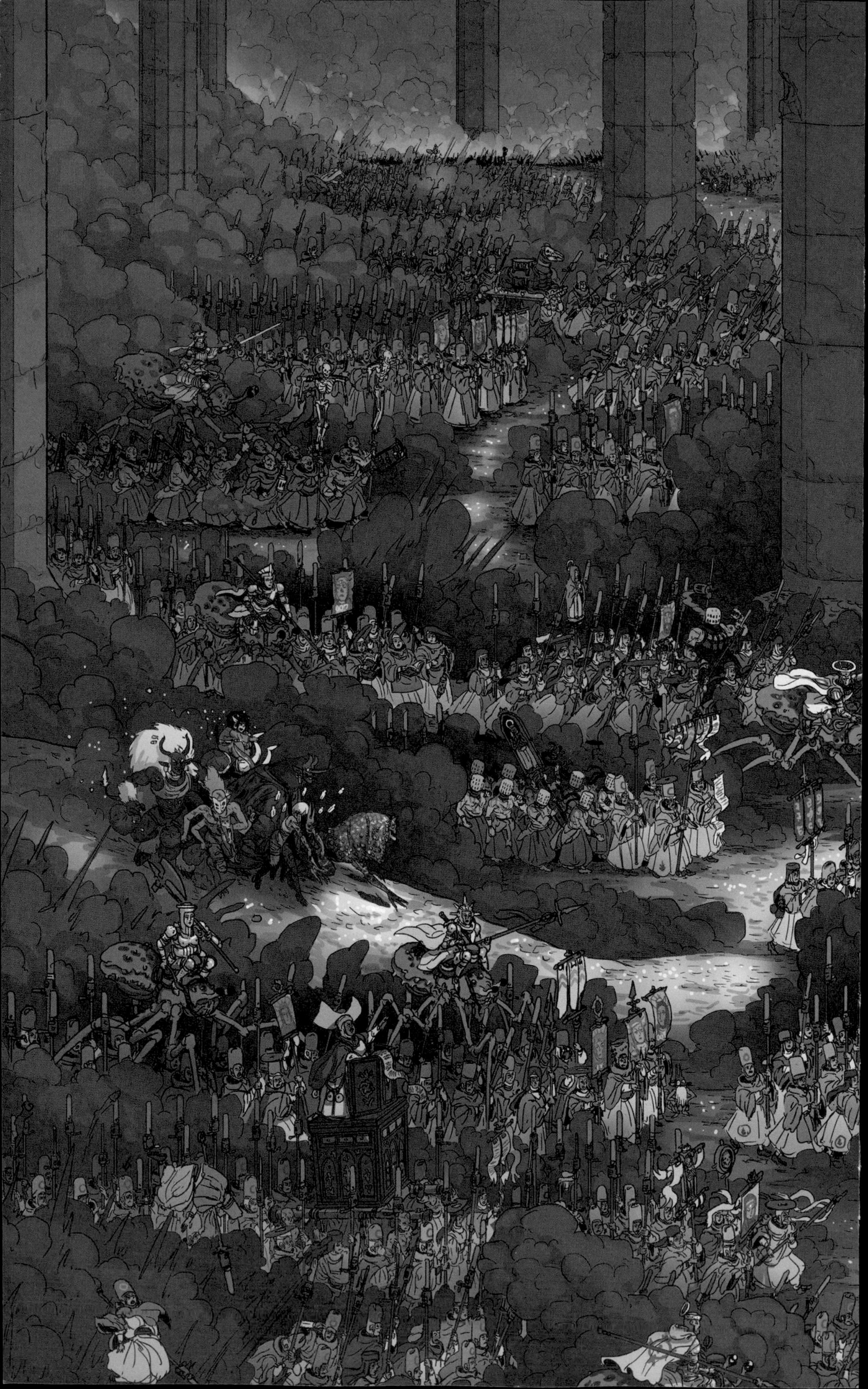

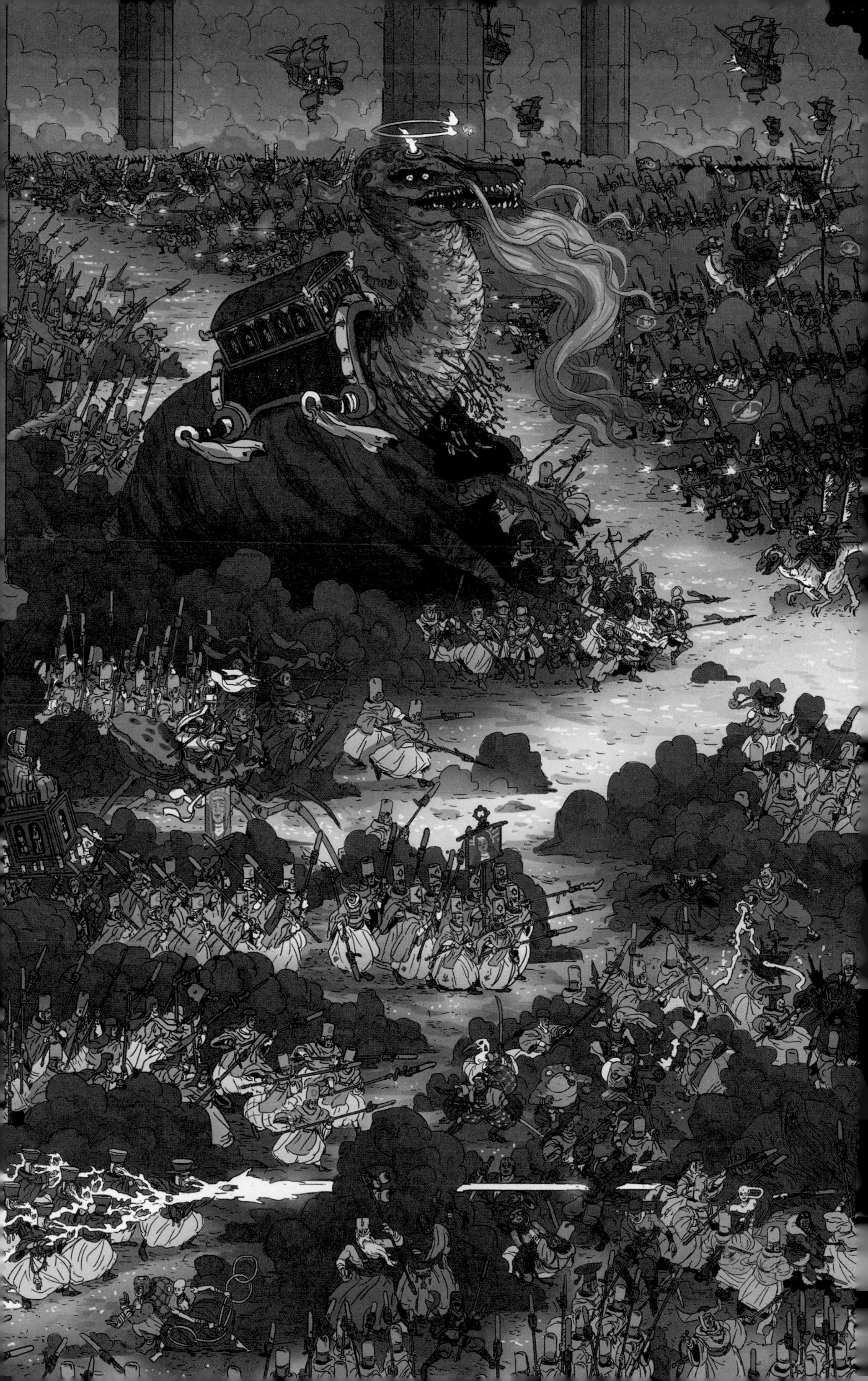

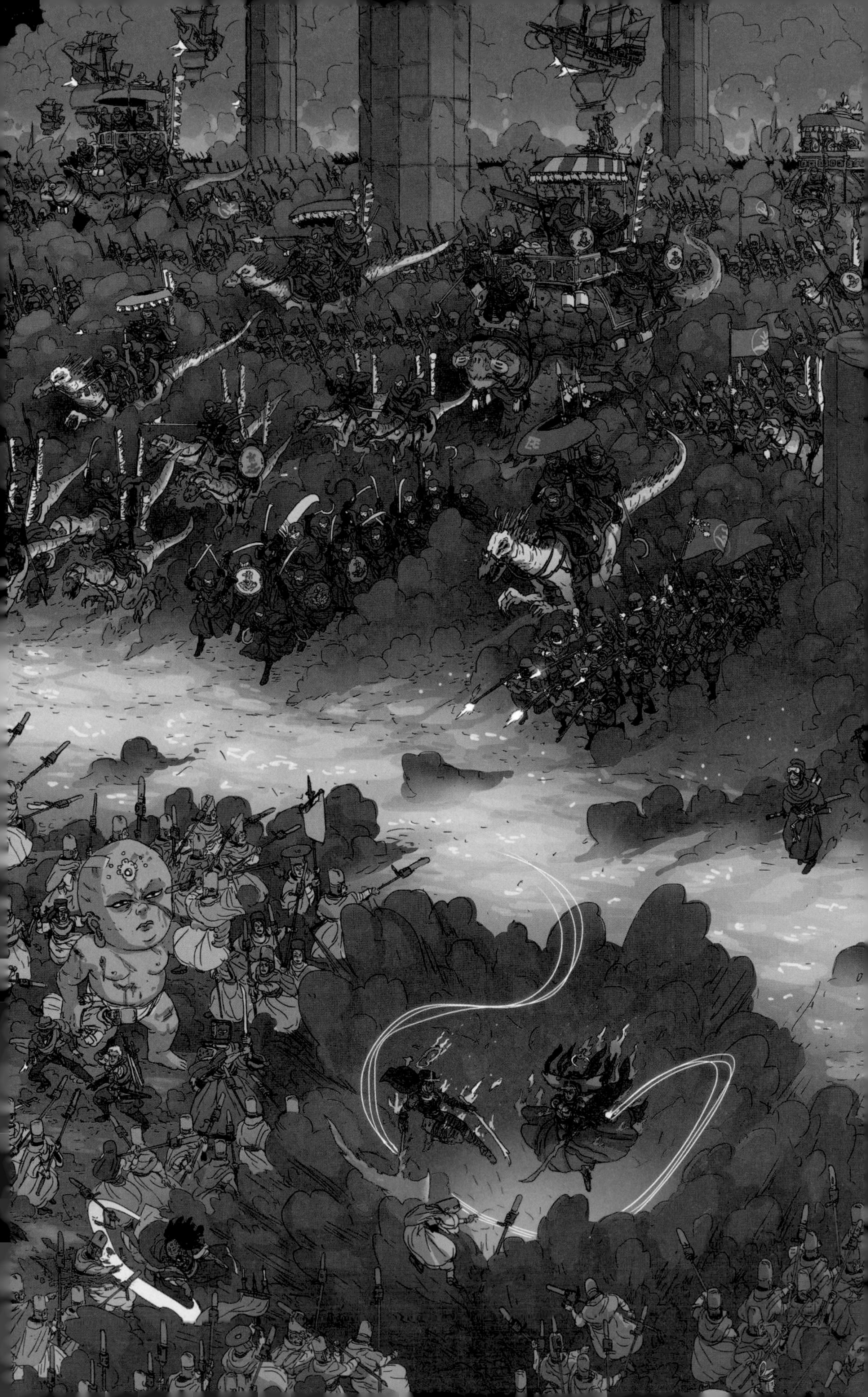

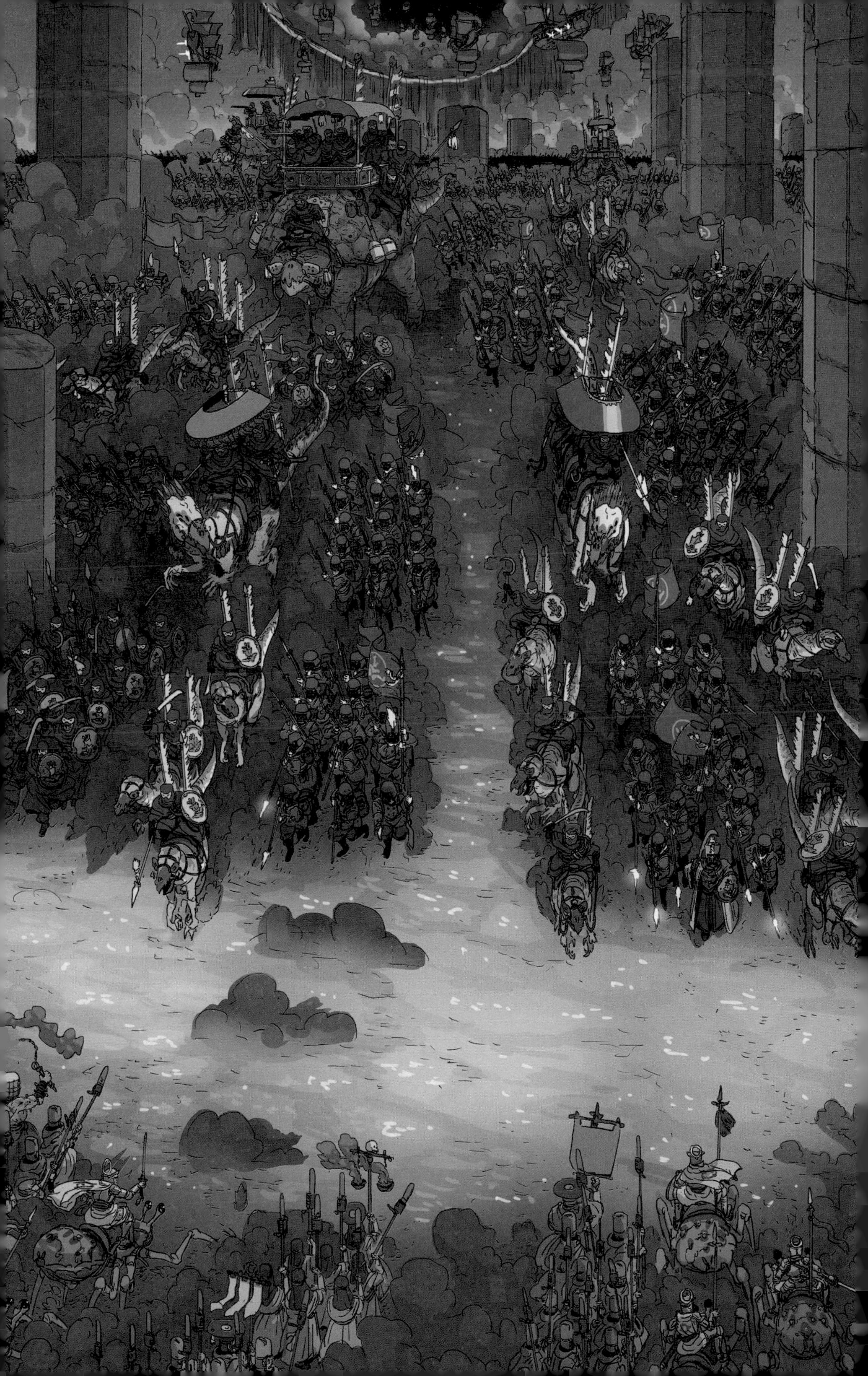

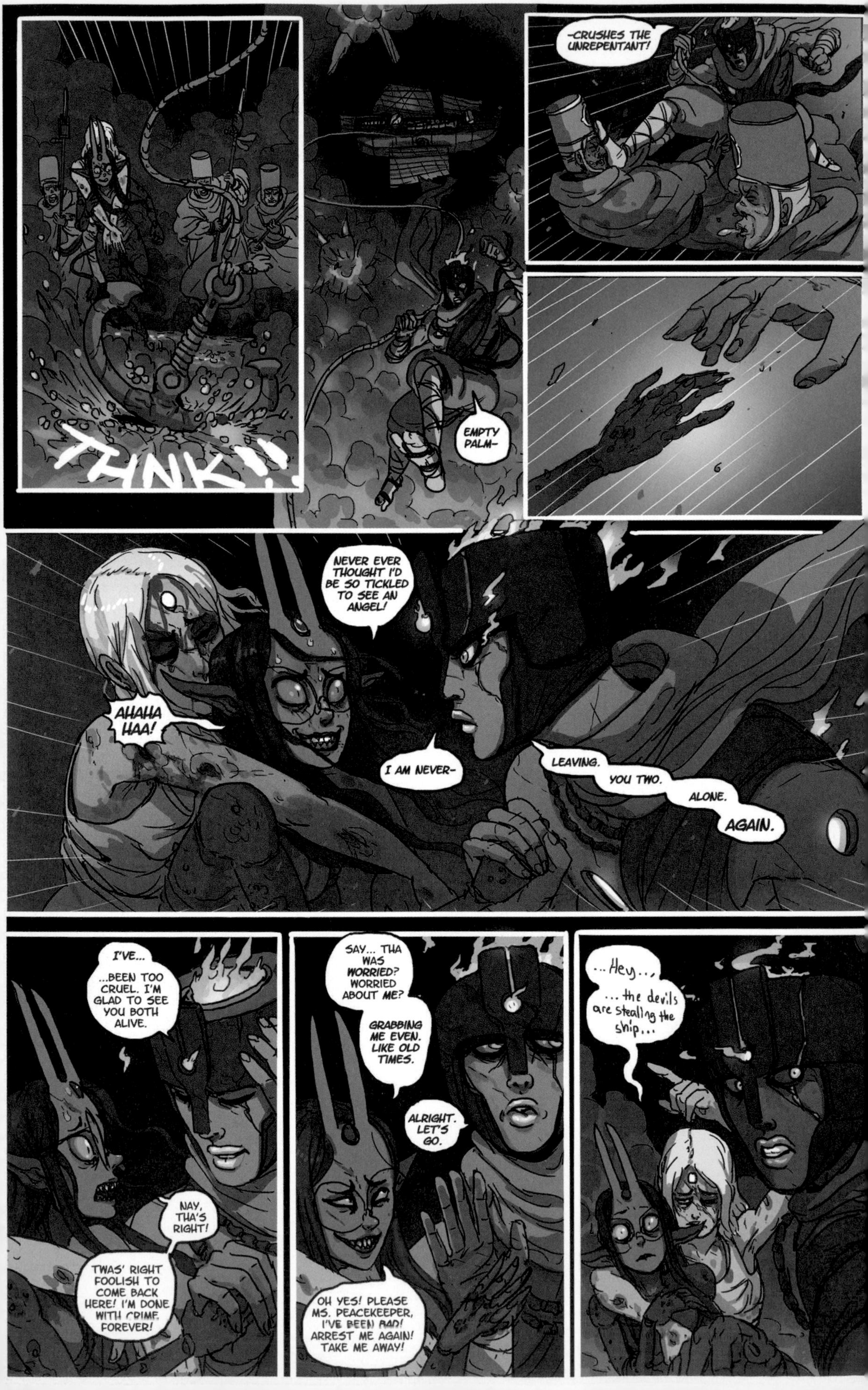
THNK!!
EMPTY PALM-
-CRUSHES THE UNREPENTANT!
NEVER EVER THOUGHT I'D BE SO TICKLED TO SEE AN ANGEL!
AHAHA HAA!
I AM NEVER-
LEAVING.
YOU TWO.
ALONE.
AGAIN.
I'VE...
...BEEN TOO CRUEL. I'M GLAD TO SEE YOU BOTH ALIVE.
NAY, THA'S RIGHT!
TWAS' RIGHT FOOLISH TO COME BACK HERE! I'M DONE WITH CRIME FOREVER!
SAY... THA WAS WORRIED? WORRIED ABOUT ME?
GRABBING ME EVEN. LIKE OLD TIMES.
ALRIGHT. LET'S GO.
OH YES! PLEASE MS. PEACEKEEPER, I'VE BEEN BAD! ARREST ME AGAIN! TAKE ME AWAY!
...Hey...,
...the devils are stealing the ship...

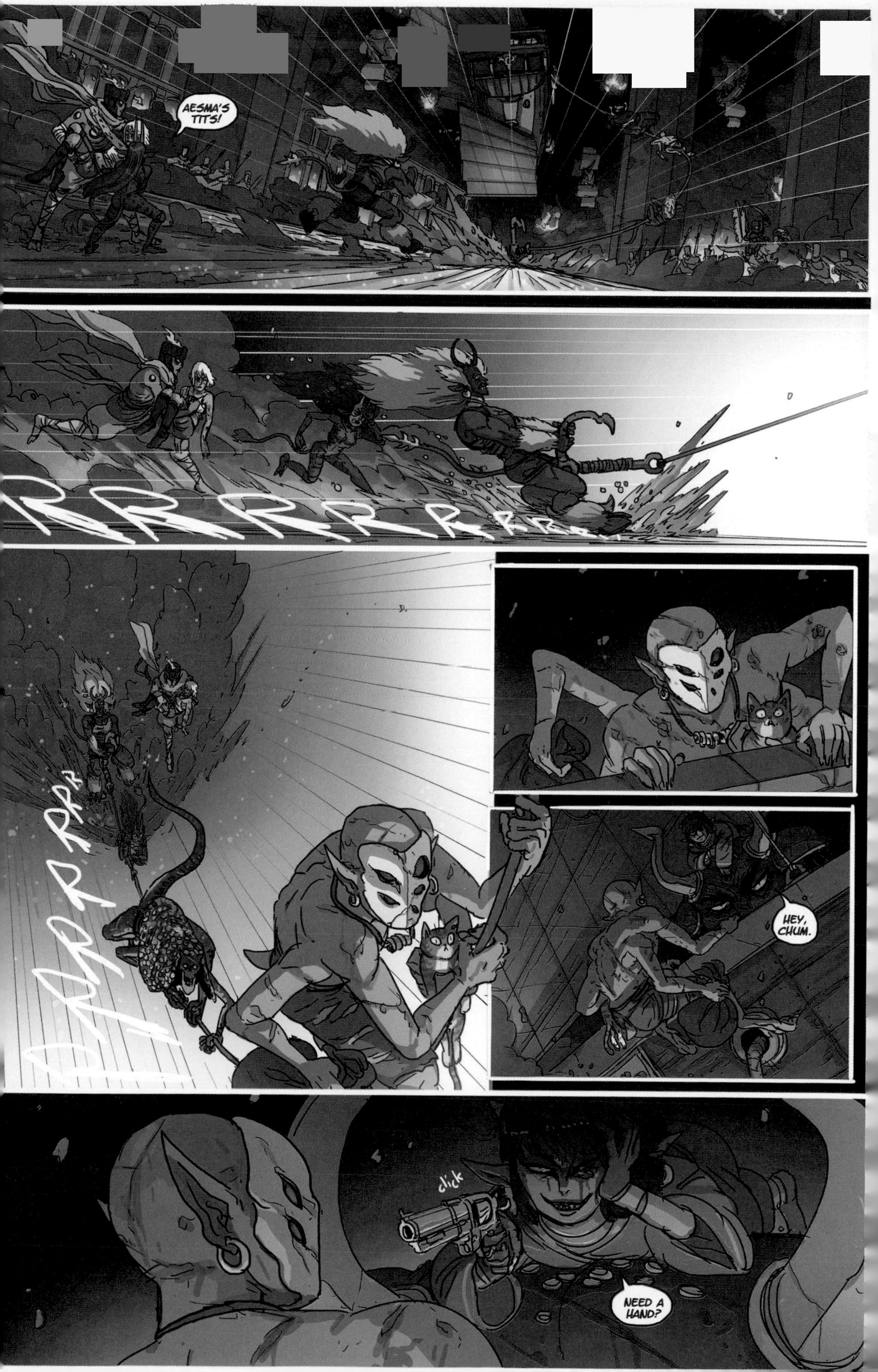
AESMA'S TITS!
HEY, CHUM.
click
NEED A HAND?

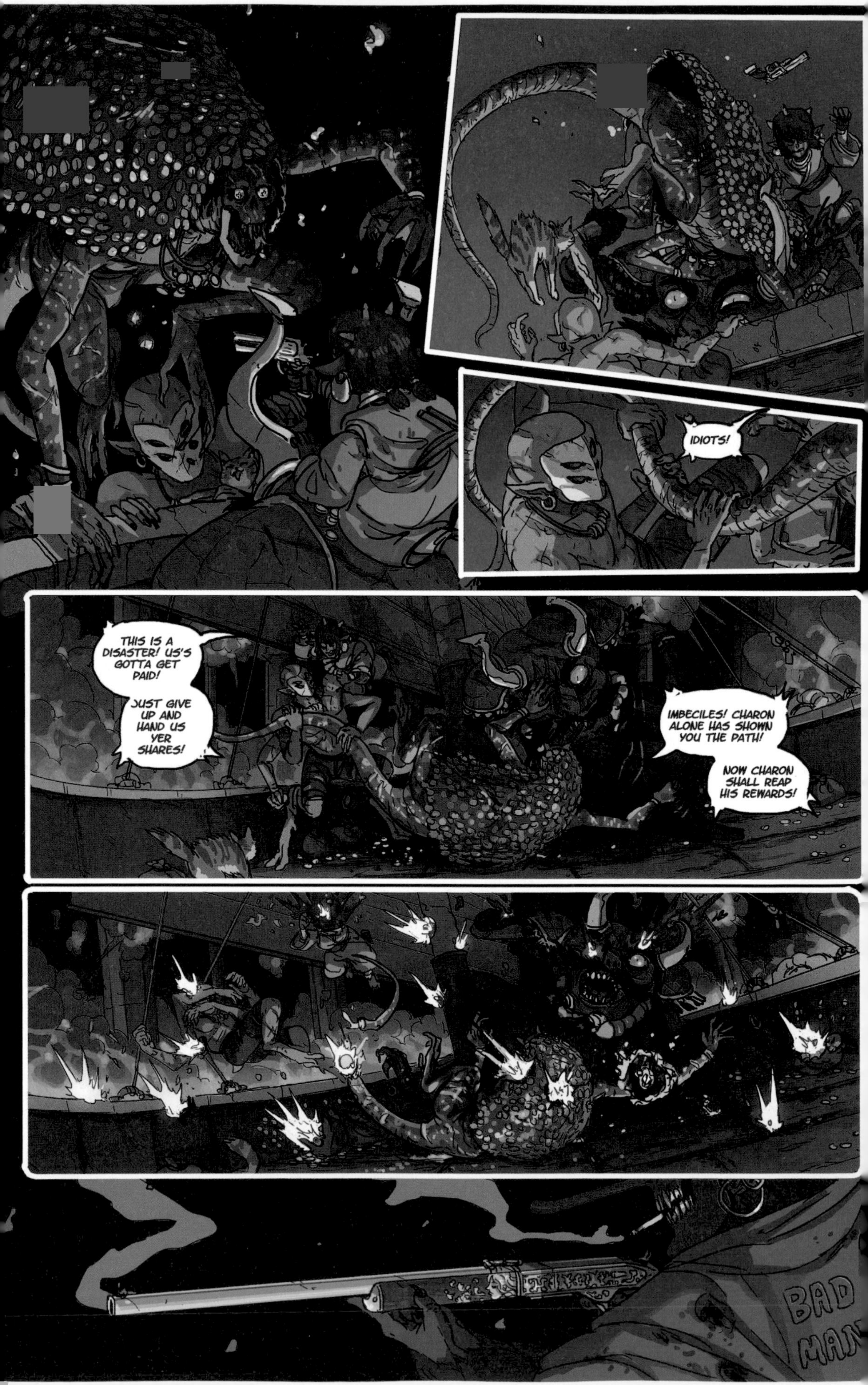
IDIOTS!
THIS IS A DISASTER! US'S GOTTA GET PAID!
JUST GIVE UP AND HAND US YER SHARES!
IMBECILES! CHARON ALONE HAS SHOWN YOU THE PATH!
NOW CHARON SHALL REAP HIS REWARDS!
BAD MAN

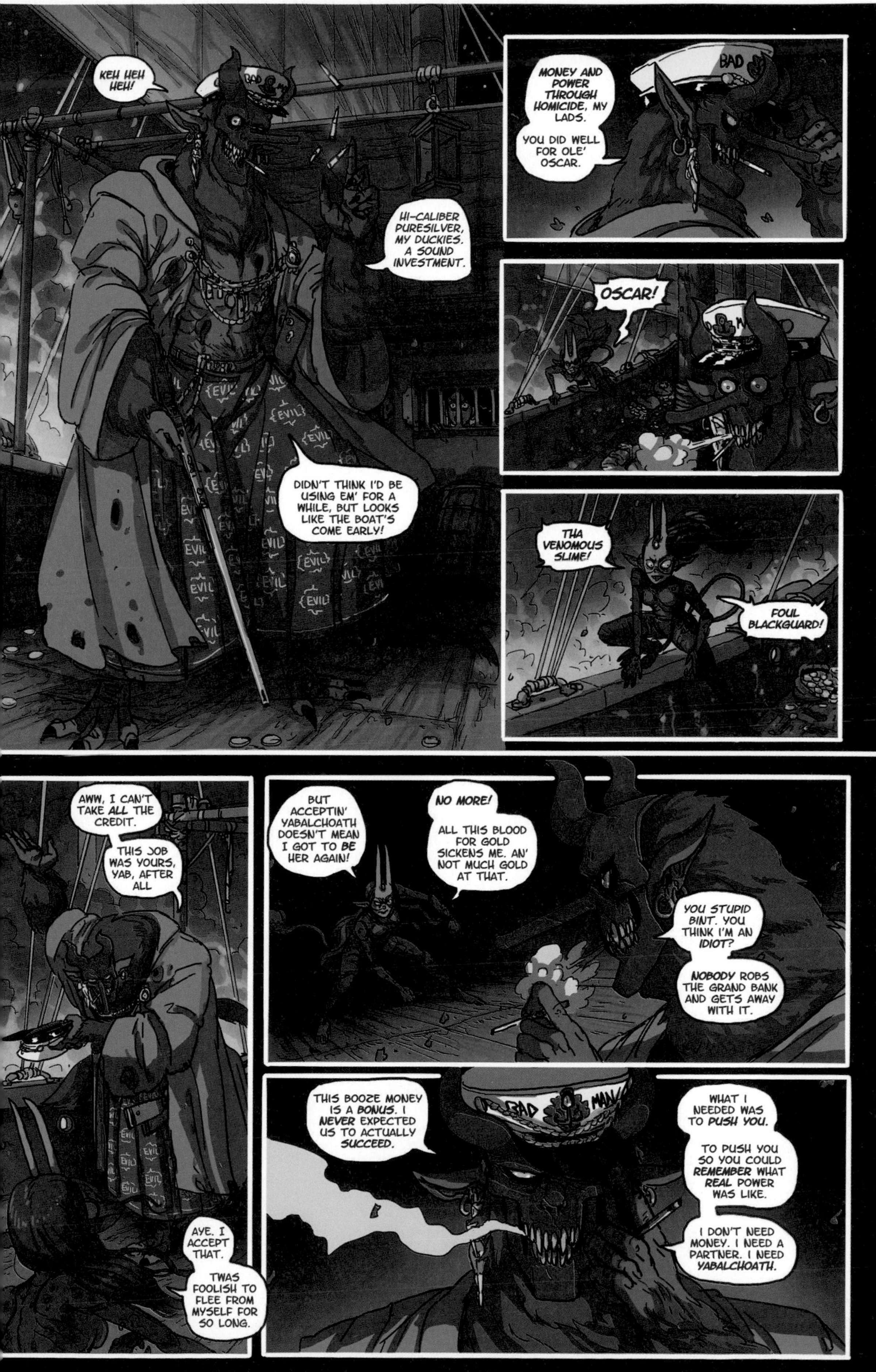
KEH HEH HEH!
HI-CALIBER PURESILVER, MY DUCKIES. A SOUND INVESTMENT.
DIDN'T THINK I'D BE USING EM' FOR A WHILE, BUT LOOKS LIKE THE BOAT'S COME EARLY!
MONEY AND POWER THROUGH HOMICIDE, MY LADS.
YOU DID WELL FOR OLE' OSCAR.
OSCAR!
THA VENOMOUS SLIME!
FOUL BLACKGUARD!
AWW, I CAN'T TAKE ALL THE CREDIT.
THIS JOB WAS YOURS, YAB, AFTER ALL
AYE. I ACCEPT THAT.
TWAS FOOLISH TO FLEE FROM MYSELF FOR SO LONG.
BUT ACCEPTIN' YABALCHOATH DOESN'T MEAN I GOT TO BE HER AGAIN!
NO MORE!
ALL THIS BLOOD FOR GOLD SICKENS ME. AN' NOT MUCH GOLD AT THAT.
YOU STUPID BINT. YOU THINK I'M AN IDIOT?
NOBODY ROBS THE GRAND BANK AND GETS AWAY WITH IT.
THIS BOOZE MONEY IS A BONUS. I NEVER EXPECTED US TO ACTUALLY SUCCEED.
WHAT I NEEDED WAS TO PUSH YOU.
TO PUSH YOU SO YOU COULD REMEMBER WHAT REAL POWER WAS LIKE.
I DON'T NEED MONEY. I NEED A PARTNER. I NEED YABALCHOATH.

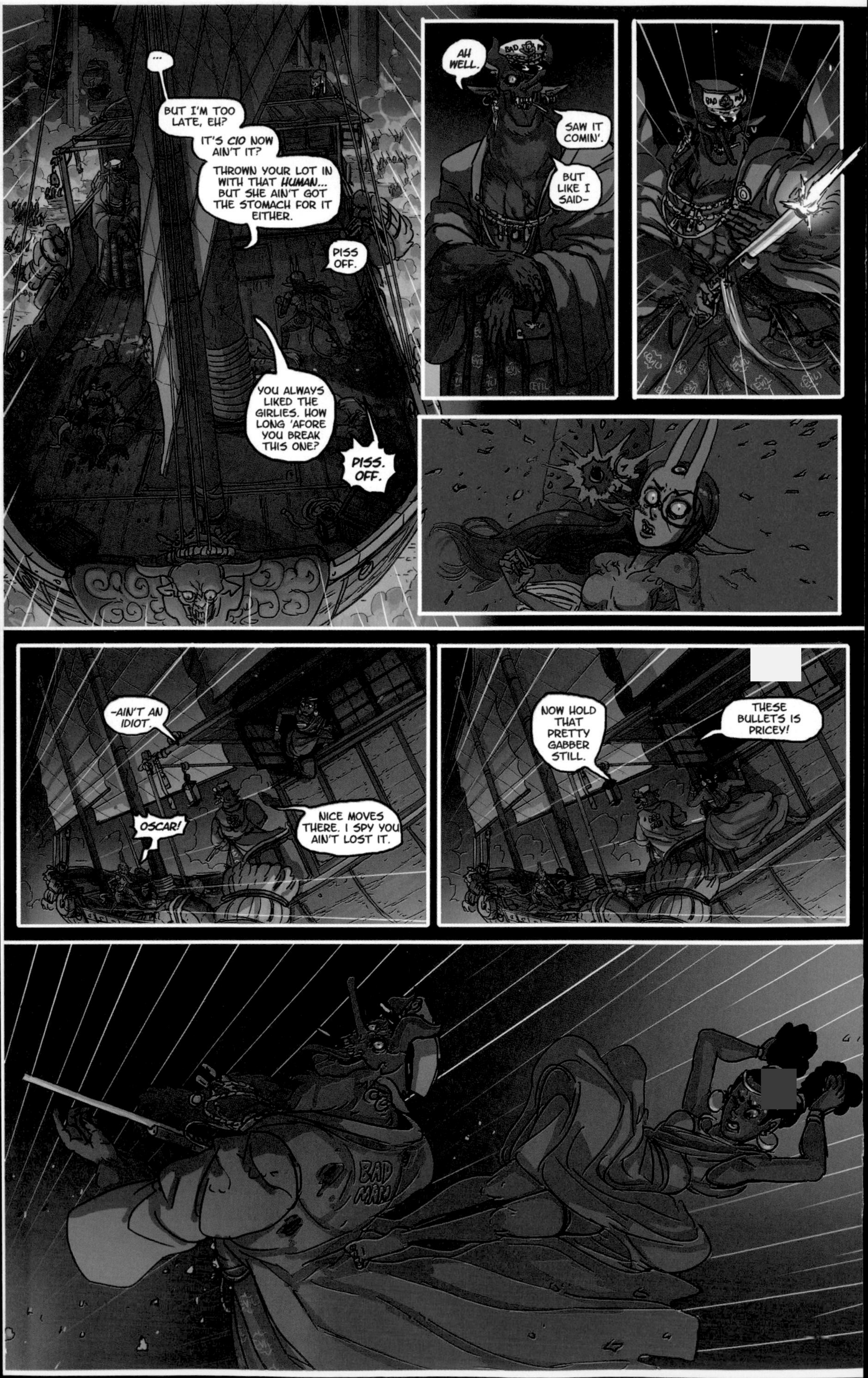
...
BUT I'M TOO LATE, EH?
IT'S CIO NOW AIN'T IT?
THROWN YOUR LOT IN WITH THAT HUMAN... BUT SHE AIN'T GOT THE STOMACH FOR IT EITHER.
PISS OFF.
YOU ALWAYS LIKED THE GIRLIES. HOW LONG 'AFORE YOU BREAK THIS ONE?
PISS. OFF.
AH WELL.
SAW IT COMIN'.
BUT LIKE I SAID-
-AIN'T AN IDIOT.
OSCAR!
NICE MOVES THERE. I SPY YOU AIN'T LOST IT.
NOW HOLD THAT PRETTY GABBER STILL.
THESE BULLETS IS PRICEY!

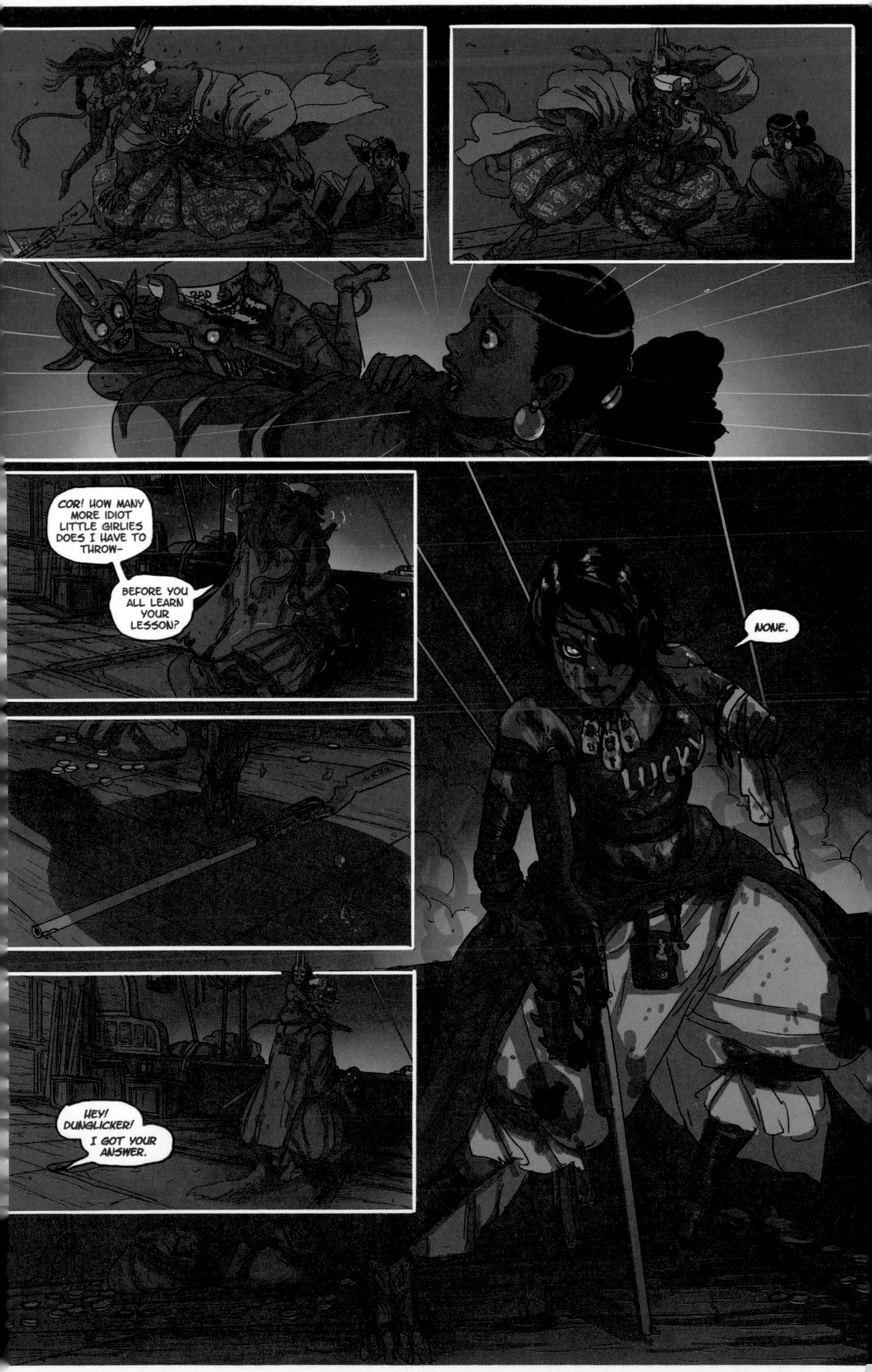
COR! HOW MANY MORE IDIOT LITTLE GIRLIES DOES I HAVE TO THROW-
BEFORE YOU ALL LEARN YOUR LESSON?
NONE.
HEY! DUNGLICKER!
I GOT YOUR ANSWER.
LUCKY

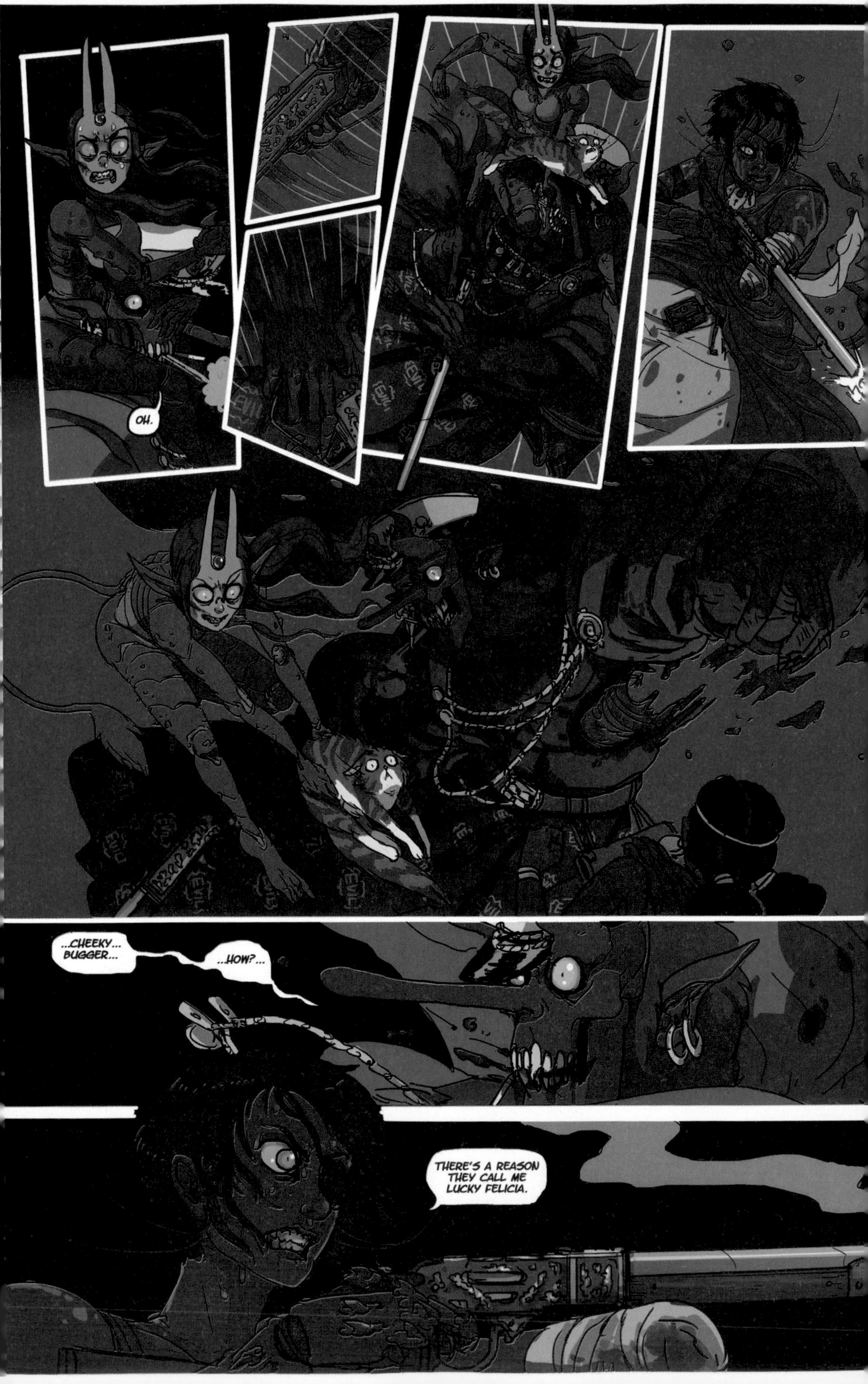
OH.
...CHEEKY... BUGGER...
...HOW?...
THERE'S A REASON THEY CALL ME LUCKY FELICIA.

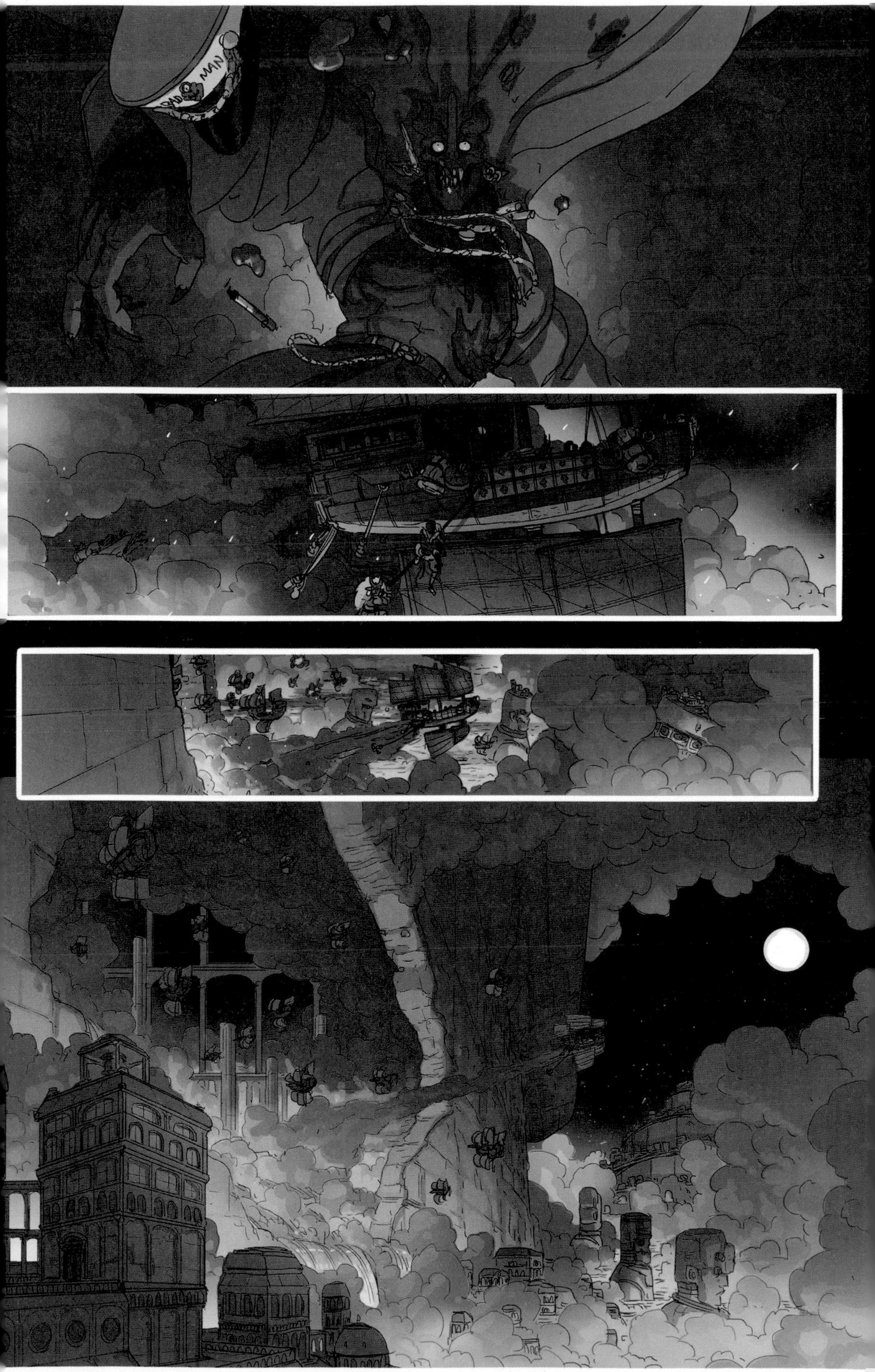
MAN

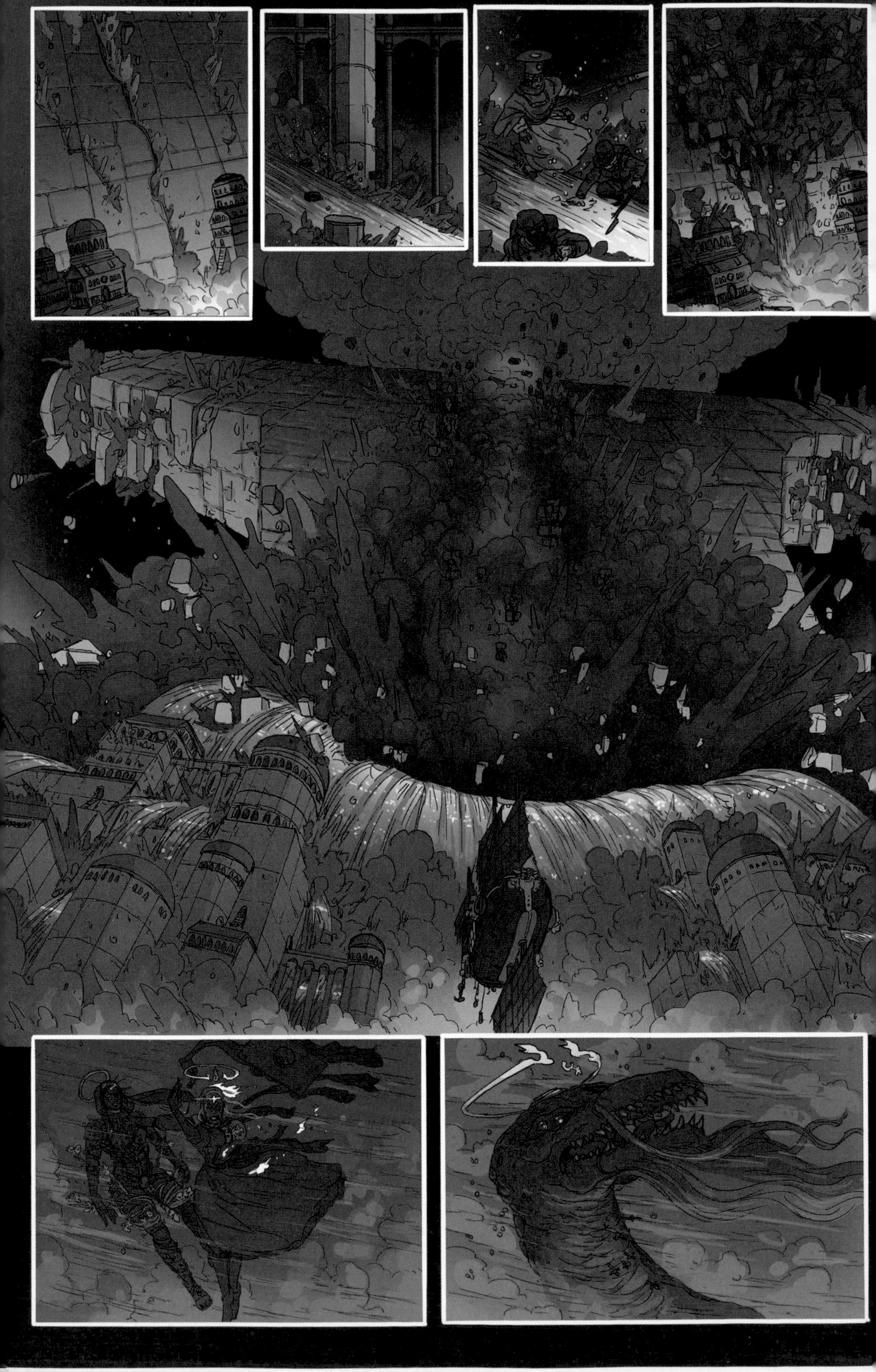

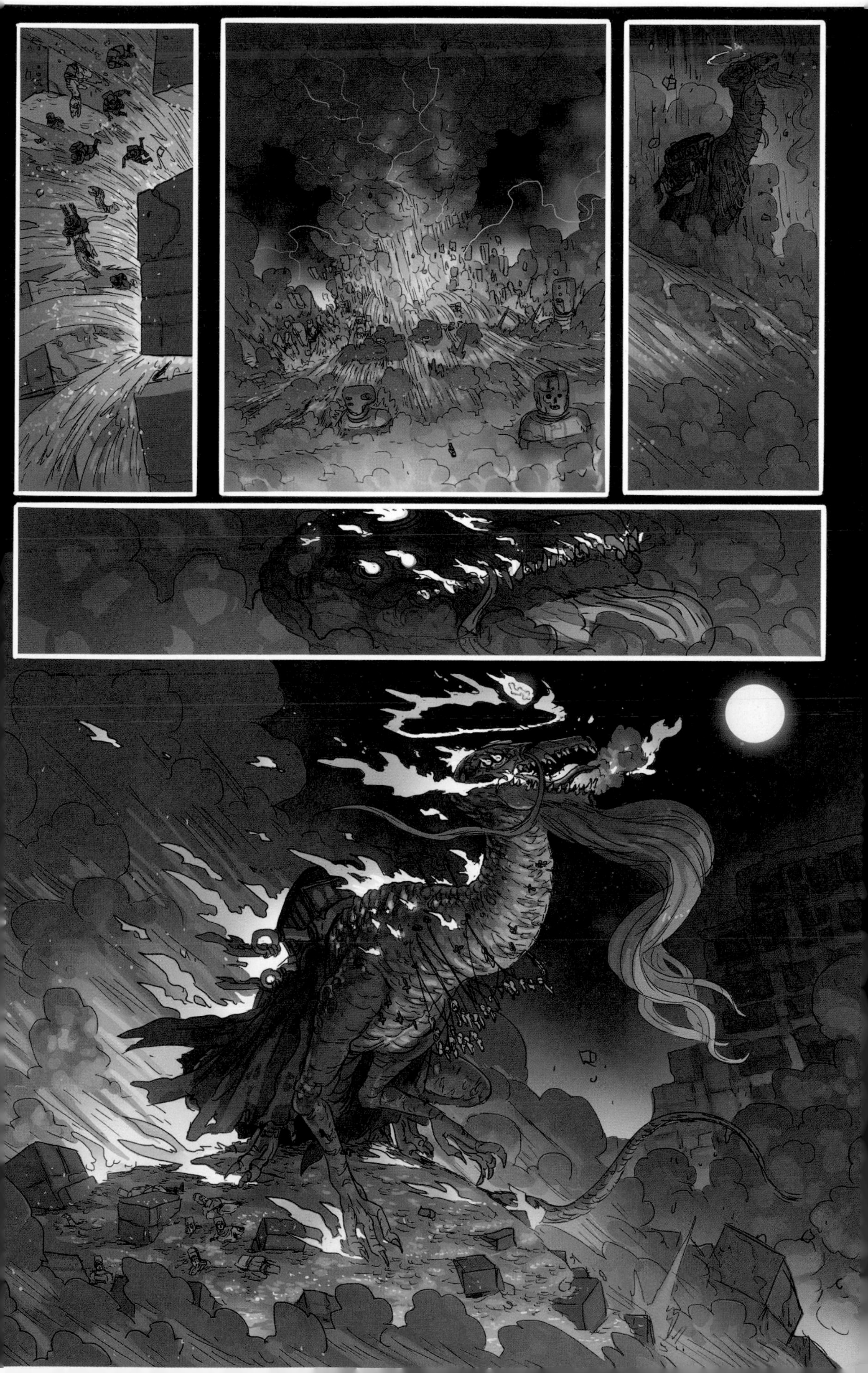

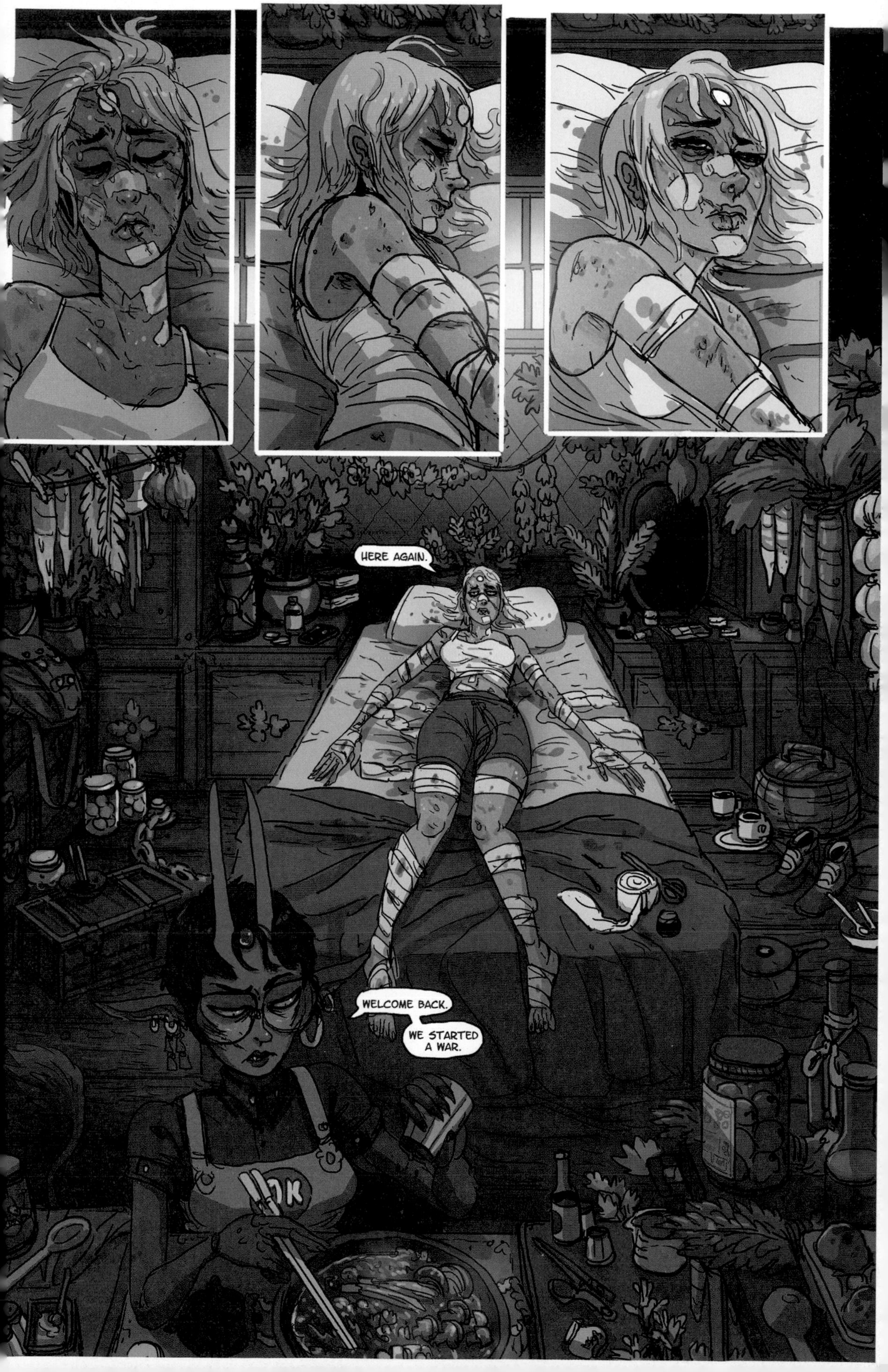
HERE AGAIN.
WELCOME BACK.
WE STARTED A WAR.

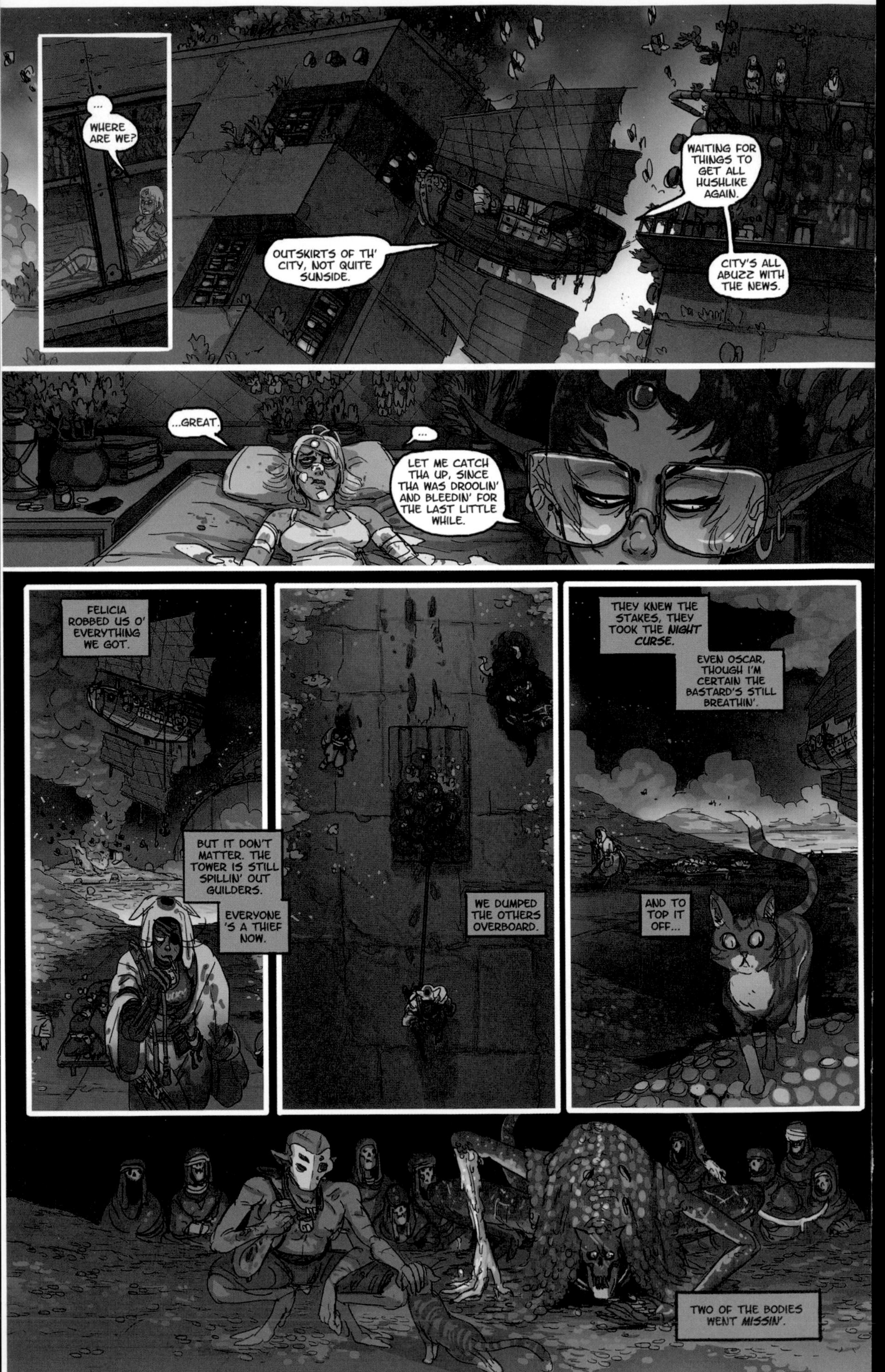
...
WHERE ARE WE?
OUTSKIRTS OF TH' CITY, NOT QUITE SUNSIDE.
WAITING FOR THINGS TO GET ALL HUSHLIKE AGAIN.
CITY'S ALL ABUZZ WITH THE NEWS.
...GREAT.
...
LET ME CATCH THA UP, SINCE THA WAS DROOLIN' AND BLEEDIN' FOR THE LAST LITTLE WHILE.
FELICIA ROBBED US O' EVERYTHING WE GOT.
BUT IT DON'T MATTER. THE TOWER IS STILL SPILLIN' OUT GUILDERS.
EVERYONE 'S A THIEF NOW.
WE DUMPED THE OTHERS OVERBOARD.
THEY KNEW THE STAKES, THEY TOOK THE NIGHT CURSE.
EVEN OSCAR, THOUGH I'M CERTAIN THE BASTARD'S STILL BREATHIN'.
AND TO TOP IT OFF...
TWO OF THE BODIES WENT MISSIN'.

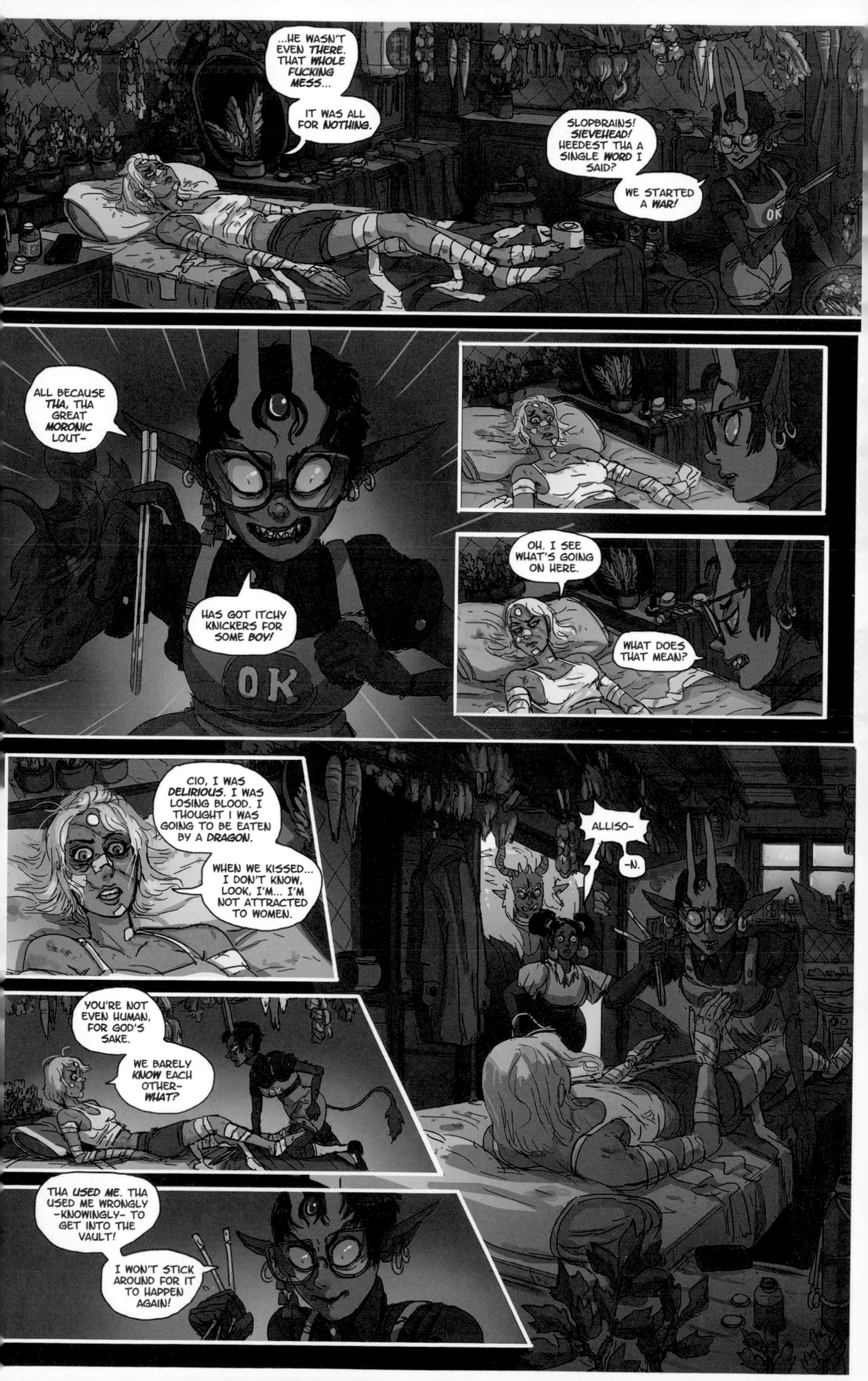
...HE WASN'T EVEN THERE. THAT WHOLE FUCKING MESS...
IT WAS ALL FOR NOTHING.
SLOPBRAINS! SIEVEHEAD! HEEDEST THA A SINGLE WORD I SAID?
WE STARTED A WAR!
ALL BECAUSE THA, THA GREAT MORONIC LOUT-
HAS GOT ITCHY KNICKERS FOR SOME BOY!
OK
OH. I SEE WHAT'S GOING ON HERE.
WHAT DOES THAT MEAN?
CIO, I WAS DELIRIOUS. I WAS LOSING BLOOD. I THOUGHT I WAS GOING TO BE EATEN BY A DRAGON.
WHEN WE KISSED... I DON'T KNOW, LOOK, I'M... I'M NOT ATTRACTED TO WOMEN.
YOU'RE NOT EVEN HUMAN, FOR GOD'S SAKE.
WE BARELY KNOW EACH OTHER-
WHAT?
THA USED ME. THA USED ME WRONGLY -KNOWINGLY- TO GET INTO THE VAULT!
I WON'T STICK AROUND FOR IT TO HAPPEN AGAIN!
ALLISO-
-N.

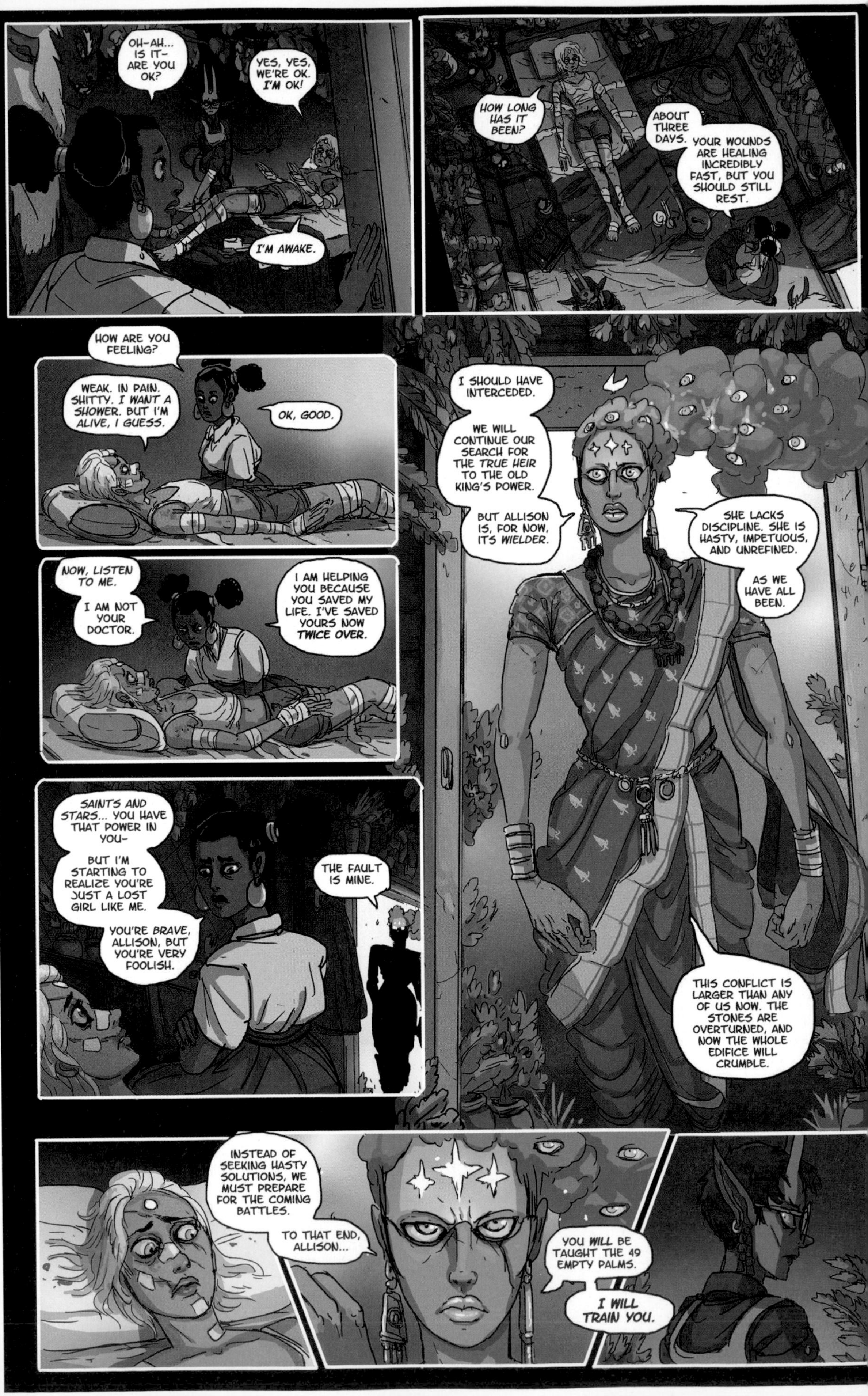
OH-AH... IS IT- ARE YOU OK?
YES, YES, WE'RE OK. I'M OK!
I'M AWAKE.
HOW LONG HAS IT BEEN?
ABOUT THREE DAYS.
YOUR WOUNDS ARE HEALING INCREDIBLY FAST, BUT YOU SHOULD STILL REST.
HOW ARE YOU FEELING?
WEAK. IN PAIN. SHITTY. I WANT A SHOWER. BUT I'M ALIVE, I GUESS.
OK, GOOD.
NOW, LISTEN TO ME.
I AM NOT YOUR DOCTOR.
I AM HELPING YOU BECAUSE YOU SAVED MY LIFE. I'VE SAVED YOURS NOW TWICE OVER.
SAINTS AND STARS... YOU HAVE THAT POWER IN YOU-
BUT I'M STARTING TO REALIZE YOU'RE JUST A LOST GIRL LIKE ME.
YOU'RE BRAVE, ALLISON, BUT YOU'RE VERY FOOLISH.
THE FAULT IS MINE.
I SHOULD HAVE INTERCEDED.
WE WILL CONTINUE OUR SEARCH FOR THE TRUE HEIR TO THE OLD KING'S POWER.
BUT ALLISON IS, FOR NOW, IT'S WIELDER.
SHE LACKS DISCIPLINE. SHE IS HASTY, IMPETUOUS, AND UNREFINED.
AS WE HAVE ALL BEEN.
THIS CONFLICT IS LARGER THAN ANY OF US NOW. THE STONES ARE OVERTURNED, AND NOW THE WHOLE EDIFICE WILL CRUMBLE.
INSTEAD OF SEEKING HASTY SOLUTIONS, WE MUST PREPARE FOR THE COMING BATTLES.
TO THAT END, ALLISON...
YOU WILL BE TAUGHT THE 49 EMPTY PALMS.
I WILL TRAIN YOU.

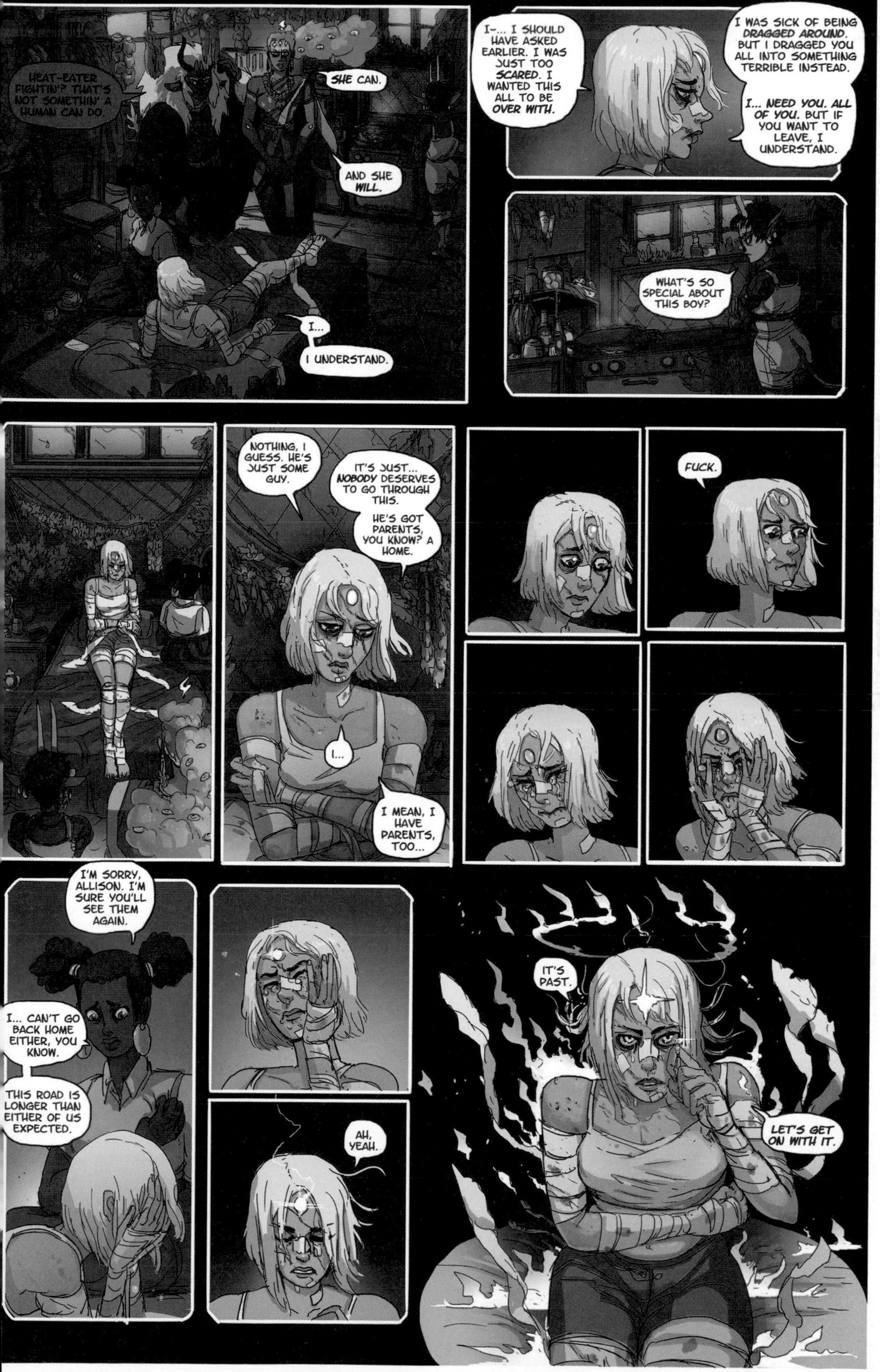
HEAT-EATER FIGHTIN'? THAT'S NOT SOMETHIN' A HUMAN CAN DO.
SHE CAN.
AND SHE WILL.
I...
I UNDERSTAND.
I-... I SHOULD HAVE ASKED EARLIER. I WAS JUST TOO SCARED. I WANTED THIS ALL TO BE OVER WITH.
I WAS SICK OF BEING DRAGGED AROUND. BUT I DRAGGED YOU ALL INTO SOMETHING TERRIBLE INSTEAD.
I... NEED YOU. ALL OF YOU. BUT IF YOU WANT TO LEAVE, I UNDERSTAND.
WHAT'S SO SPECIAL ABOUT THIS BOY?
NOTHING, I GUESS. HE'S JUST SOME GUY.
IT'S JUST... NOBODY DESERVES TO GO THROUGH THIS.
HE'S GOT PARENTS, YOU KNOW? A HOME.
I...
I MEAN, I HAVE PARENTS, TOO...
FUCK.
I'M SORRY, ALLISON. I'M SURE YOU'LL SEE THEM AGAIN.
I... CAN'T GO BACK HOME EITHER, YOU KNOW.
THIS ROAD IS LONGER THAN EITHER OF US EXPECTED.
AH, YEAH.
IT'S PAST.
LET'S GET ON WITH IT.

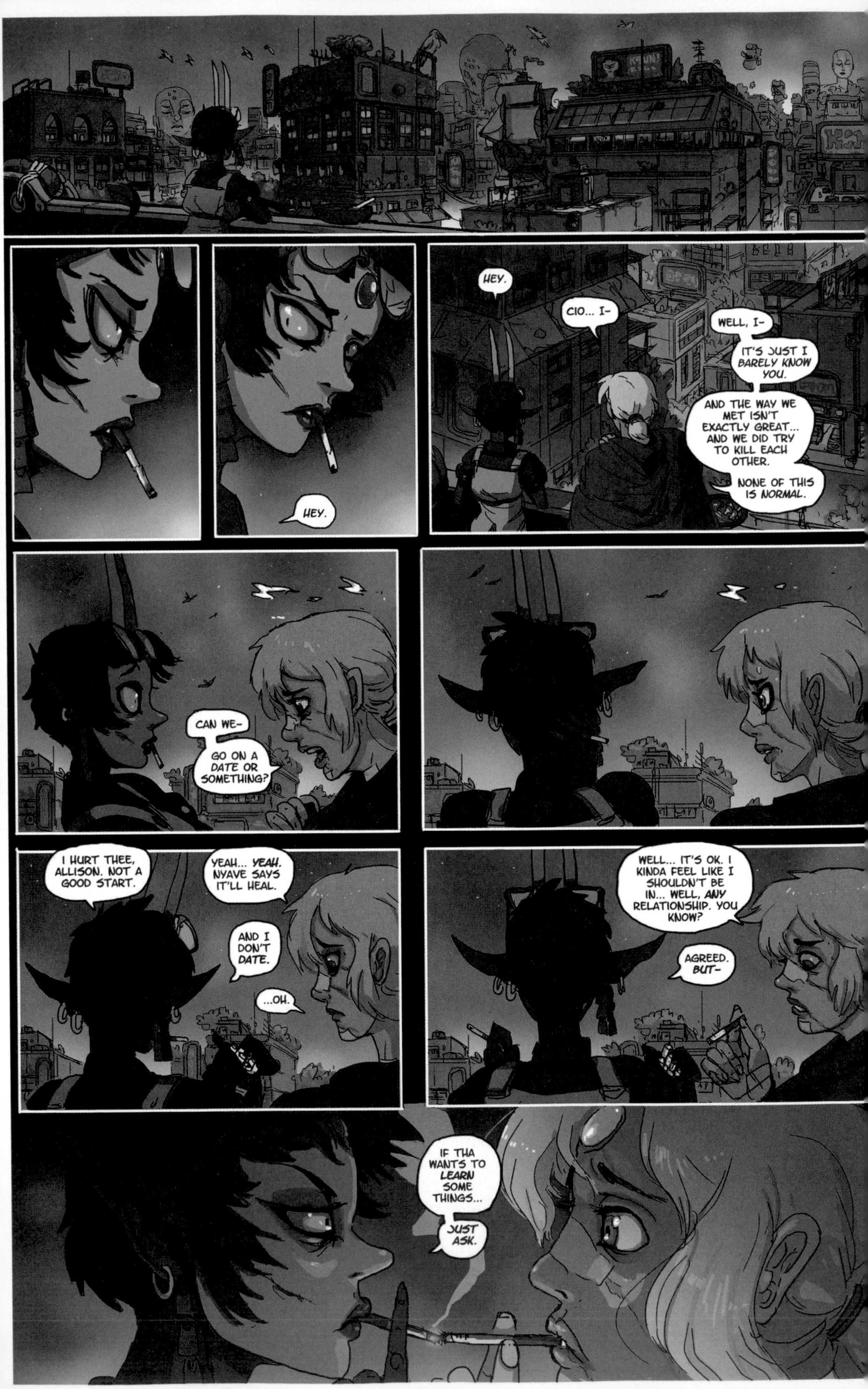
HEY.
HEY.
CIO... I-
WELL, I-
IT'S JUST I BARELY KNOW YOU.
AND THE WAY WE MET ISN'T EXACTLY GREAT... AND WE DID TRY TO KILL EACH OTHER.
NONE OF THIS IS NORMAL.
CAN WE-
GO ON A DATE OR SOMETHING?
I HURT THEE, ALLISON. NOT A GOOD START.
YEAH... YEAH. NYAVE SAYS IT'LL HEAL.
AND I DON'T DATE.
...OH.
WELL... IT'S OK. I KINDA FEEL LIKE I SHOULDN'T BE IN... WELL, ANY RELATIONSHIP. YOU KNOW?
AGREED. BUT-
IF THA WANTS TO LEARN SOME THINGS...
JUST ASK.

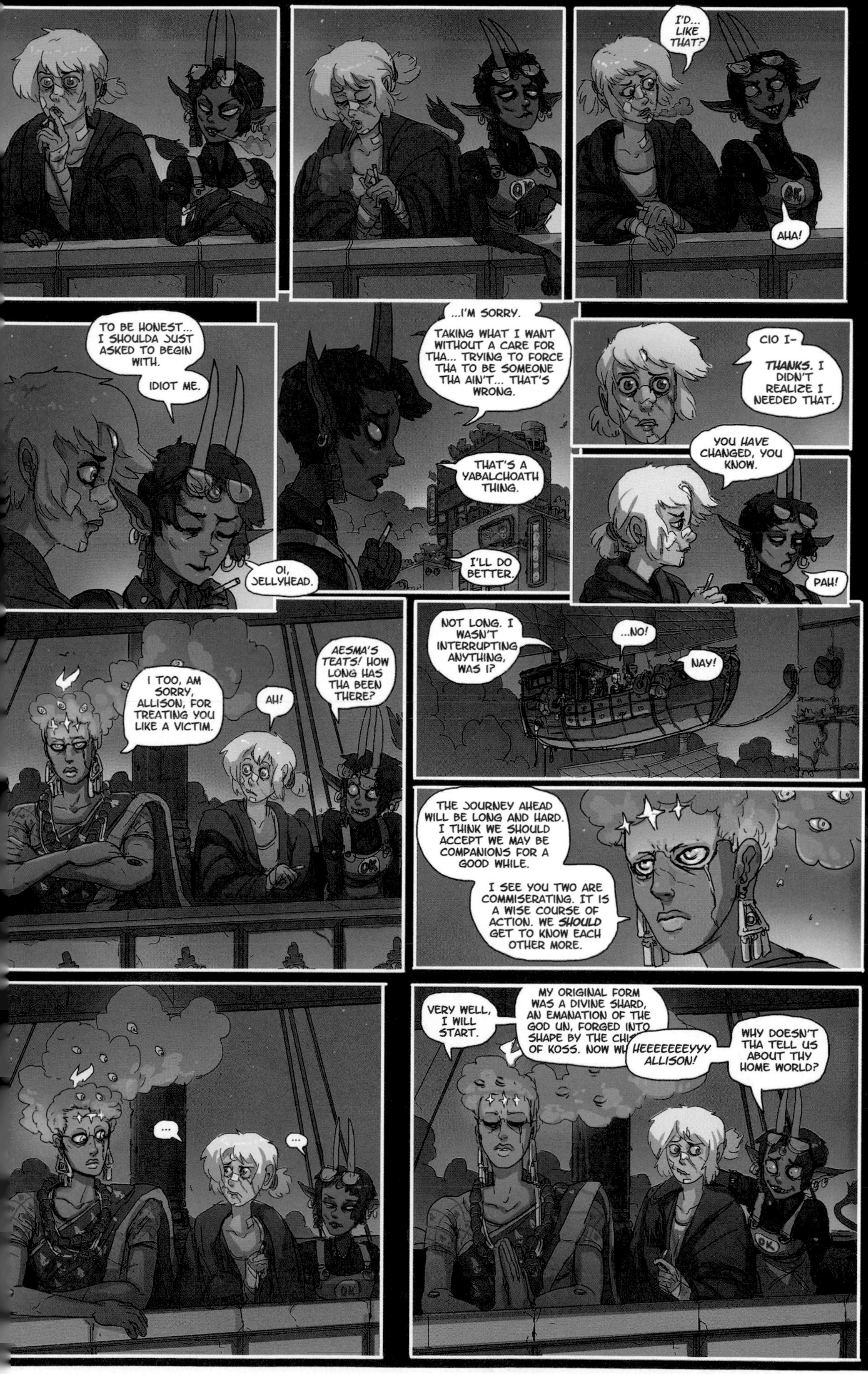
I'D... LIKE THAT?
AHA!
TO BE HONEST... I SHOULDA JUST ASKED TO BEGIN WITH.
IDIOT ME.
OI, JELLYHEAD.
...I'M SORRY.
TAKING WHAT I WANT WITHOUT A CARE FOR THA... TRYING TO FORCE THA TO BE SOMEONE THA AIN'T... THAT'S WRONG.
THAT'S A YABALCHOATH THING.
I'LL DO BETTER.
CIO I-
THANKS. I DIDN'T REALIZE I NEEDED THAT.
YOU HAVE CHANGED, YOU KNOW.
PAH!
I TOO, AM SORRY, ALLISON, FOR TREATING YOU LIKE A VICTIM.
AH!
AESMA'S TEATS! HOW LONG HAS THA BEEN THERE?
NOT LONG. I WASN'T INTERRUPTING ANYTHING, WAS I?
...NO!
NAY!
THE JOURNEY AHEAD WILL BE LONG AND HARD. I THINK WE SHOULD ACCEPT WE MAY BE COMPANIONS FOR A GOOD WHILE.
I SEE YOU TWO ARE COMMISERATING. IT IS A WISE COURSE OF ACTION. WE SHOULD GET TO KNOW EACH OTHER MORE.
...
...
VERY WELL, I WILL START.
MY ORIGINAL FORM WAS A DIVINE SHARD, AN EMANATION OF THE GOD UN, FORGED INTO SHAPE BY THE CHI OF KOSS. NOW WH
HEEEEEEEYYY ALLISON!
WHY DOESN'T THA TELL US ABOUT THY HOME WORLD?

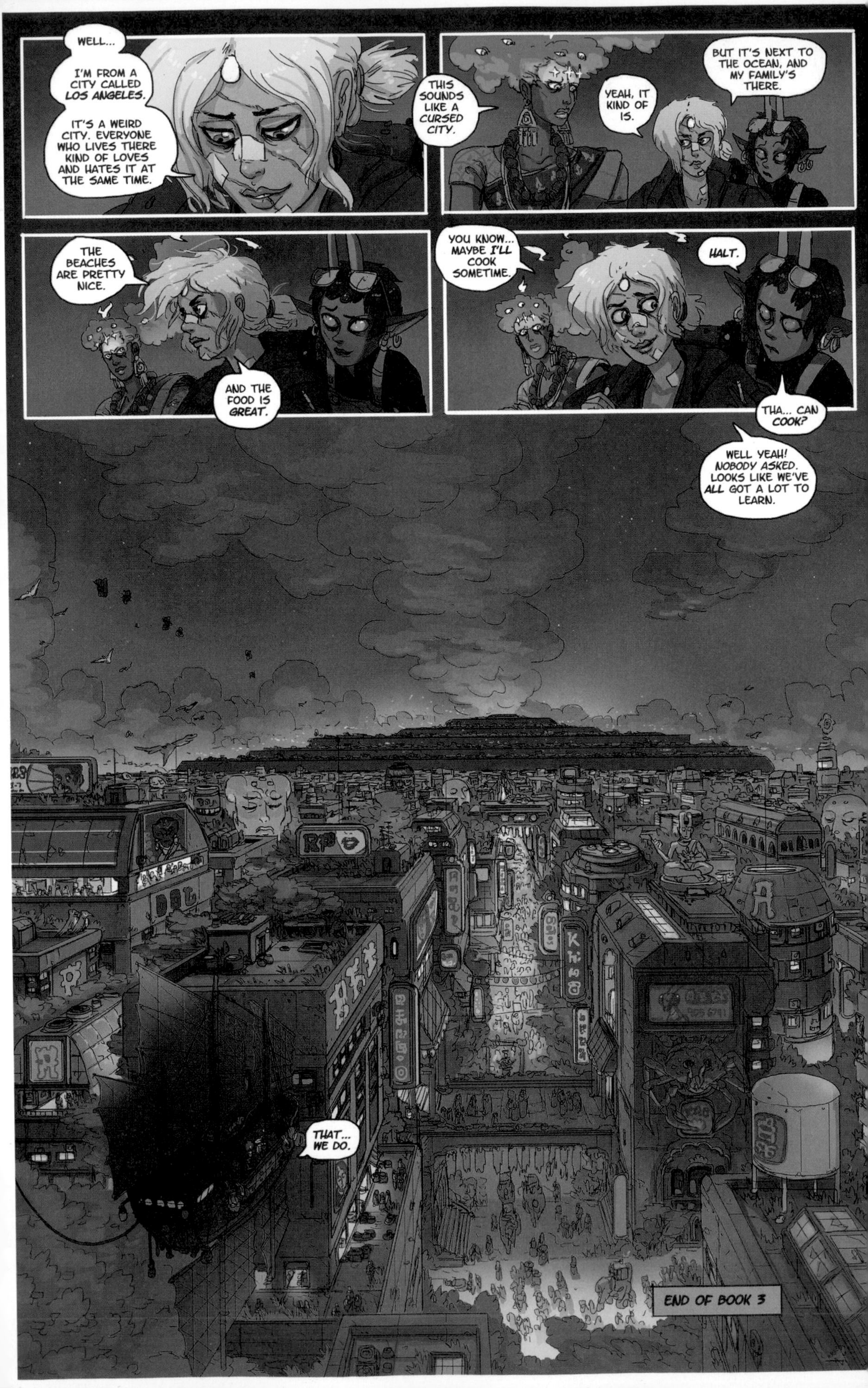
WELL...
I'M FROM A CITY CALLED LOS ANGELES.
IT'S A WEIRD CITY. EVERYONE WHO LIVES THERE KIND OF LOVES AND HATES IT AT THE SAME TIME.
THIS SOUNDS LIKE A CURSED CITY.
YEAH, IT KIND OF IS.
BUT IT'S NEXT TO THE OCEAN, AND MY FAMILY'S THERE.
THE BEACHES ARE PRETTY NICE.
AND THE FOOD IS GREAT.
YOU KNOW... MAYBE I'LL COOK SOMETIME.
HALT.
THA... CAN COOK?
WELL YEAH! NOBODY ASKED. LOOKS LIKE WE'VE ALL GOT A LOT TO LEARN.
THAT... WE DO.
END OF BOOK 3